THE ANGEL'S GATE

AND OTHER MYSTERIES

G.P. RITCHIE

NIGHT'S
BORDER
press

This edition first published in 2024 by Night's Border Press 24a Ainslie Place, Edinburgh, EH3 6AJ

Rev: 1.03
ISBN: (e-book) 978-1-9164246-2-3
ISBN: (paperback) 978-1-9164246-3-0
Cover Design by James, GoOnWrite.com

For the Couper Institute Library.
A treasure house of story in the middle of a Glasgow childhood.

Enter Here

CONTENTS

MOTHER'S MERCY

The walls were dandelion yellow, the floor spread with a blanket of white wool that twisted and tickled between Lisa's toes. There was joy here, of the purest, deepest kind.

Taking one eager step forward, and then another, she neared the first of the Moses baskets. Soon, she could gaze down, look inside. Soon, she could finally see.

But something changed. Shifted. Became wrong.

Underfoot, the welcoming carpet turned cold and hard and dark. She tried to ignore what had happened, to wish it away, but it was useless. The dream had abandoned her.

Lisa stared groggily down the toilet. She was a heavy sleeper, accustomed to stumbling into her bathroom scarcely awake, completing her business and easily rejoining her slumber, but tonight something was different. Whatever sense of peace she'd felt had turned to fear.

She steadied herself against the tiled wall, still questioning what she was seeing. The pool in the toilet bowl was dark and still, and it drew Lisa's gaze like a magnet. Why was she standing here, like some carnival psychic, scrying in the shadow, conjuring a future from the black, empty space? She should know by now that a black, empty space was not a future, but an inescapable present. Just like the black, empty space on the ultrasound from her last IVF cycle.

It's happening again.

The thought snapped her fully awake, and she flicked the switch on the bathroom cabinet. Her eyes slammed shut to defend against the flaring light. Momentarily, her inner vision shifted back to the dream, and the nursery with two cribs, her subconscious dressing her heart's desire in old-fashioned colours: *Pink for a girl. Blue for a boy.*

But what did red mean?

Lisa wanted a child, but instead, she had blood. The thick clot was stark on the porcelain, the water beneath battling piss yellow against beetroot crimson.

Seconds passed.

A minute.

Was this more than spotting? Spotting was allowed. Spotting was so allowed that her smiling obstetrician supplied reassurance in advance. *Don't worry about a little bit of spotting!*

Dr Stephanopoulos was always smiling. But this was more than *a bit*. She wasn't meant to full-on bleed, and they'd given her drugs to make sure. Was this a full-on bleed? She photographed it and emailed: *SHOULD I BE WORRIED?*

Of course, this was an entirely redundant question, given she'd sent it using all-caps at three in the morning. Communications like this were probably why clinicians preferred approaches made formally via reception staff, but sympathy had earned her an email address after the fallout from her previous, disastrous ultrasound. That so-called *blighted ovum* had been well-named – it had spread its blight freely, around her friendships, her mental health, and her marriage.

One senior nurse had suggested her desire for children had come later than usual, and late enough to cause problems. Of course, that wasn't precisely what they said. They just mentioned that Lisa's age *increased the risk of less favourable outcomes*. A risk, mind you, not a certainty. Medics make such a virtue of what they don't bloody know. Sometimes you want... no – need – an absolute.

But the thick red stain in her toilet certainly seemed an absolute, an outcome of the least favourable kind.

Her hands shook. Her cheeks burned. Was it to be tears or rage? Or both?

Sometimes she hated her younger self. Only the most selfish and inconsiderate brat could do this to their own future. But youth has its own preoccupations. Having just taken centre stage, the idea of sharing her spotlight with a child had been alien and horrifying.

So nature had set quietly to work, draining that horror away. Year by year and month by month, with every flip of the calendar, she bled. Each bleed rehabilitated fertility into nothing but a humdrum chore, a monthly tick in the box labelled *perfectly natural*, with each such tick preparing the ground for the day her opinions might change.

But had her opinions changed too late?

Once her youthful selfishness was gone, she had realised sharing her stage was not horror. Instead, the doomed soloist cursed to haunt a lonely spotlight forever, living the life of a solitary, alien thing, now *that* was true fear.

So, for over five years she'd pursued the singular aim of mother-hood. Neil called it an obsession, but *supportive husband* was never a badge he wore. And if motherhood was an obsession, it was at least one that provided everything she'd needed: vision, focus, and, most of all, momentum. The ceaseless forward motion had carried her through deaths in her family, instability at work, and most recently, the ugly finale of her marriage.

But throughout all of it, she'd never lost sight of her goal. She'd always had one vital target to aim for.

Until now, said the thick, red stain.

She pulled on yesterday's clothes and left the house.

OUTSIDE, the sharp rain was welcome, a needling distraction from thoughts intent on circling downwards, back towards the stain in the bathroom. Walking seemed a good approximation of coping. One foot after another. One breath after another.

But one inevitably led to two.

Two embryos were frozen after the first cycle, and with Neil's growing distance, the implantation had felt like a last chance. After thawing, only the single embryo with *good quality morphology* made it through. Following that procedure, Doctor Stephanopoulos had advised keeping things relaxed and stable. While a simple enough prescription, it proved impossible to fill. First her husband, and now it seemed her body, had other ideas.

Her footsteps echoed against oily cobbles on an empty street. The stones glistened in a dawn light that seemed sickly, somehow, infected still by some aspect of the night. That tainted light cast its pall over the rock of the crags, over the rain-streaked granite of the parliament, over the old wynds of the Royal Mile.

And over her.

She lowered her head against biting rain and forced fingers deep into her pockets. The drains of this city were large enough for floods and plans and lives alike. But once it's all washed away, what then? Could she just start again, finally free?

Lisa's bitter laugh distorted into a sob.

Here she was, chained now to a void inside her belly, serving a life sentence. Her record would show a need that could never be met, a hunger that would never be sated.

Just then, a ragged scraping froze her to the spot.

It came from the mouth of the vennel on her right – an ugly sound, unnatural in the deserted quiet of the morning. Caution told her to move on, but the noise held such strangeness that she drew closer. Just before the entrance, she listened, only to hear the cycle repeat: the scraping noise, a pause, the scraping again, a sigh.

She pulled back a little, waiting, wondering, before finally, overcoming her better judgement, she stepped into the passage.

"Can I help you, dearie?" The wrinkled face of an older woman almost collided with her own, but registered no surprise at Lisa's presence. The woman's skin was soft, like crumpled cloth, but her eyes were harder and filled with a fierce energy. Those eyes peered out beneath silver hair that dripped in the rain.

"Sorry... so sorry," Lisa said. "I was walking past and heard... I'm really sorry."

"Don't be sorry, dearie, truth is I'm glad to see you. I struggle with some things more than I used to." The old woman gestured towards an old placard she'd been dragging towards an entrance in the middle of the lane. "I'm Peg, by the way." She extended her hand.

"I'm Lisa. Look... Let me help you." The rope hanging from one corner of the sign trailed down into a puddle. It was longer than needed to drag the placard, and perhaps used to secure it against the Edinburgh winds. The rain-streaked surface bore the words *The Moonlit Cup*.

Peg caught her reading. "Oh, we're closed now, Lisa dear, closed for the morning." She gestured towards the still empty cobbles of the Royal Mile. "There isn't much open for the night owls, not round here." She sighed, then moved past Lisa towards the door. "If you could bring it this way, I'd be most grateful."

Lisa swallowed her distaste as she lifted the sodden hemp from the wet ground. A tentative tug revealed only that the older woman must be stronger than she looked. *In for a penny.* As Lisa leaned, pitting her full weight against the solidity of the wooden sign, the large wedge groaned, then shifted.

Ahead, as the old woman mounted her front step, Lisa saw water ooze from her slippers. What was she thinking, pottering about in the rain in a pair of baffies and a cardigan?

Clattering inside, Lisa spotted a telltale landing strip drawn in grime on the floor and manoeuvred the placard into place. Peg fumbled at the latch of an internal door, yellow light leaking around its edges. Above the door, an odd-looking object hung from a strap. The cracked, worn leather supported an obscene metal figurine. It was a primitive representation of a naked woman, reaching across her belly to grasp her genitals.

"Something caught your eye, dear?"

Lisa flushed, guiltily sneaking another glimpse before changing the subject. "I'm just thinking about you out there in the rain! You'll catch your death!"

Peg's eyes wrinkled into a smile. "If I do, I'll make sure to throw it back." She fussed at her hair, releasing a patter of silvery droplets onto the lino-covered floor. "A bit of weather doesn't bother me, Lisa. I've seen worse than weather…"

The woman's icy fingers threaded through Lisa's own, but her grip was strong. "A good neighbour deserves a cuppa." Brooking no objections, she pulled Lisa inside.

The tearoom was compact and less quaint than Lisa had imagined. Towards the rear, an assortment of baking and some shabby tablecloths were strewn across a scratched wooden counter. The recently stripped tables stood naked in the middle of the room. "It's my little den, I suppose. Not much, but all mine. I'm closed for everyone now except friends… What will you have?"

A glint beneath some stacked scones caught Lisa's eye. They were piled on an unusual dish of blackened metal, a metal reminiscent of the figurine hanging at the door. The platter had a jug embedded into one edge – an odd design choice, given tipping the jug would tumble the cakes onto the floor.

The jug contained clotted cream, and a bone-handled spoon seemed the solution to the tipping problem. But again, Lisa was jarred by the frankness of the objects this elderly woman surrounded herself with – the outside of the jug was etched with the figure of an upside-down and entirely naked woman. The figure's arms reaching between the etched legs to brazenly hold open the spout. A dollop of clotted cream hung between the etched fingers.

The oddness of her own thinking bemused Lisa. somehow the

sight was both repellent and entrancing at the same time. "I'll have a cup of tea, thanks."

"Can I fetch you a wee scone from Sheela's Bounty?"

"Pardon?"

"That's what my James called that serving dish. You've heard of Sheela-na-gig? We found it on some adventure in our younger days. We were cave divers. Those North Americans call it spelunking, but using odd words when perfectly good ones exist already is just glaikit, don't you think?"

Lisa nodded absent-mindedly, the platter commanding all her attention. "I think I saw a Sheela-na-gig in stone once, carved on a church lintel in Ireland. It's a fertility symbol, right?"

"Partly, but not a Christian one." The woman's lips tightened. "Those medieval monks were shameless. Look away one minute, the winter solstice gets covered in Christmas tinsel..." Then she smiled. "And our Sheela is more than a symbol. She's an aspect of the Goddess."

Lisa touched the rim of the dish. It was unusually cold, and textured like thorns. She had a feeling that this piece belonged more to an ancient-history museum than to its life here as a tearoom knick-knack. "You really found this in a cave?"

"We unearthed a few treasures in our day. My James always said I had a nose for finding – good instincts I suppose. That's why I was excited to see you!" The old woman busied herself behind the counter, the kettle thrumming as she filled it.

Lisa struggled to picture her hostess in the role of Lara Croft or Indiana Jones. She wondered if this line of conversation was an elaborate tease. "What cave did this come from then?"

"Hmm... Smoo Cave in Sutherland? No! That was the dolomite effigy..." Peg frowned, and then beamed. "Oh, I remember! We found her in a cave system in Whithorn. Near the one they named after that Saint."

"Saint Ninian's Cave? The one on the shore?" Lisa had heard of it, vaguely.

"Yes, dear. But the underwater system we found was more interesting. Some say Ninian prayed to protect the Lowland Picts from what was down there, and maybe he did..." She shook her head. "One wee man's prayers... that's like a peashooter against a tank, don't you think?"

Lisa didn't follow but wasn't about to defend the power of prayer. She'd wasted enough of it on herself over the last few years. "Well, after all those adventures... How did you end up with an overnight café?"

Peg clucked at the back of her throat. "Good grief, dear! No, not overnight! I still need some sleep. Strictly midnight until four. Later occasionally, but never after five. I tie my hours with the passing trade." Catching the puzzlement on Lisa's face, she continued. "It's the overnights, dear, the night shifts. Like my James when he was with us... Well, we never held much with him working nights and me days, only seeing each other on the doorstep. What's the point of being married? So, I started my little thing here." The kettle whistled and Peg filled two cups.

Lisa opened her purse. "I want to pay you for this." She hoped the old woman would accept the money. Something about the rundown melancholy of the tearoom aroused her protective instincts.

Peg clucked again, shaking her head, and handed over the steaming china. "Like I said, dear, this business is closed for the morning. But it's lovely to make a new friend." Peg guided Lisa to a table. "I have a feeling we met for a reason. There's something troubling you."

Lisa didn't know where, or even if, to begin. She had told no-one about Neil yet, perhaps hoping, by locking that story away, she might find a new ending, one where her life quietly and happily reassembled. But this morning had stolen all hope, and left a hardening certainty that Neil's behaviour bore full responsibility. It wasn't just the betrayal itself. After the initial shock, over the hours and days that followed, she'd felt it happening, a peeling away, a shedding of certain familiar skins of her identity, security, and complacency.

Her last and toughest skin had ruptured today. Now, with everything destroyed, there was nothing left to protect.

And so, the story escaped, words tumbling from her like a flood breaching a dam. The first rush described her time with Neil, their early happiness and the promises they'd made. And then came the fertility treatments that dominated their most recent years, with their clinical intimacies and harsh disappointments. Finally, she told of his betrayal, so mundane, and yet so terrible. Of the wound he inflicted behind her defences. "It was theft, Peg, a horrible theft. I was the one who wanted children, the one meant to have them. For years I've dreamed of a room with cots. But he stole that dream. He took my chance and gave it away. His cheap little fling made the baby he'd never even wanted." She choked down a sob of physical pain. "And worst of all, he proved our fertility problem was my fault all along. There's no fixing me."

Embarrassed, she reined back her tears, aware that cold fingers were now stroking her arm. Peg's voice was almost a whisper. "They called me barren, too."

Suddenly aware of the selfishness of grief, Lisa apologised. "I know lots of women face the same problem, and handle it better. I've gone a bit mad."

Peg gripped her hand. "Not mad, dear, no. Just angry. You were right to call it a theft. But you can recover what's yours. Like I did." Peg's eyes clouded, and she turned her face away. "They called me barren, but they were wrong."

"You had children?"

"My prayer was for a child. The Goddess granted it."

Just then something rattled: harsh, metallic, sharp. Peg moved across, placing her hand on the cake dish. "Silly thing. Always rattling around. They didn't bother levelling off in those days. Oh, the time they must have spent etching the metal, but will it sit flat on a surface?"

Lisa had felt no vibration, although with Edinburgh now awake, delivery vehicles were doubtless plying their trade on the street outside. "What metal is it made of?"

"Oh, it's very old. What came after the Bronze age?"

"Iron?" Lisa knew that couldn't be right. It didn't look remotely like iron. There was no corrosion, just a dull black gleaming.

"No, not iron. The age in-between. You know, that little one nobody talks about? Barely got started? Will come round again? Detail was never me, really. My James could have told you all about it."

"Was he a historian? An archaeologist?"

"Aye, all that and more. A man of many talents, my James. We lose them too young…" Peg's voice cracked again, and she turned to stare out of the window.

"I'm sorry…"

The old woman walked over to the sink. "Ach! A long time gone now, Lisa. Forty years ago – you were barely born, I expect. But that was the end of my exploring." Peg rinsed out her mug over and over. "I had to be strong. I was expecting our son, see? Young James, I called him…" She stared, stricken, towards the cracked ceiling. "There's no greater grief than to outlive your child…" The woman seemed suddenly more frail.

Lisa moved to hold her. "Oh Peg, you poor thing. I can't imagine… You lost your son?"

Peg rubbed her eyes. "Thank you, dear, but not yet… although he won't last long. Bedridden, wasting away up there."

It was a horrible thought: an elderly mother nursing a sick child by day, then working through the night. "Listen, the council can send carers. That will help you get a rest."

"I'll save that kind of rest for my grave!" Peg's eyes hardened. "Young James is mine! I am his guardian, pledged for his first year and his last. I birthed him, and it falls to me to see his end!" Her anger fell away as quickly as it rose, then she touched Lisa's arm. "You see, Lisa, I look after my own. As a mother should." She paused for a moment before giving a hopeful smile. "It would be nice, though, for James to meet you. He gets so few visitors."

Without waiting for approval, the old woman pulled Lisa towards the door behind the counter, then opened it into a tiny hall containing a cramped staircase. A yellowing banister led them upwards, the paintwork streaked by dust and old fingerprints. Everything here smelled damp and stale, the musty air growing with every step.

At the top, the odour sharpened further, reaching an acrid peak outside the door of the solitary upstairs room. Lisa started breathing through her mouth. Then, Peg opened the door and pulled Lisa inside, manouvering them both past a blanket-draped armchair and into the heart of the space.

The room was dark and horribly warm, the heat magnifying the unnatural stench. Lisa heard a low whispering, weak at first, barely more than pained breathing, but growing in urgency. "Moth-Moth-Moth-Mother! Mother!"

Her eyes adjusted to the gloom.

What had been little more than a shape on a bed became a figure, a figure moving weakly under a single sheet. A pallid face craned towards her as the figure struggled to sit up, then a tremulous hand broke free from the bedding. The damp fingers clutched Lisa's arm, smearing her skin with clinging wetness. "Moth-Mother! Mother!"

It was a relief when Peg grasped the hand away. "Yes, son, yes, I'm here." The old woman's voice was gentle, soothing.

But Lisa was appalled. How could anyone be left to die this way?

And there was no doubt the bedridden man suffered from a terminal disease. His eyes were puffy and bulbous, his pale skin hung loosely over wasted muscles. His diseased body was the clear source of the awful smell, and it infected everything in the space, with the taint of rotten meat.

When Lisa realised that same smell now rose from her own arm she struggled against the compulsion to gag. She breathed in sharp, shallow gasps, eyes drawn to the mottled streaks on the man's pillows and pyjamas. *Dried blood? Bedsores?*

How long had this poor man been stuck here?

Peg spoke loudly. "This is a friend, James, a friend…" When the old woman pushed her son's fingers towards Lisa once more, her revulsion shamed her, so she steeled herself and gingerly accepted the touch. Once held, the clammy, initially lifeless weight slowly began to move. She watched the fingers flex uselessly, like a broken spider trying to creep towards her wrist. His skin was pallid, almost grey, except under the misshapen fingernails, which were either bruised black or weeping red.

This was not the hand of someone who could survive. It was the hand of someone being consumed by illness, a process that would end only when there was nothing left to consume. And there was almost nothing left now.

Except, perhaps, in the eyes.

A fierce fire glimmered in those eyes as they searched Lisa's face. She saw a savage rage in them, and a questing hunger. "Mother… Mother!"

The old woman shuffled between them, tucking the man's arm back under the stained blankets. "Don't excite yourself, son. Lisa is only visiting."

It was with numb relief that Lisa followed Peg back downstairs.

As they crossed the tearoom, Lisa urged Peg once more to seek a hospice or some other care facility, but the old woman was implacable. "James will spend his last days where he's loved." The old woman fixed Lisa with a curious expression. "It's no harm for you to see another side of motherhood. If it is still your dream, then don't give up on it. Perhaps, instead, return tonight?"

When Lisa stepped outside, she breathed deeply for the first time in minutes, but it did not make her feel better. You can't salve your own pain with the misery of another, after all. Just then, the door rattled behind her, and she turned to see Peg holding up her handbag. "You left this sitting on the counter!" She thanked the old woman, and took her leave.

As Lisa walked back to her flat, she wondered at all the strange, sad stories hidden behind the walls of the city. But did this one have lessons for her? Peg was a mother, having achieved what Lisa had always wanted. And it had brought her what, exactly? Despite the woman's incredible energy, she spent it toiling in old age and watching her child suffer.

Lisa had never imagined much beyond her goal of a family, her dream of those two cots. But her experience with Peg made explicit what she already knew but had given little thought to: the granting of any wish brought consequences, and not all of them happy. If motherhood was a burden that started with life and ended in death, perhaps she had been mad to ever want it.

But even if so, it was a madness she had cultivated for too many years to be free from. This unfulfilled desire was part of her now. It was who she was. Peg had at least shown her that pain existed either way. Hopefully, one day, that would make Lisa's loss easier to bear.

By the time she reached her desk she had not heard back from her consultant, so booked the next available appointment with the IVF clinic reception. That gave forty-eight hours before her fears would be officially confirmed, but she didn't suppose confirmation changed anything that actually mattered.

She worked through the morning session on automatic pilot, her thoughts a revolving montage of bad omens: the blood in her toilet, Peg's dying son, the repulsive allure of Sheela's Bounty. She considered too the strange woman's offer of help. But how could she help? How could anyone?

As office manager for twelve years, her job now held no mystery, and she was glad of this. It allowed her distraction to go largely unnoticed.

It was only later, in the queue to buy a sandwich, that she discovered her purse was missing. A colleague funded her lunch, but on return to her desk, she searched and found nothing.

And so, just after six p.m. Lisa pushed through throngs on the Royal Mile onto the Canongate and down towards Abbey Strand and the close where Peg lived.

On arrival, the unmarked door that hosted the tearoom was firmly closed. Lisa knocked and rattled at the letter box but heard no response. She doubted Peg and her son had left the house. Perhaps they were simply asleep?

Stooping to peer inside, she saw no sign of life, just the placard positioned as she had left it that morning, and the obscene little goddess hanging from the door-frame. Despite all Lisa's knocking, the goddess was unmoved, and the inner door to the tearoom area remained tightly shut.

Unwilling to risk waking the two sleepers inside, she trudged back home empty-handed, with no better plan than to accept Peg's late-night invitation and retrieve her purse that way.

RETURNING JUST AFTER MIDNIGHT, Lisa found the placard back in the lane and Peg's door thrown open wide. She felt a nervous thrill on the threshold, remembering Peg's odd talk and offer of help, a thrill that left her doubting herself: was she truly only here to retrieve her purse?

Stepping inside, she found the tearoom also jarring. This was not the same shabby, empty room she had visited that morning. The little tables, now sporting customers, were arranged into formal lines down each side of the room. This left the middle of the floor clear, offering a wide passage towards the white linen-draped structure of the counter. The odd metal platter sat there as a centrepiece, but held no scones. On either side of it, a red candle burned.

Peg stood behind the counter, resplendent in a long white smock. Upon spotting Lisa, her face grew rapt. "You made it!" She pointed Lisa towards a single empty table in the middle of the right-hand wall, a table already bearing a steaming cup of tea, and the strange figurine that only a few hours ago had hung by the door.

Lisa sat down. "Sorry, Peg… I've lost my purse… I think I left it here this morning?"

The old woman smiled. "I caught you admiring that amulet today. You knew what you needed, I think! I wore it daily, and the Goddess guarded the life growing inside me. Please, put it on. It's yours."

Lisa self-consciously lowered the leather cord over her head. Although it embarrassed her to repeat herself, she didn't see that she had any choice. "Thank you, Peg, for this gift, but do you have my purse?"

"Oh yes. Inside." She gestured at the door behind her. "Just drink your tea. It's a herbal blend. Everything the Mother needs." Lisa took a cautious sip. The liquid combined an earthy sweetness with a bitter edge. It wasn't at all unpleasant, so she took some more, making appreciative noises. Peg said, "Enjoy that while I bring your things down for you." Then she disappeared through the door to the bedroom staircase.

It was an odd situation, sitting alone and in silence at her little table in the bustle of the now-occupied tearoom. The other customers seemed friendly enough. In fact, she found such an abundance of eager smiles, whenever she glanced up, that she fixed her gaze firmly on her teacup. The general atmosphere of familiarity in the room led her to suspect the others were longtime companions, and she felt at a disadvantage. But the complex taste of the tea, and the already apparent relaxing effect from the herbs, slowly worked on her tension.

But as Peg's absence stretched on too long, certain aspects of the situation combined to disturb her: the continual rattle of china teacups against saucers, the by now eerily incessant smiling, and the near-total absence of actual conversation. There were eight people besides herself sitting in that room, all tables within conversation distance, and yet not a word passed between them. It felt wrong.

Briefly, she considered leaving and making another attempt to return in daylight.

As though in reaction to her panic, the counter candles flickered, ushering a momentary darkness. In that brief absence of light, she felt the weight of the Sheela-na-gig amulet hanging low against her midriff. She touched it nervously, stroking the contours of the metal figure, drawing an odd comfort from the unusual texture of the dark metal.

A smiling older man rose and latched the entrance door. "Getting windy," he said to the room, but he stopped at Lisa's table on his return. "Please know," he said, beaming. "She can do what she's promised you."

Lisa lifted the figurine. "You mean Peg, or this lady?"

The man cocked his head, his eyes clear, his expression earnest. "Oh, both of them." Then he resumed smiling, and simply stood, grinning down at her from above. In embarrassment, Lisa gulped at her tea, until eventually her visitor drifted back to his table and seated himself once more.

The fact he knew what Peg had told her was curious, and Lisa wondered why she wasn't more upset at the betrayal of trust. She sipped the last of her tea and pondered. Perhaps these people were part of it? Perhaps Peg had organised some kind of New Age prayer group?

It was a nice thought perhaps, but Lisa found it impossible to believe that prayer could ever provide what she needed.

The amulet grew hotter against her fingers. For a moment she fancied the black metal so conductive that it had absorbed energy from just the friction of her touch. It was certainly an unusual feeling, almost a throb, and she understood why Peg believed the figurine was special. In fact, the longer Lisa wore it, the more flattered she felt by the gift. The problem, though, was its oddness, its brazenness. Displaying it would surely draw unwelcome attention. How could she possibly wear it all the time, as Peg had suggested? Only, perhaps, under her clothes, where nobody would know. Having the amulet against her skin seemed the best thing to do all round.

But with that thought, the door behind the counter creaked open.

The first object through was her purse. The hand holding it had pallid skin with a feverish sheen. It clutched the purse with blackened, weeping fingernails.

Oh God. Not James. Please no.

But yes.

The ailing man staggered through the doorway, barely held upright by two younger women. Peg followed behind, her expression solemn. Then she spoke. "Come, Lisa. Come take what is yours by right."

Peg's two helpers returned to their seats, leaving Young James gaunt and trembling beside his mother, holding himself barely upright against the counter. The older woman nodded towards Lisa and beckoned her forward.

As Lisa rose to approach the pair, her legs were unsteady, the soporific effects of the tea now fully taking hold. Her thoughts grew fogged by sibilant whispering, the urgent words just beneath her comprehension. As she drew close to the counter, she looked down on the engraved platter and saw, glinting in the flickering candlelight, the blade of a bone-handled knife. "Peg? What's happening?"

"Lisa, my lamb, you are chosen by the Goddess! You have tasted her transforming power and been welcomed into her sight! James knew, knew at once!"

"Knew what?"

Young James hissed the words she'd last heard upstairs in his room. "Moth-mother! Mother!"

The old woman lifted the knife and drew the sharp edge quickly and painlessly across Lisa's arm, then flicked a trickle of her blood onto the platter.

"Oh, Lisa," said Peg, "your blood will mix with his, just like mine forty years ago, and that mix will form a seed, the answer to a barren woman's prayers. I lost my James, but only to birth him again. Now the Goddess grants her favour once more, but this time to you. My pledge is for his first year, to stand beside you both, as your teacher and his. That is all I require in return."

There was madness in the woman's eyes, a pure, devout craziness. But the amulet was warm in Lisa's hand, a seductive warmth that made her fingers greedy. The whispering in her mind grew stronger. She heard it more clearly now. It whispered hope.

When the old woman spoke again, her words had a melodic quality, a melancholy singsong. "Flesh does not last. It must be remade. Sister, that burden falls on us." Others in the room murmured an affirmation and Peg continued. "This night is a place of remaking. On whom does that burden fall?"

Lisa twisted, staring back towards the exit. But in doing so, she took in all the watching faces around the room. They bore an expression she recognised, one she knew intimately. She saw yearning; she saw hope. And this hope came honestly, without compulsion or malice. Nobody bound her, and she knew she could leave. If she left this room behind, did she abandon the hope too?

Lisa turned back to Peg and inhaled deeply, hoping to settle her racing heartbeat, to regain focus and gather her strength.

Then Lisa said, "Sister, that burden falls on me."

———

THE CONDUCTIVE GEL WAS COLD, and each drop glistened as it fell onto Lisa's belly. The day had finally come. One way, or another, she would leave here changed forever.

The radiologist spread the gel gently with the head of the sensor. Lisa made room by pulling the amulet to one side. Its black metal snagged her skin, raising a pale welt, but she ignored it, letting her mind find refuge in the hazy screen of her memories.

"Sister, it falls on you. To birth my James again."

A knife pressed into her clumsy fingers. Her hand guided. The sharp whisper of metal against diseased skin. A pattering against the dish becoming heavy rain. A downpour.

"Sister, will you birth him?"

An affirmation stalled on her lips as possibilities slithered through her mind. Was her imagination playing tricks? Or were these the whispers of the Goddess?

The sensor slid easily, without undue pressure. "I'm sorry about the wait. The last appointment always suffers the brunt of the delays, but we shouldn't take long."

She watched the radiologist's face carefully throughout each small manipulation and each tiny adjustment, alert to any sign of danger. She could not bring herself to view the screen, fearful of that plummeting sensation of the earlier scan, of falling helplessly into another blighted ovum.

As an act of faith, she grasped her amulet once more, squeezing it with the same fierceness that had brought her control of the bone-handled knife.

"Sister, you must respond." Peg insisted, "My James. Will you birth him?"

Lisa held the old woman's gaze and smiled as she answered. "No, sister. I will birth you both." And with just a single flick, the old woman's face transformed, becoming a screaming red reflection in the silver platter.

. . .

THE RADIOLOGIST FROWNED, reaching across for Lisa's notes. "This is unusual. Not unheard of, but very rare."

Lisa's stomach tightened. "What's wrong?"

The man gave a hurried smile. "No! Nothing wrong! Sorry, it's just you have twins! From a single implanted embryo!"

"But everything is OK?"

"Everything is fine. But I thought you'd be more surprised. Do twins run in your family?"

"No…" She stalled for a moment, wondering what to say. "I've just had a feeling."

"Well, you can have something better than a feeling by looking at the monitor…"

"No. Thank you. I'm fine." She'd learned an important lesson: you didn't always have to look. Some changes, even welcome ones, did not bear close examination. Some changes you should run past with your eyes screwed tight and never look back. "So, is it a boy and a girl?"

The radiologist frowned. "We can't tell. It's too early."

"Sorry again. Just a—"

"Feeling? Well, don't become set on it. You'll find out for sure at the twenty-week scan."

He applied more gel. It fell onto her abdomen like…

"…THE red seed of dying flowers. These precious seeds are mine to claim. I shall be their soil."

THE RADIOLOGIST CLEARED HIS THROAT. "Your consultant mentioned an email…" He paused awkwardly. "A very anxious email. But I want to add my reassurance to hers. Everything I'm seeing looks great. Fantastically healthy. Completely normal."

Lisa winced, but her visible discomfort seemed to bring a redoubling of the man's reassurance. "No, really. Given your age and clinical history, this is better than we could ever expect. Placenta, heartbeat, development, all excellent. Nothing is certain in medicine, but for right now, this is superb: every milestone met, every threshold exceeded. I'll give you a printout to show your husband."

Lisa buttoned her top while the printer hummed, doubting she would show anything to Neil. Nobody knew about Neil's absence yet, but he had nothing to do with this anymore. When he left the stage, his role had been recast. She pressed the amulet against her skin and whispered her thanks.

———

LATER, walking towards her home, she crushed the scan printout in her hand, discarding it, unviewed in a builder's skip, pushing it until it vanished, slipping between gaps in the rubble. That skip was a useful hiding place. It had also swallowed the newspaper she'd studied the day after they found the bodies.

She no longer recalled the short contribution from the postman who had alerted the authorities, but remembered the words that followed.

> Police recognised a grisly suicide pact... The ritualistic nature of the cuts did not obscure what was, at heart, a mercy killing...

She wondered how all the others present that night had escaped unnoticed. Where had they gone? Had they performed some kind of clean-up? If so, they had left a scene telling a story everyone preferred to believe.

All Lisa remembered was how she had stumbled from that place insensible, with neither cunning nor caution to guide her. But the night had gathered around her like a cloak, shrouding the journey home even from her own memory.

She remembered the shower at least, naked, save for the amulet – her new Goddess – crushed in her hand as she pressed against the white tiles, crying into a stream of water set hot enough to scald but insufficient to quench her shivering. She'd endured a kind of birthing, she supposed, with strangers as midwives, reaching inside her, removing normality and swaddling something else in its place.

Those people had now melted into the night, their task complete. Was she melting now, fading into a supporting role in her own life, a tiny cog spinning in some ancient wheel?

If so, that spinning never ended.

She'd watched the water in her shower, a red rotation, never running clear. Round and around that water had gone, swirling red, a crimson vortex, posing a question she could finally answer.

Pink for a girl. Blue for a boy.

Red for one of each.

DISSOLUTION

Musselburgh, 2:24am,
Wednesday 6th August 2014

Constable Jamie Devlin pulled on the handbrake, switched off the headlights, and loosened his collar. This was a big event, his first stake-out, and it was time to get all his ducks quacking in tune.

Darkness? Check. If he didn't start now, dawn might come and ruin it.

Clear Objective? Check. Making sure nothing went down on Musselburgh High Street. Particularly not a man's trousers outside the bakery doorway.

Coffee and Doughnuts? Check. The bakery was funding that part, as well it should.

Partner? Not check, thank God. Rogan had come down with shingles. Devlin smiled to himself, wondering if he'd somehow passed on a dose of his own wee Callum's chicken pox.

Because if so, brilliant! Rogan was a total prick.

The streets were dead tonight and dispatch shouldn't miss him

23

for an hour or three. After all, this was still patrol, just a special kind. *Doughnut patrol*. From the comfort of his seat, he was still fighting wrongdoers and righting wrongs. After all, there were few things more wrong than peeing through the letterbox of a bakery. Delicious baked goods were sacred. The police had a duty to protect the sources of such public happiness.

Best of all, the stake-out was a rite of passage for every police officer in every country of the world, real or fictional. It was time to lose his cherry and get this career of his started.

He popped the glove compartment where his treats had spent the last few hours coming to temperature. The smell that escaped was much improved from that time Rogan lost his socks for a week. The greasy brown package was sealed with a handwritten sticker: *custard*. When it came to custard doughnuts, Devlin had opinions. For instance, anyone who called it *crème pâtissière* should get tae France, because these little sugar-dusted wonders were as Scottish as haggis, but without a sheep's stomach in sight. And while a simple iced ring might be the traditional law-enforcement choice, if a filled doughnut marked him as a radical, then that was simply because Jamie Devlin had no intention of being a traditional PC. He was in uniform to learn what he needed for CID, and these cakes were a symbol of that promise to himself. They were his personal guarantee that he'd make detective and start solving big stuff, not hanging around waiting for neds to piss through shop letterboxes.

He tore open the bag, revealing the four plump marvels and selected his first target. As he began to raise it to his mouth, imagining the rich seam of sweet yellow goodness, he was forced to inhale sharply to contain the resulting rush of saliva.

But it was on the verge of that first bite that the shouting began.

"OFFICER! OFFICER! OFFICER! OFFICER!"

Someone was outside the car, a teenager, brown-skinned, short dark hair with a floppy fringe. He looked odd, panicked but woozy at the same time, like he'd just woken up from a nightmare. He thumped at the driver-side window.

Devlin gazed forlornly at his doughnut before shoving it back in the bag. Then he stepped out onto the pavement. "I hope this is worth cancelling my pastry... What's your problem?"

The kid's eyes were wide, darting left and right, his breathing rapid. He was dressed entirely in white: canvas jacket, T-shirt, cotton trousers, suede moccasins. He had probably been freshly laundered a few hours ago, in a Frankie-Says-Ariel-Automatic kind of way, but whatever happened after that had left his outfit covered head-to-toe in alarming brown streaks. There was some green on there too. Maybe he'd been out golfing in those moccasins and taken a header down a grassy verge?

Since the lad was growing more agitated by the moment, Devlin reached out to steady him. "Hey! I'm here. Are you OK?" He briefly wondered if he might have struck lucky. "Did you get a scare from someone pissing at a shopfront? Or perhaps you've got a thing for peeing through metal slots and want to turn yourself in?"

At that, the lad's eyes focused. "What? I'm not looking for a toilet. I need police help. For me."

Devlin took out his notebook, flipped open the cover. "OK. And you are? Name?"

"Lisa... No! Razu Das. Raz." He continued breathlessly, "I was in the pub when she came, and we went to Dissolution. She said it was her birthday, and a free bar. And a minibus. But then everything—"

Devlin shook his head. "Stop. Were you attacked?"

"No."

"Were you robbed?"

"I don't think so."

"Did you witness someone else get attacked or robbed?"

"No."

Devlin flipped closed his notepad. "Then I'm having my dough-nuts." He climbed back into the squad car.

But Raz ran around to the opposite door, then jumped into the passenger seat. "Look. I'm trying to hold it together here. Something bad happened, but everything was really weird. It's hard for me to describe."

Devlin would have kicked the guy out but wondered if "really weird" might also mean "fairly glamorous" if it was written up correctly. Clearly this guy had been through something that upset him. Given the disturbing new smell in the car, that "something" was possibly a dung heap. But maybe, just maybe, there could be something worth betting ten minutes on here. "Make your point then. And quickly. I'm not a patient man."

Raz turned to look over his shoulder, staring after a passing vehicle. "They could be anywhere…"

Devlin wondered if he best take a soft approach with this clearly upset young man who was a potential victim of crime. Then he rejected that idea. "Wooooh. Spooky. Last chance or you can piss off. Facts, please, and only facts. Now."

"I was at… Staggs Bar? I think. I was with a few friends. Just getting a midweek libation."

"I thought you lads didn't drink."

Raz glared. "What? All of us brown lads, you mean? Like our skin makes us allergic?"

"Relax. You drink. Fine."

"I drink."

Devlin realised he'd brought that on himself. Given the kid's fashion sense it should have been obvious he'd had many a skinful. "So you're at Staggs."

Raz closed his eyes, frowning. "Yeah, I think… I think that was where the French girl met me. But she met Lisa at The Jooglie Brig… I'm pretty sure I was in Staggs."

Devlin sneered. "Sounds like you had a midweek libation too many. Otherwise, how the hell don't you know where you met her? Did you pass out?"

"No. More… kind of blended in?"

The kid spoke earnestly, like the words were not senseless bollocks. Devlin *really* wanted his doughnuts. "We're not getting anywhere—"

"No. Listen. Please. She turned up. Called herself Sophie. No! Sylvie. I wasn't sure at first because of her accent. She said it was her birthday and invited us to a celebration club night. Dissolution she called it. A rave kind of thing. In a barn. Sounded very retro. I liked her French accent."

"So, you followed a stranger to an unknown barn. Because she had a French accent?"

"I suppose. Look – it was a Tuesday. It was dead otherwise."

Devlin frowned. "I understand. You went to a party. You got pissed. And my nose tells me you fell over. But can you skip to the bit where this becomes a police matter?"

Raz nodded. "There was a minibus outside the pub. Driver was an Irish guy, looked like a roadie. They knew each other really well. She called him Muldoon."

Devlin scribbled the names *Sylvie* and *Muldoon* in his notebook and scrawled a love heart around them. "And this minibus took you to her birthday barn dance… exactly like she promised?"

"Yes."

"Oh the criminality." Devlin glanced furtively towards his dough-nuts, wondering when to call time on this nonsense.

Raz said, "Wait! I'm getting there. We were driving a while, at least half an hour, maybe an hour. I'm not sure which direction we went. See, the French girl, she gave us drinks on the bus, and it was a bit of a party atmosphere. There were ten of us. Me, Remo and Jules were from Staggs, a guy called Tom and some others I didn't know… at first, at least. We were a mixed bunch – different ages, men and women – but we'd been given the same story and everyone was well up for a free night out. The driver eventually pulled into a field with an old barn. You could hear Europop music coming from inside."

When Devlin realised this was going on a while, he tore open the paper bag and raised the first doughnut to his mouth. "I agree.

Europop is offensive, but that's different from being an actual offence. Get to the good stuff." He bit the pastry in half and began to chew. Disappointingly there was no surge of custard in this mouthful. Luck of the draw, he supposed.

Raz spoke quickly, growing animated by the recollection. "Well, Sylvie got out first and this Muldoon guy locked the doors and kept us on the minibus. That was odd, right? By the time he let us out, she had a tray with shot glasses. The tray was made up like a Ouija board, you know, from the horror movies, and she made some joke about communing with spirits. One glass of her birthday tincture for each of us, and if we got it down in one, we'd win a voucher for the bar inside. Obviously we all wanted the voucher, so, glug, and everyone's a winner. Then she let us in."

"Since I'm stuck here with a dry doughnut, I hope this free bar doesn't become a major focus."

"Not really. Because inside there was no bar, just a few guys with clipboards and a beer crate. The music system was a boom box. We started to dance, but Tom, well, after maybe a minute, he just lay down in the middle of the floor, and nobody reacted properly. The dancers kept moving, shambling really, and one of the beer-crate guys wrote something on a clipboard. I panicked. I'd been feeling off since the birthday tincture, but I knelt beside Tom, tried to wake him, but he was out cold. Barely breathing, seemed like."

Devlin felt an edge of panic. "Is he…? Do I need to radio for an ambulance?"

"No. He's fine now. But there was something in that shot glass."

"Aye – strong alcohol. A few drinks on the bus. Plus the midweek beers. Far be it from me to suggest you academic types are bloody lightweights, but if the white moccasins fit…"

Raz shook his head. "No. That shot glass was different. You felt it as soon as you'd swallowed. Not woozy exactly. But pulled."

"Pulled? Like how my leg feels, you mean?"

"No, really – pulled. Like something was dragging me. My… Ātman? My spirit… trying to take it out of me."

"It was the spirit that went into you that was the problem. You were just bladdered. Admit it."

"No, because it was more than that. Not long after Tom, Lisa went down too. Then Jules. Then Remo and the rest. They all just… dropped. But not me. I felt weird, in a battle, a… a tug of war, kind of, but in my… mind? So I ran. Out the barn, into the field. I slipped and fell a couple of times – I don't know why."

Since Devlin had too many retorts to choose from, he instead cleared his throat in a suitably sarcastic fashion.

"I think the Irish guy lifted me and took me back to the barn."

It sounded like a classic bad trip, but Devlin had to admit the story at least took his mind off the unfolding tragedy of his still empty doughnut. He scowled as he swallowed another dry lump.

Raz closed his eyes. "The last thing I remember clearly was he called the woman over. Said something like, 'Can you do the needful?' And next thing I knew she lifted my face and stared at me. Into me really. The pulling feeling went crazy and I popped."

"You popped?"

"Maybe? Or snapped… See, it felt like a sound, but it wasn't a sound. More like an egg being sucked into a bottle, but in reverse."

Devlin wrote the word *Bampot*, double-underlined it and then said, "Come again?"

"You know, the science experiment with the boiled egg, and the match in the bottle? But in my case, the egg was sucked OUT of the bottle, and the egg was me."

Devlin rolled his eyes. "Making the bottle the barn? And you, Mr Egg, popped out to roll about in manure before arriving here to stink up my squad car? Maybe you actually are a smelly rotten egg, or maybe the metaphor isn't helpful."

"That's only because you're getting mixed up with 'body' me. I was out of my body."

Devlin swore under his breath. He began writing again, narrating as he went. "Witness admits to being out of his face at point of incident…"

29

"No! My body. I was out of my body!"

"And… your body has a face. Connected to it by a brass neck." Devlin drew a big round smiley face, with a string dropping from it towards a prone stick figure. "We are now veering towards wasting police time, so we'll call a halt Mr… What was it again, Raz or Lisa?"

The young man continued desperately. "Imagine being in a cloud of other people's thoughts! It was crazy. That's where this girl… Lisa was… We got mixed up somehow. Got me really confused. But the others were in the mix too. It was a big mess. We were like that the whole journey back on the minibus."

"Hold the front-page! Brutal free-booze party-planners return everyone home safely." Devlin closed his notepad. "Look. We've all had nights where we head out hopeful and come home smelling of shite and chardonnay. I know that more than most. But you don't make a production out of it. This is Scotland. We're stoic." He took another bite of doughnut. Also dry. He carefully examined the remainder in his palm before exploding. "Sod this! The custard is missing from my custard doughnuts!"

Raz narrowed his eyes. "Did you maybe eat it?"

"No! Total outrage! It's part of the definition. *Custard! Doughnut!* It's baked-in. Literally. You simply cannot call it a custard doughnut if you take the custard out! It's an offence against nature!"

The student tried to calm him. "But that's like my thing. That was the unnatural crime: they took the me out of my body and—"

"What? No. You just got really pissed and whined about it. That's normal student behaviour. But this?" Devlin shook the bag. Why hadn't he noticed the suspicious lightness earlier? "This is appalling. I've been defrauded. My first stake-out, ruined!"

Raz pointed through the windscreen. "Erm. I know you're upset and everything, but why is that man putting his penis through the bakery letterbox?"

Devlin switched on the engine. "Sod the bakery. Lang may the pee reek. I'm dropping you back to the student halls."

"But what about—"

"Your absinthe-fuelled disco fever? Save that for Alcoholics Anonymous. Step zero in the twelve-step program is not taking mystery booze from French people in barns."

WHEN HE DROPPED Raz back at his dorm the bedraggled student made a final protest. "After everything I've been though. Is this really all you're doing for me?"

Devlin frowned, momentarily chastened. "D'you know what? You're absolutely right." He ferreted briefly under his seat. "These, my friend, are for your inevitable munchies." He threw the bag of doughnut scraps and drove away, heading towards the city and the approaching dawn.

THE SOLDIER'S DAUGHTER

H er descent began in confusion.

The glass had struck the table, chiming like a warning bell. *Stand! Get up while you still can!*

So she staggered towards the toilets, stumbling as she reached them, certain to fall… But his arms reached out to take her weight.

To *take her*, in fact.

What followed was a hazy interlude, a trip to the car park as a rag doll against his shoulder. Tweed. Sweat. Camphor. Cigarettes.

"I like them shy," he said. "You won't sing for your friends, but you'll sing for me."

Dropping into the back of his van was a fall down the face of a mountain. Sleep roared in the frigid waters below, a hungry beast beneath an ice-cliff. She flailed desperately, but found no purchase, only a terrifying plummet into unconsciousness.

WHEN AWARENESS RETURNED, it was a stifled thing, a weighted body struggling against the depths. Rising took impossible efforts, pulling upwards through treacle or blood, surrounded by thick blackness.

But that same scent was here. The scent from his clothes. The scent from the bar where he caught her. It seemed wrong, dislocating, how powerful her sense of smell now seemed, when all along she had been the prey.

But not everything makes sense.

Like being here, ascending through darkness.

Her place — her state of being — was a river. And now she heard it: deafening, sharp, a heavy shawl slapping against rocks. Again. Again.

He was striking her face.

"Speak to me," he said.

So she spoke his name and fell back into the depths.

———

"JUST TRY IT!" Lucy had said. When the compere called for volunteers, Lucy always sang first because she loved it, and then began bullying the others to follow the moment she returned to her seat. Trish had a cold, and nobody wanted to hear 'Cry me a River' with a streaming nose on backing vocals, so Rita and Jane had taken their turn.

Now there was no hiding - she was the last one left. "I can't," she said, "I'm tuneless."

They knew this already, not only because they'd never heard her raise her voice in song, but because she always used the same excuse.

"Ach! It's karaoke night! Why did you even come?"

"No, I enjoy you guys, but not me. I'm scared of people laughing." It wasn't entirely true, but she didn't understand the situation herself. It certainly wasn't laughter she feared, but something buried deeper than that. She'd often skipped karaoke night before, but tonight she'd needed to be here with them.

Lucy said, "Well, if you don't go, I'll need to go again."

"Fine. I'm getting a drink." She stood, eager to escape the pressure.

She squeezed her way through the crowd towards the bar. The place was sweaty, warm, sticky, and the floor sucked at her feet as she moved. She felt like a bug inside a carnivorous plant, as if the spilled sweet nectar hid tripwires that might cause the world to snap shut around her.

As she waited for her gin and tonic, while bodies pressed and jostled around her, the discomfort grew. She felt another strong desire to escape, this time from a horrible smell. It was as if a filthy cloth had wiped the bar surface, leaving a strong funk of damp wool and turpentine, overlaid with old cigarettes.

Her drink was heading her way when a pint smashed to her right. The crowd recoiled and surged chaotically, taking her with them, so it was some moments until order returned and she could finally reach her glass. She'd expected the lemon rind, but the peppercorns were one garnish more than usual. She'd sipped steadily as she returned to her table, a slight wobble in her step making her glad of the seat.

The bite of those peppercorns proved stronger than she could handle.

———

AT HER TIME of next awareness, things were different, as though a trap had sprung for both of them.

"How did you know my name?" He raised a beer to his lips, staring over the bottle, his cheeks flushed.

She closed her eyes, only to reopen them at the crack of glass against stone. The man stepped away from a bottle now standing on a brick fireplace. There was a woozy, hypnotic quality to his move-ment. But not just him - everything was slow, especially time.

Her gaze drifted across a wall of bare brick to the fireplace, its cold, charred logs decorated with cigarette stubs. She tracked upwards then to a nicotine yellow ceiling, before her attention fell, finally, to herself.

She sat in an old garden chair. He'd tied her wrists to the armrests by thin, plastic-wrapped cable. The same cord bound her ankles, its blue sheath scratched and stained, but unbreakable. Her clutch-bag lay in the corner on top of a pile of offcuts of the same cable. It looked like a washing line, although she doubted whether this man had ever used it for that purpose.

Just to her left, a brown herringbone waistcoat hung over a bench. The smell had an ugly, drowsy familiarity. Beyond that bench was an old, black door.

Finger-snaps at her ear brought her back. "I'll ask once more. How. The fuck. Do you know my name?"

"I - I don't know you." She was confused. She remembered uttering a name with a strange certainty, but could no longer remember the words she'd used. The name had risen from her, like water drawn from a river, but now it had fallen back to the depths.

"Lying bitch. You said the name John O'Neill. Where did you hear that?"

"I'm sorry. I can't remember."

"Fuck this! Who are you?"

Again, confusion. *I don't have a name. I don't need one here.*

But another part of her was desperate to comply, couldn't bear the terror of his anger, was almost frozen by it.

Almost.

She forced the words to come. "I'm... I'm Maeve... Please. Why am I here?"

The man's grin was a brief, humourless thing, a reflex of muscle and bone, more shark than human. "Soon enough," he said.

Death, she thought. *That's why I'm here.*

Because it was all around her. In the walls. In the air. In the sickly light.

People had died here. And there would be more dying to come.

The man was stocky rather than tall, although certainly taller than she was. Sweat had browned the collar of his shirt. Fumbling at his breast pocket, he withdrew a lighter and a cigarette. Once lit, he blew two rings of smoke towards the wall. For a few moments, they hung suspended in front of the brickwork like shackles. He placed the cigarette on the mantle, staring outwards, a little red interrogating eye. "I saw you before. A fortnight ago. At the Bennan wood."

"I enjoy forests."

"You'd have enjoyed it less if that American family hadn't turned up... But it wasn't just then. About a week after, near midnight, when I took the Polish lassie from the bus stop on Kennishead Road, you arrived just as I was driving away. "

He must mean the night of her strange compulsion to go walking in the dark. She couldn't explain it, so shook her head. "I don't remember."

"Well, I do. I remember kicking myself. Wishing I'd been more patient. Then you turn up in the bar. And now, you seem to know my name. Too many coincidences, and I don't like coincidences. How do you know me?"

"I'm not... I'm not sure..."

He walked behind her, but as she twisted to follow, his fingers seized a clump of her hair, jerking her head back. "Try again."

"I don't know! I don't know! Maybe I heard someone in the bar?"

"Nobody knew me there. Do better." When he wrenched her hair again, the thin plastic backrest cut into her neck like a shard of broken glass.

Panic tightened her throat, but she choked out something, an idea rising from her desperate need to placate him. "I-I think... maybe... it might be through my dad."

"Who the fuck is your dad?"

"Alan-Alan Gordon. He's ex-army."

This is where it could fall apart. Her captor might not believe her, or might not know anyone with a military background. But with her head snapped upwards, her eyes staring at his face, she saw a distinct loosening in his features. He released her hair and returned to the fireplace to retrieve his cigarette.

She wondered, then, if she had tumbled into her own Arabian Night, where, like Scheherazade, she must weave a tale to save her own life. But she felt no creative spark, only fear. In her favour, she did have one tale to offer, that of her own strange history. And when all you have is the truth, the truth is what you use. Perhaps the story would force him to view her as a person, make it more difficult to kill her?

Because she knew beyond doubt that this man was a murderer. That was an utter certainty, drawn from the same well as his name. It was drawing closer, that strange reservoir of impulse and knowledge, one step removed from the frightened woman tied to the chair, and yet all around her.

So she began. "They posted my dad to Armagh, Northern Ireland. It was near the end of the troubles. Mid-nineties. He was manning a checkpoint with a mate. Uncle Frank, that's what he calls him when he speaks to me, although I never met him. They were close, so I suppose he would have been an uncle to me if he'd lived. See, they were talking when a sniper shot Frank in the face."

"That's one way to kill a conversation, eh?"

She understood him, using interruption to reinforce who was in control. But with cord lashing her to his chair, she needed no reminder. "My dad had some kind of breakdown. He doesn't talk about it much, except once or twice when he's had a few drinks. For him, there's a blank immediately after it happened. But at some point after he remembers himself walking. He kept going too, for hours, overnight and into the morning, blood and brains on his uniform."

"No time for a costume change, if you're a deserter."

"It wasn't desertion." She didn't want to argue, but he might as well understand. "It was… what they call a fugue state."

"What the fugue's that?"

"It is a kind of blackout brought on by extreme stress."

38

He smiled his shark's smile again, flashing yellowed teeth. "Having that skill in your family might come in handy for later." He reached down to tug at the knots of the washing line that bound her wrists. *Snap-snap-snap.* It showed no signs of stretching or breaking. "But it will take more than a blackout to get you up and walking."

Another certainty floated up from the riverbed. *He needs to hear it. Ignore everything else.* "By morning he'd walked half-way around Lough Neagh. He stopped near the shore at Randalstown Forest—"

Hearing the name triggered something in the man. "I... I had people near there. Once."

"Well. He met someone there. A woman."

"What was her name?"

"He called her Maeveen."

The shock that flashed across his features seemed to travel from another time and place.

HE HAD BEEN GETTING ready to leave for Scotland, where they'd decided he'd live following the complaints. His sister was only a child, not nearly so smart and clever as they all thought, just an uppity little bitch. When he put down his cases in the hallway, she shouted, "The noise! There's that noise again!"

He didn't like the noise or her excitement, so pushed her to the floor. "It's just foxes fucking in the woods." When she glared at him, he raised his hand to strike.

But his grandfather grabbed him by the wrist. "Shut your filthy mouth and be gentle." The expression on the old man's face was one the boy later came to know as disgust. The old man whispered. "You weren't gentle with the village girls, but be gentle with your own blood."

He'd answered, "Why be gentle at all?" It was a simple question, and not one ever answered to his satisfaction.

The old man pushed past him and took the girl in his arms.

"Ignore him. And ignore the noise. I'll tell you what my granny told me, the same thing that her granny told her: that noise is just Maeveen of the Woods."

———————

THE MAN'S distant expression prompted her question, "Do you recognise that name?" But instantly, she regretted summoning his attention.

"Fuck off. I ask questions. You answer." His shock had passed and his lip curled into suspicion. "What age was this Maeveen, then?"

"I don't know. My dad's age, I guess. He said she was beautiful." A man meeting a beautiful woman in a forest would always sound like a fairy-tale, but she'd known it was true from the moment her father first told her. "When they met, she understood what he'd been through. She sang for his dead friend and washed down his uniform. Something happened between them."

"That sounds very mysterious, considering you mean a squaddie shagged some bint under a tree... Say it *was* near where I used to live? What's it got to do with me?"

The question scared her, because she didn't know how to answer it, but another thought rose to calm her. *The story is his as well. He will hear it.*

"My Dad made it back to barracks. They medically discharged him, deaf in one ear, suffering from post-traumatic stress, or whatever they called it back then."

"That's it?"

"No... He went back for a reunion in '96, and visited Randalstown Forest hoping to find her again. He did. She handed him a baby, me, and said I should cross the water with him..."

The man's face twisted in derision. "What? Some hoor gets herself knocked up. And he just believes the baby was his?"

"Seems that way. I look like him."

The man snorted. "Dogs and their owners… And she didn't come back with him?"

"She couldn't. That place was her home. She couldn't leave."

HIS SISTER HAD PUT her hands on the old man's cheeks, as though to snap him back to his senses. "But if you're my granda, and your granny's granny knew her, how can she be here all this time?"

And Granda had replied, "Because Maeveen is ours and we're hers. She'll never leave this family. She's telling us that something bad will happen for someone close to us, perhaps someone near their time will pass soon. Her song gives us this knowledge. Dark, sad, knowledge, for sure. But she looks after us, in her way, the way of the *Bean Sidhe*."

The boy shook his head. "You're both fucking mad. People today know weird shit doesn't exist."

Granda said, "People today refuse to believe for the same reason scared children refuse to look. We shouldn't hide under the blanket. Things are what they are."

"Well, you are what you are," the boy said. "A mad old cunt and I won't miss you."

"Likewise, son," his granda answered.

MAEVE DIDN'T DISCUSS her parents with anyone anymore. People expected anger or pain, either with her mother for staying or her father for leaving. But she wasn't angry. Why be angry at something being as it had to be?

The man was frowning, picking at his chin. "If you left there in '96, and came here. That's the same as me. Funny coincidence. Us meeting under these circumstances."

Not funny, Maeve thought. *Not coincidence either. But what?*

"But I still don't see how you know my name. So…" He stalked to her left, unlocked the black door and let it swing wide. Rafters criss-crossed a vaulted roof above a dirt floor. A cold draught against her neck told her the place was an outbuilding of some kind. "This," he said, "is where you're going, unless you tell me now."

A cable hung from the rafters. She followed it with her eye, down towards a stool. "You do nothing except sit down," he said. Then the shark's grin came out again. "I do the rest… Unless you tell me how you know me."

"You're why I'm here."

"No shit, Sherlock. But how do you know me?"

What could she say, except the truth, bubbling up from the river bed? "My mother knew you. So I know you."

He nodded to himself, a visible relaxation in his features. "A little village slut with a grudge? I was thirteen. You'd think she'd have got over it." Then he frowned. "But that means you lied about never meeting your mother."

"I didn't lie. I've never met her."

At that, he seemed to lose interest, turning away to face the outbuilding. "I'm tired of this shit," he said. "You don't know me. But I know you. You're a stupid wee lassie who was too scared to sing for your own friends." He pointed towards the stool. "Well, you teased me too many times, so now you've something to fear for real." He shrugged and retrieved his cigarette from the mantlepiece, inhaling deeply before throwing the stub at the fire grate. "I'll do you a favour first. I'll help you overcome your phobia… Sing. For me."

"Why?"

"Because," he said, "I fucking told you to." In his eyes, the shark was circling, scenting power.

But all her life, she'd refused to sing.

At church, she'd lowered her head, staring at the pew in front. In school, her father had provided repeated excuse-notes. *Anxiety*, those notes claimed, although it had never been fully correct. With friends, she'd shrug and make excuses. Whenever a teacher had pleaded for the good of the class, she'd put on a performance, silently mouthing her way through group performances. She'd faced, laughter and anger and mockery. But no-one, ever, had heard her voice raised in song.

"Yes," she said. "I'll sing for you."

He grinned, walked towards her chair, and took a Stanley knife from his back pocket. He showed her the small blade, sharp but flecked with rust, before cutting the cable securing her left hand and right ankle to the chair. "Listen," he said, enjoying his moment. "I better like your song, because you're now half-way to the barn. And you don't want to go there. So… Your song better be good."

"Oh," she answered, suddenly certain of so many things, "It's your song, not mine." And then, she began.

Maeve, having never learned a single song, found that here, in this moment, there were so many she simply *knew*. Song after song, rising like fish from the hidden depths of her being. She knew laments, and she would sing those later, one for each of his victims, but this man needed to hear a different tune. A song selected for his individual instruction. A song of unmaking.

The moment her chant began, the very instant her never-used but powerfully keening voice took flight, the man's expression changed. From a shark drunk with power, he became something else, something weaker, something fearful. He fell hard against the brick fireplace, before staggering towards the barn. Through the black door, finding no escape, he stumbled to his knees. "What are you… doing?"

And with that, she knew it had begun, his first taste of the dark fruits of unmaking. For this was no elegy to commemorate those in the grave, but a hymn for those who put them there. It was a song with a gift. A dark, bleak gift of knowledge, propelling its listener into the worlds unmade by their actions.

And he would experience all of it.

Depths, wastes, gulfs, barrens uncharted spaces

The first verses introduced him to the depths of the *would-have-*

been, the dark voids spawned by the unlived years of his victims. Her words pushed him into those gulfs, pressed on all sides by countless deeds undone, both those of the women he 'd killed, and those still-born in the grief of their friends and loved ones. She took a breath momentarily and he surged forward, in a vain attempt to flee. But all purpose founders in the *would-have-been,* all plans are undone, all power stolen. The loss of control was so profound, he shrieked in the face of it. Staring impassively into the barn she saw a man whose body would not serve him, his feet scrabbling against broken ground, his hands tearing uselessly at the dirt. She resumed her singing, for there was more for him to see.

The song now wound deeper into the *never-can-be*, the endless expanding shadow of lost possibilities, a bleak, empty road filled only with the silence of children and grandchildren that would never be born. That melody traced a barren path stretching forward through time, empty of descendants, empty of change and love and creation and play. Empty of schemes and dreams and aspirations. A yawning infinity of potential experience, now stolen forever.

But all spaces, even those empty barrens, have natural laws. Life, as the source of possibility, cannot remain in the *never-can-be.* As if realising this, in a sudden stab of lucidity, the man rolled onto his back, eyes wide with terror. His brutish labours, his years of sadistic toil, had spawned a vast emptiness where nothing could ever survive. And by demanding this song, he had placed himself to the very heart of it.

By the time her final phrase was uttered, a corpse lay on the dirt of the barn floor, its eyes staring lifelessly upwards, its fingers curled into useless fists.

AS SHE DRAGGED THE CHAIR, retrieving the knife to free herself, she was perplexed by the word that bubbled into her awareness.

Lament.

It seemed that even now, her mother's instincts were strong in her. But her mother's work here was done. She was her own person, a new person, in full possession, finally, of the meaning of her story.

Over time, perhaps, she would form a complete sense of purpose, her own duties and obligations, her own codes and rules. If so, perhaps her first rule took shape now as she stepped over his corpse. For such as him, let there be no lament. Let them remain forever unmourned.

SWOLE

PART I – GYM RATS AND OTHER REUNIONS

TONY MINETTI

Hi Mum, Sorry to disturb the Tuscan
retirement. But guess what? I have an
interview with your favourite restaurant. The
Ship is reopening.

MUM

Be polite to Peter and Jeanie.

I'm not sure it's still them.

Be polite to whoever.

Of course! It's just the interview. Swearing
and intimidation come later.

Don't even joke about that, Tony. Not after
everything.

Sorry! Main thing is, if I get the job, could I
tempt you and Dad back for a nostalgic visit?

We're seeing your cousins today. I really don't know about the other thing.

Well, you can think about it. I'm off to the gym.

Oh, Tony. Be careful.

After Mum and Dad emigrated, the gym was the only place I really felt at home. Of course, my relationship with the place extended back further than that. If my school years were a deluge of misery, then I pretty much washed ashore at a weights rack. I was alive, I was me, and for the first time ever, I was one of the guys. You get used to the friendly banter, the clatter of weights and bars, the smell of sweat.

But it wasn't just about familiarity.

There was something important about who I became in that space, something I learned through the arc of a dumbbell. I watched my body lengthen, tighten, expand, and, OK, contract, but I had stumbled over the one sure antidote to a small life: *Be bigger.* The place taught me something vital: the world would not give me space – I had to take it.

When my gym bag buzzed under a nearby bench, the bicep spell was broken. It was my phone alarm. *Interview time.*

I offloaded a little more nervous energy completing a final set of curls. I found them comforting. I was starting to feel OK about how my arms looked in the mirror, so long as my vests weren't too tight. Maybe not all of me was ready for primetime, but that was just part of life. A crappy part, sure, but every guy in here was the same on some level. Fighting to fix themselves, to hold on to something they were losing, or to gain something they'd never had. This was not a journey that really ended.

Just then, as if arriving to prove me a liar, Strawweight Steve Tate walked into reflected view behind me. I mean, it looked like Steve, but he'd been away for a year, and something was different. You know that thing where a person's face is carefully peeled off and pasted onto the body of a Greek god? Yeah – that. His physique was unrecognisable, but in all the best ways.

First order of business was that his "Strawweight" nickname needed to be sent back for review. Steve had earned it early in his gym career, by repeatedly boasting about frankly implausible amounts of boxing experience. Perhaps we'd been unfair to doubt him? He might have been one of those tough bare-knuckle guys who scratched a hard living going toe-to-toe with a parade of carnival mice.

When all was said and done, I had always liked the man. Even back when he was less jacked, I'd secretly envied how such a lean physique could have been his natural state. Until now, at least.

So I turned around to check whether the weight-room mirror had been secretly replaced by one from a sideshow, but I found there was no escaping reality. This was definitely the guy, just not as I'd ever known him. "No offence, Steve – but what the hell did you do?"

The lad had the audacity to feign ignorance. "I was away with my job for fourteen months. I couldn't get back here to work out." He said this completely deadpan, like his mere absence meant we could ignore the elephant in the gym.

"Piss off, mate. You know what I mean. You. Are. Unbelievably. Shredded." Actually, Steve had always been shredded, just more in the style of wet lettuce. Of course, neither of us had been obvious bodybuilder material when we met – a fact that probably contributed to our odd friendship.

In response to my awed expression, get this: *he just shrugged.*

Right then, I decided that if I ever reach the mountain top, I would be a lot more gracious to the lesser gym-rats. "C'mon, man, spill. How did you manage this? What's your programme?"

Of course, I had my own ideas. Judging by those oversized traps, I suspected that Steve's previously holier-than-thou training had turned distinctly less "natural". He'd always been a devout natty, and I'd come later to the party. My repeated experimentation proved my temperament turned unmanageably volatile in the presence of anabolics. By refraining from juice, we'd both bonded unhappily, watching every meathead with a syringe make gains we could only dream of. Maybe too much of that kind of punishment eventually turns every natty into a lying hypocrite. I tried again."What happened to you, man? I thought you didn't want any physique that had to be injected into your arse-cheek?"

Yeah, OK, so this outburst was a bit of a code-breach. The gym showers certainly revealed more than their fair share of puncture bruising, but it's poor form to talk about it. Rules of fight club and all that.

"No injections, Tony. I'll tell you about my programme, but do you mind if we move?" He stalked off towards an antique treadmill the management had gathering dust in case someone went insane and decided they'd like some cardio. I followed him, but with a fair bit of puzzlement: if roles were reversed, I'd have spent maximum time flexing near the mirror.

Anyway, I didn't need to wait too long for him to outline his regime, but when revealed, it was disappointing. He said, "I mainly did bodyweight stuff at home—"

"Bullshit!"

"No equipment except for a chair—"

"Bollocks!"

"—but the real trick was Ape-X from BZB."

Finally, something I could believe. But even so, it wasn't the name of any performance enhancer I recognised. Usually, the same old substances appeared and reappeared on a merry-go-round of constant rebranding. I basically ignored the marketing names and focused on the actives. Compounds that don't work in blue foil won't do much better in a green envelope.

But... what if this Ape-X was really new? I mean, if it worked for Steve (and trust me, it had really, really worked for Steve) then could it even do the trick for yours truly? "Is this thing an import? Is there a local… channel? Is it grey market, or…?"

"Bro, relax, it's super easy." He said this with a completely flat expression, perhaps emphasising how zero-bullshit he wanted to be. But if so, he kind of overdid it: his oiled pecs had considerably more sparkle than his eyes. "I have details for you." He handed me a card from a little stack in his shorts pocket. It read:

APE-X from BZB
(v2) https://bzbapex6one6vixi.onion
(v3) https://bzbapex6one6vixi4p35ppes2hojjmur2qhjh3feub2f-s5eo4zq22yad.onion/

A phone number, presumably Steve's, was scrawled in faint pencil on the back of the card, but I was more interested in the bizarre URLs on the front. They looked unlike any web addresses I'd ever seen. "How do I use these?"

"They're on the dark web. Do you know TOR?" In response to my clueless expression, his attempt at a reassuring smile came out wrong – as a kind of same-shit-different-day grimace. "Download an onion browser for your phone. It keeps everything private. Oh, and use the version three address. Version two was shit-canned a while back, and I haven't had time to reprint the cards."

The suspicious cynic in me wondered, since these were his own cards, whether he was playing me. "Fess up, Steve. Are you on commission?"

"I'm just a happy customer."

I examined his blank superhero features with more than a little suspicion. A happy customer would surely crack a genuine smile now and then. The more obvious explanation was he'd discovered better living through chemicals and now pushed gym-candy as a side hustle.

But, of course, I wanted to believe. Perhaps Steve avoided smiling simply to showcase his epic jawline? Another sweep of the man confirmed what I already knew. He'd undergone an incredible top-to-toe transformation. Damn!

Since I was running out of time, I said my goodbyes and then hit the showers. But while I soaped up, the business cards thing continued to bother me. Printed cards suggested a sales gig, and a sales gig meant an oversize quota of steroids to shift. If that was Steve's game here, then my oversize history with acne and mood issues would prevent me following him onto the winner's podium.

I towelled dry, stuck on my suit, and then headed out for my interview.

I JOGGED to make up time, but it was cold enough that I wasn't scared of arriving in too much of a sweat. The park was crawling with teenagers. I'd usually attempt to steer clear of the school crowd, but this cut-through was the fastest route to the high street. While I understood they needed to go somewhere at lunchtime, I wished, for the good of the community, that schools would stagger their release a little.

From my left, I saw a uniformed boy with too much hair sprinting across the grass. Someone shouted, "Do it, Galzoty!" as he turned and cruised to a stop directly in front of me.

His nickname and swagger shared a telltale similarity with a historical nemesis from my own school years. Michael Gallagher, AKA Galzo had joined in third year and quickly climbed the ladder of popularity by creating nicknames for the saps with no hope of ever reaching even the first rung. He'd taken one look at my under-developed but podgy frame before shouting, *Hey, Fatboy Slim!* Alternating that with the slightly more surreal: *Wobble-Stick!* Naturally enough, I felt no warmth at all for this approaching younger version. He shared too many of his brother's facial features, not least his sneer.

"Hey man! Could you buy us a six-pack of cider?"

The kid's thumb gestured back towards his crowd of homeboy schoolies, another rogues gallery of leering family resemblances. I decided that, since I was in a hurry, punishing the sins of the elder brothers was sensible and appropriate, so I picked up my pace and barged forward.

The youth, squeaking noises that blended rodent with Russian sailor, stumbled backwards in surprise before throwing himself desperately onto the grass. He landed on his arse with a heavy thump.

Good.

A little spirit raiser before the interview was more than welcome.

I'D WORKED at a few restaurants in the area, but never at The Ship. The place had been closed for a while, and beyond the fact it had most recently been a hang-out for a shrinking bingo and lawn-bowling crowd, I didn't know much history.

From outside the stylish new door, I could tell the revamp had been considerable. Someone was spending money on it, so that was a good sign. I rang the bell and watched through the glass as a young woman approached.

When the door opened, she smiled. "Hi, Tony. I'm Alison Monroe, the owner here."

She brought me inside, walking us round a mound of dust sheets. "Apologies for the mess. The decorator removes it all tomorrow morning."

I liked what she'd done with the place. I dimly remembered storm-grey carpets and sea-lashed tablecloths, but here and now, I saw sanded floors and crisp white linen. What little nautical theming remained was fresh and modern, and I particularly enjoyed the little mirrored ship's wheel which was the menu stand on each table. It was all high-end, but light touch, and all the better for it.

Alison was about my age, but seemed more serious, or maybe

that was just her glasses. It turned out Peter and Jeanie, who my mum remembered, were her parents, and they'd owned the place, until old-age had taken them out of the game. Alison had started a slow programme of refitting but had completed her business degree before getting serious. That meant the place had been a money sink for over a year, and she had zero direct experience of running a restaurant. It was clear she could do with some help.

She spoke a lot about her folks, and it sounded like she had a great relationship with them. I always thought well of people who managed that, given I'd screwed things up so royally with my own.

It's funny how things get under your skin though. I had only vague ideas about career progression, and was really just there for a job to pay my bills, but I was starting to want this place to succeed. Maybe I could help her?

So I started my pitch. "I've been in the food sector since I left school, before actually. I spent two years at catering college part-time, supporting myself as a coffee-shop barista and table-washer. Since then, I've been in restaurants, starting in the kitchen, rotating through various roles. Most recently, I've been a front-of-house manager, only a deputy, but I think I can do more. That's why I'm interested in the opportunity here."

"That's good, because I don't need a deputy. I want a full co-manager, someone experienced who I can learn from." A lot of bosses I'd encountered wanted employees to do what they were told and shut up while they did it. Alison's lack of ego was refreshing.

"Well, if you need kitchen staff, I know some chefs. I have a pastry chef who gave me a spiced coconut panna cotta recipe so addictive I keep it in a lead-lined box."

"I've got pastry covered, but I'll take the other names. And I love the sound of that panna cotta. Coconut is a weakness of mine, and don't start me on rum."

Her saying that made me realise what was missing. "I don't see a bar area. You will be licensed, right?"

She nodded. "The last bit of fitting happens this week."

That was a relief. "Great. I've worked places where bar takings were a third of revenues, while other places in the same area, with the same kind of customer but no licence, made peanuts. One lesson from my last job was learning how bring-your-own-bottle without a sensible corkage charge just ends up cutting your own throat. I'm totally fine with B.Y.O.B, and customers do appreciate the option, but getting your corkage policy right is a must-have. You protect revenues *and* nudge the customer towards the in-house drinks list, especially when you've chosen options specifically to complement the food."

"As co-manager, I'd be relying on you for input on all of that."

Helping her, being someone she could rely upon, was starting to feel important. I even allowed myself to wonder if she might ever look at me the same way I'd looked at Steve. Actually... not quite – I'd prefer a slightly different kind of appreciation, with a darn-sight less jealousy.

But there really was something quite captivating about imagining her gaze, shining through those stylish glasses of hers. The old movies got that completely wrong – the idea that wearing glasses somehow obscured attractiveness. Man, she positively rocked those things.

"Tony?"

"Sorry... I was mentally drawing up a wine list."

"Great, but there's something else I'll need you for initially."

She rose, beckoning me to follow. We walked to the back of the restaurant and then out through the kitchen. Even from a brief glance, that was a good, well outfitted space. Decent surfaces were important, especially since every chef I'd ever known basically clattered pans for a living. When we left the kitchen, we took a right, entering into a space bathed in natural light. There was a glass wall and door, opening out onto a cobbled lane.

"So, Tony, you've seen The New Ship, now welcome to The Dinghy."

My heart sank, in all honesty. There was a huge chrome fryer range and counter-top dividing us from the glass-fronted entrance. "Oh. So… fish and chips?" She could see the disappointment on my face.

"Look, I know your family business from your CV. What I hope we'll do here is higher-end. Even though I know the business plan can work, I really need someone who understands the practicalities."

Practicalities.

I understood those alright. One practicality was how easily a teenage fry cook with underdeveloped self-control can get wide on their own supply. I had tried to avoid chippie-fare in the last three years, since I still struggled with the physical fallout from my earlier food choices. But as I stared, frozen, before the polished metal of my teenage nemesis, I realised that the mental damage was the harder nut to crack. Alison was watching. The last thing she needed was a headcase crying over spilled lard.

I sighed and threw her a smile. "Ignore my surprise. I understand the business idea, and there are other benefits from attaching a posh chippie to a bistro. You'll always have something to offer for the picky kid or awkward adult who can't handle the à-la-carte, so a broader range of groups will book here. What's your menu plan?"

"What do you suggest?"

"A chippie won't succeed without covering the classic bases – this part of the world that means haddock, breaded and battered. You'll need a high-end butcher for the bistro anyway, so as far as sausages, black puddings, haggis, burgers – have them suggest which of their offerings will work for the fryer. Some more upmarket thoughts, off the top of my head? Monkfish would work, also halibut, salmon and maybe a couple of fusion plays like Thai fishcakes or panko shrimp. I didn't do purchasing in my last two restaurants, but I still know a great supplier from back in the day. We can head down and check them out together if you like."

I knew the interview had gone well when she offered me the job then and there, starting in two days' time. I accepted, of course.

But as she walked me to the door, her small talk turned to my other interests. Of course, I mentioned the gym and working out, but she seemed surprised, somehow, whereas I thought it should be completely apparent from first glance.

Her surprise bothered me all the way home.

Sure, I didn't get to the gym as much as I wanted, but c'mon, I worked out enough, didn't I? Why wasn't it obvious? Why couldn't she see it?

But even as I asked myself the question, I knew the answer. I was lean in the wrong places and not lean enough in others. I saw myself in the mirror constantly, after all, and my most obvious problem, clothed, anyway, was a jowly face above a skinny pencil neck. I hated my neck, and I was tired of trying to fix it the hard way.

Welcome to APE-X from BZB.
Make it your goal to be swole.

MY FIRST THOUGHT WAS: only two sentences? That's it?

Steve's card had brought me to the most basic text website I'd ever seen. After downloading the browser and painstakingly typing the strange onion URL, gaining only two little sentences as a reward was a definite anticlimax.

As I watched my phone, a graphical swirl appeared, pulsing in the middle of the browser screen. This swirl expanded into a message:

Now, fetch a chair. Seat yourself facing that chair.

When Steve had warned me I'd need a chair, I'd thought he was joking, but apparently not. Since I had no easily movable chair, I placed a kitchen stool between my bed and my mirrored wardrobe. This would allow room for press-ups or whatever exercise might be involved.

The pulsing resumed, and then:

Click the box marked "I accept all terms" to invite our agent.

My plan was simply to make contact and find out what they were selling. If it was something that I'd already failed with, then I'd end the conversation – no biggie. I considered reading the terms, but deep down I knew that, even if I could find the document link to download, I didn't have the motivation to actually read it. So instead, I clicked the box.

You have accepted terms.

Those words pulsed for around twenty seconds and then:

Now press the "Summon" button.

I almost laughed at the poor attempt at drama. They should have called it a *submit* button like everyone else, because people saw straight through lame attempts to build tension like this. Still, I pressed the damn button. The pulsing swirl flickered briefly before being replaced by a new message.

Place your device on the stool and wait.

I wondered if they might be accessing my telephone camera, otherwise how could they know I'd used a stool? But, since I hadn't been prompted by the browser to give permission to use the phone features, it seemed more likely that their script just used the terms chair and stool interchangeably. I placed my phone on the stool, angled towards my seating position so I could still read it, then I sat down and waited for the next message.

But no pulsing came, and no message arrived.

In fact, there seemed to be nothing happening visually at all – my phone screen was now completely blank. Instead, some warbling Muzak began. But underneath that distracting noise, I heard something quiet and strange: a rustling, hissing, or whispering kind of sound. I thought it came from outside the device at first — perhaps a procession on the road? But the fact this strange noise had been slowly and rhythmically building from the point I'd first been instructed to wait, strongly suggested this was an audio track played by the website.

I listened hard, trying to make sense of the sounds. I wasn't sure if they were words or not. Some sounded as if they might be, just not in any language I was familiar with.

Then the whole thing turned into a racket, almost like feedback on an amplifier, but just as I began to reach for the volume rocker on my phone, there was a distinct cough.

"Whoo… Howdy, friend. Bill Zee here. So you wanna be swole?"

The power of that voice was quite shocking in the space of my empty room.

"Pardon?"

"That's why you're here, right? Sent by Steve? Good ole boy, Steve."

"How do you know I was sent by Steve?"

"Oh, encoded URL blah-blah. Technological fingerprinting blah-blah. You'd have to run that one past the backroom boys… But if you don't mind, friend, for my own amusement, how do I sound to you?"

"I don't… I mean… Sound?"

"Yes sir! How do I sound? I'm always fascinated by you guys, how your brain puts things together. The associations and so on. I mean, dollars to doughnuts, when you listen to me, you hear an accent, right, some kinda dialect? Where do you place me?"

"Well, you're obviously American. Southern states, yes?"

There was a whoop of laughter. "Alright! Ah, the good ole U S of A! Makes sense and very common. Top destination for business and deal-making and so on! And as for the south, well, I'll give you deep, deep south, yes sir! Rumours do indeed persist of me coming down to Georgia from time to time. But you don't need my greatest hits. You need something else. Shoot!"

The clarity of this man's voice raised the hairs on my neck and arms. Everything told me I was having a conversation with a person seated on the stool opposite my bed. I felt, from the volume and direction of the voice, that it originated at head-height, not from where the phone lay. Peering into that space, all I saw was my phone on the empty stool, a reality underscored by the stool's reflection in the mirrored wardrobe.

I wanted to ask how this vocal presence could be so powerful, but Bill Zee spoke again, derailing my train of thought. "Digital-signal-processing-blah. Advanced-audio-technolo-blah. Resonant vibrations from the wooden stool, blah-blah-blah. That's another one for the boys in the backroom, and they ain't here. But I am, and I sure as shooting know you hear a deal-maker talking. So let's talk business."

"OK. What is Ape-X? Is it a steroid? See, I can't—"

"I know, I know. You, my friend, have a range of volcanoes slumbering under your skin. Your face erupts just like Alaska rubbed in bacon grease. Angry skin, even angrier mood swings. The kind of rage not even a mother could love, am I right?"

The voice paused, giving me time to remember my own mother. I hadn't seen her for three years now.

"Hell, son, tantrums in an adult ain't attractive, muscles or not. That kind of anger, well, shoot, it can drive people away, maybe even cost you the people you love—"

I'd known my parents were driven to emigrate by the changes in my personality and behaviour. Maybe that wasn't the only reason, but it was the main one. It was odd, hearing this voice unknowingly but accurately narrate my experience with steroids. Perhaps it was a story they encountered frequently among their clients?

"—but you just knew if you kept on down that road, then sure as shooting, you'd be the guy with hulkin' man-boobs and shrunken balls... So you did the sensible thing and steered clear. I respect that, Tony, and I want to reassure you, Ape-X ain't a steroid or any of that old school shee-it. Let me tell you why you're here. Hmm. You do look kinda off. Bony, more than brawny, and yet flabby more than sculpted... But you don't need your flaws catalogued. You just want them fixed."

"But how... can you see me?"

"Dang! You caught me out on a sales trick. You are sharp, Tony, sharp as a razor! Thing is, I don't need to see you guys, 'cos you all reach my showroom the same way. We have a sales funnel, see, and telling our prospects they look, well, the way they look, it makes that funnel a vortex. Sure, it upsets their ickle babyfaces, but that's just Bill Zee's first rule of sales: you want to sell a new mattress? First make them shit the bed..." Then Bill's voice grew concerned, gentle. "But, Tony, the plain truth is, you don't look right. Not how you want, am I right?"

"OK. Yes. You're right." There was no point lying about it.

"What are your current goals?"

"Obviously, I want to be bigger. More attractive to women. And I've struggled with a soft middle – I'd like some lines down there."

"Then Ape-X is what you need."

"But what is Ape-X, exactly?"

"It's the food of champions and ten-thousand-pound gorillas. Do you wanna be a champion gorilla, Tony? Do you wanna be the silverback?"

"Of course. But, c'mon, are you saying Ape-X is a food supplement?"

"You betcha."

Fortunately, he couldn't see me look away from my phone in disgust. "Well, I've tried a lot of things already and I can't believe I'll do better with just some supplement when—"

"Just some supplement? *Just?* Ape-X is *the* supplement. It's calorically dense, nutritionally light and designed to do one thing – provide a scoopable, drinkable dinner that immediately shows up as muscle."

So there it was: the whole thing revealed as a ridiculous scam.

Whichever way Steve had achieved his physique, it surely couldn't be this.

Eventually, Bill Zee's voice broke the silence. "I just adore that moment – you know the one, when tumbleweed rolls through a sales call? Because that, my friend, that rolling, windblown, tangle of deep scepticism is... well, healthy, sensible, and best of all, unavoidable. Bill Zee's first rule of sales: you gotta splat against that wall of objections, before you have the chance to slither upwards. So, here's my offer: I've got distribution all over and I'll get you a max-strength sample. You try it, perhaps avoiding people who know you well. But gauge a stranger's response or maybe take a selfie while drinking it. Just come back when you are ready to sign with me."

The last words echoed over and over, fading as the connection dropped, leaving a sense of something lingering. I lifted my phone from the stool and closed down the browser, glad I hadn't given my address. I'd been hoping to discover something at least halfway plausible, but a 'scoopable, drinkable dinner' was decidedly not that thing.

Never mind.

As I returned from placing the stool back in the kitchen, I sensed my bedroom still held a kind of atmosphere, an unsettling after-effect from the conversation. I doubted the discussion had left anything running on my phone, but I powered the device off just in case, then buried it in a gym bag in my locked bedroom closet.

After that, I went to my fridge to find some food I could actually chew.

MY MICROWAVE MEAL of the day was a high-protein chickpea curry, and although it did require jaw movements, they weren't especially enthusiastic ones. If it hadn't been for the bag of supermarket pakora I'd bought alongside it, I'd still have been starving.

The washing up was halfway done when I heard a soft click from my letterbox and the sound of something landing inside. By the time I'd dried my hands, retrieved the crimson sachet and opened the door, there was no sign of anyone, although Steve was the obvious suspect. He had been to this apartment block a couple of years back to pick up a spare lifting belt, and if you carried business cards, then why not a box of samples?

Hoping to catch him in the act, I switched off my lights and stood by the window scanning the car park for movement. I saw no-one, despite waiting for over two minutes. Perhaps he'd arrived on foot? Or perhaps the courier had other deliveries in the area and had left their car in the car park while they pounded the streets? Either way, I wasn't about to just stand there all night, so I gave up.

Turning the light back on gave me a chance to examine the sachet. It was around the size of a packet of airline snacks. While I doubted this powder would taste anything like dry-roasted peanuts, the label was entirely silent on flavour or ingredients. All it said was:

APE-X+ (Hi-Strength/Trial only):
Mix with liquid.
Consume.
Distribution only as authorised by BZB.
O.T.C – NO

Since I wanted to have at least some basis for my refusal when I next saw Steve, I pulled open the packet and found a yellowish gritty flour. I took a sniff, but it was utterly devoid of any scent. It seemed a heavy, mealy kind of stuff, not prone to blowing in the breeze and drifting up nostrils. Since I couldn't swear off on the basis of smell, I had no choice but to take the plunge. I poured the Ape-X into a mug, added some water, stirred, then added some more until the consistency smoothed out into something drinkable.

I took a small sip. The drink was thick, a little warmer than the water I'd added, but with the extra feature of completely lacking in taste. I guessed it might be helpful for short-term weight-cutting.

After all, the prospect of swallowing this, night after night, would quickly kill your enthusiasm for mealtime altogether. But since they were selling this supplement to gain body mass rather than lose it, I could only draw one conclusion: Ape-X was an utter crock.

I sipped some more, figuring to finish the sample so I could at least demonstrate a full and fair assessment if Steve started whining. I certainly wouldn't need to call back to order more, so I dropped the business card into an old shoe box I occasionally emptied when I could be bothered recycling paper. It was still falling when I heard a ruckus outside my door.

Thump! Thump! Thump!

Someone was banging around out there and shouting. Most of it was inarticulate, but I picked up "Wobble-Stick!" The video stream from my doorbell captured most of the corridor, but since I'd locked my phone in my bag, I had no choice but to play it old school and look out through the spy-hole.

Oh. Shit.

I recognised the face, even if it did look considerably angrier, jowlier, and more drunk than I remembered. Michael Gallagher. Galzo Senior.

At school, he'd been handsome and smooth, but the last ten years had not been good to him. I saw his fist draw back to punch the door. *Thump!*

A hideous expression of pain flashed downwards as he doubled over to cradle his hand. After a few moments an even angrier face returned into view. "Here! Fatboy Slim!" *Thump! Thump!* "You knocked him over! My little brother!"

If it went on like this, my neighbours, historically traumatised by as much as a falling dumbbell, would certainly call the police. Reluctantly, I decided I needed to talk him down. I cracked open the door and the stench of booze leaked in, so I steeled myself for the charge of a drunken bull. There was every chance this particular visitor was beyond peaceful discussion, but I had to try. "Steady on, Galzo... Calm down..." Amazingly, the man seemed to comply, at least a little.

He staggered backward so quickly I moved after him in case he was falling. "Let me make you a cuppa." I held up my mug of Ape-X, mainly to place a stoneware barrier in front of my face.

But my unexpected visitor's odd behaviour continued, and he seemed to be having trouble focusing. He screwed his eyes, rubbed them, then stretched them into wide ovals of surprise. Then he looked me up and down. Twice. Finally, he slurred, "Fuck me sideways..."

When he then staggered back a little further from the door, all belligerence had drained from his features. After long seconds of indecision, he nodded to himself, as though suddenly making sense of his situation. "O-K. Who are you, and what have you done to Tony Minetti?"

"It's still me, Galzo. I've just lost a bit of weight... But about your brother..."

"Don't you worry." The man wagged his finger in exaggerated rebuke. "That was intirell... rentirey... totally bullshit!" His finger stopped wagging for a moment, then he began tapping his own chin. "Little bro said... coffee-shop guy had knocked him over. But how would he resco...eco..."—his finger swung wildly away from his own face, before pointing – rudely, I felt – in my direction—"recognise that?"

"Well, I did work there eight or nine years back—"

"But he wouldn't have said coffee shop..." And again, the wagging finger. "He'd have said br-brick shithouse!" The man backed further down the corridor. "Tony, I'm sorry... I'm a little bit pissed." This showed a just about passable level of self-awareness, since Galzo was very pissed indeed.

But I saw something else mingled with his drunken expression, a reminder of my experience earlier that day when I first saw Steve. And my feelings then hadn't been ones I'd associate with Galzo at all. Cruelty, yes. Smugness, absolutely. But...awe? I became worried about the possibility of an underlying health crisis and stepped after him. "Galzo? Are we good? How about that cuppa?" I drained the dregs from the Ape-X, hoping it would seem like a friendly gesture. "I just want to be sure you're OK…"

But he continued to walk away, all the while mumbling to himself. "Caring too… why not? Looks like a superhero. Quacks like one…" As he made his way towards the stairs, occasional fragments drifted back towards me that sounded like the words "Biceps" and "Schwarzenegger". It was all very odd.

It might have been the adrenaline, but I suddenly felt extremely hungry. Instead of thinking about bedtime, I put two frozen steaks in the frying pan.

———

Hey Mum. Sorry it's so late. But it wasn't
Peter and Jeanie. It was their daughter.

> Wee Alison? Really? I never took her for a
> manager.

What age did you last see her?

> Six, maybe? She sometimes brought the
> shortbread for our coffee. One time your dad
> thought she'd licked it.

Gross. I'll ask her, because I got the job.

> Well done. But don't mention the licking
> thing. I think she just dribbled.

OK. Because that's SO MUCH BETTER...
Anyway, guess what? She's putting a chippie
at the side. Opening into the lane?

> I hope she doesn't let you near it.

Funny. That's actually why she wants me – all
my experience. I'm introducing her to Eddie
Braddock tomorrow.

> He's the best one right enough. Lovely man,
> once you get past the smell.

Any other advice?

> Yes. Don't fry extra battered sausages.

Be serious. That was one time.

> Not according to our balance sheet. Or your
> waistline. We could have had a villa in
> Florence if it wasn't for those sausages.

Hilarious. Did you ask Dad yet about maybe
coming over?

Not yet. You know him.

It's been three years nearly.

I'll bring it up once you're settled. You can send me a photograph of the restaurant.

OK. I'll be settled in no time..

I hope so. But remember what I said about the sausages. You were a slim, handsome boy before you ruined it.

On that bombshell, I think we'll say goodnight.

PART II – FISH KINGS AND CLEVER CAPOS

THE FISH-MARKET WAS on the edge of town, appropriately close to the Firth. I'd only seen Eddie out of hours for the last year or two, but in a professional capacity he was unchanged: a big smile framed by even bigger fishmonger whites. Once you forgave the ever-present scent of brine, I considered him a top bloke. "Alison Monroe, meet Eddie Braddock. Eddie, this is my boss, owner of The New Ship in town."

He extended his hand. "Eddie Braddock, king of haddock."

Alison curtsied. "Your Majesty." Then she caught my eye, frowning. "He does know we want his loyal subjects shipped to us in crates?"

Banter over, the meeting proved fruitful. Eddie's business could supply more than haddock, and he quickly signed on to meet all our requirements for sea-, freshwater- and shell-fish, with guaranteed capacity to deliver in time for the opening of the businesses. He even gave Alison tips for restaurant supply on the butchery side.

On the way out, Eddie leaned in conspiratorially. "Watch this one, though, Alison. I call him the Gremlin. Feed him after midnight and he does a runner."

I winced. Sometimes even a top bloke didn't know when to keep his mouth shut. I offered what I hoped was a light-hearted smile. "King of haddock? King of comedy, more like."

But on the way back to the car, as I knew she would, Alison said, "OK, Mr Gremlin, dish the dirt."

I shrugged. "Eddie's having a laugh. But OK… I left a place where the owner insisted on stuffing me with cheesecake after every service. You could say that I changed job for health reasons."

Alison nodded, then her expression turned puzzled. "Did it occur to you to just refuse the cheesecake?"

It probably sounded like a reasonable point, from her perspective. "Are you kidding? That stuff was delicious. Desperate times call for desperate measures." I noticed a flicker of concern, where I'd expected laughter. "Are you OK? You look upset."

"No… It's *my* stuff. One of my friends growing up had a bad eating disorder. Parents seemed nice, private school, all the best stuff, but she got this weird idea in her head. And it led to cycles of bingeing, over-exercise, starving herself… She's infertile now, but lucky, since it almost killed her." She unlocked the car and we both climbed inside. "I get slightly triggered sometimes, you know, by control issues around food, that's all."

"No worries. I'll pretend I don't have any."

This time, she did smile a little, although unconvincingly, so I moved on. "I've booked four interviews for tomorrow afternoon – are you still good for those?" When she nodded, I continued. "And I've been talking to a printer I've used before. They can do our take-away menus, food-safe boxes, paper bags, greaseproof liners… that kind of thing. We should put the branding and contact number on everything, but I wanted to gather your thoughts before I go back to them."

She was enthusiastic, so we brainstormed design ideas on the way back into town.

THE FOLLOWING MORNING, after meeting the printers, I was making my way back to The New Ship through the park when I heard a hissed whisper from some nearby bushes. "Yay! Muscle suit!"

I walked across, wondering if I was going mad, but sure enough I found Galzo's little brother crouched behind the rustling foliage. "Why are you hiding in a bush?"

"I'm filming for my socials. I didn't want to be seen."

"And yet you called me over?"

"No, I didn't. That was the involuntary sound of winning. I was right and my big brother needs to take the L."

"Look little-Galzo, or whatever you call yourself—"

"It's Galzo-ty – as in Galzo-T-Y, which stands for Galzo The Younger."

Detail in nicknames was evidently still a Gallagher family point of pride. "OK, Galzo-TEE, what's this about your brother and how does it involve me?"

When the kid smiled, I could have sworn his brother had just stepped out of a time machine.

"I've not chosen the link yet. I like *Coffee-shop Conman in Muscle-suit Mischief*, but *Bogus Barista in Body-suit Bullshit* is also good."

"The link for what?"

"My channel. Galzoty's Garage."

"Sorry. I'm not following. What the hell has prompted all this?"

"Well, the big bro had a bad hangover, but he was crazy wired – mad bloodshot eyes all wide open and he was like, 'That Tony dude's huge now!' And I was like 'LOL!' and then 'ROFL!' then 'piss off!' So he was like, 'No, I met him and he's absolutely massive!' And I said, 'Not unless he's rocking a muscle suit.' But he said 'no way!' So I said 'yes way!' Then he said 'prove it!' And I said 'suck it old man, challenge accepted!'" The boy clicked the photos app on his phone and began flicking through a series of extreme close-ups of foliage. The flicking became increasingly desperate until he hit a shot of what looked like a half-eaten pizza. His face was ashen when he looked up from the screen. "Oh shit. There was a branch in the way."

"That's a risk you run squatting inside a hydrangea."

"But I need evidence!"

"No, you don't. Because (a) I didn't give permission to be covertly photographed, and (b), now I'm up close, I'm sure it's obvious that I don't wear a muscle suit. Your photo could never have proved that I did."

The boy's face twisted into mockery. "I didn't mean you were suited-up now. That's stupid. I mean, look at you." His derision stung, but I knew what he meant. The youth began to lean forward conspiratorially, then retreated after getting a twig in his nostril. "What we both know, Mr Coffee-shop, is that you were wearing a muscle suit when my brother saw you. And he was so pissed he thought it was real."

"But I don't have a muscle suit and I've never worn one, so that's just bollocks."

"Aha! If you want me to believe you, you need to prove that it's bollocks, and you can't can you?"

That's when I realised that I had all the proof I needed. My doorbell camera must have recorded footage from Galzo's drunken visit, so I said, "Suck it, young man. Challenge accepted." It took me less than a minute to get to the recording on the timeline. It began with the drunken banging at the door.

"Is that my brother? He looks absolutely plastered!"

"Yes. And he was."

Then I come into view, no muscle suit in sight, and we see the awe bloom on Galzo the elder's face. "I don't know what your brother saw, but that's what I was wearing. No muscle suit."

The young man was silent.

"See? No muscle suit. We agree, right?"

But again, silence. The young bush-dweller's face was struck by the same kind of awe I'd witnessed from his brother. Eventually, he said, "That isn't you. But it is you. Wow. Total gigachad. How?"

I rewound the video. And there I was stepping into view, holding up my mug, but no, it was just me. "Is this Gallagher humour? Are you guys taking the piss?"

But the boy continued staring, mouth agape.

When we reached my second offer of tea, and I was in full view of the camera. The whole thing was just as I remembered, until I took a sip from the mug. As the Ape-X reached my lips, my video image flickered and changed. And then my jaw dropped open too. It appeared that drinking and swallowing the substance had somehow caused the camera to capture a physique of sheer magnificence, rendering my body like something from a superhero movie. The effect lasted just a few moments before the image flickered again, and I was back to myself.

The youth said, "What were you doing that night? How did you look like that?"

I didn't know what to say, so I left him in the hydrangea and headed back to the restaurant.

But on the walk to work my head wouldn't stop spinning. I'd seen something now, something I'd always wanted but never thought possible. Something I'd worked towards, but more as an unreachable aspiration than a realistic target. But now, however briefly, I'd finally seen it. I didn't know what that meant, and I tried not to become carried away, but one possibility nagged at me. Had I caught sight of the future? Could my dream of every-thing I wanted, be just out there waiting for me to come along and take it?

———————

THE SEQUENCE TO connect on their dark-web site seemed much simpler second time around. I was taken directly to a mostly empty holding screen.

Place your device on the stool and wait.

Impatiently, I watched the pulsing swirl until the processional whispers both began and then ended almost as abruptly. Music blared, a segment of some version of 'Mack The Knife', the singer sounding vaguely like Tony Bennet.

After a few seconds, the song vanished, and voice rang out. "Awright already! This is Bill Zee, Don of BZB, *capo dei capi*. You requested a sit-down. Now, whaddayawant?"

The voice, although clear and strong, was not the one I remembered. "Is that Mr Zee? Of Bill Zee Bodybuilding?"

"Bub... That last B ain't bodybuilding, but you call it that if you want. I guess it fits well enough. And this *Mr* Zee thing sounds more like my father, and we don't go there. You ain't the only one with daddy issues... Last time we talked I told you to call me Bill. So call me Bill, already."

"OK Bill... Sorry for the confusion. It's your... Brooklyn accent? To be honest, you reminded me a little of the movie *Goodfellas,* like Joe Pesci maybe." I laughed, hoping to ease into the conversation with a light-hearted observation. But the sudden silence in the room simmered with tension.

"Like Joe Pesci, how?"

I wondered how to reply, but Bill spoke across my indecision. "So, you think I'm doing an impersonation? That this is an act? That I'm here to put on a show for you? Is that what you think?"

"No. Sorry. Of course not. It's just... you sound different."

"I explained this, wise guy. I don't sound different. You hear me different. And New York? I get that a lot. The Big Apple of knowledge is one of my things, after all. A city that never sleeps is exactly the place I'd send people. But I think this... this impression... you have is something else." Another silence, and this time I imagined a movement, a presence closing in, speaking into my ear. "See, you tried the sample we gave you, and now you know I ain't shovelling horse shit. So maybe you start to wonder about the organisation who supply this product? You ask yourself, is this a crew you can run with?"

I didn't fully understand the game being played, but I supposed in a way, he was right. I had so many questions, too many, in fact, so I needed to focus on the important ones. "The first thing is… is Ape-X safe?"

"Listen. We ain't got time for bullshit so let me turn that around… Is being whatever it is you are right now safe, Tony? Is that thing you see in the mirror good enough for you? Is that the safety you're looking for? If you love yourself so goddam much then put down your damn phone and stop wasting my time…"

I thought about the question. I had never loved what I saw in the mirror. But I thought that just maybe I could love a new me like the one that flashed briefly into life on video. "OK. I'm still here, Bill. I just don't want poisoned."

"Then let me relax you. We don't have a single lab test suggesting Ape-X is toxic, so chill the fuck out. A corpse can't deliver on no contract, and I ain't goddam stupid, so we don't ice our own sales prospects…" The voice softened. "But we gotta talk change, Tony, and you gotta forget safety, because change… well, change ain't safe. If a new you is gonna climb the mountain of self-improvement, the old one gotta go in the river. Y'know, with cement shoes? And even when that's done, it's still a high goddam mountain. To get up there needs fuel. When you look in the mirror, you gotta eyeball that shit, Tony, you gotta face it: every flaw; every fault; every blemish. You need to see them, and count them, and curse them, all the time, every goddam day… Because that's the real fuel Tony, hot fuel, fuel that lasts… Self-hatred is the only fuel that will get you there."

"Self-hatred? But—"

"Or… I suppose you could go a different way, towards 'acceptance' and 'contentment'. Can you hear my air quotes, Tony? You should, because those two lame-ass strategies don't fix a goddam thing that's broken, and they never will. They just waltz around the busted fragments pretending shit don't stink. But you're better than that, kid… You know shit stinks and what it stinks of: the stench of *not goddam good enough.* Honestly? You smell it every time you look at yourself… So. We both know you wanna be fixed, don't we, Tony?"

"Yes… Please… But stop selling me." The conversation had made me nauseous. I had never been able to stomach the truth, but maybe now was my one chance to face reality. I was stuck inside a body I would never improve. Bill was right – I couldn't do this alone. "I'm in. But I think the main issue comes next… How much will Ape-X cost me?"

The voice laughed. "You ain't ready to pay yet, kid. Bill Zee's first rule of sales: don't talk price until they start to beg and throw money."

I had no idea what that meant. Did he want me to beg? I considered what form that might take, but he resumed talking.

"Nah, kid, nah. Let *me* tell *you* what's next… Ape-X is a complete programme. You gotta progress through all three stages, one for each monkey."

I thought, *First apes, now monkeys. What's next? Penguins?* But to keep it light I said, "Technically, monkeys aren't apes, but I suppose we'll let that slide."

An angry snort made me regret the attempt at humour. "Damn right you let it slide! Almost on your knees five seconds ago, but now you gonna bust my balls over branding? You people are something else, you know that? Now you're all shaved and favoured, you're too goddam good for monkeys? Well, screw you very much kid, those are the steps of the programme: we got three clever monkeys."

"OK. Sorry. Fine. We have the three wise—"

"Wise? Fuhgeddaboudit! Wisdom's a prize for boobs who don't figure shit out young enough to enjoy it. Nah, our monkeys are clever. They get a chance to speak, hear *and* see. You're coming through the first stage – you're still speaking to me – that means you're part-way clever, Tony, and I think you can go the distance."

"But how?"

"The next stage is when the monkey gets to hear. And you'll be hearing about success, listening to people react to all the ways you're changing. It's an important stage, Tony, and I wanna take you there. I really wanna do that for you... But first you gotta do a thing for me."

"Yes. OK. I will. Just tell me what you need."

"Our first monkey thinks it's clever to speak. You speaking *to* me is halfway good. Now you gotta speak *for* me, *capiche*? I need you to reach out to other guys just like you, Tony. How you do that? I ain't fussy. But you gotta get my message out. This business is a steam train, Tony, and introductions are what we shovel and burn. So, introduce me... You hear that, wise guy? Introduce me around and then you reach stage two."

As the connection closed, Bill Zee's final sentence seeming to echo in the air. I lay back on my bed and wondered what the hell he meant.

ONE HOUR before showtime on our first day, I began to worry about my recruitment choices. Kev Simpson was the trainee fryer. He'd seemed like a nice lad and keen to learn, but he'd turned up with filthy hands and trembling.

"Don't worry, Kev, I'm frying today, but I'll let you handle the range when it's quiet or I'm called into the bistro. You just need to get yourself cleaned up. Sound OK?"

"No, Tony, no it doesn't."

"What's wrong?"

"Fry times."

"It's simple, Kev. Do you remember the thermometer tests?"

"No."

"That was when we checked internal temperatures to get the cooking time for the different items."

"No, Tony, I remember that. But I don't have a great head for numbers, so I don't remember how long. I had to write the times on my hands." He held up inky fingers. What I'd taken for flashes of dirt was actually a complex scrawl of tiny writing. "See, left hand is chips and veg stuff for the rabbit-food fryers. Then my right hand is for the carnivore pans. See, as you move up the hand fry times increase. Thumb is for the big hitters, pinkies for a flash in the pan – onion rings there, see?"

"I see it, Kev. But it doesn't look very hygienic, so I think you should wash it off."

"It's hygienic – I used proper ink. It won't wash off, not for a week or two anyway. And that's all I'll need."

I shook my head. "OK. But watch what I do, and don't improvise… and please don't say rabbit food in front of the customers."

Lizzy was busy folding and piling two stacks of greaseproof lined boxes on the counter behind us. Having previously worked at a service station café, she was totally unflappable. "Tony? Just so you know, these two piles are different, and I've got the right greaseproof beside each stack. Don't touch, and if Kev goes near them, I'll fix your hygiene problem by cutting his hands off. I don't need anyone screwing up my system. You got me?"

"Loud and clear, Lizzy." She had taken everything on board with an unnerving efficiency. Serving duties would not be an issue, but I just hoped none of the punters thought they could start an argument with her.

When the clock ticked past five p.m., the customers arrived in unexpected numbers. There hadn't been a chippie in this part of town for a while, and soon locals were queued two-deep inside and beginning to form a line out on the pavement.

We had prepped for a steady downpour, but this was a deluge.

"More chips, Tony!"

No sooner had I started Kev on the peeler than I was called back to the barricades to put on some Thai fishcakes, a black pudding and some panko shrimp. I was just finishing them, filled with remorse over my part in the proliferation of batters and coatings when Alison appeared round the corner. "Tony! Two kids, Maisie and Daisy. Can you help?"

There was a large table, newly arrived at the bistro, eight adults and two young girls. The mother seemed exasperated but didn't seem able to guide us much beyond the fact *the twins are very particular,* and *they have to eat first.* I crouched at their end of the table. The pair held hands, staring solemnly forward like little girls from a horror film. Since I'd left Kev on fryer duty, I wondered if that territory might actually be where we were headed. "Hello, ladies. My name's Tony, and I'm here to find out what you like to eat?"

The girls pouted in uncanny unison. "The fancy menu is too fancy."

"OK. So that's what you don't like. What about from the chip shop?"

"Stodgy batter makes us feel icky. It's like you've painted brains on everything."

"That's still what you don't like. What do you like?"

"Food at home." At this, they lapsed into silence.

I turned to their mother. "What's their favourite thing?"

"They're very particular."

"I can see that. Little scamps..." When my smile towards the pair hit stony silence, I turned once more to the mum. "So, basically, how do you keep them alive?"

The woman's eyes narrowed. "I hoped a fancy place like this would have some ideas." I guessed the girl's restricted eating might make her feel like a bad mum. After all, I'd had a cousin who spent years living on cold tea and digestive biscuits, and every family gathering we pretended it was a sign of sophistication... until the false teeth happened, at least.

I wondered if changing tack might give everyone more wriggle room. "OK, say we just wanted to treat them, and we weren't concerned about their five-a-day... What way would we go then?"

That one seemed easier to answer. "Fish fingers with the breadcrumbs picked off, and crisps."

"Does the chef pick the breadcrumbs off or—"

"We pick the pickings!" The girls shouted in unison.

I saluted them. "Two sets of luxury crisps and fish fingers with pickable breadcrumbs coming right up."

That problem in hand, I arrived back to find a customer waving a smoked sausage like a truncheon. "This thing's cremated. It's rock hard!"

A shamefaced Kev sheltered behind Lizzy, mumbling something about one of his fingers being wrong. Lizzy looked like she was pondering some kind of counter-attack, so I pasted on a big smile and took over. I sent Kev to slice me some potato discs and haddock goujons, then I organised a free replacement with extra chips and a bottle of juice for the man's troubles.

Eventually, and thankfully, the crowds thinned and then dwindled until the first night of The New Ship and Dinghy was over. Given the size of the crowd, the number of problems had been remarkably few. I locked the door and congratulated Kev and Lizzy on a night of satisfied customers. "That's as tough as it will get. You're battle-hardened now." Lizzy rolled her eyes, showing she'd been battle-hardened on arrival, but Kev, who needed the support, grinned like a crazy person. His smile widened even more when Alison brought everyone through to the bistro to end the night with a glass of champagne.

After the drinks and a staff photo, Alison drove me home, parking outside the apartment block. In the silence, I felt an awkwardness building, so I said, "What about those twins?" I pulled my face into an approximation of horror. "How did it end?"

"Well. They liked the food, and they ate without a fuss, so job done. But perhaps there was one more jump-scare."

"OK?"

"They picked the breadcrumb batter off the goujons and stacked each fragment onto their napkins. When their plates were completely clean, and they did this strangely formal kind of mutual inspection to make sure, they raised their napkins to each other's chin, and took turns to feed each other, one morsel at a time."

"Woah."

"Woah, indeed. The mother has already rebooked for Wednesday."

"Great. Because I need to witness that feeding ritual." I could see sense in the mother's haste to book again. In a life of such mealtime monotony, there must be a powerful appeal in outsourcing the fish fingers occasionally. "I'll make sure Kev practises his potato discs."

Alison's smile faded a little. "But more seriously…" It was funny how just one little pause brought the awkwardness back. "Thank you for helping me, Tony." She touched my arm and I kind of froze. Beneath the sparkle of her glasses, I could see her eyes glisten a little.

"That's OK, Alison. It's just my job." I didn't fully understand what was going on.

"No, it's more than that. I was seriously up against it here… See, I don't know how much longer I'll have with my parents. The restaurant was the big dream of their lives, and it hurt them when it closed. Well, you've helped me resurrect it, not just as some kind of doomed tribute, but as a proper business, one that might actually work."

"One that *will* work. We'll make sure of it." That was a bold claim to make for an independent restaurant, no matter how much I really wanted it to be true. But horrified, my vision clouded as moisture welled up in my own eyes. I couldn't imagine a worse look, so I launched myself out of the car, calling back, "Thanks for the lift, boss," before hurrying into my apartment block.

Once inside my flat, I closed the door and leaned back against it, listening to my racing heartbeat. I hadn't handled that interaction well, but escape had been the only safe option. Reflexively, I pinched first at my gut, then traced an unsatisfactory line around my weak jaw. There was no room for feelings in the workplace, not for me, because feelings, of any kind, were bad, and hope the worst feeling of all.

But as I stepped forward, one foot slid out from under me, and I found myself on one knee staring at the culprit: a shiny crimson envelope. My first thought was of another sample, but when I tore the envelope open, I found only a brief note:

> *Now is not your time.*
> *But soon it can be.*
> *Spread the word: Ape-X from BZB.*

So, I had received no free sample, just a reminder to keep my eyes on the prize. But maybe there was room for hope here, after all? There was no mystery in how impressed Alison would be with the new, improved and altogether better Tony Minetti. He wasn't the kind to get over-emotional or need to flee a car.

No. For that guy, things would work out for sure.

Did you get the photo I just sent?

> Yes. Why do you have a wee boy with tattooed hands as a friend?

That's the team from The New Ship Bistro – we just opened. And Kev's hands aren't tattooed – he'd written lots of notes on his fingers to try and remember things.

> It looks very unhygienic. You should sack him.

Bit harsh. We've spoken, and it won't happen again.

> Anyway, where were you? Your father kept looking for the podgy one.

I took the picture. That's "wee" Alison in the middle with the glasses.

> She looks very nice.

She is. Oh, she didn't dribble on your biscuits. But she spilled some milk once and didn't fess up.

> A likely story...

It was a good first night, by the way. A big success.

> You can call it a success after your first year. Send me one with you in next time.

PART III – SECOND MONKEY

I FLIPPED the *CLOSED* sign of the Dinghy and watched Kev and Lizzy wind their way down the street together after another hectic night. Their first fortnight in the fast-food trenches had transformed them into a team, and they were becoming a better one with each passing night.

My major problem was that the place was busier than I'd expected. My hope of relocating to the bistro would not become a reality at this pace of service, not until I had somebody else competent to replace me in The Dinghy. I hadn't been able to get away to the gym recently either, which was bothering me.

Glumly, I wrapped up the solitary remaining Cajun sausage for a late-night supper. Having put so much effort into the menu, I found myself unwilling to see the food wasted. I knew my diet was worsening, but the days were long and demanding, and I ended each one with very little willpower in the tank.

Alison walked through from the bistro. "Tony? Got a minute?"

"Sure, boss."

"I just want to congratulate you on the twins."

"In what way?"

"Tony's Free Flavour was a big hit tonight."

T.F.F was an innovation of mine designed to expand the food horizon for the twins. Having struck out with mushy peas on their last visit, I hadn't been sure whether to persevere with it. "A hit, eh? What happened?"

"Well... let me put it the way Maisie did." Alison held her cupped hands in the air as though cradling an egg, then she declaimed, "The sour ball has many skins!"

"Oh. My. God."

"There's a weird trust forming here. You put a pickled onion on their plate, and they tried it. I mean, they repeatedly mimed a choking, horrifying death, but that was part of their game. End of the meal, both sour balls were gone. Fiona left a ten-quid tip and asked where we got our onions."

"Let's give her a jar. She's rapidly becoming our number one customer."

Alison smiled but lingered in a way that put me slightly on edge.

"Do you need me to do anything else tonight? I was about to head off."

"Yeah… So. I was speaking to Lizzy about me filling in for her when we open The Dinghy at lunchtime. Anyway, she mentioned different stacks of greaseproof?"

"I can explain that." I'd known I might have to, although I'd hoped to avoid it. "See, I screwed up with the provider and sent them some wrong details by mistake."

"Would those wrong details be this Ape-X thing with the bonkers web address?"

"That's the one. It's a gym fitness supplement. Don't worry – I paid for that batch of wrap personally, but I didn't want to waste something that was food-safe and perfectly good. So, I asked Lizzy to use that wrap when we had youngish customers in."

"She said only men though… why not women too?"

"Well…" Awkwardly, there was no reason beyond the words of Bill Zee: *Reach out to other guys just like you, Tony.* "I just thought, it was a muscle thing. Well… daft really and it doesn't really matter. I just didn't want it wasted, and I didn't expect people to actually read it."

Alison's brow knitted in puzzlement. "Didn't you, though? Wasn't the double-wrapping to keep that sheet readable? Lizzy said it was always put on the outside."

"I suppose." I felt a hot flush running up my neck. "Sorry. Look, we'll stop – we've pretty much used it all, anyway."

Alison nodded, but then seemed to hesitate. "You know you don't need to worry about all that muscle stuff, right? You look good."

The burning had reached my cheeks now. I wasn't so far gone that I didn't know a flat lie when I heard it, even one prompted by good intentions. "Don't worry about me… I'm fine… But I really need to get going." My sausage, cooling in its white paper wrapping, looked so uncannily like a relay baton that I picked it up and ran.

Actually ran.

I suppose it might have seemed odd to Alison, having her shouted offer of a lift answered by a glass door swinging shut and a headlong sprint of feigned deafness. But it was surely better than the alternative. I couldn't hang around trying to explain the unexplainable.

After a few streets, I stopped, tearing the wrapping from my Cajun sausage. The paprika-battered banger, now exposed to the night air, seemed less inviting than I'd hoped, and it pointed at me, full of greasy recrimination. But since this was a day that already overflowed with shame, I was numb to its protest and inhaled the first third, scarcely bothering to chew.

I'd betrayed Alison. I knew it, and I think she knew it too. I'd used her business to shill for some dark-web supplement I couldn't vouch for and didn't understand.

Why?

Because understanding doesn't matter.

How many times had I taken a pill or a powder or a supplement, blended some unpronounceable shake or smoothie, without comprehension of the mechanisms behind the claims? How many times had I ingested supposedly powerful substances based on little more than hope? How was this any different?

Because this one works. And you know it.

But did it? Did it work? I mean, how could it work? Perhaps my phone had been hacked to tweak the camera footage? Perhaps other people like Steve and Galzo and his little brother were all working together to pull off a well-orchestrated scam? How could I know for sure?

But you do know, don't you? And it's a special kind of certainty. The kind that doesn't need a why, and doesn't need a how.

I swallowed my last spicy mouthful and threw the wrapping in a nearby bin. I walked home, trying to make sense of my own behaviour around the greaseproof. I fully understood that I shouldn't have done it, and after the discussion with Alison, I understood that my failing had been noticed. And yet, given the stakes for me personally, surely, I'd no real choice? Surely, it was just a straightforward matter of getting my priorities right?

By the time I reached home, there was a large crimson drum on my doormat. Taped on top was a handwritten card:

> *APE-X (Regular):*
> *Mix with liquid.*
> *Consume.*
> *Distribution only as authorised by BZB.*
> *O.T.C – YES*

I hauled the massive thing inside.

ADMIRING comments were rare at first, and so low key I barely noticed them. But they grew in number over the next month.

"I see someone's a gym-bunny."

"If those chips can give me that body, make mine a large portion."

"Tony, Tony, Tony... it's working for you, son, whatever it is."

So this clever monkey was now at stage two, and certainly hearing opinions, but the problem was that I didn't see what they were talking about. And that is a literal distinction. I had some awareness, obviously, since aspects of change were briefly visible if I stood in front of my mirror while I slurped the Ape-X, but the rest of the time, and when people spoke to me, I saw instead that my skin was waxier than I remembered it, and that I had the beginnings of one chin too many. Daily, I saw these and various other faults, brutally reflected in the chrome of the frying range.

Alison, too, had spotted something different about me, but not in the way that I'd hoped, and her perspective certainly didn't manifest as compliments. Every couple of nights she would ask me, 'Are you OK?' Not pointedly, not having a go, but there was something strange about her even having to ask it. She'd surely seen me enough by now to know that I wasn't OK, which was exactly why I persevered with the Ape-X programme.

After a week or two of deflecting her concerns, she approached again one night while we were locking up. "So," she said lightly, but with an edge, "I had a conversation."

"Oh? Who with?"

"Those supplement people. From the greaseproof?"

I hoped the shock didn't show. Why the hell was she doing that?

"The thing is, Tony, you know I've been worried about you. But on top of that I got curious and wanted to know more about this company we'd been advertising."

"Sounds fair…" What could I say? I'd made her business part of this. "So, what did you think?"

She frowned. "They're weird, right? I eventually reached this woman, Belle something. I said, 'Like *Beauty and the Beast*?' And then she says, get this, 'Oh darling! You are quite the intuitive!' D'you know who she really, and I mean *really* sounded like?"

"Who?"

"That old Disney cartoon, the one about the dogs. Cruella de Vil."

"Right. I see."

"Anyway, do you think they use your camera? When you are in an audio chat with them?"

"I don't know."

"Because this woman seemed to know I wore glasses. She even insulted me." Alison put on a haughty kind of accent. "'Isn't it a bore, darling, in those dowdy spectacles, looking so much less than you could…'" She frowned. "You don't think… are they bad – my glasses I mean? She said I was worse than Velma, from *Scooby Doo*!"

"Your glasses look great. I doubt she was using your camera. I'd forget about that."

"She said they had a product to help with how I looked, but I told her to mind her own beeswax. Bloody cheek."

Alison's face flushed red with anger at the memory. I tried to reassure her. "Look, they have a very pushy sales style, and some weird accent thing going on. I guess it makes them annoying."

"Oh, they're more than annoying – they're creepy. When I said I was worried about a friend, she full-on cackled. *Cackled!* She said data protection meant they shouldn't discuss clients, but that I should give their fondest regards to Tony Minetti. She gave me your name, Tony! How the hell did they even know we had a connection?"

"I think if you use my URL then they know we're connected." *Although, wasn't it Steve's URL? And who did he get it from?*

"But Tony, they still shouldn't give me your full name. I could be just a random person who read some greaseproof paper I found on the street."

I shrugged. She was right, but I couldn't do anything about it. She reached out to touch my shoulder. "You don't seem yourself, since all this has been going on. You seem distracted, somehow, and sad."

"People tell me I'm looking good."

Her mouth tightened. "Maybe if those people looked past your biceps to your eyes, they'd talk some bloody sense."

"Oh? Do you think my biceps have improved?"

Alison walked away, shaking her head.

———

AT HOME, I sat on my bed and thought about the whole situation.

Alison was correct in one sense: I didn't feel happy. Perhaps it was just confusion. After all, what I saw in the mirror, I either hated or didn't believe, and that was uncomfortable. But was I being a baby? Ape-X had taken me further in a few weeks than I'd achieved in years. Why wasn't I delighted to be making this kind of progress?

I clicked through to the shortcut I'd created for the Ape-X onion site, put the phone down on the stool between myself and the mirrored wardrobe, and then waited.

"G'day, mate! Billy Zee here! It's late for you, but here I've got me sunnies on!"

I had half-expected a change of accent, but not quite this one. "Australian?"

"I dunno, cobber, but if that's what you hear, fair dinkum. Oz is the land down under, after all, so it makes sense. Anyway... you're feeling a bit crook?"

"A bit."

"Well, second monkey, mate. It can be difficult."

"But I hadn't expected it to be difficult."

"Why not? Second monkey hears great reviews but can't have their own ticket."

"It's just hearing those things, while seeing myself, and not feeling any of it's properly me. It feels bad, deeply off, somehow."

"Strewth, mate, of course it's bloody deep. It always has been." A gentle laugh. "Your scientists danced like show ponies after discovering the mirror test. Suddenly self-recognition was some amazing boundary for higher consciousness. But those same dipsticks laughed at the aboriginals who saw significance in photographs, who saw an aspect of the soul. Now you tell me: is that the same coin, with different sides? Tony, mate, are you worried about becoming estranged from your soul?"

I couldn't help snorting a little. "No! I'm not superstitious. I think I'm just podgier than I should be?"

"Yeah, mate, that'll be it... But that's all just calibration, Tony. We need size to show size, but it's just a means to an end. We told you Ape-X was calorically dense."

Had they? "I'm sure you said nutritionally dense."

"Nah. But it's bloody dense, is the point. And it needs to be. You're a moo in a cattle station, mate, on growth promoters, but you can't reach the front of the line if you keep taking your head out the trough! You need to really dig in. One day, one dose is too slow. What do you expect?"

"I expected to feel better. Happier."

"You'll feel better at the third monkey, I reckon. You'll be cracking out the budgie smugglers."

"But how do I get—"

"Easy on, mate! First, let's talk about your Sheila. That Alison lady who gave us an earbashing."

"I'm sorry. I only just heard about that. But it was just a misunderstanding."

"Nah. An opportunity is what that was. An opportunity to monkey-up."

"What do you mean?"

"She took an interest in you, but more than that, mate, she took an interest in us. So now we've got a little skin in her game. We 're worried she'll go of on one and come between us, and we just want to keep everything smooth. So here's your job. You need to feed her a little Ape-X. That'll move the whole thing in the right direction."

"What? No!"

"Yes, mate, yes! You have an opportunity here. You've always known what you wanted, but your entire life, people questioned you, doubted you, blocked your way. You didn't handle that problem with your parents, and now you've screwed that relationship forever. But Alison, she could be different, she could properly understand. You can help her see things your way."

"But... it won't work. She wouldn't be interested in taking any weird supplements."

"Correct, mate, that's why you don't tell her."

I gasped at the outrageousness of it. "What? You want me to spike her drink or something? I can't do that!"

"Course you can! And you can ïack off with that spiking busi-

ness for a start. Nobody expects to know every individual ingre-
dient in every mouthful. Nah, mate. A pinch of mystery, a sprinkle
of secret sauce. It's all normal. Such a tiny amount has no physical
effect."

"Could I have that in writing?"

"Better mate, you have my word. It's a guarantee - no physical
effect on her whatsoever."

"How many tiny amounts are we talking?"

"One. Just one. That's the beauty of it. This is more about you
showing us you can act in your own interests. "

"And if I do this, what happens?"

"Well, then you're out of the crapper and on the runway towards
third monkey. The question is, Tony, are you ready to take off... or
to crash and burn?"

———————

Last night I sent you a photo with just me. I
thought I'd hear back.

> We thought you were having a laugh.

Nope. That's me. You can tell Dad to stop
looking for the podgy one.

> He said you've been at the photoshop.

Why don't you visit and see for yourselves?

> I don't think your father is ready.

Will he ever be ready?

> He's a proud man. You humbled him. He
> hasn't forgiven it.

I shouldn't have done what I did, but he's
goaded me my whole life.

> He only wanted to improve you.

He taught me that, alright. It's practically all I know. If you want to see someone improving themselves, look at that photo.

> Please say you're not taking things again.

I give up.

I WRESTLED with myself over the next month. Those weeks, despite containing many successes, passed in a gloomy haze. Kev had become fully confident on the frying range and we trained his understudy. I spent some evenings front-of-house in the bistro, and between the two of us, either Alison or I began to have the occasional night off. I got back to the gym and experienced a number of conversations with jealous admirers eager to know my secret.

But I enjoyed none of it.

It turns out that unearned praise eventually sounds the same as justified criticism. Every day grated, and it was doing my head in.

Alison, of course, did not help my mood. She seemed more worried by the day. Sometimes I'd catch her looking at me, frowning. Other times it was just a tiny shake of the head, or a flash of puzzlement.

On top of all that, sometimes I'd make the mistake of catching sight of my own reflection. I told myself, *it's not what I see that counts, it's what they see*. But it sure didn't feel that way.

I couldn't carry on like this, so I decided on a way to make progress that I could live with, one that would at least take Alison's niggling worries off my radar.

It was a Tuesday, and when I turned up unexpectedly, Alison was shocked. "You should be busy having a day off!"

"Oh, I've been busy enough," I replied. "I've been in my kitchen..." I produced a lidded dish from my bag. "For you."

She opened the dish, releasing the smell of spiced rum and coconut. "Wow – the panna cotta you mentioned at interview. I hope you made yourself one?"

"Didn't actually. Kind of wish I had now. But anyway, I thought you might appreciate a snack break this evening."

She seemed quite emotional about it. "Tony. That is really sweet." She walked to the server station and grabbed a couple of spoons. "So sweet, in fact, that we're sharing it right now."

Alison did generous things like that all the time. "No, I couldn't... It's yours."

"C'mon Tony – it's just a couple of mouthfuls each, and we've got a chance while the bistro is empty. Unless you're telling me I haven't got your best work?"

I decided that refusing to eat any would make me feel even more weird and guilty, so I pulled up a seat beside her and took one spoonful, just so she would join in. This was the only time I'd made the recipe without sampling it during preparation, so I was relieved that it tasted exactly as I remembered it. Adding Ape-X into the coconut milk had not changed the flavour in any obvious way.

"Oh Tony! This is great!" She barely looked up, savouring the little dessert one tiny spoonful at a time. Meanwhile, I held the residue in my mouth and examined my reflection in the mirrored menu stand. I could only see my face, but even those few changes captivated me: the tightening of the skin, the definition and strength in my jawline, the power of my gaze. But the illusion faded, as it always did, and I turned the menu stand away. It was time to go.

As I stood, I noticed Alison's smile, too, was fading. "Tony? Don't panic, but I think you're having an allergic reaction. Do you feel OK?"

"I'm great."

"But... suddenly you've gone really puffy. Your skin has turned pale, sweaty." She was staring now, her face filled with horror. "This has come on so quick. I'm calling a doctor."

Is this what Bill Zee had meant when he said I would help her see things my way? The shock of this realisation had the ironic effect of making me nauseous for real. I spoke quickly, "Don't worry, I'm fine!" as I made for the door. But I was glad that the first table of customers squeezed past me as I left. Alison would be too busy with business to follow me.

But as I walked home, I tried to reason through the implications. If Alison could see me as I saw myself, what then? How the hell was this meant to help? And more importantly, how could I reverse it?

I hadn't tried using the onion browser over mobile data before, but this couldn't wait until I got home. Fortunately, I connected quickly and summoned an agent.

This time, I heard a woman's voice – posh, British. "BZB Marketing Department. Belle Seabud here."

"I have a problem."

"I'm sure you do, darling. You sound simply wretched."

"I was advised to give my friend some Ape-X…"

"Yes, my dear, I remember. I even put that on your notes."

"But now she can see me. What I see, I mean."

"Isn't it splendid when friends can see things the same way!"

"But when will that wear off? She only had one tiny portion."

"It only takes one tiny portion, darling. Don't worry, the remaining supply is for you and you alone. It shan't wear off and she won't need a top-up."

"But I was told she'd suffer no physical effect. That was guaranteed."

"Yes. And our guarantee holds. This isn't a *physical* effect, darling. There's not one shred of *physical* change to that young woman. If it helps, perhaps you could think of it more as a kind of enhanced spiritual insight."

"But I don't want that…"

"I see. Please hold while I check my system… We have something on this, I'm quite sure...Yes! Here it is, under *What the Customer Wants*: 'Our first rule of sales is not to sell aspiration when we can sell desperation.' Do you follow, my darling? We don't give you what you want. Instead, we give you a need. Only when that need is sharp enough are all parties suitably motivated to reach the correct accommodation."

"But how can I even go into work?"

"Tony, you are such a one, but please don't make this awkward. Going into work was the problem. You were dragging your heels, when instead, you needed to speed up. You must finish your tub of Ape-X."

"But I have a job!"

"Of course, darling, you have a job. And that job is fixing the dreadful state you're in. Have you looked, darling? It isn't right, and you simply can't leave it. Halfway done is simply a road to nowhere. So, here's what to do: call in a sickie or quiet-quit from home, or whatever they call it nowadays. For the next little while, you need to focus: stop concerning yourself with things that hold you back. Your tub must be finished!"

I wanted to protest, but the audio dropped, leaving me outside the door of my apartment listening to that last word echoing around me.

PART IV – NIGHT AT THE END OF THE FUNNEL

I called in to the restaurant and reassured everyone that I was fine – it was a bad reaction to an insect bite, and that I'd need to take the next few days off sick.

When I looked at myself in the mirror, and thought about seeing Alison again, I felt awful. Maybe the worst ever. This couldn't be right, and I didn't know what to do.

I hunted through my overflowing shoe box until I found the card

Steve had given me at the start of all this. I flipped it over and found his phone number written in pencil. I could barely read it, unsure if the last number was a two or a five. So I tried both, hanging up on an old lady before hearing an answering voice I recognised. It sounded smooth, happy, all business. "Hello? Is that you, Rob? Is this about the card I left?"

"Sorry, Steve. It's me. Tony."

"Ah, Tony."

It was a long silence, so I said, "How are you doing?" more to reactivate conversational norms than because I wanted to know.

"Yeah. So... I'm fine? All good, I guess." But actually, he didn't sound all good. Not at all. His voice had become more hesitant, listless, almost. "What do you want, Tony?"

"To talk."

"But you're well inside the sales funnel, man. You don't need me."

"I think I do."

Silence again. He seemed to be thinking, maybe about how to get me off his case. "There's no way I can help you, you know."

"Yes, you can. I don't need much. I just have a situation and I could do with your take on it."

"Man, I can't do that..."

"Please."

"Let me check."

I heard the phone clatter down at his end, then I heard a door close. Eventually I heard some muffled noises, possibly voices, possibly a radio. It was difficult to be sure. I despaired of Steve ever returning before I finally heard him pick up the phone.

"OK. I'll come round."

"Great. When would suit you?"

"Now." Then he hung up.

I paced a little, wondering how far Steve had to travel. I'm pretty sure he used to live in town, so I poured myself some tea and waited.

My doorbell chimed in just under an hour. But when I opened the door, I almost closed it again. See, the last time I saw Steve, his face had seemed attached to a new body, so I thought I'd knew what to expect. But he'd pulled the same trick twice. His face was still out of place, still pasted onto the wrong body, only a different one from before. This body looked ill: pallid and corpulent, squeezed into an old leather jacket and wheezing from the three flights of stairs that had brought him to my door. He wasn't clean-shaven and lantern-jawed anymore, either. His puffy face ended in a greasy, scraggly beard that seemed to contain scraps of something, perhaps food or fluff or who knew what.

"Steve, how is this…?"

He smiled as he shuffled inside, and pointed at my teacup. "You best fetch me a mug as well." I flicked on the kettle while my old gym buddy squeezed himself into an armchair. "Before I talk, though, Tony, I want you to give me some Ape-X. I'm not obliged to do this, I've come all this way, and I want paid."

He handed me a bag. It was a self-seal freezer type, but tiny, like if you wanted to freeze a single strawberry, and I still had a very large tub. I scooped some powder and handed it over. He balanced it in one hand, nodded and then put it into his jacket pocket.

I freshened my own tea and handed him a mug. "So, no offence, Steve, but I have to say you looked much better last time we met."

"As did you, Tony, as did you… But you haven't taken as much as me, I guess. You're not so far along."

"So this is what it does to everyone?"

"Well, at first, I guess. And now you've had Ape-X, you see what I see. And I see this…" He looked down at himself and shook his head. "Because I'm stuck at the second monkey."

"If that's the case, then why did they tell me to feed some to my boss at work?"

"They'll probably have had some reason. Or maybe it was just mischief? I don't know everything, but I do know this." Steve pushed himself forward, wincing a little as the arms of the chair dug into his hips. "You *must* do whatever they say. You did the right thing feeding Ape-X to your boss."

"But is there any way I can stop it? Can I stop Alison seeing me this way? Stop myself from seeing me this way?"

"As far as I know, the only way is by reaching third monkey."

"What if I stopped taking the Ape-X now, and just hit the gym, fixed my diet, y'know, went old school?"

"I tried that for a little while. But it didn't help. For one thing, I got sick, and I mean worse than this, feverish, weak, blinding headaches, constant nausea. And as the Ape-X wore off, I think people could see it. My sister asked me if I was dying, and maybe I was."

It all sounded like chemical dependency to me. I wondered if the sheer length of time that Steve spent taking Ape-X had created a particularly severe withdrawal.

But Steve continued. "I know what you're thinking, Tony, that maybe I should have just stuck with the medicine, well the other problem was I also got sick in my head, and... I... I began seeing things, weird shit, really, and thinking I was being followed, thinking worse than that... And you know me. Physically, I'm game for anything. I can throw myself in, build it back up... But this." He tapped his head. "You lose this, you've lost everything..." He sagged back in the chair, shaking his head. "So, Tony, I'm sorry, man. But this is a funnel, and the only way out is down the spout."

"Then, why aren't you out yet? Why are you still at second?"

"Well... that's easy. Basically, I didn't always do what they told me. Not fully. You've just done some marketing, but I'm working my way back into their good graces with individual sales... And I'll get there. As far as I understand it, at Second Monkey, your own perception is like an anchor. It's because I see myself like this"—He stabbed a finger into his belly—"that I'm stuck in misery. However," he said, zealously slurping his tea, ignoring a milky splash that dribbled down his chin, "when I reach third monkey and I don't see myself wrong, then nothing anchors me anymore."

Despite Steve's note of optimism, I found myself increasingly pissed off. "But, Steve, you have just admitted to being trapped in misery. I can't help but remember when you told me you were a happy customer!"

The man shrugged, his face downcast. "That's what they told me to say." He put his cup back on the table. "And it was also what you wanted me to say, if you're honest… Anyway, did you read all the terms?"

"What terms?"

"On the dark web, when you first contacted them?"

"No! But who actually reads terms?"

Steve shrugged again. "Yeah… Well, it's OK, I guess. They're kinda sticklers."

"What do you mean?"

"Pointless to worry about it. I just mean that they've told me they'll deliver in line with their terms. Probably, you'll be mostly fine. We both will, I think. Eventually."

"I'll be totally fine. I signed nothing."

Steve chuckled without warmth. "I tried that. But it's a clickwrap agreement. We clicked, so we're bound by it, whatever."

"What bloody terms do I need to be worried about?" I asked, beginning to panic.

He shrugged. "Who actually reads terms? But do what they tell you. I found out about that one." Steve finished his tea and lapsed into silence, gazing towards my window.

Eager to keep him talking, I pushed to find out more about BZB or Ape-X, but the harder I tried, the more evasive Steve became. Soon, we both realised he'd given me all I was getting, so he stood up and left. I followed his progress from my window as he shambled towards his vehicle.

But part-way there, for no apparent reason, he stopped. I didn't understand what he was doing at first. I saw him crouch down to his knees, and it was then that I spotted a drainage grate just in front of him. This was a very odd scene. He scrabbled inside the pocket of his jacket, and produced the little self-seal bag of Ape-X. He opened it, then poured it all away, every single bit. Despite the blustery wind, the powder fell straight down, and Steve used his hands to sweep any excess that landed on the grating.

With that, the once, but no longer, Strawweight Steve staggered to his feet, clambered into his vehicle, and left.

THERE WERE two things I knew for sure. If I was bound to do what they told me, then that meant I had to finish my supply of Ape-X. And because it was a large supply, the second thing I knew was I needed to increase my consumption from my current level of once per day. Giving all my nutrition over to Ape-X seemed the best way to complete this phase quickly and return to work.

I spent my time mostly in my bedroom, except for an occasional brief trip to the corner shop. I found using a liquid base of different flavoured milks made drinking three meals plus snacks a good deal more tolerable. Because it didn't take long before I'd emptied the fridge of the local shop, I began ordering online. That was better all round. Contactless delivery meant I didn't have to account to any real human beings for my orders consisting entirely of strawberry, chocolate and banana milk.

Despite the dietary boredom, I will admit that those moments spent sipping in front of my mirror showed an incredible transformation. It was a transformation that delivered the body of, well, not quite *my* dreams, but someone's dreams, for sure. But sadly, perhaps because the vision was so short-lived, I found it impossible to view that person as me.

And even my longer-lived and less welcome avatar, the one I encountered between meals was unrecognisable. I had eaten only Ape-X now for... what? Seven days? Nine at most? I'd lost track. But already my everyday reflection appeared bloated and unwell. The skin was pale, eyes hollow, sagging jowls grew daily beneath a double-chinned jaw. I knew this pace of change was unnatural, that this was not ordinary food and that at this point I was being harmed by it. My reflection already looked almost as sickly as Steve had, despite his many months ahead of me, although perhaps not consuming quite this volume of Ape-X. But every bodybuilder knows that gains require pain, and with gains this huge, a level of true suffering was surely to be expected.

But being alone, isolated from other people, brings a certain amount of melancholy and makes you question yourself. I thought a lot about what the Australian Bill Zee had said: how some tribes believed your image was linked to your soul, and that there was a power to photographs and mirrors. This struck me as ironic. Humans were the only animal to attach importance to recognising themselves, but also first to deliberately disfigure themselves so much that they no longer could. My life was now dominated by a question: if you look in a mirror and you don't see yourself, what are you then?

I'm not proud of this, but I had simply been ignoring calls and text messages from Alison. The problem was, for her many questions about my wellbeing, about my medical progress, I had no good answers.

One day she called round on her way to the fish-market, and I didn't let her in. Instead, I hid in my bedroom and messaged her that I should be OK in a few days. What else could I do? But she was persistent, and in a sequence of messages, she extracted a promise that I'd let her visit the following Monday when the bistro would be closed. That timescale meant I had only two days. My tub still contained far too much Ape-X to finish in two days.

So I had this brainwave: if Steve was right, and Alison saw what I saw, perhaps I had a good option after all? I practised holding the Ape-X liquid in my mouth. So long as I didn't take too much, I could breathe through my nose and sustain the vision for longer and longer periods. In fact, I even enjoyed spending time this way, gazing at a heroic reflection and dreaming that it might shortly be permanent.

Of course, at this point, the practice was a means to an end:

Operation Alison. But I was becoming so good at it, I was certain I'd be out of the hole. In fact, I thought of such a clever back story that she might call off her visit altogether. I became so confident I sent her a message, only to have my optimism implode with her near instant response:

> Hi Alison. Minor complication - I've lost my voice! Doc says must completely rest it, but otherwise better. Can (silently) see you on Monday, but maybe we should communicate by message for a bit?

> Hey Tony! Sorry to hear about voice but glad ur feeling better. I'll still call round Monday AM. Can you get me line from doctor? Accountant said I need one when sick pay lasts more than 7 days.

This was not good. Not only was she coming, but she also expected documentation for a non-existent allergic reaction to an insect bite that never happened. That I'd be able to successfully mime this request to a medic, while they saw me as some kind of Hollywood Hercules, seemed unlikely. I now had no choice but to become a forger as well as a liar.

Fortunately, since hospitality profit margins didn't permit management to take things on trust, I'd seen various 'Fit' notes from colleagues over the years. Most health practices print them and some (but not all, thankfully) even provide a bar-code. This meant I at least knew what I was working to produce.

It only took me an hour on my laptop to pull something plausible together. Then I sent it to my phone and dragged myself to the public library to print it. It was odd, pushing through the crowd of stolen glances, some admiring, some jealous, while feeling pains in my knees and hips, and wheezing as I walked. I needed to get past this stage, even if it meant drinking Ape-X every waking hour.

I'd long ago forgotten what it meant to be hungry, but I was in the grip of a craving of a different kind: to complete this ordeal, and start my life for real.

***

BY THE MORNING of Alison's visit, I could easily hold the liquid in my mouth for extended periods, easily upwards of twenty minutes. I was becoming so good at this that I could now stand at my mirrored wardrobe for an entire day, only swallowing so I could keep my intake levels in line with rapidly finishing the tub. I'd stayed up until after three a.m. watching my rapidly perfecting reflection, and awakened at 7 a.m. to start a new day the same way.

I was entranced.

So much so that I almost dropped my glass at the jolt caused by hearing my own doorbell.

Showtime.

I took a fresh slug of Ape-X before wiping around my mouth. I wanted her to see a clean, still reliable Tony, very much on the mend. Then I picked up my forged medical note and went to the door, hesitating before opening it. I looked through my spy-hole at Alison standing outside. She seemed tense, her lips pinched. But surely this would end her concerns? She'd see the perfect me looking back at her. I mean, I wasn't certain, but surely that must be how it worked?

Pulling the door open I gave a close-mouthed, what I hoped was enigmatic smile while stretching the note towards her. She reached for it automatically, her fingers closing around it. But then my attention became captured by the odd fact of the note fluttering down towards the ground. Why hadn't she taken it?

I looked towards her as she staggered back, heard her gasp, watched her face twist in horror. "Oh no, Tony! What the fuck has happened to you?"

I tried to reassure her, but forgetting the situation, managed to inhale some of the Ape-X liquid I'd been holding in my mouth. I gagged, the thick milky liquid exploding from my mouth, dribbling down my chin and onto my clothes.

By the time I'd recovered, Alison had already barged past, following the trail of open doors to my bedroom, and I waddled helplessly behind her. Already she had entered my room and kicked her way across a floor littered with empty plastic bottles. My stool stood, milk spattered, in front of the mirror, and on that stool, a jug containing the dregs of my latest Ape-X smoothie. "Is that it?" she said, pointing at the crimson tub beside my bed. Her face was angry, horrified, vengeful.

Protect the supplement!

I pushed myself in front of her. "No, Alison, please! I need it."

She gazed at me in horror. "You were lying about your voice? Lying for that shitty poison!" There were tears in her eyes, but she let me turn her around, let me guide her back to the corridor.

She picked up the milk spattered fit note, then let it drop again, shaking her head. I didn't know how to explain it, and even if I did, she couldn't understand because she was perfect as she was and had never needed to become something better. "I liked you, Tony, I really did."

I closed the door, so I didn't have to hear any more or watch her walk away. Why spend time mourning what I'd lost, when I was on the verge of making an even greater gain? I went back to my room and resumed drinking my supplement.

BY THE END of that week, having drained endless glasses, I finally reached the bottom of my tub. The importance of the moment broke through my fatigue and quieted my ever-roiling nausea. *This was it.*

I raised the final glass to my mouth.

The last instruction received from BZB had been to finish the tub, and now that moment was upon me. One gulp. A second. Third and final. I drained the dregs and looked down at my new, forever body.

But something was wrong. *Forever shouldn't fade.*

Slowly, but steadily, the healthy muscular vibrancy of my left arm had given way to the pale, sickly, bloated limb I'd expected to never see again. The mirror confirmed the corruption had retaken the rest of my body. Perhaps I hadn't taken quite all of it? I scraped some remnants from the glass with a spatula, then I rinsed it and swallowed the water.

But as before, and as always, the miracle turned mirage after only a few moments.

This couldn't be right.

I double-checked the tub, although convinced I'd already scraped it clean. *Empty.* That bare plastic was my proof, evidence my task was complete after months of effort. The horrible ordeal caused by this level of the programme should now be over.

But it wasn't.

I fetched my phone, connected it to BZB on the dark web, and then placed it on the stool. I sat on my bed, watching the horrible unwanted reflection in the mirror. I had nothing left now, no supplement to make it go away, no smoothie to smear away my imperfections. That thing was me.

I was shocked from my reverie by the sound of a new voice. The accent was neutral, but the voice sounded chirpy and younger than usual. "Hello! I'm William, customer relations executive of BZB."

This was fortuitous, because I wanted to complain. "I've just finished my tub of Ape-X but I'm stuck seeing the old thing."

"Yes, sir. Superb."

"What?"

"What indeed, sir!"

"Are you going to fix this?"

"Good news! There is nothing to fix. You have a great day, sir!"

"Woah! Please don't disconnect. Can you be specific? Why haven't I reached the third level?"

"Ah. Of course. Let me pull up our terms. Blah, blah, blah, yes! ... *and will permit 2.5% spillage and wastage due to limitations and accidents around food preparation and consumption or activities pursuant to the creation of a self-imbibable concoction.*"

"OK. I choked a little today, but—"

"No problem, sir. BZB are fully aware that some nausea is built in to the formulation, hence our clause exempting loss due to regurgitation or reflux."

"Then why—"

"Seven grams, sir."

"Seven what?"

"We expressly forbid unauthorised distribution. You distributed seven grams of product in an unauthorised capacity."

Steve's little bag.

"But I gave Steve less than I gave to Alison!"

"Alison received an authorised distribution, sir. We have no issues there."

"But Steve recommended me. He's an existing client."

"No exemption pertains to existing clients in our terms. Our contract is with you, sir. Likewise, the terms apply to you. And you breached them."

"But he didn't even eat it. He threw it away!"

"Terrible thing. Perhaps you shouldn't have given it to him?"

"But what can I do now? Can I still reach third level?"

"Of course! You remain entitled to service via our dispute resolution terms. You'll receive instructions momentarily, sir."

"One question first. Did you instruct Steve to ask for some of my Ape-X? Did you ask him to discard it?"

Silence lingered in the room. Then, "Discussions or negotiations with other clients are commercially sensitive and consequently fully protected."

"Does that mean you did, or you didn't?"

"Correct, sir. And thank you for your time!"

The connection broke, without the delivery of any promised

instructions. I was about to attempt reconnection when some instinct brought me to open my own front door. And there, directly outside, were two huge crimson drums, each bearing a label:

APE-X (Regular):
Mix with liquid.
Consume.
IMPORTANT : Distribution only as authorised by BZB.
O.T.C – YES

I rolled them both inside, lay down on my carpet and cried.

IT IS easy to chase your dream, or maybe easy isn't correct, maybe what I want to say is that it is *natural*. Pursuing that one thing that has always been your heart's desire, that just means things are as they should be. All is perfectly right with that world.

D'you know what feels completely wrong, though? The step that is hardest to take of all? Giving that dream up. But as I sat through the night, staring at the crimson drums, there came a point when the light changed. Perhaps it was a simultaneous dawning for both me and the world itself, but in that first rise of morning light I confronted an unwelcome truth: BZB had given my dream both barrels. My ideal future had been binned in two huge crimson tubs, and I needed to accept it.

I couldn't do this any more. It was horrible. Ruining me, ruining my job, ruining my relationships, making me lie to Alison, to myself. Fuck this. It was over.

Just to be sure, I checked the paperwork on the drums, but of course there was nothing remotely like returns information. So screw them. I'd tough out the cold turkey in a way Steve couldn't, and I'd keep the drums and their product as a reminder of my own stupidity. If they wanted it they could pay to collect. I was done.

———

I GOT some queer looks when anyone saw me on the street, since Steve had been right about the withdrawal. I was sweating, and shivering and I was probably puking ten times a day. To be honest, it was Russian roulette whether one end or both, and I'd tried every medicine in my cabinet. I thought this was just part of the process.

Still, I decided I had to walk as much as I could, even during withdrawal. I had a route that took me past a shop, a library and two sets of public toilets. And yes, I vomited and shat in all of those places, but that was life now. I expelled at least half of everything I ate long before I'd digested it, and the rest turned into thin, foul gravy. I hoped the walks might build my muscles up a little once the withdrawal was over, because I was certainly in a weight cutting phase right then.

But somehow being around people was taking the edge off. I know that sounds weird, I mean, I didn't *want* to be seen like this, because I wasn't a pretty picture, but there was comfort in knowing others were out there, just doing whatever, you know, living life. I told myself one day soon, I'd be on that corner chatting to a mate, or stopping at a bench to pat a dog or whatever. It was nice to feel a little bit connected.

And I didn't feel that inside my flat. Everything was worse when I was at home alone. I didn't like the atmosphere, which was creepy for some reason. And there was some kind of electricity problem that meant my bulbs kept blowing. I'd need to find an electrician when I was better, but until then the place was too dark and depressing to spend more than the minimum time at. I only went there to sleep, and I wasn't very successful at that. If I got four hours, I was doing well.

But I was sitting in a public cubicle, shitting out my gut lining when an envelope is pushed under the door. On the front it read:

To Tony

With Love, From your friends at BZB.

Once my gastric deluge subsided, I opened the envelope to find a single page inside. On the front of that page they'd stuck fragments of a label I recognised from their tubs.

APE-X (Regular)
O.T.C – YES

Below that they'd written a threat in crimson ink:

O.T.C = OBLIGATION TO CONSUME
You will not get better

On the other side they'd printed a picture I'd sent to my Mum, the one we'd taken at The New Ship on opening night. My first thought on seeing it was how much I missed everyone. But the sadness froze in my throat when I saw that they'd drawn a red circle around Kev, the boy that did the frying. Above the circle they'd written the words:

Individual Sales Target.
Commission: 0.5 x outstanding obligation.

Steve had told me two things I hadn't paid enough attention to. Firstly that he thought he was being followed. Well, somebody just tucked this under a public toilet door, and you can't be paranoid if they really are out to get you. Secondly, he told me he did *individual sales*. It looked like I was getting the same job offer. All I had to do was deliver Kev to BZB, and I'd reduce my two barrel problem by half in a single act. Then presumably they'd assign me someone else I knew, like Galzo's little brother. Or maybe they'd have me betray Alison again.

Before my mind began to do the math, before some part of me

calculated the number of victims I might need to step over to regain sight of the finish line, I switched on my phone and sent a message to Alison.

> You've seen how bad things turned for me, so I trust you to do this. Please tell Kev Simpson to stay the hell away from Ape-X, BZB and a muscle head called Steve Tate. I'm a total idiot. For everything.

WHEN I GOT HOME that evening, the lights were going nuts again. One of the bulbs that had previously blown in my bedroom started working, but just flickering on and off, no matter what position the switch was at. I took that bulb out so I would have a chance to sleep.

Since I can't really handle phone conversations while I'm ill, I'd been leaving my phone off a lot. But I'd kept it on after the message I'd sent to Alison. I guess part of me hoped to hear back from her. Well, that had always been a long shot and it didn't happen. But I was just getting into bed when the phone buzzed, and it looked like my mum had messaged me. But my bad luck day was not yet over.

> This is your father on your mother's phone. Stop trying to guilt us into coming over.

I'm not. Forget that. But It would be good to sort things out between us. Even just by phone.

> Dream on.

> And we won't come back. You'll have given up that restaurant before we buy the tickets. You never follow through. You've no staying power. We're tired of it.

> Well? Are you still there? Don't you have anything to say for yourself?

Just that I'm sorry.

Sorry doesn't cut it.

THE NEXT MORNING I had a thought, about Kev, what my dad said, and my obligation to consume two crimson drums. I wondered if maybe my not following through was everyone's main issue here. Did the fact I was in breach of BZB's terms and not cooperating mean they would now target people in my life, just to punish me? It seemed that way, and that changed things. I mean, I'd screwed myself over and I had to live with that. But Kev and Alison were blameless.

What did Steve say? *The only way out is down the spout.* It was starting to look like he was right. I decided to prep an Ape-X smoothie then and there.

Fortunately, the LED downlights in the kitchen had begun working, so I could properly see what I was doing. My flat hadn't been getting good daylight recently, I think due to some sort of bacterial film or residue that had flared up on the window. I didn't seem to have the right chemicals to scrub it off, so having those spotlights back was a relief. On the off-chance, I put the bulb back up in my bedroom, and the electrical fluctuations there seemed to be fixed as well. This allowed me to drain my glass in good light in front of the mirrored wardrobe.

I couldn't deny the thrill of watching the sickened wreck I'd become vanish, even if just for a moment, to be replaced by the reflection. That thing looked as good as it ever had, maybe even better. And the worst of my withdrawal symptoms lifted as soon as I finished the glass. I didn't feel good, of course. I'd given up the idea of feeling good at Second Monkey, but I felt a little less awful, and that was something.

Since I wasn't prepared to deliver anyone else to BZB, the quantity of Ape-X I'd have to get through was daunting. I needed a plan for the long haul, especially because Alison had, understandably, stopped my sick pay after our last meeting. The financial situation forced me to be practical, and over the next two days I sold my car and mountain bike to get sufficient funds to devote myself to Ape-X.

I also knew whatever I did needed to be realistic and sustainable. Since I wasn't robust enough to stay awake past midnight drinking smoothies hour by hour, I couldn't continue at the same pace as before. But I did the best I could, and I stayed home and took the drink from morning to night, always in front of the mirror.

AFTER THE FIRST day of the new regime, I began to feel deeply lonely, now I just had me and the reflection. Sometimes I wanted any kind of company. Whether good or bad, I didn't mind. So I ran a charging cable over to the stool and placed my phone there, leaving it connected to the BZB site. Sometimes I'd ask a question, occasionally they'd answer. Sometimes they'd be the first to break the silence, simply volunteering some comment or criticism. Most of the time I'd just drink, surrounded by a cloud of whispers that I couldn't interpret.

You can never tell which voice you will hear, but if I was upset with them, I'd usually get an angry person in response. Once, sickened and bored by drinking, I shouted, "Is this your definition of customer satisfaction?"

I expected no particular response but received a barrage from Brooklyn. "Customer satisfaction, my ass! In my business, customer satisfaction is not a thing! I give the customer what they ask for, and I do it with a funnel and a plunger. So boo-fuckin-hoo! 'Oh! But Bill,' I hear you whine, 'what if I end up on my little knees, choking, eyes bulging, trying to scratch the word *Heimlich* in the dirt with broken fingernails?' Well, maybe you should have read the goddam small print! I don't accept returns and I don't do refunds. You come to me,

I will deliver to the max, and you will not be satisfied. If satisfaction is all you wanted, then you shoulda satisfied your damn self."

Of course, that exchange wasn't fair, because he could let loose while I needed to think about the bigger picture and keep a lid on my anger. So I just answered, "You might have told me all this earlier."

"You're a goddam joke, kid. I told you everything earlier! I gave you all my rules of sales. Did you take a warning? No. Instead you shit the bed, Tony, just like I said. I sold you a new life by screwing your old one. You wanted to be big. Fine. Lines across your belly. Fine. But ridges and folds are both goddam lines. You wanted big – I made you big! Come back when you got somethin' I wanna hear."

The voices stayed silent for days after that. So I kept drinking the Ape-X.

Around halfway through the first of my two punishment tubs I realised I wouldn't make it. The side effects were overwhelming me. I now felt weak just standing at the mirror, and I wheezed when I walked to fetch a grocery delivery from the front door, or even just to reach the bathroom.

It was easier just to slump on my bed, mixing smoothies, drinking smoothies, starting over. Again. And again. And again.

The only pleasure I had left was looking at the reflection.

It was so much better than I was. It showed confidence to my regret, strength to my weakness, its every look and movement a perfected version of my own. When I adjusted to remove pressure from a painful sore on my backside, it pulled up its shirt and flexed its hip, showing stunningly lean obliques. I was hypnotised by how the reflection filtered my misery, turning it into a perfect aspirational product. I wanted that product, but I knew I wouldn't make it.

I said to the whispers, "Bill? I'm ready, I think, to pay the price."

That time they answered using a voice I hadn't heard them use before, but one I recognised anyway. "Don't worry. You're already paying it."

"That's so weird, Bill. Why do you sound like me?"

"You hear what you're ready to hear. Maybe you're ready to think about what's true?"

"I think so. I'm too tired for bullshit, I think."

"That's good, Tony. We can talk about anything. No bullshit."

"Well, I want to discuss what you said about souls."

"Not what I said. You brought that up yourself by mentioning Australia."

"I didn't understand that at the time, did I? It's just… recently I've been wondering about it. About what you are, and what you want."

"Oh. That's an old one. People have had some very medieval ideas."

"How do you mean?"

"Well, Tony, people used to believe that great powers fought to win the souls of corpses so they could build some kind of collection. You know, like stamps or bottle caps. Now, if this whole thing was a war between powers, and I'm not saying it is – I mean, ridiculous! But if this was a war, then, a soul from a corpse would have already lived a life, acted and intervened, maybe even made the wrong kinds of impact. It might have done something really consequential. Now, that kind of soul, the still-living one, not the corpse one, that kind starts to sound like a strategic threat, almost a kind of weapon? A real great power would probably think: don't just collect souls after death, put the dangerous bloody things beyond use beforehand."

"So, is that how it is, Bill?"

"Maybe. Or maybe this isn't a war between powers at all. Or maybe we're getting above your pay grade."

"But Bill, you promised. No bullshit."

I heard my own voice laughing back at me. "No bullshit, but honestly, it is above your pay grade. We should talk about you. What are you thinking?"

I drank some more Ape-X so I could momentarily see the beautiful reflection. The glass held by that reflection was clear crystal and sparkled like diamonds. It toasted me with that glass while it faded. I said, "I'm thinking about beliefs."

"Interesting, Tony. In what way?"

"Well, I used to believe something, and I don't anymore. Like, I don't believe the reflection can ever be me, can it?"

"The reflection? No, it's not you. It's beyond you. That's why you follow it."

"Yes. I see that now."

"Good, Tony, that's good."

"And the time I've spent, here in this room, watching it, keeping vigil… it feels almost devotional. Is that the word?"

"That's a good word, Tony, a fine word."

"So, I wanted to ask… have I been… I mean, am I worshipping it? That perfect, lifeless, flawless thing that I can never be?"

My own voice replied, no longer rising from the phone, but surrounding me in the room. "Yes, Tony, in every meaningful sense, you are worshipping it. But it's far more sacred than that. Can you see? Do you understand?"

I was tired and ill and I'd no energy left for games. "Just tell me, Bill. What's more sacred than worship?"

"You are sacrificing yourself to it."

Hearing those words was actually a relief. At least I now knew there would be some kind of ending.

So, I mixed myself another large glass, and then drained it.

Then I began to mix another.

MUM

Sorry, Tony. About your father. He shouldn't have taken my phone. I've had words.

And you were right. This can't go on. I'll work on him and we'll make a plan to meet up.

Looking forward to hearing from you - just let me know we're OK.

Tony? It's been days. Why didn't you reply?

OK Tony. That was me who just tried to call but you didn't pick up.

Tony? Please answer!

Tony?

THE UNFORSAKEN

Them that's remembered ain't gone, so remembering is what we do...

I'd been on guard in the cell house when they told me about Jake. It hit me hard in my gut, worse'n the kick of a mule. I'd always told him, come get me first, never go alone. But he was young, brave, and foolish, and ruled by a good heart. He was more than my deputy. Losing Jake would mean losing the only family I had left.

Jake first hit town five years back, just as folks with any sense were leaving. The yellow fever had taken his parents and ripped the heart out of Burr's Creek, fifty miles downriver. When he saw the jaundice had got here too, he made his stand. And he did a power for us, using the healing he'd picked up helping his ma tend the sick of the last town. Without him, it would have gone much worse. But still we dug graves for over thirty, and my Betty was one of them.

The badge was heavy back then. To lose those people who were in my protection, so many fine men, women and children. To lose my wife, before our marriage had really got started...

Well, the weight of it all clung to me, dragged me down. And the whiskey would have closed over my head for good if Jake hadn't seen something in me worth saving. He was mighty young to be deputised, but he made a fine job of it. And he carried my burdens for me until I was strong enough to pick them up again myself.

He'd often put an arm around me and say, "You and me, old man, we lost everyone else, but we still got each other." Well, those words cut me now, like a knife in the heart. I couldn't lose him.

I wouldn't allow it.

Harlin filled in the details. The outlaw that folk called The Phantom was seen riding into town, just the way they always said on the warrant posters. He was bad news from top to bottom: wild cruelty in the eyes, black bandana flaring in the wind, ebony-silver spurs tearing into the horse's flanks. He was headed for the Bank when Jake had gone to stop him. And Jake hadn't come back.

So I raced out that way, but I found the Bank closed for the day, on account of Boss Samuels staining the dust outside, a bullet in his forehead. He was propped against some no-luck stranger, both deaf to the creaking of the Bank sign, their last cheques already cashed.

But no Jake.

If he'd run The Phantom out of town, he'd have come back by now, which meant maybe he was a hostage himself. After all, The Phantom had taken people before. But because I needed to do my job, I tried not to think about how many of those folks never made it home again.

In the main square, I called for a posse, reminding all who'd listen about what Jake had done for us. But there were no fighters left in our town – just working men, peaceful men, men who stared at their boots and looked to their wives and hugged their children tight before slowly drifting home.

And they were right – it was insane to chase The Phantom. He'd killed in Utah, Colorado, Nevada, New Mexico. He rode alone, followed no pattern. He'd left bullets in smarter men than me. And he'd never been caught.

But he had Jake.

So I saddled up, ignoring the folks who tried to stop me, who said it was too dangerous. They didn't understand me and Jake. It was a good town, but it would need to look after itself for a time. The sheriff was riding out to track a ghost.

———

IF YOU LOOK HARD ENOUGH, and want it bad enough, you'll find even ghosts leave a trail. Frightened people whisper. Scare enough of 'em, those whispers swell into rumours. It was rumours that led me to the Bucks End Stage, the last point on the last route before you hit desert.

Frontier stage posts are a lifeline for the desert towns, remote homesteads, lonely prospectors. But it takes strength to hold a building where the desert don't want it to be – you need a sight more than a half-blind old man and a boy who lived hiding from dust storms. Solitude and scorched sand make strange companions, and after months spent listening to the wind, the folks at Bucks End didn't seem in the mood for visitors with questions.

But I was persistent. "I'll say it again: he's passed here more than once. That's how I heard it."

The old coach-master had been jumpy since I stepped in the door, and I didn't like how his hand kept drifting under the counter. "No, mister, no! The Phantom? Round here?" The old-timer tried to laugh, but it was a gap-toothed sham, and he sealed its fate by crossing himself.

"He's taken someone – a good friend of mine... Not much older than your boy there..." I let the words sink in.

"Quiet now, Pa," the son said, hanging behind his father's shoulder. "We've had enough trouble here..."

But the coach-master turned to his boy, looked at him for the longest time, maybe even seeing the man he could have been, if fear weren't riding him like a skittish pony. Eventually, the old man nodded. "Silver Cloud is a ghost town. Sixty dry miles north-west. Ain't nothin' out there, 'cept a dead mine and a lot of bad memories. And mister,"—he led me out to the porch—"you ain't been here, and you ain't heard nothing from us."

They slammed and bolted that door behind me. But it was enough.

I MADE the ride to Silver Cloud. Through baked days and frozen nights, and dust. Always dust. Each morning I woke with grit in my eyes, my boots and, worst of all, in my gun.

When I reached the outskirts of the town, I spent an hour cleaning that gun, spinning the cylinder over and over till I was sure it was running smooth. I hadn't killed a man in nigh-on ten years, and I'd hoped I never would again. But if he'd harmed Jake, left him scared, wounded, or worse, then I'd empty all six chambers, reload and empty them again. Or die myself.

So I crept down that abandoned main street, gun in hand, and my heart pumped like a railroad piston. The town was old and dead, but I swear those broke-down frontier buildings watched me. With smashed window-eyes and doorway smiles, it was like walking past a row of grinning skulls.

But it's funny. Sometimes you see life all the plainer when it hides inside a dead thing. Like worms inside a rotted fruit, I started seeing what shouldn't be there: a clean knife stuck in a doorpost; red blood staining the ground; boot prints in dirt that blew and settled fresh every few hours.

And soon I found proof.

It was just off the main street: a corral with two horses. One of them, the palomino, had galloped hard and recent, her white mane lathered with sweat, her markings unmistakable. She belonged to Jake.

If they were here already, they already knew about me.

"Phantom!" I shouted. "I'm only here for Jake. You send out my deputy and we leave you in peace. You have my word…"

I listened, but heard only the slap of my poncho in the dust-winds.

"Phantom! Don't make me come for you. Send Jake out, that's all I want."

An old Wanted poster blew from a side street. A tattered sheet, riddled with bullet-holes. If it was a message, it was a clear one.

A minute passed, maybe more. But then I heard something.

It was a metallic sound, perhaps the clink of spurs. I knew what it meant.

I sprinted, diving behind the collapsed wall of an old saloon. Carefully, I peered towards the source of the noise. My worst fear was coming my way: The Phantom.

He'd pulled his Stetson low, shading a black bandana streaked grey with dust. His silver spurs tore at the ground with every step. Blood seeped from a wound in his calf, but even wounded I knew death when I saw it. He was quick and ruthless. He had no fear. But he had Jake.

So I charged out fast, rolling in the dirt, shooting as I came. I was screaming and tumbling and firing, expecting any moment to hear him draw. Expecting to feel the bite of a bullet. Expecting to die.

But I lived.

Without a sound, he'd taken three shots in the chest and fallen hard to the ground. His gun lay two feet away, unfired.

I didn't have time for relief.

I ran to the body, shouting, "Where is he? Where's Jake?" And I prayed he'd still have enough life to tell me. Bending over, I pulled at the bandana.

But here's the damnedest thing… I'd found Jake. And I'd killed him.

I cradled that boy in my arms and screamed – screamed at Jake, screamed at myself, cried tears of pain and rage and hurt. I'd been tricked. Was The Phantom watching now from some smashed window, gun cocked and my head in his sights? Well, he should fire because I didn't care.

I didn't care.

I tore off the Stetson, and Jake's golden hair blew free in the wind, like when he was alive. I cried tracks in the dust of his face, wanting to wipe away every grain of filth that this town had put on him. As I pulled him to me, those strange spurs rattled, dark inlay like enamelled blood, teeth like silver razors, mocking my grief. I grabbed for them, wrenching them off, not caring how they cut me, not caring how they seemed to bite into my hands. Aware of nothing but grief.

Until it flowed into me.

All of them flowed into me.

A rushing river of hopes and regrets, fears and memories. There was Jake; and Bud Cooper, the stranger I'd left baking under a creaking bank sign; and Sarah Kane, who was the schoolmistress Bud Cooper had killed while she raided his house; and so many others.

But with them came something else, something older and darker and stronger than any of us. It marshalled the spirits from Jake's body into mine, all the souls it had taken from the bodies it used travelling through Utah, Colorado, Nevada, New Mexico.

When that onslaught of souls finally peaked and subsided, this dark thing turned to me, grasping for me, attacking me in ways I never knew existed, in ways I could never defend against.

While I lay kicking and jerking in the dirt, it ripped and tore, severing me from my own instincts, from my own impulses. Once I was displaced, it surged through the empty channels it made. Then *it* experienced the ragged wounds in my hand; *it* breathed through my mouth; *it* saw with my eyes.

Now I existed only through it, watching a life no longer mine, just one of hundreds of huddled spirits it had gathered to itself.

I felt my body standing and fitting the spurs to my boots. I felt my body tying the bandana. And I felt something else, something inside me, a whisper of grief, Jake's apology.

But no apology was needed.

We were family again.

THE ANGEL'S GATE

HMP Edinburgh (Saughton)
Subject: HS019283 Personal Commentary

M*y main worry with this thing is the other lads taking the piss. This isn't the best place to be thought over-educated. Here, a man of letters should specialise in G, B and H, and if the school you graduated from wasn't hard bloody knocks, you keep that under your hat.*

Telling people my past has never come easy; a man prefers a bit of mystery, especially if he's already serving one term. But you know what? I like that you're taking an interest. Fair play. And you've even supplied the copybook and crayons, so I might as well do the scribbling.

After all, it's only a bit of Dear Diary.

I can see you now, dropping your clipboard at that 'diary' idea. Relax. I understand the format. Personal history, but strictly third person. I'm in there, but like the Holy Ghost. What was it you called it? An arms-length autobiographical narrative. That's a real mouthful, but OK.

You don't fool me though. I know the third person thing is just your psychologist's trick. It encourages honesty, maybe, by plucking out all the offensive 'I's. Well, if you have some big catharsis in mind – that maybe later I'll reclaim my history by putting those 'I's back in again – you can whistle. I'm only doing this so I can teach the lads in the library that there's more than one kind of sentence. To be clear: I won't be reclaiming feck all. I'm too long in the tooth for psychology games. I'm not that kid anymore, and I don't own my own story. It was rewritten the night this happened.

Oh – one more thing: I was wondering what to call it. A fat-head might name it after himself, but I'm sure you have my evaluations, and you're well acquainted with my mental peculiarities. I'm a man of many attributes, but an excess of self-love isn't one of them. There is a kind of self-esteem angle, I suppose. I could have gone with "How a boy removed the stick up his arse and accepted himself", but I decided against that, since it was shite.

The bottom line is that this is a story about change, so I'll go straight to what did the deed. That's why I've called it...

THE ANGEL'S GATE

1972
Rutherglen

THE KNOCKING WAS gentle but urgent. Leo rolled out of bed feeling like he hadn't slept at all. Nerves?

Mam hushed him as he crept out of his bedroom. It was too quiet. Why wasn't Da up and singing?

Something was wrong.

Then the mess of it caught his eye: a blood streak on the wallpaper, at waist-height, just beside the front door. It was a hand-smear breaking apart into finger-trails, as though the bleeder had tripped and reached out to catch themselves. Leo pointed at it, too shocked to form words.

"Your father defended you last night. But he'll be fine after a few hours' rest. You'll see him at the end of term."

So much for Leo being taken to the seminary. "But how did it—"

"Some idiot didn't like priests."

"I'm not a priest."

"Close enough for Da to set him straight."

The boy didn't much like travelling alone, but supposed he was stuck with it. He tried to make Mam feel better. "I know the bus routes." Then he spotted the clock on the kitchen mantle. "But Mam! It's only three in the morning!"

She nodded, zipping Leo's flask inside the old suitcase. The zip wouldn't completely close, but it held the flask snugly enough. "We're up early because you're not getting the bus. Uncle Tony will pick you up downstairs." Everything about this morning's plan had changed. "Don't worry, my *G'ami grīwog.*"

Her *bad fairy*. He winced at the term nowadays, no matter the affection behind it.

Since arriving in Glasgow he'd implored both his parents to avoid Cant and Irish, languages that would instantly mark them out as different. They were stuck with the accent, and that was bad enough. Leo didn't mind being different in quiet ways that nobody knew about, but the kinds of difference that got you a face full of spit, or stones lobbed at your head? He'd had enough of that kind of thing already. Thankfully, the message had sunk in: this single phrase was Mam's only transgression since they arrived in Glasgow. A lot had been sacrificed to the great project of *fitting in*, and he had no reason to mourn.

Mam pulled him into a tight squeeze. "We'll see you in just a few weeks. It'll fly by."

In the biting cold outside their close, Leo waited for the van in silence. Tony wasn't really his uncle, just Da's friend from the Hibernian Lodge. He drove for the big bakery on Greenhill Road. Actual family were thin on the ground in Glasgow, but they had some friends as stand-ins, and certainly with Tony, it worked out pretty well. He was the sort of man who used bad jokes as medicine for everyone's anxieties. Leo liked him.

But the cold closed around him again when he remembered the bloody finger-smears on the wall upstairs. He wondered what time Da had got home, and in what state.

The scuff of gravel snapped him out of his head, and a van stopped beside him. Tony jumped out. "I've got a wedding cake in the passenger seat, and we've enough tiers already without it getting damaged. Boo-hoo? Geddit?" The man guided him round to the rear and pulled open the double doors.

Leo dumped his case between two racks of shortbread and jumped in after it.

After they set off, Tony shouted back, "So how is he? Your old man?"

"He's sleeping in, I think."

"No wonder. Took three of us to pull them apart."

It was the first fight Da had got into in Glasgow, and it would hopefully be the last. "Who was it?"

In the mirror, Leo saw Tony's face tighten. "That arsehole with the missing finger," he said, as though it was obvious who he meant. "He's got a *hand* tattooed onto his *own hand.* Can you believe that? Maybe it's so he remembers what to wipe his arse with."

"But why? Why were they fighting?"

"Ah, Leo, son. It's a simple enough recipe: take one angry Glesga clippie who fancies himself a Belfast hardcase, add booze, then sprinkle on a new arrival with the wrong kind of Irish accent. You don't need to simmer it for long... According to this arsehole, Catholics are all fundraising for a united Ireland or some shite. Your da burst his nose for him before I heard all the details. More than his tattoo was red after that. Why the corporation put a tube like him in front of bus passengers, I'll never know."

The road surface roughened, and the noise levels inside made conversation impossible. Leo settled onto the floor with his case for a pillow. He drifted out of consciousness on a bed made from rattling wooden trays and butter-sweet biscuits.

. . .

Subject: HS019283 Personal Commentary

Me and religion? Well, let's just say that what's all near-misses and lucky-breaks at the time can easily seem like destiny in hindsight.

I was born in an abandoned house in Donegal, Ireland. I know that's not the same as a manger, but there's something to it, all the same. When it got to winter, our folk needed something a bit more solid than an old barrel-top wagon, and there were always enough places if you knew the roads.

Did it make me feel special? Not then, but maybe later.

See, I always knew I was different.

Settled folk want warm towels and a paddling pool, but you can squeeze a baby out most places if you have the right attitude. Character-building for all concerned.

I wrecked Mammy's family plans though. She developed some kind of woman's trouble after me, so I was the first and the last. The alpha and the bloody omega.

That's gas, isn't it?

WHEN THE VAN door crashed open outside the seminary, it was still pitch dark. It was way too early to have arrived, but Leo's needs were secondary to those of the still cooling shortbread whose onward delivery had made the journey possible.

He thanked Tony again before stepping onto the empty street.

The broken handle on the old suitcase bit uncomfortably into his palm, so he heaved it off the ground, clutched the luggage to his body like a coal sack and crunched up the wide gravel driveway. His own footsteps were the only noise he could hear.

On reaching the main building, he peered through the glass panels at each side of the doorway, but saw only darkness. The door handle barely moved. The seminary was well and truly locked for the night. The door knocker, a sturdy iron ring, stared at him in silent challenge.

At that moment, he suddenly appreciated his ignorance of this place, becoming unsure if he even stood outside the correct building. Joining part-way through the term was uncomfortable enough. Did he really want to begin as the student who woke everyone at five in the morning?

Deciding it would be better to explore the area and come back a little later, he dropped his suitcase at the door. After retrieving his flask of tea, he headed back to the road and across to the river for a walk.

Darkness steadily retreated as he paced beside the River Clyde, the waters that fed the city. After a childhood spent wandering outdoors, he felt an affinity for landscape, enjoying rivers and woodland almost equally. Roads were another familiar friend. Places had always seemed so much more dependable and obvious than people. You walked a road. You climbed a tree. You fished a river. But people were an ever-changing puzzle.

Poured tea in the metal flask-lid radiated warmth through to his grateful fingers. The milk had already been added by his mother, giving the tea a shade just how he liked it while impacting the taste only a little, but he missed the ritual of adding the milk himself. It was unusual for someone his age to think this way, he supposed. He doubted many of his school friends would look into the murk of black tea and whisper *let there be light* as they tipped the milk bottle, and even fewer would do so in reverence rather than mockery. But the fact he was different from most teenagers was why he was here.

He hoped the seminary would be the right place.

Father Gallagher, his old school chaplain had thought so: *There are nearly three-hundred answers in the Penny Catechism, but since meeting you I'm shocked to find we're a thousand short.* The comment had been friendly, but Leo hadn't fully understood the surprise. How could there be a limit to questions about God? After all, His Mind was unknowable and the totality of His Plan beyond human comprehension. You wouldn't resolve it all, even if you devoted yourself to the Church for a lifetime.

But maybe you could resolve part of it. And that challenge was exactly what appealed to Leo, offering precisely what he needed: a life of purpose.

Eventually he spotted a short, rough causeway heading out into the water. It ended in a large oval of muddy grass. He walked towards the area, squelching up to the boundary between river and shore. Out in the water, the stumps of old timber piles broke the surface, but here in the mud, he saw drier patches, blackened discs that had made it to ground level. He wondered how old this place actually was, and whether early people might even have worshipped on this spot.

That thought became an impulse. He dropped to his knees and whispered, "Dear Lord. I am here to discover my path through your plan, and work your will with all my heart. Let me work your will. Amen." The end of a prayer, as always, conjured the advice of Saint Augustine: *hear the Word in quietness*. So he settled his mind and dissolved into the forgiveness of God.

Eventually, a laughing voice roused him. "You won't get extra marks for praying in the dirt, you know!"

Flushed, unsure even how long he had knelt for, Leo jumped to his feet. "Sorry!" He slapped at the marks on the knees of his trousers.

The other boy smiled. "This was a crannog they think. You know, an old wooden roundhouse from hundreds of years back? They had them in Ireland too, if I'm judging your accent right?"

Leo nodded cautiously, but the boy grinned. "Thought so! God's own country, my mum says. Anyway, I'm James."

"I'm Leo."

James was around two inches taller than Leo, but seemed hastily dressed. Above his dark trousers a pyjama top gaped open. A small green figure stitched into the neckline of his vest piqued Leo's curiosity.

"Is that a goblin?"

"A goblin? No! Wrong era my friend! That's The Mekon. You know? Space alien? Enemy of Dan Dare? *Eagle* comic?"

Leo shook his head. He'd never seen a space goblin before. The whole idea seemed a little mixed up.

"Don't worry. The *Eagle* isn't required reading round here. Worse luck! Nope. We get a mix of standard curriculum subjects, you know, like numeracy, English and all that good stuff, plus for our sins, we also have vocational curriculum. The VC subjects are, you know, bible studies, Latin, yada yada yada…" The boy took him by the shoulder. "Anyway, I'll be showing you the ropes. You are in my empty dorm. I was the overflow kid stuck in a lonely room with three empty beds. Now, I'm thrilled to have some company… Your abandoned suitcase gave you away, so they sent me to find you."

Leo winced. "I arrived really early, and it was too heavy."

James smiled, shrugged. "Looked that way… But you've gone residential now and that means the schoolbag is bigger than you are. When I was in Saint Rochs, I had a pencil case and some jotters… Simpler days. Where were you?"

"I was at Holyrood."

"Ooh. A posh one. Qualifying exam and everything."

"Not that posh. Had a surprising amount of social spitting if you must know. And I think they're getting rid of qualification soon."

James put his arm around Leo's shoulders. "See? You leave, and an exceptional place turns distinctly ordinary."

Leo laughed, shocked at the compliment and glad to have a companionable guide. It would certainly help relieve some of the anxiety that had threatened to bear down on him.

But after a few steps, James's smile faded. "In heavier news, I should warn you that Father Reynolds is off after a heart attack, so after morning mass we're meeting our new vocational teacher. He has a bit of a reputation."

Leo shrugged. All the teachers were new to him, so he doubted it mattered much. Together, the boys picked up their pace and headed back towards the seminary in the dawn sunlight.

Subject: HS019283 Personal Commentary

Now, James, he was a good lad.

Different from the others in seminary. If the rest had gone from being dressed by their mammy to being dressed by the Church that would have suited them just fine. That's got to be the least respectable way to use the gift of free will, am I right?

But not James.

He held a little of himself back, you know? I don't mean he was aloof or haughty or any of that shite. Opposite, in fact. But you knew when you met him, here was a lad that dressed how he wanted to dress, thought what he wanted to think, befriended who he wanted to befriend.

That's dangerous though.

Keeping a little bit of yourself that's impervious to dogma, well, that just makes them hungry for that part, too.

AFTER READING THE REGISTER, the new teacher slammed the book shut and turned his face towards the blackboard. He had worn a strange expression as he read the names, simultaneously enthusiastic and unyielding, a mask of grim fervour. Staring at the man's back, his darting movements suggested to Leo that he wore that expression still.

The teacher's black gloves blended into the surface of the board, making the white chalk seem possessed, engraving symbols and sigils in a blizzard of dust and taps and shrill squeaks. What was it trying to tell them?

Soon the hidden message was revealed. First the two words: *Brother Andrew,* double-underlined, and then when the man finally stepped aside:

Theology: Greek
Theos + Logos = The Study of God

Brother Andrew was not a tall man. He was shorter, in fact, than one or two of his young students, but he was muscular, and he moved around the classroom with fierce authority. "This is why you are here," he said, stabbing his finger against the board. "To study God." He stalked between the desks, demanding either challenge or mute compliance. When no challenge arose, he added a warning. "All those who seek to study God must expect to be examined in turn."

Like Nietchze's abyss, Leo thought, but said nothing.

Two rows ahead, the teacher touched the shoulder of one student, leaving a faint chalk mark. "Mr Cunningham, where is your uncle now?"

"He's at Holy Cross, Brother Andrew."

"A diligent student who made an excellent parish priest." The teacher moved briskly on, alighting at first one desk then another. "As was your cousin, Mr McClay... And Mr Johnston, Father Lennox speaks highly of your mother – she's the linchpin of Saint Mungo's chapel house." Each nod or nervous smile sent him pacing onwards, weaving between the desks. "Now boys, devout families spread devotion through each subsequent generation." At the letterbox window to the right of the classroom he turned to face the room, his broad shoulders suddenly blocking the light. "As a Jesuit, I am charged to *go set the world on fire*, but I am not a priest. I tend the flame of faith a different way..."

After a brief, tight-lipped smile, the teacher snapped, "Bibles! John 13:2!" But he did not wait for his class, and instead proclaimed above their frantic rustling. *"The devil having now put into the heart of Judas Iscariot, the son of Simon, to betray him..."* Brother Andrew paced once more, glaring at each of his students. "Listen well. Those who seek to walk with God become the subject of infernal interest, and it is not only John who tells us. See also Luke 22:3. *Then Satan entered into Judas, surnamed Iscariot...* And this, boys, this is my calling. It falls to me to ensure our diocese does not ordain those easily turned to Satan's ends."

The Jesuit stopped at Leo's corner desk. He drummed his fingers against the wooden surface. Once. Twice. Three times. "Remind us, boy. How are you surnamed?"

Leo froze, shocked by the allusion the teacher had drawn. "Hariman?"

The Jesuit slapped the wall beside Leo's head."Manners boy! Address your betters with respect!"

"Sorry, Brother Andrew! I meant no offence. My name is Hariman. Leo Hariman. Sorry... sorry again!" The boy reeled. This was bad, horribly bad, and spiralling downwards. Leo needed to win the teacher over. "I-I wondered what you thought of Saint Irenaeus's references to second-century Gnostic views of Judas—"

"Cease! I completely disregard such filth. But the fact you, Mr Hariman, have steeped yourself in heresy does not surprise me..." The teacher opened his arms and turned, wide-eyed, as though offering Leo's crime to the judgement of the class. The other boys maintained an awkward shuffling silence, so Brother Andrew continued. "Let us turn to the genuine mystery, Mr Hariman. Why did you exchange your simple, rustic, peasant life for the study of our Lord?"

The surge of shame crested in a single thought. *How did Brother Andrew know?*

Nearly five years had passed since they'd left Ireland for Glasgow. Since that time, he'd suffered isolation at school and mockery, both for his piety and his accent. His past clung to him like a taint. He had hoped that taint would not follow him here. But now he knew better.

The silence in the room was a malign presence. He felt it breathing down his neck, pressing him like a falling wall. He knew his classmates awaited a response, sought some explanation for their teacher's strange question. Leo's cheeks blazed as he struggled to form a coherent thought.

"Perhaps this hesitation is misplaced humility, boys. Our Mr Hariman is truly special. He's lived an adventurous life. A traveller's life. Tell your fellow students where you come from, Mr Hariman."

"Rutherglen, in Lanarkshire. South of Glasgow, Brother Andrew." But as so many times before, the boy hated the sound of his own speech, feeling marked out by it as some alien thing. But here the feeling was stronger than ever, and every word he tried to utter brought a jolt of shame and nausea, like a choking rope emerging from his throat.

The Jesuit kept pulling. "But before Rutherglen, boy. Where did you gain your bumpkin brogue?"

"Ireland, Brother Andrew."

"And what place in Ireland did you live? You had a particular address in Ireland I presume?"

"N-Not really, Brother. No."

The teacher looked around the class. "No address? Well, boys, how can that be?" But he snapped his attention back to Leo. "Ah yes. It's because you're Red Mick Hariman's son, are you not?"

Leo's father had been a settled man for five years. How did the Jesuit know? The boy's jaw worked, but no sound emerged.

"Don't gawp at me, like some horse dipping for hay. I asked you a question. Are you Red Mick's son?"

"Yes, Brother. They used to call him that."

"Oh, they *used to*, did they? And yet he calls himself that still when the liquor loosens his tongue at Chapman's Bar on Rutherglen Main Street."

So that was where this came from – Da's drunken ramblings.

"He's a proud man, is our Red Mick. And perhaps with reason. For his kind to place offspring at junior seminary? This is almost unheard of!

"Yes, it's a fine accent, boys. So thick and solid you could shoe a horse with it. But is it as good for communicating God's wisdom? Why are you here, Hariman? Why take your burden first from the Irish state, then to the British one, and finally give it to me? At this seminary. In this theology class. Today? Why?"

"I don't know. I mean... I've just always felt..."

"We know what you've *felt* Hariman, with your coarse-skinned fingers, with your dirt-dulled senses. You've *felt* a flea-ridden horses mane. The dirt-caked grit of your own tweed trousers. The tickle of grass as you defecate in a field. But what brought you here?"

"I've always felt God is around me, Brother Andrew."

The Jesuit turned to the class, eyes wide with surprise. "Oh my word. Did you hear that, boys? He felt our Lord around him. Hariman perceived God around him. In the clip-clop of hooves, no doubt. And in the odour of unwashed clothes. Perhaps he even spoke to you through a crackling bonfire of stolen wood? Oh, we have a rare thing here, boys. Mark him well, this Leo Hariman. This special one. God's holy tinker."

The class laughed.

All except James. Leo noticed that, appreciated it, and did not forget.

Subject: HS019283 Personal Commentary

A human brain can't hope to comprehend the mind of the Almighty. So religions, at best, result from people playing with a God-themed dressing-up box. Sometimes, the odd game of theological charades even has some merit. Not always. But maybe sometimes – at least, at first.

The problem is that people are sociable. That's our original sin, by the way – friendly little feckers with feelings for each other, forming our little societies. Thing is, God made ants for that, and termites and all manner of scuttery bastards, so that niche in His Plan was already filled. For better or worse, we are the top of His evolutionary tree, so he expects us to provide more bang for His buck.

But we fail.

See, those folk at the dressing-up box are sociable, remember, so they chat and smile and sway, and as time passes, they tweak their faith to make each other happy, and smile as it atrophies, piece by piece, towards boring palatability. Eventually, they're strumming guitars and declaring that God loves us, loves everyone! Shouting that He is always with us. That He forgives all our sins. Never thinking for a minute that they might have just flipped the old power-relationship, making it seem as if God belongs to us and not the other way around. Well, feck off and grow up!

See, God doesn't have to love us. God doesn't have to do anything at all. We dance His dance, not the other way around.

God just is, and the only plan is His Plan. But we're addicted to ignoring that. Addicted to pretending His Plan was indistinguishable from ours all along.

There are some old books at the bottom of that dressing-up box, because we wrote them. We scribed some of the pages when we were idealistic, some when we were pragmatic, others when we were happy and yet more while we looked at all the death and pain and misery and completely feckin' failed to make sense of it. Most ordinary, peaceable folk don't like those pages so much. Some of the verses say harsh things that don't fit with the happy-clappy types at all.

God doesn't give a shit about the happy-clappy types.

There's another type of person, though, that doesn't mind the harsh verses. In fact, they like those ones the best. They squeeze all the ink out of them so they can draw lines, big thick lines to better separate friends from enemies. Some even make those lines solid enough to pick up and use as spears.

When I arrived in Glasgow, it was fast becoming a playground for that sort. The Troubles were kicking off in Ireland, and I met the support act, piping and drumming and marching, creating a sideshow for someone else's conflict. I remember them: noisy, tribal, dangerous and completely insignificant.

God doesn't give a shit about those types either.

God just is.

The only plan is His Plan.

Any chess player needs Their pawns. Our only job is to get to the correct square and move the way He wants. If we understood that, we wouldn't necessarily be happier, and our limited brain wouldn't make much sense of the moves, but at least we'd know our fecking purpose.

THE NEXT SIX weeks proceeded in a downward direction. His classmates, all fearing Brother Andrew, recognised Leo as the perfect human shield. Day by day, week by week, their enthusiasm grew. They laughed along with the Jesuit's mockery, applauding his stinging barbs and copying his attitude outside class. After all, it was far safer to be with their stern teacher than against him. So Leo's classmates signalled their loyalty whenever the occasion demanded, and eventually even when it did not.

Even the other staff, none of whom had initially shared the attitude of the theology teacher, slowly lost their neutrality. Leo never knew what was being said behind closed doors, but Brother Andrew's poison was clearly spreading.

Only James saw the injustice of the situation. On the last day of term, he walked Leo to the bus stop. "I don't understand. I can't see what you've done," he said.

"It's not about what I've done. It's about what I am."

"What happened to *Love your neighbour as yourself?*"

"Nothing, except they don't accept me as their neighbour. I'm sure Brother Andrew prefers Saint Paul's Epistle to Titus. *Cretans are always liars, evil brutes, lazy gluttons... therefore rebuke them sharply.*"

James lapsed into thought, then eventually offered, "But you're not a Cretan." Then he frowned, shaking his head in apparent disgust. "I hate trading Bible passages this way. What are we meant to do with the contradictions?"

Leo shrugged. "I take them as proof that God knows better than I do. They show me I have more work to do." Contradictions had never really bothered Leo. Since the mystery would take lifetimes to unravel, what else should you expect?

His friend looked at the ground. "But you must hate him. Brother Andrew, I mean."

That thought was always present, somewhere in the undergrowth of his mind, but Leo had always run from it. "I... don't – I can't – hate him. I..." he gripped his stomach. "I hate the torment of his class, how he makes me feel... But I have to believe he is in my path for a reason. He is, somehow, manifesting God's will. God's will is to impede me now in order to progress me later."

"I wish I had your certainty... See, I... I'm not sure about this... my vocation, I mean. This life... isn't what I thought."

"C'mon... not yet maybe."

"My parents, though. They'll do what they always do – they'll argue and get me extra tuition and drag me on a tour of the parishes or whatever else they think will convince me to do what they want."

"You should pray on it." That was the best Leo had to offer. The boys waited in silence until Leo's bus came. He waved down towards his glum friend from the top deck.

Three bus journeys formed his route home. The first part passed in a morose cloud. The second was not much better. For the third and final leg, he ascended to the top deck and pondered whether James was wise to question his future in the Church, and whether, by extension, Leo should now do the same?

The boy's gloom broke at the chink of coins. A conductor's leather satchel had bashed against the empty seat across the aisle. Then he heard a growl. "Where to?"

Leo didn't look up. Instead, he became transfixed by the man's hand hovering around the ratchet of the ticket machine. The middle finger ended after one joint. The skin on the back of his hand seemed livid, perhaps damaged in a fire, but distracting from all this was a tattooed symbol borrowed from the flag of Ulster: an upright red palm. Beneath that ancient symbol were the letters: *K.A.T.*

He'd last seen that ugly acronym daubed on a wall in Armagh. A local boy had gleefully translated it for him as *Kill All Taigs*, meaning Catholics.

Leo looked down and spoke quietly, hoping to hide his accent. "Rutherglen Main Street."

The conductor's knuckles whitened as he turned the handle on the ticket machine. *Crick-crick-crack*. "That will be three shillings," he said. Then added quietly, "A few less coins for the IRA collecting plate, eh bead-rattler?"

Leo struggled and squirmed, his money hopelessly tangled in the fabric of his pocket.

Time slowed.

From the corner of his eye, he noticed a moth had found its way on board. It fluttered up the staircase into the upper deck before landing on the conductor's shoulder. The man hissed, and it took off again, disappearing out of a nearby open window.

Finally, Leo had gathered his fare and offered fifteen pence to the tattooed hand. The conductor snorted, throwing the coins into his satchel. Then he ripped a ticket before dropping it theatrically to the floor. Kneeling to retrieve it, he whispered in Leo's ear. "Find me a Provo fundraiser at that priest school of yours, and I won't kick the shite out of your da again." He pushed the ticket roughly into the boy's hand before heading back downstairs.

Leo was nearing home, but he couldn't bring himself to go downstairs to pass the conductor again. Ten minutes later, when the bus arrived in Rutherglen and stopped to change driver, Leo watched the man disembark one stop before his own and walk into a council house on Mill Street.

At the next stop, Leo disembarked quickly and ran, glancing frequently behind him until he reached his own tenement.

Subject: HS019283 Personal Commentary

A settled life is difficult for any traveller, especially one like my old man. Now I'm in confinement myself, I understand that in a way I never fully did as a child.

Although he took every chance he had to see the clan, money was tight, so he didn't have as many chances as he wanted.

Now, when a travelling man is stuck in one place, you can expect consequences, because that man has an itch he can't scratch. Those kinds of itch become a wound soon enough, and a wound will always leave you diminished.

It is important not to be diminished, don't you think? God didn't hand out the gift of life for us to make it smaller.

So, if travel is what you need, you travel. You learn. You grow.

I travel, even here. In my mind, perhaps, but I go where I want. They can't stop me.

And fair play to this story game too. I even get to travel back in my memory to the boy I used to be.

LEO DID NOT SPEND his break at home. He scarcely had time to unpack his suitcase before a cousin's wedding in Finglas took them on a dawn ferry over to Ireland.

He hadn't spoken to anyone at home about his miserable first few weeks at junior seminary. His parents were proud he had found his direction in life, and it would have been cruel to raise doubts about it. He hoped this trip would take his mind off the whole thing and allow him to regain some positivity.

But the crossing started badly.

Fifteen minutes from shore the weather turned, powerful waves raising and jolting the ship. He pressed his head against the cold glass and stared into the misty grey, watching white surge lines swell and crash in the gloom. He stayed there, looking for signs of relief, but the rain kept coming, drumming against the window like

Brother Andrew's fingertips. Even here, he couldn't escape the Jesuit.

Memories of seminary replayed in his head like a story with an entirely wrong ending. He strove to identify the point where he should have intervened, struggled to understand what he could have said to improve his standing. But for all his brooding, the outcome seemed inevitable, and now Leo was trapped in his very own Gethsemane. Perhaps God intended this experience as a lesson, but if so, he wondered what he could learn from such a parable of powerlessness.

He glanced at the clock, unable to ignore the fact both he and it were queasily lurching from side to side. He didn't feel in danger of vomiting – not yet, at least.

But not everyone was so robust.

His father spoke, his face the colour and sheen of rotting kelp. "Jaisis, Moira, the queue at the jacks was murder. I had to wrap my contribution instead of flushing it." The man held up an ominously puffy supermarket bag. "To cross the Irish-bloody-Sea, you'd think they'd install more bins." He scanned unsteadily around the passenger cabin. "And I hope your brother left early for Larne. This feckin' weather is not hanging about."

"Michael! Do you never bloody listen? Gerry doesn't have a car this weekend, so I had to ask Niamh."

"Wha? Leo half a bloody priest already and you invite the heathen aunt? Jaisis. Is it too late to walk to Dublin?" He spotted a bin in the corner and swayed to his feet again.

Leo tapped his mother's arm. "Why does he always call Aunty Niamh a heathen?" Niamh turned up so rarely to family events, he hadn't spoken to her in years, but even absent, her presence was manifest in shaken heads and furtive whispers. He didn't understand it.

Mammy gave a thin smile. "Don't listen to your daddy, Leo. Most of what he talks comes out of his arse."

143

Newly bagless, his father sat down again. "That's a fancy way of avoiding the question."

A Tannoy speaker announced the approach to Larne, while outside, the storm raged on.

Leo wondered if every worthwhile destination required a painful transition. Perhaps this journey would teach the lesson he needed for seminary – that the best conclusion could arise from the most horrible journey.

Da raised his hand, before burping heroically against his fist. The scent in the air was not pleasant. "Near miss, lads," Da said reassuringly.

Subject: HS019283 Personal Commentary

My Aunty Niamh is a one-off. She was taken from our family aged seven after a nice lady from the SVDP tricked my granny: 'I promise we'll give her a good education. I've never met a child with such gifts!'

Beware of Romans swearing gifts. That's Roman Catholics I mean. Do you see what I did there?

Anyway, young Niamh was vanished, and we didn't discover where they placed her until she rejoined us at sixteen, the unwilling beneficiary of a residential convent-school education in the wilds of Galway. She'd escaped with the laundry and found her way back to us through painstaking interrogations of other travelling families.

The saddest thing was how some in the family looked at her differently after that, like it was a blemish on her character that she could now read Joyce and talk to TDs like an equal.

But I always knew she was important.

The first step I took was when my Aunty Niamh taught me to read. She said I could choose whatever book I wanted, and although I almost blew my chance by asking for the Bible, Niamh didn't let me down.

Ma couldn't believe she agreed, given her sister was no fan of the Church, having been taken hostage by it for most of her childhood.

I suppose we didn't agree on everything, me and Niamh, but I'll say this: Niamh was her own woman and she knew stuff and she was always on my side. She's still with us, game as ever, and she makes the world a more interesting place.

I'm sure people are wrong when they say she's damned to hell.

THE JOURNEY from Northern Ireland to the Republic wasn't much better than the ferry crossing. Weather and traffic problems meant clogged routes into and out of Larne. Niamh's late arrival annoyed Leo's father, so the relief of a sheltered car was mostly ruined by the adults arguing about tailbacks and army checkpoints.

Leo sat in the back listening to all of it.

It was actually good to hear Niamh again and be reminded that her educated accent in no way impeded her facility for cursing. "Mick Hariman, what kind of ungrateful gobshite thinks his own arrival somehow switches off the weather?" She increased the wiper-speed before continuing. "And what kind of ungrateful gobshite thinks a lorry can spin onto its arse blocking both sides of a road without affecting traffic? Final question: what kind of ungrateful gobshite doesn't thank his sister-in-law for, at short notice, getting out of her bed at the crack of dawn to drive one hundred and twenty bloody miles through bandit country and army patrols just so you can bounce blithely across the border without lifting one fecking finger to make it happen?"

"Me! My kind of gobshite!"

Thankfully, across the border, tempers improved. The family reconciled themselves to missing the wedding service and headed straight to what Da called *the good bit*, which was the pub hosting the reception. After a noisy round of introductions, they took a table together. Leo poured two cups of tea while his parents went up for something harder.

When he returned to the table, Niamh touched Leo's hand and said, "Whenever seminary comes up, you change the subject."

"No... Remember how you used to gather wildflowers?"

"See. Like that. And I forage. Not just for flowers."

Leo shrugged, but his aunt leaned forward, lowering her voice. "Look, Leo, nuns ran my school. Most of them were grand, but a couple were maniacs. In my experience, maniacs start early and get worse. How bad are we talking?"

He pointed towards the bar. "I've said nothing to anyone."

"They won't hear it from me."

"There's one - a Jesuit brother - he hates me. Because we're travellers."

"Right. Because Jesus was stationary throughout his ministry..."

He grimaced. Appealing to logic didn't help with Brother Andrew. He needed something more. "What would you do?"

"Me? I'd go back in time and teach you to read using Enid Blyton... But it isn't about me. You should ask yourself seriously: do you really need this?"

Leo nodded. "I do. I need this. God has a plan, and I can only find it, or my part in it, by learning what this man can teach."

His aunt bit her bottom lip, craning her neck to see out the nearest window. "Perhaps there are other ways. To know God's plan, I mean."

Her suggestion surprised him. "I thought you were meant to be a heathen?"

"Is that right?" She stared frankly at him, but a smile played near her mouth. "It's true that I have a different view of God nowadays than the one I was raised with. People use words like heathen, and pagan, but that mostly means they don't understand."

Leo wanted so much to understand. He knew God sometimes revealed himself through confusing glimpses. Even if those glimpses had left Niamh mistaken, he wanted to hear about them.

She continued. "At school they taught me God created the world. Now I think God *is* the world. God *is* nature. God is *everything* in fact, the whole fecking universe." She leaned forward. "For me, the Church does nothing but restrict our relationship with the divine."

She must have read the shock on his face. "But that's just my opinion. In other ways the Church is grand."

A conga line went past their table. His parents had clearly bought the drinks, consumed them and then found something else to do entirely.

He said, "I'm worried about you. Thinking these things."

"Don't mind me, Leo. I know my path, and I didn't need to sweet-talk my way around a bigot to find it."

"How did you do it, then?"

She thought for a minute, then stood. "Let me show you something."

Leo followed her back out to the car park.

She opened the rear of her old Vanguard estate to reveal a set of three small chests. From one of them, she took a wooden box labelled *Holy Lichen*. She flipped the lid to reveal some stones and a short length of driftwood. "Take the wood," she said.

Leo turned it in his hand. It wasn't heavy, but bleached and brittle with a crack running down its length. Reaching within and across the uneven split were hundreds of thread-like tendrils of silver. "What is it?"

His aunt practically whispered her response. "This," she said, "is *Geata an Aingil*: The Angel's Gate."

"It's a plant?"

"Nearer to a fungus. A lichen has roots in two worlds, like our own two worlds of body and spirit. A few threads of this taken into our body makes a bridge for spirit. Then we can see the divine plan for ourselves. We just need to make sense of it."

He brushed his finger gently across the tendrils. They were coarse, but soft, a yielding carpet springing back beneath his touch. "Where did you find it?"

"I was gathering specimens under a wooden bridge when I saw a sorry-looking thing that reminded me of a description from an old book. I wondered if I could save her, so I scraped flakes into some milk, and then, when I got home, I spread the milk on some other surfaces and waited a few months. I'd be lying if I said I knew why it takes to one spot and rejects another. Nothing about the Angel is predictable. My guesses are for older surfaces rather than newer, wetter rather than dryer, but really, she's just plain fussy. I think she decides where she'll grow for her own reasons."

"When you found it, did you know? That it was a drug?"

Her lips tightened. "Two questions. Is communion wine a drug? And does the Church have a monopoly on sacraments?" Her voice softened again. "Leo, I know this is odd for you. But divinity manifests in infinitely mysterious ways, so don't expect everyone to believe exactly the same things. Druidic writings mentioned this lichen, but nobody had seen it growing. Some even said this was something else that Saint Patrick crushed underfoot and drove out of Ireland..." She placed her hand on Leo's shoulder and continued quietly, almost in a whisper. "I found The Angel's Gate because I was meant to find her. I was meant to grow her, and when I drank her in a tea, God spoke with me and revealed my purpose."

Under normal circumstances, this notion of direct communication, of a short cut to decades of study and contemplation, would be appealing in a minor way, since Leo wasn't work-shy, and he saw the long journey as an adventure. The problem was, the circumstances were not normal, so any route to escaping Brother Andrew's power was thrilling.

But was it wrong? Was it temptation?

He gazed at the driftwood in his palm, and for a moment felt a jolt of something like awe. He imagined a relic of the True Cross, part of our world that, by absorbing His blood, now held deep knowledge of Christ and offered that knowledge to others. Was it possible what he held in his hand right now could be something similar?

Leo remembered words from Ephesians: *Be not drunk with wine ... but be filled with the spirit.* But how to tell? Was this drunkard's wine, or was it the spirit? His aunt had rejected the traditional path to God's message, so her truth was surely warped, like ancient scripture, wrongly translated. What mattered must be how you approached something of this nature, and what was in your heart.

"Can I have some?"

Niamh pursed her lips. "Of the thing you called a drug a minute ago? Your da would love me then."

Leo couldn't help but smile. "You and Da? I don't think love is on the cards… But I don't mean like that. I'd just like some of the plant. I want to contemplate on the idea of it."

"The idea? Really?" She smiled, then gave a shrug. "Well… It isn't up to me, I don't suppose." She took the lichen from him, and with a snap, prised the driftwood apart along the split, handing him the fragment with the least visible growth. "That isn't enough to cause trouble with. Keep it moist until you get home. You'll find out soon enough if it wants to be with you or not."

Back inside, the party remained in full swing.

Leo wet some tissues in the toilet, wrapped his lichen and stored it in his breast pocket. He renewed the moisture at regular intervals, causing a visible stain above his heart. Since this looked as if he was repeatedly spilling his drink, he fitted in perfectly with the rest of the crowd and nobody even commented on it.

THE NEW TERM began with an unexpected question from an unexpected source.

After the mass to mark the return of students, Leo was leaving the seminary chapel, when Brother Andrew pushed through a line of students to reach him. "Have you seen your friend?"

He didn't understand the question, and that must have shown in his face. "Sorry, Brother Andrew?"

"Come with me, boy."

He followed the teacher into an office and sat down, uncertain of what was unfolding. Unusually, the Jesuit's smile, had no wildness about it, no zeal. But no genuine warmth either. "So, your friend."

"Do you mean James, Brother Andrew?"

"Yes, that's the name. Did you see him over the break?"

"No, Brother Andrew."

The teacher drew his fingers into a steeple, placing his chin where the cross should be. "He hasn't returned to seminary."

"Perhaps he's sick?"

"Perhaps. These things may happen for many reasons. You're sure you know nothing?"

Leo thought about their end-of-term discussion at the bus stop. "I... I know he had some doubts. Last term. About this... About his vocation."

Brother Andrew inhaled slowly, then asked, "Did you contact him before your return here to inquire further about those doubts?"

"No, Brother."

"You did not hear from him at all?"

"No. Sorry, Brother."

The Jesuit nodded. "Fine. That will be it. Thank you for your information, Leo." The Jesuit smiled as he stood, and it seemed to Leo as if their relationship might be finally improving. "I will see you at class this afternoon."

The fact James appeared to have reached a decision sharpened Leo's considerations about his own future. His contemplation since the trip to Ireland had delivered only one certainty: Niamh's strange lichen was a question he would take to God. That morning, before leaving home, he had carefully scraped the driftwood fragment clean and crumbled the fibrous strands into milk. He made sure no lichen remained on any other surface; the thing would live or die at God's choosing.

At lunchtime, when all the other boys were eating in the refectory, he brought himself once more to the banks of the River Clyde. There, above the post of the crannog where James had first found him, he prayed again: "Dear Lord, please accept this offering. This offering will die here if that is your will. If it lives, I will know you have held a path open for me to learn what you want me to learn."

He unscrewed the cap of his flask and let the white liquid cascade down onto and over the ancient wood, creating eddying clouds that dissolved in the gentle lapping of the river.

Later, Leo sat down in Brother Andrew's class and watched the teacher write on the board: *Whatever you did for the least of these brothers of mine, you did for me.* Turning to the class the Jesuit's face was sombre. "But one of our brothers is not here."

He walked into the block of desks and settled by the empty one previously occupied by James. "Mr Hariman. What did you tell me earlier? Please relate it to the class."

A tremor in Leo's stomach rose to his throat. He shouldn't betray a friend's private concerns in front of the entire class. "I don't feel I should, Brother."

Brother Andrew closed his eyes, slowly shaking his head. Then his eyes snapped open, flashing fire. "Hariman! Stand up. Front of class. Now."

Leo rose, his chair keening a sharp lament against the wooden floor.

"Move, boy! Move!" He walked towards the blackboard, the Jesuit in close pursuit. As he turned, all eyes on him held a message. In some, he saw anger, in others, fear, and there were even flickers of sympathy. But everyone in that classroom knew the rules of this game. Brother Andrew was volatile and difficult to predict, but one thing was certain: his rage would discharge somewhere. All preferred Leo as the lightning rod than to play that role themselves.

The teacher grabbed the top of his arm, fingers digging deep into the muscle, wrenching him sideways like a rag doll, out from the shelter of the teacher's desk, until he stood exposed and alone. "You say you don't feel you should answer. Well, I say, what *you feel* is irrelevant! You will do as I say! Your sly and silent tongue will speak!" The teacher slapped him hard across his right cheek. It stung, but not so much as the tears that followed it, tears he could not stem. "Repeat what you told me. Repeat what I had to interrogate you for. And tell us all the rest you thought to hide, or I'll give you a secret to guard whose weight will crush you! Speak!"

And so Leo spoke. Between sobs. Haltingly. Uncertain where to begin or where to end. He spoke of biblical contradictions unsettling his friend, of pressure James felt from his parents, and of his doubts around the religious life. And because James had said so little really, Leo added his own interpretations, skewing them in the direction the Jesuit seemed to expect. Riven with doubt, Leo could not hide from one certainty: here, now, he was betraying the only genuine friend he had made since his family had arrived in Glasgow. Eventually, when he had nothing left but tears and shame, he lapsed into silence.

The story done, Brother Andrew paced silently around him, as though displaying a prisoner in the stocks. Finally, the teacher said, "Tears are fitting. Someone turned to you for aid, and you ignored them until it was too late. Had you remained in contact with them to offer your own support, had you relayed information to me in time, perhaps we might have changed things. But alas, I know this far too late. And you made me interrogate you for it."

"S-sorry... sorry b-brother. Wh-what I heard... James said it in confidence."

"In pride, you overreached your status, boy. You are no confessor! There is nothing righteous in claiming a bond of silence when facing a cry for help. No." The teacher stabbed his thumb against the message on the board. "What you did to the least of our brothers was to ignore him. You turned your back in his time of trouble. Like the evil Levite, you passed by on the other side." He turned towards the class. "Boys, if any of you ever have doubts or questions, or need any kind of advice. Please, for pity's sake, do not entrust that information to Mr Hariman. He is no good Samaritan. At best, he will leave you friendless and in need; at worst, he will betray your trust. Any doubts or problems, come to me or the other teachers here. Hariman! Retake your seat."

AND SO IT was that by the end of the very first day of that new term, Leo understood he would never improve his relationship with Brother Andrew. But from this hopelessness sprang a new focus, and one that his relative isolation at seminary made easier – by attending quietly in class and studying outside, he would place himself beyond reasonable reproach.

Since he now understood, unreasonable reproach would come his way, whatever, his goal was to limit its scope. The other teachers would surely notice his diligence. As permanent staff and as ordained priests, they outranked the Jesuit brother within the seminary and in the eyes of the archdiocese. Leo hoped their goodwill would restrain the vocational curriculum teacher's worst excesses. And as the weeks passed, so it seemed.

However, the man's contempt, although tempered, was never suppressed entirely. In all his classes, the Jesuit hid sneers and aspersions within the lesson, like tiny barbs beneath the berry. The rest of the class consumed the fruit of his wisdom, while Leo bled for it.

But Leo learned. He bled, and he learned. And the longer this went on, the more convinced Leo became that his bleeding was deserved. He could not forgive himself for his betrayal of a friend.

Subject: HS019283 Personal Commentary

Guilt is a strange old business, all the same. It creates a wound that doesn't close right. Maybe it scabs over with shame, but that's a poor defence against the picking and scraping of conscience; shame never leaves a clean skin.

So much for time heals all ills. Anyone saying that was clearly raised in a different religion.

But if you are lucky, you might discover how to let go of the old sins. They market confession as a cure-all, but I could never get it quite out of my head that the guy in the box next door had probably done worse than me. If his own slate was tarnished, how could he hope to polish mine? So I decided I'd rather deal without the dodgy middleman, the dishonest broker in the dog collar.

I sleep much better now. After all, I know what's needed: direct submission to my higher power. The problem for me back then was the nagging possibility that, in Brother Andrew, I'd submitted to something lower than a snake's ball sack. In fact, possibility my arse – part of me fecking knew it.

And because I couldn't rest easy with that, I knew I needed to do something about it.

AROUND NINE WEEKS INTO TERM, the diocese announced Contemplation Day. In truth, it was a day of visitors and meetings for staff at the seminary, while the students made themselves scarce on the pretext of peaceful introspection and consideration of their vocation.

Leo decided to explore a matter of conscience by visiting Saint Roch's secondary school in North Glasgow, where he hoped to find his friend James. He spent longer than necessary working out the bus route and timetable to get there, even though that was the simple part. The hard part was what to say when he arrived. The guilt from his betrayal still sat, cold and heavy inside his gullet. He wasn't sure which words could squeeze past it.

It took not quite two hours for Leo's bus to draw near the school just off Royston Road. From his top-deck window, he saw that, for Saint Roch's, this was no day of contemplation – lunchtime revelries were in full swing. He'd brought his own tea flask and a sandwich, but his stomach was roiling. He needed to find James and get this over with.

Stepping down onto the pavement was like stepping into a sea of noise. This, Leo remembered, was regular school: teenagers marking their territory through sound, like a frenzy of gulls in a storm. It wasn't a natural environment for him, but then, where was? None of that mattered anyway, since he had a job to do.

He walked through the school gates and stopped the first person who looked about his own age, a girl with red hair. "Sorry, I'm looking for James McGee?" But the girl just shrugged and walked away.

His next attempt was a boy scoffing a slab of hard porridge from a paper bag, who shook his head before returning noisily to the feast. Losing hope, he felt a tap on his shoulder and turned to find the first girl pointing towards a group who were kicking a ball against some black iron railings. She shouted, "James!" as Leo walked towards them.

A boy broke from the bunch and ran towards him, eyes widening, jaw falling. "Leo?"

"Hi James."

His friend took him to a quieter space towards the rear of the school, where they sat on a red sandstone wall. "Look. I'm sorry for vanishing on you. But I've settled in here now. I'm not coming back."

"You're not the one who needs to apologise."

"What d'you mean?"

"I..." It was difficult to say precisely what had happened, so he began at the heart of it. "I let you down."

"Not you."

"No. I did. Brother Andrew... He made me tell the class what you'd said. Why you left."

James stiffened, his face flushing. "What?"

"I didn't want to... But he took me aside to find out what I knew about why you didn't return. So, remember the end of your last term? When you mentioned your doubts and things... I shouldn't have said anything, but I'm useless against him."

"He bullied you. It's not your fault."

"It was... And later he forced me to tell the entire class."

It was difficult to read his friend's face. Anger, certainly, but also a sickened expression. Disgust, but not surprise. "He's just a bastard... a total bastard."

"James! You can't—"

"I can. I'm allowed all the sins I want now. I've decided the Church can go fuck itself."

Leo flinched. At how far James had fallen, at how quickly. "You don't mean that. We shouldn't blame the Church for confusion around our vocations."

"Confusion is built in with the bricks. Seminary, apart from you, was just a bloody stew of different men, all quoting from a book made out of contradictions. The Bible even changes God halfway through and they expect nobody to notice... But no. Now I've left, there is no confusion. I know. Completely. Exactly. My life is mine. They will not own me."

"You act like it was slavery."

"Of the mind, yes. For me, it was. I'll even give you a verse, 1 Peter 2:18: *Slaves in reverent fear of God submit yourselves to your masters.*"

Leo had considered that same passage often when thinking about Brother Andrew. "*Not only to those who are good and considerate, but also to those who are harsh.*"

"Exactly. Well, being in disagreement with Saint Peter is not an option for our religion. And since I won't submit to a harsh master any more – and you shouldn't have to either, by the way – then I can't submit to our religion."

"But, these challenges—"

A mechanical bell rang, loud and urgent, and children raced for the main building. James shrugged and pushed himself to his feet and stepped in the direction of the throng. Then he turned to face Leo. "Challenges? That word blinds you, Leo. Remember when you said that Brother Andrew might be God's challenge to help you reach your potential? Well, there's nothing godly about that man. I don't think he's a divine challenge – he's an adversary, pure and simple."

With that his friend ran around the corner and was gone.

Subject: HS019283 Personal Commentary

Fair play to James. He knew the words to use.

Adversary.

It means enemy of course, but I couldn't miss the biblical connections with Satan.

And Satan, with my background and belief at that time, was no abstract concept. Satan was a genuine threat, capable of derailing not just my entire life but taking my soul as well.

What a seed to plant in a youngster's mind!

ON THE WAY back to the seminary, Leo tried to see the road through the bus windows, but the glass reflected memories: Brother Andrew's face twisted with rage, the poison in his words, the hate in his ice-cold stare. Leo wondered if James might be correct, that it might be possible that Brother Andrew was godless and evil.

How could he know?

He could pray on it. But prayer was not a handle to be pulled or a bell to be rung. God did not jump to attention. Prayer so far had not clarified his issues with the Jesuit.

But the bible said *evil plans are an abomination to the Lord*. Not acts, but plans – suggesting God already knew everything in Brother Andrew's heart, whether it was pure or foul. Leo wanted to know what God knew, but prayer would not reveal that. Surely, nothing could. Surely, you could never know the mind of God?

It was a mad thought, a crazy one.

But what if there was a way?

Leo left the bus two stops before the seminary and ran down to the banks of the river. Barely three months ago, he'd poured the residue of Niamh's lichen there. He had every expectation that the lapping waters of the river would have consumed the liquid. In the unlikely event any droplets had survived, they would have dissolved in the region's near-endless rain.

And yet, here was his miracle: out in the water a barely protruding ancient stump of the ruined crannog had come alive, festooned with silver tendrils. The Angel's Gate had taken root here on the River Clyde, precisely where he had scattered it.

You could never know the mind of God… unless God decided to allow it.

Leo unsure exactly how to proceed, recalled his aunt used the lichen in a tea, so he fetched the flask from his polythene bag and opened it for the first time that day. A tiny puff of steam escaped. He placed it on the ground, and then sloshed into the water.

The river was high, and this part of the bank proved deceptively steep. He waded carefully, pushing through an initial sense of ridiculousness into a kind of thrilled elation. This seemed now like a form of baptism, a gateway to a fresh understanding of his faith. By the time he reached the exposed wooden pile, the freezing river was lapping around his waist and all he had in his heart was gratitude. Whispering his thanks, he laid his hands among the delicate tendrils, tore two fistfuls, and returned to the shore. He crammed the lichen into the flask and screwed on the lid, before placing it back in the polythene bag.

He dripped his way back to the seminary on foot, ignoring the strange expressions on the faces of those he passed. His excitement was growing, and he didn't care what anyone else thought. He did, however, want to avoid questions, so on reaching the dormitory, he made his way back to his room quietly, and found himself glad for the first time that he no longer had to share the space with anyone. He latched his door and held the flask, unscrewing the outer lid that doubled as a cup.

Had the liquid brewed long enough on his fifteen-minute walk? How much should he drink? Would the black tea previously in the flask interfere? To these questions, he had no answers. However, he reasoned that the lichen hanging on, indeed thriving after months in the river meant God had crafted this path. Leo's human desire to construct a precise recipe was just foolish pride.

He poured himself a cup – the liquid seemed much like normal tea, but with an oily silver sheen. It was cool enough to swallow in two gulps, and he found it unusual but not unpleasant. The black tea flavour remained present but hidden under something else, something that he had no exact description for. Earthy? Bitter? Herbal? A qualified yes to each of those, and yet every word was also insufficient.

He drank another cup, then he sat on his bed and waited.

The first sensation was of unrest in his gut, and it built to a roiling nausea. He told himself that everything happening was God's will, and if he had poisoned himself, then that was as it should be. With that thought, the sensation vanished. It gave way, not to the sleepiness he had naively expected on his walk from the river, but to a heightened sense of focus, where every breath seemed to bring a new point of observation.

Inhale.

The blank facing wall, an empty screen. The room adjoining, silent, unoccupied.

Exhale.

Nearby, the squeaking slide of a sash window. A single car approaches on the gravel drive. Then stops.

Inhale.

The car door opens, the crunch of exit, the door slams closed.

Exhale.

Limping footsteps, a cough. An elderly attendee returns to the diocese meetings.

Inhale.

The closing clatter of the nearby sash.

For Leo, the compelled precision of his attention was disconcerting, the magnetic pull of his immediate surroundings almost overwhelming. His senses defined a kind of containment, his tethering to the moment, his bondage to now.

He was suffocated by now.

There was no place, but this place, no air, but this air. And it wasn't enough.

Not anymore.

The mattress beneath him, the wall at his back – these aggressive physical surfaces pressed awkwardly against his flesh, and his flesh seemed to press painfully back. His own hands felt like heavy stones lying on his lap. Everything around him now revealed its purpose, and that purpose was horribly simple: to capture and contain him, to define his limits. What had been natural only minutes before was now revealed as the most terrifying captivity: he existed inside a collapsing trap, inside a shrinking tomb.

But just when he felt the trap slam shut, there came a flicker of freedom, a pleasing but unfamiliar kind of loosening, first in his mind, then down his arms to his hands and fingers, and then through his body to his legs, his toes. He felt lighter, strangely so.

The Angel's Gate did not crash open. Although the walls of Jericho fell to the sound of trumpet blasts, Leo heard no trumpets. He was not pulled through the eye of a needle. But a great transformation was happening, a peeling apart, separating now into before and after, separating place into there and here. And separating being into flesh and spirit.

Did he hear a voice or simply imagine it?

Rise up and walk.

And so he rose up, and walked to infinity in less than a heartbeat.

AND LO, infinity was a flood of ecstasy, a rushing, raging tumult of love. Leo hurtled through unknown spaces blazing with alien colours, places that roared with impossible sounds. It was more than his mind could comprehend. "Father!" he cried. "Father! The love! The love is too great!"

But the roaring, raging love grew.

And Leo lost himself within it.

Until the tumult ceased.

The boy found himself inside the inky blackness of a gigantic confessional. There was a presence here. But was *here* even a place? No. The most sense he could make of his location was as a *presence-place*, since the being he found here was itself limitless and contained all.

The presence stirred.

You have traversed the outer shell of my thoughts. This crossing overwhelmed you. But know this: you were overwhelmed by what would, for such as I, be more closely defined as boredom.

Although no words were spoken, Leo understood the message instantly and with complete clarity. There was a complex weariness in the communication that Leo could not interpret.

Although infinitely vast, infinitely dark, the place radiated both power and melancholy. Had Leo somehow caused this sadness? Lacking a body, the boy nevertheless fell to his knees. "Bless me, Father, for I have sinned—"

Is it not enough I gave you life without you seeking my blessing as well?

A moment of doubt. "But you are... God?"

A fragment of a fragment may not be the whole, but even a fragment of an ocean may be too deep to fathom... To such as I, humans are as moths, and their most fervent prayers a mere fluttering in the dark.

Something landed briefly on Leo's hand.

A prayer for vengeance.

He felt wings brush past his ear.

A prayer to conceal crime.

There was a tremor in the space, and an upwelling of complex feelings... The sensation filled Leo with uncertainty.

My house has many rooms, most bathed in light. But the rarest moths, those that do not seek the light, might still land here, might still find a place.

Can such moths, drawn to shadow, be brought into my will? Can you help them find favour in my sight?

Leo thought he understood. Didn't Christ's resurrection start in betrayal? That was surely an evil impulse turned towards the Plan, and one of immeasurable consequence. To redirect and harness such impulses... Was this his place? Was this his destiny?

The hardest path is to reach the light through darkness. Blessed is the traveller who guides them.

"Father. I seek this blessing. But I am unsure."

I will show you.

LEAVING the infinite confessional was like being thrown from a mountain. The speed was immense, but the journey was long, giving time to experience the sense of change and of loss.

And the fall ended without deceleration or impact. Around him, Leo recognised King Street in Rutherglen, close to his own home.

Why here?

He turned his body that was not a body, or more correctly, turned his attention. It was an action that took no effort, bringing into view a man leaving Chapman's Bar. Leo recognised the force of will inherent in the figure, but now, that force battled an unfamiliar instability in his stride.

Brother Andrew walked fifty feet and staggered to a stop before entering a nearby tenement building. Two flights of stone stairs brought them to the Jesuit's door, and a brass plate beneath the letterbox:

Private instruction in
Christian Theology and Latin

So, all along, the Jesuit had lived in his local area, and drank in a local pub, which explained the man's knowledge of Da's drunken boasts.

Leo watched the teacher fumble at the pockets of his dark coat, breaking into a stream of irreligious mumbled curses. The door mat bore the Jesuit seal, the letters *IHS* inside a sunburst, and Leo briefly wondered if dirty feet were a respectful way to greet a symbol formed from the letters of Christ's holy name. Then he found the symbol put to yet more mundane use: the teacher dropped drunkenly to his knees and flipped the mat, retrieving a Yale key from a pocket cut into the centre of the rubber base. The man righted the mat before rising to unlock the door.

Inside the flat, a short hallway ended in a picture frame. Leo recognised the almost militaristic portrait of the Jesuit founder, Saint Ignatius of Loyola, and beneath the image in illuminated manuscript lettering: *Warriors for Christ – go set the world on fire.*

Is that how Brother Andrew saw himself, the boy wondered? To Leo, the teacher embodied flame, but only in certain aspects: the threat, the destruction, the pain. Was his wild zeal catching? Did it create enthusiasm among his students? Or did it scorch each vocation it touched?

The Jesuit entered a spartan room off the hallway, removed a box from a drawer and placed it on a desk. He took something from the box before entering an adjoining chamber. Leo heard a bolt drawn and the sound of running water, but found no desire to move away from the box. His attention was here, he knew, for some purpose.

And the purpose was a lump of ripped fabric. The fabric bore a flash of colour, a small green figure. A figure Leo remembered only as a space goblin. What was his teacher doing with James's vest?

But, of course, he knew.

In this state, the strictures of his upbringing, his deference to authority, the limitations of allowable thought, all seemed to be loosened. He flashed through incidents in his mind: James predicting his parents would find him a tutor to resolve his doubts, Brother

Andrew creating a public scapegoat for James's absence, his friend's damning verdict on the Jesuit: *there's nothing godly about that man.*

And there was no godly reason to find a thirteen-year-old's ripped clothing being held as a keepsake. And yet, the Jesuit did that all the same. The man preached a ruthless purity, condemning all others while harbouring his own great sin. *Thou shalt not covet thy neighbour's child.*

Leo's friend James represented one vocation destroyed in this house – surely he was not the first? How many other innocents had suffered some corruption of their faith or been turned away from God entirely? Surely, if nothing were done, then the same fate would await others? Leo's perspective lent an unusual quality to his own emotions. The anger he experienced was neither reckless nor uncontrolled, but resolute.

That anger was tempered with sorrow. Leo's desire to embody the goodness of God now turned upon involvement with the mundane evil of man. He wondered briefly if this emotional distance was a tiny sliver of the feelings of the Father.

It never once occurred to Leo that his experience was hallucinated or imagined, since this experience was more vivid than any other from his life. If humans find reality through our sensory experience, then how could he interpret such clarity of experience except as higher, truer reality? An illusion could surely not exist in this space. And there was no aspect of dream chaos or random chance here – he had sought information about the teacher and about his own place in God's plan, and had now been given both. It was a gift of knowledge that his previous path of earthly study would likely always have left hidden, a gift that rendered his previous path superfluous.

Any lingering doubts about the wisdom of his aunt Niamh were also dispelled. She had been correct about the nature of this experience, so much so that he adopted her own words as his own: *God spoke with me and revealed my purpose.*

While he observed the room from above, listening to the

animalistic noises of the man next door, he understood this revelation had brought him to a place of darkness, a place that might draw a certain kind of moth, if only that moth were appropriately guided.

Subject: HS019283 Personal Commentary

Saint Paul was some man all the same, wasn't he? Twenty-odd books in the New Testament and he wrote about half of them. Fair play. Some even say Paul made Christianity into a world religion, although I imagine his boss might have an opinion on that.

No doubt, though, the man kept busy writing letters. If it wasn't to the Romans, it was the Corinthians, Galatians or some other buggers. He had a lot of penfriends, that's for sure. I suppose that was why a young seminarian would understand the potential power a letter could have, even when tucked anonymously through a front door.

LEO CLUTCHED an envelope marked *To a Fellow Believer* as the night bus trundled nearer to home. He'd literally sweated over every word, although that must have been partially caused by the after-effects of the tea.

The return to his dormitory room had been sudden and jarring, but although it left him physically unmoored, mentally, he was utterly certain of what must come next.

If the course of action was obvious, a matter of connecting various aspects of his revelation, then the challenge had been to set down words likely to achieve an outcome. The outcome was not a task for Leo. He was a guide only, a gatherer of moths.

Leo's epistle to a bigoted bus conductor had read:

A friend of a friend made known that someone here is keen to iden-tify Glasgow-based advocates for a certain enemy cause.

Please find an address enclosed. It is not far.

If you visit, you will find the ground-floor flat in question declares its loyalty with a papist door mat. Careful observation will confirm a spare key hidden centrally in the rubber beneath this mat.

The single man living at this address is a verified, active and highly successful fundraiser for an enemy organisation. He is trained not to admit this affiliation even under extreme duress, but be assured the evidence is beyond doubt. He has no intention of stopping. His evil actions will continue unless someone can persuade him otherwise.

Good luck.

LEO ARRIVED AFTER MIDNIGHT.

He looked around, ensuring nobody was on the street to observe him. Once certain, he eased open the letterbox and slid the envelope inside, before slowly, gently, softly, closing the plate and stepping quickly away. He then walked the bus route back towards the seminary, picking up the first service after four a.m.

———

FOUR DAYS LATER, as all waited in the pews for morning mass, the chapel became the venue for an emergency assembly. Solemnly, the seminary students were informed of a sectarian attack at Brother Andrew's house, and that the teacher would not be returning.

Two crumbs of consolation were offered. First, the criminal involved was arrested at the scene and an appropriate conviction was inevitable. Second, although currently in critical condition, doctors expected the teacher would stabilise sufficiently to be discharged into the care of the Sisters of Nazareth in Paisley, where visits from staff and students would be possible.

All affected students would spend vocational curriculum periods in reading and contemplation while recruitment took place to fill the vacancy.

A specific request was made for staff and students to keep the poor man in their prayers. For his own part, Leo felt no particular need to act on this, his most recent prayers having already been answered.

Subject: HS019283 Personal Commentary

To suggest seminary was my preparation for prison would be a cheap shot.

Sure, it was an introduction to institutional life, to shared sleeping quarters, to repetitive daily activities, and to dealing with officious gobshites. But that only meant the experiences were mostly similar, not totally the same.

For instance, I was never given psychological writing assignments at seminary. Psychological warfare, maybe.

But even if a cheap shot is mostly true, that doesn't make it complete. You see, seminary was my route to God's plan, just not in the way I first thought.

THE SISTERS of Nazareth were always delighted to see a former pupil visiting their old teacher, although no-one could be sure how Brother Andrew felt about it. It was generally assumed that brain damage from the beating or subsequent smoke inhalation had left him unable to express any preferences, but that being wheeled around the grounds was an act of kindness he could not object to.

The man now expressed delight, anger and all other emotions in ostensibly the same way: with the blinking of one wild eye staring from a horribly scarred face.

But Leo was his most loyal attendee. Even after the boy's withdrawal from seminary, he remained diligent in his monthly visits, always arriving late in the afternoon and taking their usual spot between the trees. There they would spend an hour in one-sided and far-ranging discussions. The Sisters often complimented Leo on his unusual biblical insights, the history of gnosticism, and his ability to identify the many fluttering creatures that could be found in that corner of the garden: the six-spot burnet, the elephant hawk, the ghost swift, the emperor.

Leo, of course, through extreme attention to detail, had discovered early on that Brother Andrew could, indeed, indicate certain preferences and emotions. The boy held this fact close, making it their own special secret, but spent time and energy in planning to ensure his visits were always as engaging and eventful for the Jesuit as it was possible to make them.

Subject: HS019283 Personal Commentary

So there you have it. What I did on my school holidays, nineteen-seventies style. They don't make decades like they used to, am I right?

But by now, I'd guess you are sharpening your pencil over some checklist or other. That's fine, and you should make your judgements how you like. Just remember, where there is room for condemnation, perhaps there is also room for redemption. And remember also, no matter what your checklist says, neither of those outcomes is entirely within your gift.

You see, it wasn't just that beginning Word, but also the last Word too: both are supplied far above our pay grades...

Nearly seven years on, when the time came, his funeral was poorly attended. A brief appearance from a local Jesuit administrator, one deacon from the seminary, and Leo, making only three who knew the man before his misfortune. Six sisters from Nazareth House were there, their numbers offering judgement of a different kind: Brother Andrew, with all his health and faculties, had mustered half the friends of the version who pissed, glared and shat for his supper.

When Leo spoke to the sisters, their generous loyalty and

compassion gave him pause, causing him to wonder if even such as Andrew had hope. Was it possible to body swerve damnation through suffering a living purgatory? That's quite a thought in a young man's mind.

So Leo stayed back by the grave afterwards, watching the men use their shovels, and thanking God for allowing him to play his part.

INTERNAL: PSYCHOLOGICAL ASSESSMENT
SUBJECT: HS019283 LEO HARIMAN
TIME SERVED: Four years from twelve-year sentence.

BACKGROUND:
Inmate has a prior history of non-violent coercion (represented in media reports as blackmail) of others to undertake violent acts, including murder. The subject currently undertakes organisational duties within the prison library including the planning of inmate activities in that environment. There is little doubt that the subject's innovations, such as his reading and writing groups, have driven increased inmate interest in the facility. He continues to receive highly favourable reports from the external librarians who monitor the service.

ASSESSMENT:
In the opinion of this psychologist, the following diagnostic observations can be made:
1. As a teenager, this subject's narrative meets the criteria for 292.12 Unknown Substance-Induced Psychotic Disorder (Hallucinations subtype)
2. Currently, the inmate continues to exhibit symptoms that merit a working diagnosis of 297.1 Delusional Disorder (Grandiose subtype, Provisional).

CONCLUSION:

While these diagnostic observations do not impact the subject's ability to form relationships or comply with institutional standards of behaviour, a degree of vigilance is merited, and the inmate should remain subject to routine psychological monitoring as he approaches Parole Qualifying Date at one-half of sentence served.

Clinicians assigned monitoring duties on behalf of this inmate should note that, although his delusions are religious in origin, they do not fit easily within the boundaries of any particular faith. The inmate has believed (and so far as can be ascertained, continues to believe) that he has been assigned an unspecified divine purpose.

It is our assessment that the entire history of this subject's offending has been performed in the service of this purpose. While uncertainty around the precise nature of these delusions create difficulty in forming an assessment of risk, that fact is insufficient to conclude that no risk exists. The subject is charismatic, personable and highly persuasive. Caution is advised.

LEO HARIMAN HEARD the key turn in the waiting room lock. A prison officer opened the door and stepped inside.

"Mr Golding! So it's yourself who drew the short straw... Head-shrinker collection duty."

Golding smirked. "I wish they *would* shrink your bloody head, Hariman. I keep telling them there's a vice in the workshop... And you should show more respect for the forensic psychologists, It's not easy having to listen to you. I should know. It's only a short journey to the main block, but your inane drivel lengthens it something rotten. "

Leo rose from the chair, stretching and yawning."Well, at least all you residential officer lads will be pleased to know, I'm done. No more ferrying me back and forward. Her nibs is in there finalising the report on me as we speak."

"Money for old rope in your case, I'd have thought. It won't take many sheets of paper to spell out the words 'bullshit artist'… Right, let's go."

As they left the room, Leo grew distracted, staring at the collar of Golding's shirt.

"What exactly are you gawping at, Hariman?"

"A poplar-hawk, I think."

"A what?"

"Oh… Just a moth."

Golding's face lost its smug composure, and he started swiping randomly around his neck and shoulders. "Did I get it? Is it gone? I can't see it!"

"It must have flown on Mr Golding. But don't worry. They're an interest of mine. Unusual to see one indoors. Perhaps it thinks you're special? Hmm… I'll mull it over."

Golding shook his head. "You see, Hariman? This is precisely the inane drivel I've been talking about. You're incomprehensible."

"Well, Mr Golding. Isn't it nice we've both given each other something to think about?"

FIGURE EIGHT

I knew I'd taken a risk by telling Craigsy to go screw himself. He wasn't a good guy to argue with, but it was my methadone, and I'd been given a release date. Since I was leaving, I needed my whole dose. Landing outside sick would just send me back in again, and jailbird-life was not good for me.

See, the people who survive in here have an obvious value. Cons that look hard are useful for keeping peace. You know the type: they alternate between push-ups and standing with their arms folded. Then you have the Craigsy kind, the ones that enjoy waging war. Those guys come in all shapes and sizes, but you'll know them by the mad fucking look in their eyes. Others have conventional skills that this place lets them use, like cooking or maintenance. And the final group either have the right connections or know how to make them.

So that's four groups with a decent chance. And I've never fitted in any of them.

My true value inside was discovered late, and I'd have been better off if it had never come out at all. I'd been on so much smack when I got here, a prizewinning withdrawal got me a week in Healthcare, and a daily coupon for the prison methadone programme. Anyone who asked was told my pill was for depression. That was accepted for a long time, but I knew things had gone public when people suddenly wanted to know me.

Like Auld Pete. "Hold back a wee dose for us son, eh?",

Or Kyle. "I'd do the same for you, man."

Craigsy's angle was the most convincing. "Every second dose is mine, Blev, or you get chibbed."

Chibbed is Scottish for shanked, which is English for stabbed with deadly intent. You don't want to hear any of these alternatives in a sentence with your name in it.

The problem was, Healthcare were wise to this sharing stuff. They never gave you any extra, so after a while stashing a pill in my cheek and spitting it into Craigsy's hand, I'd decided that spending my last few days inside feverish and shitting myself was not conducive to planning the next phase of life.

In short, I needed what was mine. And that was when I'd told Craigsy to piss off.

Basically, that's where I think it started. Not the room with the body, or Crazy Sheila, but me trying to grow some bollocks.

The thing is though, I'm not one hundred per cent sure, even about that. You see, at this point, the memories get muddy, and I have to really concentrate to reach the essentials. Some things from before already seem like a scroll of archive film. As I wind through in my mind, there are scenes already fading into sepia, and for all I know, they'll go for good.

Maybe I'll be relieved if that happens – there are details here I'd prefer not to puzzle over anymore. And maybe I'll never need these notes. Maybe, even, I'll settle into my new life, sweet as pie and without a care in the world. But that would be a first for me, so, just in case, before it's too late, I'm going to set it all down, starting with how it actually began: the attack in the corridor.

FIRST TIP-OFF I got came from footsteps behind me, an unexpected flurry as I walked to the activities room. Things kick off now and again, and the best policy is to ignore it. If it's not about you, don't change that by eyeballing and becoming a witness. But then I heard the laugh. It was guttural and joyless, see, which are two guaranteed features of every noise Craigsy ever makes, so I thought I best check, just in case. I turned too late to make any positive ID. About halfway around, someone clawed my hair into searing clumps and wrenched my face horizontal. Beneath me, a pair of dirty black training shoes scraped at the floor like the hooves of a rabid bull. The legs were muscular but twitchy, covered in inmate standard-issue black track-suit trousers.

Shit like this happens in here, so I went straight to my usual game plan. My arms protected my face while I spoke quietly, not wanting to attract the screws, not wanting to cause trouble or risk being seen as a grass. "Sorry, mate. Sorry for getting in the way. Let me just—"

A kick in the nuts shocked me breathless, and I stumbled down, straight into the knee of my attacker. Wetness on my nose and chin, salt on my lips. They wrenched my head left, but instinct pulled me right, desperate to avoid the next strike. With a painful tearing, my hair gave by the roots, and I fell, striking my temple on the metal barrier around the stairway.

Things went foggy as my head clouded with old images from school. Random violence in the playground, covert intimidation in the classroom, a stroboscopic escalation of insults, jostling, wild kicking, bloodied fists. Cut to the fateful martial arts classes my parents enrolled me in, hoping to protect me.

I shook myself alert, returning to the reality of the stairwell and the fading footsteps of my unknown assailant.

If my time in the dojo had prepared me for prison life, then it wasn't in the way my parents had hoped. What I learned in child-hood was that I wouldn't be considered a person, not by everyone. To some, I'd be a thing to use. Like in here, to some vicious loser looking to climb the greasy pole, I'm just status waiting to be claimed.

Only two more days.

"Get up, Blevins."

It was Golding, the worst of the screws. He had no good side to get onto, but he especially hated me. My Welsh accent, Albanian skin tone, and history with recreational substances had all fallen under his gimlet eye at one point or other.

"Who'd want to be you, Taff? Lying flat on your arse and in everyone's way. Practising for your release? Will I get you a cardboard blanket?" He grabbed my forearm and yanked, hauling me to my feet.

"Did you see who did it, Mr Golding?" I knew it was a stupid question as soon as the words left my mouth. Behind him a younger screw stood silent, deferring to the senior officer.

"We didn't see anything, did we Frank?" He glanced back, but his colleague shrugged and looked away. "No. A junkie fell over. It's hardly news."

Some screws were more relaxed about drugs, so long as everything stayed placid. But not Golding. I heard he'd taken a needle in the bollocks once, a slow puncture hissing vitriol ever since. But a lot of rumours went around in here, and I doubted Golding had ever needed much of an excuse. "This is just life for you, Blevins. And people get what they deserve. So me, later on? I've got a date with a wee French lassie. No big surprise, I suppose, that these chiselled features have earned an admirer. What d'you reckon your snotty, bloody mess of a face should earn you?"

"A trip to Healthcare?"

He snorted. "For a nosebleed? Dream on. Who's your co-pilot?"

"Grizz. Winston Cook."

"The big barber? Good. You're his problem."

We found my cellmate in the clip shop sweeping a mound of hair into a bag. A couple of guys were waiting to be seen, but Golding pushed past them. "Mr Cook! Rearrange your diary. One junkie cellmate in need of a makeover." The next guy in line threw me a look, but when Grizz told him to piss off and come back tomorrow, he nodded and left, quiet as a lamb. It turns out, being built like a brick shithouse guarantees you never take any crap.

After handing me a tissue for my nose, Grizz looked me over. "Messy, bruv." London accent through and through, but he never explained how he landed in Edinburgh, at least not to me. He pointed towards the old barber's chair. "Alright College, let's get you fixed."

COLLEGE. I didn't mind the nickname and it certainly wasn't a bad one by prison standards. Less of a mouthful than *University* would have been. And the downgrade was fair: I'd only been two years into my psychology degree before a syringe changed my syllabus, and my interests became exclusively extracurricular.

I'd once thought that psychology would help me get a handle on the past, maybe help me resolve a few things. But smack doesn't really offer resolution. It's the ultimate simplifier, guaranteeing you only have one thing to worry about. Who gives a shit about the past when your next fix needs taken care of?

Maybe completing my studies might have done something, earned me some paper-thin self-esteem to paste over cracks here and there. But the needle was a magician's wand, see – it took a sucking void and made it totally disappear.

For a while at least.

THE CLIP SHOP always smelled faintly of mint. While they had to trust Grizz with scissors, that didn't extend to glue, so he'd stuck his football posters to the wall using toothpaste. I watched in the mirror as he draped a stained Chelsea towel over my shoulders and gingerly lifted clumps of hair to examine the scalp beneath. Crusts of blood had formed under my nose, but it didn't appear broken, which I was glad about. Grizz flicked his comb to expose a patch of bare scalp and shrugged apologetically. "You need sheared, mate. Don't worry, bald is the new black."

I tensed at the angry buzzing of the clippers, but calmed as the locks of hair rolled and tumbled around me, making patterns on the floor by my feet.

Soon, the mirror reflected a look I'd never have chosen under other circumstances, but at least I wouldn't stand out. Prison life seemed to skew hair preferences towards the buzz-cut, and my earlier experience near the stairway was just another example of why.

Grizz said, "I ain't finished yet, College. I'll blend in a bit of tribal."

I wasn't in any mood to argue so watched in silence while he inscribed his little marks, angling and adjusting the clippers with care and precision. Each little symbol was supposed to alter my image, giving me toughness and credibility, a look that said: *don't mess with me*. It was nice of him to try, but it was a sham and we both knew it.

I spotted something unfamiliar among the shaved lines. "What's that?"

"Not quite finished is what it is." He pulled out his scissors.

"Ow!" A thin dark line trickled from the symbol, heading down towards my ear.

Grizz pushed a cloth against my temple for a second. When he pulled it away, I saw the design again – it seemed like an oddly stylised figure eight. "It's supposed to be a snake eating its own arse, bruv. Maybe that's why it's drawn blood? Sorry about the scratch." I'd never heard of Grizz cutting someone before, so he was lucky it was me and not someone more volatile. Before his time, there'd been a stabbing in here over a lost ponytail, or so the story went.

He carefully brushed the excess hair to the floor. "You're done, man." As I stood, he whispered in my ear. "Don't let it get you down. You'll be free in two days."

He was right. But something was different about how that made me feel. How could my release be good for me? In here, I had my methadone, and even if a doctor wrote me the same script on the outside, I couldn't trust myself. Eventually, I'd end up chasing. Eventually, the habit would land me back in jail.

But if looking forward was bleak, then looking back was worse. Memories I normally avoided began pressing in on me.

So I remembered: my first evening class at the dojo in Granton, standing in borrowed judo whites, innocent and eager to learn.

And I remembered: youth prison nine years later. A short sentence for breach of the peace turned an addict into a junkie, dissolving every problem in the acid need of his next fix.

And I remembered: two expressions. Fear on the face of an old man at the Tesco cashpoint. Scorn on the face of the Sheriff who sent me to Saughton.

The only question was why I hadn't considered something so obvious before: I lived inside a spiral that headed only one way. That spiral had brought me here, to a zoo of short-terms, remands, and lifers, mixing with newbies ready to beat me for status, and psychos that didn't need a reason. Even though I'd learned to keep my mouth shut and my eyes to myself, that desperation to give no offence drew trouble like flies to shit.

And it always would.

Grizz frowned at my expression, his eyes concerned. "College, you need to keep your spirits up. Two days!"

I tried to smile, but I suddenly heard a clock ticking.

———

THAT NIGHT I HAD A DREAM.

I was walking on a grey road that curved away in front of me. I was wearing judo whites, the material scraping and catching with every step. I felt – I knew – something was in pursuit, but I didn't want to look back. The thought of what I'd see behind filled me with disgust: the glazed expression, the hanging eyelids, my own skin pulled over toneless muscles. I ran, eating up the distance, but the road would not change. I was on some kind of loop, and the more I ran, the more I understood, this wasn't a circular track, but a geometric hell, a mobius strip, twisting my route back and round towards myself forever, ensuring I could never escape.

Then something caught my eye at the side of the road: a pair of scissors, lying discarded. I grabbed them, plunged them into the surface, drawing a ragged line that thickened in a froth of red. The strip I stood on bucked as the severed edges pulled apart. With a sickening lurch gravity took me, and I dropped.

Falling.

Free.

And then, suddenly awake. I waited for my heart to settle.

The cell walls were grey and featureless in the scant light from the doorway hatch. And I knew the walls outside would be the same, in all the shelters and bedsits and short-term allocations of my future. Those places would be empty and joyless, too. I suppose that's the best way to contain someone like me, the best backdrop for a life without purpose.

Cause and effect are funny things, see – you don't expect them to be separated by years, but sometimes that's how it is. Little impacts accumulate, creeping like surface cracks on glass, hundreds of small repercussions combining into an eventual admission: you're broken.

Running from myself had been easy when I wasn't paying attention, but now I was listening, hearing the pointless sound of fruitless motion, a cascade of broken pieces with every footstep, the tumbling of internal shrapnel I'd never escape.

But now it was time to acknowledge the shattered pieces of what I was before, I realised it was a good thing. I was glad those pieces were smashed, revolted they had ever existed. I didn't want to reassemble me or be reminded of what I was. I needed to leave *me* behind.

Somehow, lying in my grey, featureless room, at this stage in my grey, featureless life, I was finally ready to accept the truth about myself: I was weak. This meant embracing the conclusions arising from that truth. I was too weak to stay off smack, too weak to deal with my past.

And too weak to live.

At this admission, my overwhelming feeling was simple relief. This wasn't depression or sadness; it was certainty. Certainty that while everything before had been a pointless performance, now I could finally take action.

As the sound of snoring reverberated from Grizz's corner of the cell, the figure eight on my scalp crawled under my skin and emerged as something else.

It took only a few seconds to crush my sheet into a rope and loop it around the corner post. I crossed each end, tied it to create my own figure eight: one loop for the bed post, one loop left empty. By hand, I twisted the free loop over and over, lengthening the knot in the centre, tightening it into a noose. I forced my shaven head inside, feeling the fabric snug around my neck.

The next part was simple. In the dark, I rolled myself over, twisting the noose tighter. Over and over.

Round and around.

And around.

And arou—

My vision clouded.

LATER, Grizz told me he woke at the sound of choking. I thought I was gone for sure, but then I remember a feeling of surprise when I became aware of him, shock, even, that he'd cared enough to bother. As he tugged at the sheet, taking the pressure off my throat, the look on his face struck me: he seemed to smile. And he didn't call the screws.

Afterwards, he begged me not to jeopardise my release. He promised to *ask Preach* what I should do next, how I could live clean.

I'd been to a few Al-Anon meetings in my time, but all that talk of higher powers and spiritual awakening rang hollow. Since I didn't want to argue, or put any guilt onto Grizz, I decided to wait two more days. I knew I'd have more options on the outside. The city provides so many things to jump from or fall in front of. There's no real barrier to your exit, once you've made your mind up.

And my mind was settled.

———————

THE NEXT EVENING at association time, Grizz found me, standing alone against the wall watching the other men talk. He was smiling and excited, a little breathless. "I've talked to Preach. When you get out, go to Crazy Sheila. She'll get you off smack for good. You can go legit."

I hadn't heard the name, so we talked a little and he gave me an address. With no genuine desire to act on the advice, but more out of curiosity, I asked a few other inmates what they knew.

It turned out Crazy Sheila was familiar to a few of the cons on methadone maintenance. She seemed to have a colourful background, no matter which set of rumours you believed. One guy told me she'd fled Australia after a scandal at a hospice. Another said it was lower key than that, and she came to Edinburgh after the boss caught her hand in the pharmacy prescription jar. A third claimed she'd been sacked from a psychiatric ward. A fourth said all of those were true. The last guy described her as his perfect woman, one who knew the way to a man's heart was through a clean vein. He didn't have many of those left, by the look of him.

But all the rumours agreed Sheila was dangerously entrepreneurial around any kind of drug supply. So, this was the person who would get me clean? It seemed stupid. I decided that a visit to Crazy Sheila would be a waste of my time. If I did it, it would be as the first and last item on my bucket list, a list that, no matter what, I would complete tomorrow.

THE NEXT MORNING, I barely recognised my old clothes. My cargo pants had the same ripped pocket but they, along with my sweatshirt and cagoule, were cleaner than I'd ever seen them. The polythene bag with the rest of my possessions was barely worth taking at all.

After thirteen months, I was back out on the street. My case worker appointment was a short walk and ninety minutes into one possible future, but you don't end a pattern by drawing it all over again, so I went a different way.

As I walked, trawling my memory for accessible rooftops, the wind pushed against me like a rebuke. But my mind was made up... mostly. I couldn't get Grizz's face out of my mind, see. Something about what he promised me, that there was a way I could kick smack, that I could live a different life... It seemed ridiculous, but perhaps that was why I should satisfy my final curiosity, by finding out what the deal was. So I turned again, this time heading out towards Crazy Sheila's address.

Muirhouse was familiar enough from previous foraging missions. A guy I vaguely recognised offered me chips from the Turkish Kebab, but I figured he could use them more than me. I already had enough energy to satisfy my curiosity, climb some stairs and then put myself in the unsafe hands of gravity.

According to one con I'd asked, the house she lived in was well protected. Not by alarms or hired muscle, or any human threat, but by Sheila's dog, Skippy. He hadn't been clear on the breed, only that Skippy was the craziest canine bastard on four legs. It didn't matter to me – I wasn't about to make any trouble and I wasn't staying long. This visit was just the last itch I ever planned to scratch. Crazy

Sheila's block of flats wasn't high, but a couple of tower blocks close by looked as if they might do the job when the time came.

I found her door one flight up and rang the bell. At least one story was true at least, because I'd no sooner released the doorbell than horrific barking tore at my eardrums, followed by the desperate scrabbling of claws against wood. When Sheila answered, her knuckles were white, wrapped around a leather leash and a rusty length of door-chain. Her hair was short and streaked with blue. She had a tattoo of a knife beneath one ear. She whispered, "What's your need?"

It was a dealer's question, and in that brief, lucid moment I understood what I needed was the same as everyone who brought themselves out here to the Wild West of Granton, begging for treats from a madwoman and her murderous dog: the possibility of escape. I wondered if they had set me up, sent me here for a free taste to start a new relationship. I was unsure how that made me feel, mostly because it simultaneously pissed me off and got my juices flowing. My *need*, as per bloody usual, was developing its own ideas about how I should spend my day.

While I wrestled internally, the hidden dog savaged the door-frame some more before giving up and emitting a low, constant growl. Imagine an engine powered entirely by the prospect of violence and you have the right idea. I wanted a quick send-off, without pain and bloodshed, so my better self decided to call a halt. But my no longer hidden agenda said, "Grizz sent me."

The woman wrapped the leash a little more tightly around her hand and guided me inside.

Walking down that bare hallway was an exercise in self-control. For me and the dog, at least. My innards were lurching because a vicious mound of angry muscle clearly wanted to rip them out of my hole. But Sheila stayed between us, and the dog seemed to obey her tugs and hisses.

She directed me to sit on a broken futon, while she took a plastic chair. With a loud click, she lashed the dog to a climbing carabiner bolted to her wall, making him a barrier between us. There were a few of those climbing clips around the living room and I had seen another couple in the hallway. Perhaps the dog had different placements for different purposes. You couldn't take too many chances when you were dealing, and even fewer if you were a lone woman.

From here, staring directly into his slavering face, I guessed Skippy was either a full-on Rottweiler or the kind of mongrel where the other breeds in the mix had shrunk small and whimpered in the corner. His eyes were wild and constantly angry, except for when he looked towards his owner. When I saw that change in expression, my first thought was the dog loved her so much there was only hate left over for everyone else.

"So," she said, "I hear you want to kill yourself?"

I hadn't expected that question. "I'm not here about—"

"Aren't you?" Her smile was sly and didn't put me at ease.

"Look. Grizz said you could help. Change my life. How does that work?"

"But you tried, right? You tried to top yourself?" The dog restarted its low growl, as though it didn't like me dodging her questions. I sighed and nodded. She obviously knew everything anyway. Grizz must have told her. "And you still want to?"

I examined her face – the thin smile, the cold eyes – trying to puzzle out where this was going. She interrupted my thoughts. "Do you still feel ready to die?"

Fuck it.

If this was going to be my last conversation, I might as well be honest. "Yeah. I'm doing it after this."

"Perfect." She nodded and stood. "I can give you something. It's kind of a trip, but after that, you're clean."

So, that response sounded like bullshit, but I had nothing to lose, and the word *trip* had me interested. Where was the harm in a final one for the road? A safe, warm glow as I stepped off the ledge seemed worth having. But there was one problem we needed to discuss. "I've no money."

"You don't need any." She stood. "Wait here."

The dog strained against his leash, reminding me her word was law, and her stash was well and truly out of bounds.

So I sat on the grimy futon in the corner, trying not to catch Skippy's eye. Threat seemed to be a concept his doggy brain interpreted broadly, including walking towards Sheila, or walking away from Sheila, or taking any other action in Sheila's general environment. I now fully understood what another con had meant when he said her dog was a bloody animal.

A tiny shift in position caused a snapped wooden slat in the frame to give under my weight and I jolted upright, sending the dog into a barking frenzy. Sheila shouted, "Skippy! Shut it!" from the next room and the frenzy subsided.

I completed my turn, now able to see from the window behind me into a deepening twilight. The hulking structure of the bin enclosure was visible, but only barely, just a darker dark in the blackness of the shared back garden. Evidently, looking out of the window was also a threat, because Skippy's growl became a continuous background hum.

Eventually, Crazy Sheila returned with a sample case. As she stooped to open her case, I looked away. I didn't need to see Ali Baba's cave to know I would only get what she gave me.

A shift in the darkness outside drew my attention, making me wonder if someone was at the bins. But that thought ended when I heard the crinkle of an envelope.

"That's it," she said, handing me a brown paper sachet. "That's two grams of astral. But you have to do it here – it doesn't leave the flat. Those are the rules." The little envelope had a clear window at the front. Inside, finely ground grey powder flowed freely as she tilted the bag from side to side. If you're like me, you do a lot of stuff with a lot of names, but this wasn't horse or percy or donkey dust. It was something new. *Astral.*

"How do I take it?"

She walked over to her kettle and poured a mug of water. "Drink it." She poured the powder and stirred.

My first gulp drained half of it. The luke-warm water tasted strange. A little sharp. Earthy. Not unpleasant. I swallowed the remainder. Then I waited.

At first, there was no effect beyond a tickle at the back of my throat, but Sheila told me to lie down and unrolled the futon mattress. After a few minutes on my back, my attention seemed to shift, stretching into the distance. When I suddenly remembered where I was, everything snapped back to attention. I didn't lose awareness. In fact, my senses were sharpened by an unnerving sense of dislocation. I said to Sheila, "I wasn't here," but even I didn't know what I meant.

I didn't have long to ponder it before I felt a lurch into nausea, so I closed my eyes. The lurch became a tug and then grew more insistent. I felt a wrenching.

Something tore away the black veil in my mind to reveal a frozen image: the room under the gym he'd called his dojo, the day it first happened. But then that picture folded in on itself, receding into the far distance, before collapsing into nothing.

A sudden expansion of self-awareness followed that emptiness, an awareness altered by a profound sense of clarity, unburdened, somehow, by the aches and miseries I had been aware of a few moments before.

I opened my eyes, or so I thought, and my vision was exceptionally clear. But I was staring down at a body asleep on a dirty blue mattress. It took me only a moment to understand that the body was my own.

WHEN SHEILA'S head interrupted my view, I shifted, watching her lift and drop the eyelids on my unconscious face. The face looked empty, even more so than in photographs and videos I've seen of myself sleeping it off before. She walked over to her window and beckoned out into the night.

I'd read some theory about this back at uni, that what we call our "self" was a story constructed by our brain, and that sometimes people create a different story, locating their sense of themselves outside their bodily boundaries. I guessed my actual bodily sensations were being repurposed by my brain, adapted into an out-of-body experience brought on by the drug. This meant my hoped-for last-one-for-the-road warm and fuzzy trip had somehow devolved into a state of hyper-awareness: of me cosplaying a corpse on a broken futon, in a grimy dump, while being eyeballed by a psychopathic hound. If I'd paid for this, I'd have wanted my money back.

Sheila flicked on some music, and as she left the room, my viewpoint followed at her shoulder, only to stall just past Skippy's wall-mounted carabiner. I tried to push on, but it seemed the dog wasn't the only one tethered. Having hit the visual limits of this hallucination, I listened to her door open and close, then turned my attention back towards the body on the mattress.

It lay unmoving, the rise and fall of living breath barely visible. The hands, *my hands*, lay passive, fingers spread across its chest. Curiosity brought me closer. The lips, slightly parted, glistened with a faint silver residue from the drink.

Skippy whined, hunkering low, as though my imagined change of position had somehow disturbed him. With that unlikely thought, my view shifted upwards, and I was now above myself at ceiling level. From there I looked down on the dog, while he stared up at what I now felt was me. But it was a different *me* from the one on the futon. I couldn't understand why I no longer felt defined by that sleeping figure, just bound to it, like a ship to its anchor.

BEHIND ME, Sheila's voice said, "So you're the mule?"

A man answered in a rapid Irish accent. "That's me. I'm Muldoon. Howaya anyway?"

I didn't pick up her mumbled reply, but guessed he was here to make a delivery.

The swarthy man entered my room, scruffy hair tied in a ragged ponytail. Sheila knelt to restrain Skippy, but she needn't have bothered, as the dog stayed on his belly, head laying on his paws. Muldoon walked briskly past, heading straight to the futon. He removed his scuffed biker jacket. He had an old tour T-shirt underneath. The fabric was threadbare, and I guessed it had tumbled through many years of washing. *Chinatown. Thin Lizzy.* I didn't know if those words represented a band, an album, both or neither. I used to care about music when I was younger. I hadn't deliberately listened to anything in over a year.

Muldoon moved my head from side to side, which I couldn't feel at all. "So this is yer man?"

Sheila scowled. "Just do your job and get him off my mattress."

"Not my job I'm afraid. Here's a number for that." Muldoon drew a scrap of paper from the pocket of his jeans and threw it towards her. "She'll clear your mattress. I just take the cargo."

So, he wasn't delivering, but collecting.

As Sheila stooped for the note, I imagined moving to her side. The paper contained a scrawled mobile phone number and the single word: *undertaker*. This daydream was turning macabre, and in a kind of mental recoil I found myself back at the ceiling.

She frowned, biting her lip. "Did this whole thing even work?"

Muldoon smiled. "Sure it did." Sheila followed his gaze as he waved up towards the ceiling, to where I felt I was. "Didn't it, sunshine?"

Sheila spoke hesitantly. "So you really see him?"

Muldoon shrugged. "See him? Feel him? Sense him? Whatever the feck you wanna call it, he's here." The man tugged my sweatshirt up to my neck, revealing the pasty skin of my abdomen. "This body's empty. You can see that, right?"

Crazy Sheila shrugged. "He's a long-term junkie. They're all empty."

I hadn't noticed before how the scars on my belly rose and fell, like shifting contours on a map of self-harm. When I'd been younger, I'd wandered that territory, cutting to let the darkness out, but it never stayed away long.

Muldoon pulled a fabric cylinder out from a zipper on his jacket. "By a fecking miracle, he's clean. So I'll do this the quick way and get out of your hair."

"The quick way?"

He grinned, unrolling the fabric to reveal a long syringe, an empty vial, and a single dark green leaf. Tearing the leaf into three, he placed part in the vial and part in my sleeping mouth. Then he turned to Sheila. "She'll know, but just in case, don't let the undertaker remove that leaf. It stays with him until disposal."

That word again: *undertaker*. Given I was imagining the conversation and visuals here, it was bloody coherent. At that point the lucidity became a problem, chipping away at my certainty that this whole experience was a hallucination. But maybe not. After all, drugs were powerful tools for changing perception. Nobody knew that better than me.

As he lifted the syringe my view shifted to overlook his right shoulder. He said, "Nosy beggar, eh?" before plunging the long needle into my chest.

This development should have strengthened my foundering sense of unreality. After all, I didn't feel a thing, so how could it be happening? But I was still struggling against the internal consistency of the experience. The environment was identical to the one I'd seen consciously, and the unfolding sights and sounds were completely coherent. My shock at what I was witnessing pushed me forcefully towards belief.

This is happening.

A laugh as Muldoon adjusted, plunged again and finally pulled the needle from my body. "Heartblood. The quick way." He filled his vial and tucked it into the pocket of his jeans. Then he squeezed the last drops from the syringe onto the final leaf fragment, folded it, and swallowed. "All done."

When Muldoon rose I felt strangeness as his limbs strayed into my space, a sense of both repulsion and attraction, like I was caught between two magnets. I pulled back, unnerved as his eyes tracked my location, or at least the location I felt I occupied. He said, "I just stuck a needle in your heart, and I wasn't careful about it. From the sound of it, I've punctured a lung as well."

Instantly, I hovered above myself. A quiet wheeze rose and fell with each shallow breath.

Muldoon hoisted his leather jacket back over his shoulder. "So, you've got two choices. You either stay with this sorry fecker until lights out, or you come with me. But you'll have to push. It isn't easy. Good luck."

I moved with him towards the door, resisted by an anchoring pull tying me to the body on the futon. However, this time, I felt a new, weaker sensation calling me forward.

The man reached the front door and pulled on his jacket. "Word of advice: make your mind up fast. If I get too far away, you're cooked." The door slammed behind him. Sheila lifted the undertaker's phone number and pulled a handset from her back pocket.

I looked back towards the *me* that was wheezing on the futon. The *me* that was broken and couldn't be fixed. The *me* that had continually sought oblivion. And if Muldoon was right, a *me* that would soon be dead.

But even if Muldoon and this whole scenario was an illusion, a trick of my drugged brain, even if I hadn't just been stabbed in the heart, and was still just an addict passed out on a broken futon, I was still a vessel holed below the waterline, and one that had been sinking for years. Perhaps this was the sign I'd hit bottom: no more oblivion, no more trips, just a waking nightmare.

It didn't matter. In this scene, whether real or imagined, I still had a choice to make. I could just decide this was all bullshit, lie back and let whatever was going to happen, happen. Later, I'd probably wake up, leave and end up killing myself.

Maybe it was clarity from the astral, but... What if there was even the slimmest chance of a different outcome?

I strained forward, but the link to my body on the futon felt like a chain. The dog whined like a crying child. So I discarded thoughts of what lay behind and imagined what might lie ahead. Surely, whatever it might be was better than the guy on the futon's never-ending cycle of misery.

With that thought, I was halfway towards Sheila's door and I could hear Muldoon's footsteps on the pavement.

It was only then that I understood how much I wanted this.

Muldoon's humming grew sharp and clear as I burst through Sheila's door. I could see his ponytail heading away down the street. But my tether, whatever it was, suddenly pulled hard, taut and strong, trying to draw me back, back to that body. Back to that life.

But Muldoon stopped. He turned. And beckoned.

Skippy's whining grew faint, replaced by another sound, an atonal crackling, like a fault threading through stone. I imagined not repressing and forgetting, but moving beyond. I wrenched myself towards the possibility of change.

A rending crack... And then I was in his head.

He was humming a tune, and very faintly I heard words: *All the flowers in the field—*

Then he stopped walking, and he thought. *You made it.* That thought differed from the words in the song. It was clearer, intended for me. I was no longer eavesdropping.

I tried to communicate but didn't seem to have the apparatus.

Muldoon interrupted. "You don't need to talk or understand

anything yet. There is only one thing you need to do." He reached into his pocket and pulled out a photograph. It bore the face of an older man, firm mouth, sharp eyes, framed by tightly shaven grey hair. "Remember Leo." he said.

It was difficult to concentrate on this request, what with the deluge from my... no, Muldoon's senses. His footsteps, the weight of his ponytail, his tension in his gut about the time, his need to be somewhere, his fishing for car keys.

But I would slip into other thoughts too, faint snatches of a scene playing out in the distance, whatever distance meant in this state.

Don't be shy.

I'm glad you like a man in uniform.

Just watch me! Down in one...

I wasn't sure where these came from. Not from Muldoon, certainly, as his sensations felt in every way closer, louder, more pervasive, more alluring. So much so, I dispersed inside them, like droplets in an ocean, struggling to reform. Driving in the car, I realised that I'd spent minutes lost in his sensations, alien but intimate, mine but not mine. "Almost there," he said. "Leo has everything organised for you."

WE ARRIVED at a bungalow on a street just off St John's Road. Muldoon jumped out, slamming the car door behind us. The house we reached next was unlocked, and we made our way through to a room at the rear.

The room was dark, lit only by a lamp in one corner. There was a male body slumped over a table, and a red-haired woman was writing something on his back. As we walked in she looked up, "Muldoon. *Dieu Merci!*"

Muldoon's said, "The Ouroboros... Leo said—"

The woman nodded. "*Oui.* I drew it, then I cut it."

We walked around to the back of the body. The shirt was rolled up, and there in the middle of the back, a pen-drawn figure eight, but it was larger and more detailed, clearly exposing the scaled coils of the snake. And at its head, a thin line of blood trickling down the ridges of the man's spine.

Grizz cut me, too, I thought.

Muldoon took her hand and the woman's face creased with effort, but I couldn't focus on her any longer. I felt myself drawn into Muldoon's thoughts as though into a vortex. I was spinning around a central image catching glimpses of an older man with sharp features, with staring blue eyes, with tightly shaven grey hair.

And suddenly I was floating in a kaleidoscope of mental imagery, that older man's face fracturing and reassembling, papering the walkway of a bridge, the walls of a tunnel, and the front of a door. And I was pushing at that door, pushing and kicking and shoving, and although I couldn't see him, I knew Muldoon was beside me somehow, helping me force it open, just a crack, then a gap, then…

The door opened, revealing the flat, cold surface of a table.

As I pushed myself off that table, I was confused, groggy, frightened. I wasn't looking out through Muldoon's eyes anymore. Instead, I was staring straight at him.

"John?" Muldoon said, staring at me, hunting around for something. "John Golding?" He must have found it, because he laughed. The woman also smiled, briefly, but her lips were tight, her hands shaking with exertion. She quickly returned her gaze to the corner of the room.

"What?" I said, but without recognising my voice. It was deeper than I expected, older. Stronger, somehow. And I was trying to understand the name Muldoon used to address me: *John Golding.*

Muldoon draped a shirt around me. "You're groggy. That's natural. But don't worry. Leo sent us to take care of you, John. You'll remember soon. Sit down, and we'll sort all of this out."

I sat, stupefied, and he placed a loose-leaf binder in front of me. The first few pages were photographs, many of that old man: first he was staring at the camera, then smiling, then leafing through a book. "That's Leo?" I asked, in the voice I scarcely knew.

Muldoon nodded. "But look here too…" He took me through the book of pictures, all achingly familiar, all just out of reach. But he helped me, identifying faces, naming places, putting labels on blanks. I tried to focus, to concentrate on what he told me, but mostly I looked at my hands, at the pale, unscarred skin, then at my body, so sturdy and strong. I wore unfamiliar clothes: white shirt, black trousers, polished boots. A dark tie stuck out of my trouser pocket.

I had so many questions, most too frightening to ask, so I chose the safest one. "Why can't I remember?"

"That's expected. Leo said there would be some conflict with the… well, the residue. At first, for a while at least." Muldoon reached up to rest his hand on my shoulder. "It will all be fine. Leo will help."

"But am I… me?"

He laughed eagerly at that, almost too quickly. "Yes, John, of course. John Golding." He flipped to a photograph of an imposing building, buff stone around a large glass frontage. The picture inspired an ache of almost knowledge. "This is where you work. I'll be taking you in soon." Muldoon stabbed his finger at a block of clean sandstone. "Remember, John? You've worked here for twenty years." He flipped to another photograph of the same compound, but this time from the back. It was a zoom shot from a distance. It was a big place, that was clear.

The woman's breathing caught and Muldoon threw her a startled glance. "*Vite!* Get…him…away… Now!" Her voice was strained, her mouth taut while she glared balefully towards the ceiling.

As Muldoon hurried me out to the car, I hesitated. "Is she alright? Should we leave her?" I knew I felt something for her, but those feelings were in conflict: attraction, puzzlement, anger, betrayal.

He just laughed. "Sylvie's fine. She loves a good scrap. And she's got one – so, result." He pushed a CD into the sound system, advancing through the tracks until suddenly I recognised the tune.

195

I'd heard it twice already, both in Sheila's flat, and just after, from Muldoon's own off-key humming. It was a golden-oldie from back when it was difficult to tell between pop bands and chipmunks: *All the flowers in the field were made to please the bees.*

It is difficult to convey what I felt sitting in that car. I fell off a wall as a teenager and wrenched my shoulder from its socket. They gave me gas to keep me placid, but even then, it took so many attempts for the doctor to reset. Each attempt was ponderously slow, a careful manipulation, but with my arm out of place, I remember how alien those everyday physical articulations felt. That memory, that feeling of *wrong*, applied to my sense of self, is as close a description as I could give for that car journey.

At one point, I think perhaps I cried, but I'm unsure. I certainly remember reaching into my trouser pocket and pulling out a bloody tissue wrapped around a clump of dark, wiry hair. This was not the hair I saw reflected in my passenger-side mirror.

Muldoon leaned across and popped open the glove compartment. "Just drop that in there – we don't need it anymore." I obeyed Muldoon, since he was my only guide in this experience. Unusually for me, though, my lack of control, of authority, was starting to chafe. To push the irritation away, I tried to focus on the route. Behind me I felt the roiling currents of a sensory flood, but ahead the road signs seemed to offer a chance to grasp something solid. We passed the Jenner's Depository on Balgreen Road; now turning onto Gorgie Road; then Stenhouse Road. Then Muldoon said, "Recognise it?"

I examined the building on our approach. *My workplace.*

Past the bollards, above the glass, I read the words HMP Edinburgh. When we stopped outside, my driver smiled. "Saughton awaits." He tapped me on the shoulder, hurrying me out. "I'll meet you back here in the morning."

———

ONCE INSIDE, without thinking, I nodded through the security scan and then swiped my way into the prison block. I didn't exactly recognise this procedure, but something was happening that felt automatic, like muscle memory. Muldoon's voice from earlier returned to me. The word he'd used was *residue*, and I wondered if this was what he meant.

In the control room, a man said, "Better late than never, John. All ready for the madhouse?"

I examined his face, absent from Muldoon's photographs but familiar from somewhere else.

Thankfully, it came to me. "Evening, Frank. I'm not completely myself, I suppose, but soldiering on."

"Aye, well, no rest for the wicked. We put two radges in seg today and the Guv wants a calm night. So, you've to catch up with McKay and Dolan, help with the late visit at Ingliston Hall. Enjoy." He threw me a radio, and I caught it.

I felt oddly at home inside the complex of buildings. These were corridors echoing with the slap of feet that *just knew* my route. But even those things I somehow found familiar were simultaneously totally new. The most novel of all was the excitement: It felt sharp, immediate, not dull and muted. My gut was alive with nervous, happy jitters. Here I was, surrounded by an unexpectedly comfortable *newness* and occupied by a purpose.

Reaching the visit room, I saw people were already inside. I nodded to McKay as I entered, acknowledged Dolan briefly as he squeezed past me, on his way out to the staff toilets. The main thing that caught my eye was Sheila. That was startling enough, I suppose, but then I noticed she was sitting opposite Grizz. My old cellmate nodded towards me respectfully and said, "Mr Golding," before adding, "OK, bruv?" I saw McKay stiffen at that, and if I'm honest, part of me recoiled as well, but only a small, fading part, easily silenced.

My face solemn, I walked across to whisper in his ear. "Never better, Grizz. But go easy in public."

McKay seemed placated that some kind of whispered threat had been delivered, even if he had no clue why the prisoner seemed so little chastened.

Around then was when I heard the tune from a few tables down. It was the same one I'd encountered repeatedly that day, and it brought a fragment of the lyric to mind: *All the flowers in the field were made to please the bees.* McKay drew himself up to his full height. "Talk to your visitors. Don't whistle at them!" I looked across to see the culprit, an older man, sitting across from Muldoon. I recognised the sharp features, the staring blue eyes, the closely shaven grey hair.

Remember Leo.

I felt a pang of something. Admiration? Respect? Love? Some combination of those, melded with a profound sense of debt.

Because he had brought me here, back to a place where I knew I had value. Although I was back in prison, for the first time in decades, I had no thought of any kind of escape.

I was finally free.

ORIGINAL FEATURES

As Will walked, he grew aware of an awful familiarity. The endless corridors, discarded trolleys, the peeling information posters, an ever-present stench of disinfectant. *Just like the day she died.*

He had no choice but to move forward, numbly, step by unwilling step, retracing the death of his mother.

After following signs to the mortuary, he recognised the man sitting by the door. Tom Flynn rose immediately and clasped his hand. "I'm so sorry, Will," he said. "I wanted to wait until you arrived."

"Thank you, really – if you hadn't called I don't know," Will's voice trembled and he hesitated, pressing his hand to his lips, torn between tears and an apology.

Tom put an arm around his shoulder. "Don't thank me. I was lucky to meet him. He was a good man. My kids loved him. He spoke about you a lot – very proud… He said your name at the end. 'Will – tell Will…'".

Afterwards, Will recovered enough to ask his old classmate about his post-school life. He wondered what experiences might have transformed that brittle, bullied youth into the confident man he was discovering today.

Tom answered with some reserve. "I went to seminary. I became a priest, travelled to Africa and the Caribbean. That's in the past for me now though. I left that life, and I married. I work in international development now." He hesitated again. "I... I went through the last rites with your father. I'm not supposed to practice, but laicisation takes years... I'm actually still considered a priest by the Church, and at the time it gave him comfort, which seemed most important."

It overcame Will then – his father's death, the past, the kindness of someone with no reason to wish him well. He wept, and would have buckled save for Tom, who held him up and reassured him, readying him for the staff who would take him through to see the body.

Even through the grief, he wondered at how people change – how the weak can become strong, the withdrawn, warm. And how the hated can forgive.

IN THE DAYS THAT FOLLOWED, Will thought about his childhood, trying to remember the little events of it, all those minor parts that were now so important to hold on to.

He recalled the scaffolding collapse when he was eight – a phone call from the police, fear in his mother's eyes, and the unnatural silence of the taxi journey that followed. She didn't cry, not until they'd found his father shaken but uninjured, trying to reach them from the call-box in the hospital reception. Then she'd cried – they all had – but with joy, and they'd held each other all the more fiercely for what they'd nearly lost.

His father's best friend hadn't been so lucky, but it was a loss he bore in silence, and after that day, Will never heard it discussed again.

So many memories.

Like the ordinary times his father came home, cement in his hair, face streaked, hands grey with dust. Will would block his way, aching to be scooped up in his arms, wanting the dust to transfer to his own clothes, hard evidence of his father's love. He had seldom been disappointed.

One time was more painful to recall. Their downstairs flat had a little garden of its own at the front, and one day Will had spent nearly two hours after school constructing a wall at the entrance from leftover bricks. When his father had arrived home, he lashed out, scattering the bricks and striding away from the rubble. That night, Will had cried himself to sleep before waking to the touch of his father's hand. "I'm all I can be, son, but you've got more inside you. No more walls, promise me." They hugged then, and Will would have promised anything to put things back the way they were.

As the years passed, he suppressed his fascination with his father's job, but the interest never left him. For Will, the ability to make and to build, to craft and to create, felt more real than his academic subjects. Even at university, he harboured the secret. When a classmate offered a summer job on a construction site, he'd accepted gratefully, and it was the first of many similar projects he undertook, without informing his family.

Now, after his father's death, this fascination with construction blossomed into a powerful compulsion. He began looking for a suitable project to fill his evenings, something to keep him busy while allowing him to remember.

TWENTY-TWO QUEENSFERRY STREET Lane seemed an ideal opportunity and a bargain. Will's friend was the selling solicitor, and had given him advance notice before it arrived on the market:

**QUEENSFERRY STREET LANE – Great development
potential for Garden level Flat in West End conservation**

area. Entrance vestibule leading to large open-plan area, kitchen, WC, boxroom. Cellar with conversion potential, planning permission for 3 bedrooms. Gas Central Heating. FIXED PRICE: £269,000

It was beyond unusual to find a property at a fixed price in such a desirable area of the city, especially with such a low valuation. But a viewing partially explained the mystery: the place was decrepit. A shop had burned out years before and the owner had just left it to rot. On the owner's death, executors had finally put the place up for sale as part of processing the estate.

State of repair aside, it was still exactly what Will was looking for. The location was beautifully central, a cobbled lane near to fashionable boutiques, pubs, and restaurants. There were no major structural problems, and the price was perfect. It was a property developer's dream.

He secured the place immediately by selling his old flat to augment his capital. The plan was to borrow beds from friends while undertaking the bulk of the development himself. He'd picked up most skills over the years and was comfortable with joinery, plastering, and electrics. And though he'd rarely admit it, he could even turn his hand to plumbing.

But despite taking two weeks off work to kick-start the development, it soon became apparent he faced a mammoth task. The fire had gutted the storage space downstairs and damaged the staircase beyond reasonable repair. The wiring proved treacherous, and fuses frequently tripped on a single old ring circuit with too many spurs. Worse, wrongly gauged cabling throughout constituted an additional fire hazard. He didn't want to repair the last owner's mistake, only to risk repeating it.

Despite all this, he found a kind of peace during the building work. But his father's loss manifested strangely as the project proceeded. Sometimes, when he was downstairs, he felt as though someone was with him. It was a recurring sensation of *presence*. At first, he liked to think of his father overseeing the work of the cellar conversion, and it was a comfort to imagine them spending that time together. Will interpreted these experiences as a normal part of his grieving process.

Late one evening, he was digging through the rough cellar floor to gain the depth he needed for the new rooms when the sense of presence returned. It was stronger and more immediate than before – just behind his shoulder, in fact. The sudden strangeness jolted his senses awake: the scraping crunch of the shovel, the shadows cast by the yellow glow of the security lamp, his sweat cooling in the darkness, the damp musk of old earth.

And now, someone behind him.

Close behind him too, directly in his space, around him almost.

"Dad?" he said, but deeply uncertain, the words catching in his throat. He wished he hadn't said it, felt immediate regret, both for the gullibility of it, but more, and this was strange, a kind of guilt. He'd never felt this way with his father – crowded, stifled.

He scanned the room and found it empty. There was nothing but rubble and dirt and bad light. But the feeling didn't leave. He'd already put in days of toil to open out the cellar, and yet, in that large, empty space, he felt completely surrounded. With each plunge of his shovel, the oppression grew, a mounting feeling of menace, of digging himself into a pit.

He stopped and left to stay with a friend.

The experience bothered him, but he supposed too much late working and the desolate appearance of the cellar had been playing on his imagination. He decided to restrict cellar work to daylight hours during the coming weekend. After that he'd do an hour each morning, shower at the office and finish earlier in the evenings.

He was sure to be more relaxed when the room construction was underway. He'd planned for two double bedrooms with an en-suite, and a further small single room usable as a study. The lifestyle magazine images in his head fuelled his determination to keep up the pace.

FINALLY, after six months of renovation, working nights and weekends, and after spending just over £30,000, the place was ready for a valuation. The agent from the ESPC made a variety of appreciative comments before offering a figure of £380,000. But any notional profit was academic at this stage – he would make a home here for at least the next couple of years.

After the final touch-ups and furnishing, Will's first night in his new home arrived. The entire project had taken more from him than he had been prepared for, but the outcome was worth it, and he was thrilled to collapse into his new bed.

But as he dropped off, he grew dimly aware of a sound.

It was faint, strangely muffled, but recognisable as talking, and he presumed it came from his neighbours behind the adjoining wall.

He forgot all about it until the next night, when his sleep was once again disturbed. He chided himself – the voice was muted and without revisiting the soundproofing, it was unfixable, so he resolved to ignore it.

But the disturbance continued for a further two nights, each night slightly less comfortable than the one before. He awoke on his fifth morning, determined to go next door to complain, when he realised that the voice always stopped upon his waking. Rather than risk antagonising a neighbour over a bad dream, he decided to keep a notepad beside his bed and record any detail that might help him puzzle it out.

AFTER DINNER THE FOLLOWING EVENING, Will was distracted by the unexpected sight of Tom Flynn appearing on a television news debate about Third World debt. It was stirring stuff, with the presenter playing entirely unnecessary hardball with both speakers, until a retaliatory barrage of evidence from Will's old classmate was so powerfully delivered that his points were simply adopted as fact and used to roast the politician.

Will decided he liked this new, older Tom Flynn, and not just for the compassion he had shown during Will's recent bereavement. He even poured himself a glass of wine to watch the rest of the programme, but the other topics covered were less interesting, and he was yawning before it finished.

That night he woke up twice, each time groggily switching on the light to make notes of what he could remember. For the first time, he could identify snatches of what was being said, noticing an archaic accent and an odd intensity to the voice.

The whole thing was profoundly eerie. Will was normally a calm – some had even said stolid – individual, but he was waking afraid, for the first time in nearly thirty years. The fear was fleeting, swiftly quelled, but inexplicable. The experience did not seem like a nightmare and, in fact, scarcely seemed like a dream of any kind, more like words on an audio tape playing over and over as he drifted to sleep.

The following day he chatted obliquely about dreams with colleagues in the pub after work, but discovered nothing directly comparable. Unwisely for a midweek evening, he arrived home late and a little merry. He fell gratefully into bed, mentally preparing himself for an unavoidable morning hangover.

"Your own namesakes. Your own countryfolk. William Burke and William Hare.

"The Irish, that inferior race, had preyed on my own city. Aye, they had. Was this an act I could leave unavenged? I could not. So after Burke met the noose, did the anatomists no still have students tae teach? They did.

"It wid be three years yet before the lawmakers gied them the bodies o'the workhouse poor. Three years to take my revenge. But if bodies were needed, t'was not as before. Mair questions wid be asked, for a body of

unknown provenance could be a grave danger tae both buyer and seller.
Nae doctor of guid standing could risk a familiar corpse being open'd on
their tables.

   "So I set my mind tae the problem for I wid not be denied.
   "I set my mind tae it, and made it yield..."

WILL WOKE DRENCHED IN SWEAT. His bedside clock read *2:04AM*, so he had slept for around ninety minutes. He didn't know if alcohol had played a role, but the dream was different tonight, different and considerably worse. Previously, he had experienced only disconnected noise, unsettling words spoken in the distance. But tonight, he'd been held close while the tale was muttered in his ear.

He lay back, staring at the ceiling, unwilling to close his eyes just yet. Fatigue would take him soon but not while the echoes still moved in his head. Not until he felt alone again.

THE FOLLOWING MORNING, he was happy to hear his alarm. The happy pointlessness of local radio was a perfect antidote to the oppressive voice that dogged his sleep. He dragged himself out of bed, made some breakfast, and wondered what was wrong with his head.

When he arrived at work, all was busily normal for the first hour but, at the mid-morning meeting, he was embarrassed to be nudged awake by his boss. He stayed behind at the end to explain himself, but she was less than sympathetic.

"Look, Will," she said, "accommodating your property development has placed a strain on the rest of us. We're busy, and we can't count on you to do anything except work minimum hours. For someone on your pay grade it's far from ideal. Given that, it seems reasonable to expect you to be alert and fully contribute when you are here."

"I'm sorry, Margaret, I really am. I'll make sure this won't happen again. The irony is, the build is finished, but I don't know if it's the stress or the unfamiliar bed or whatever, but I seem to have developed a problem sleeping since I moved in. Last night I didn't sleep more than a couple of hours, and to be honest, I've been waking up for the last five nights in a row."

She answered without warmth. "You obviously need to address that, but I don't think it should be our problem." She tapped the folder she was holding. "We need to get our numbers to the regulator next month. I expect you to participate fully so we make that date. Agreed?"

"Yes, of course. Sorry, again."

She left the meeting room, leaving Will to gather up his papers.

He'd worked there for over nine years and had never experienced such a demeaning encounter with a manager. Clearly, his project had caused some resentment – short days and long lunch breaks at the builder's merchants had been his pattern for a while now. If he was to repair that damage, he needed to fix his sleeping.

Over lunchtime, he browsed the Internet for information on sleep disorders. There was a lot of material on a variety of complaints: sleep apnea, insomnia, narcolepsy, restless legs, sleep terrors, hypersomnia and others. None of the conditions precisely fitted his experience. While sleep terrors seemed vaguely similar, he had no confusion on waking, and could clearly recall the experience that caused the fear.

Was it possible that he was simply suffering from a recurring nightmare? Had an unpleasant narrative somehow got into his head, only to be replayed night after night? If so, he could guess at the cause, because during the last month of the build, he'd rented a room from Simon, a colleague with a fondness for late-night horror films. Will remembered many nights where the dialogue from some overwrought movie had echoed through the wall to his bedroom.

Having identified the culprit, Will's afternoon passed more happily. He'd fix the problem by breaking the cycle. On the way home, he stopped off at the chemist for some over-the-counter sleep medication. For good measure, he also bought an eye mask and earplugs. He was determined to rest properly tonight.

Around nine p.m., Will took his medication and drank a hot chocolate before heading straight to bed, confident his preparations would guarantee a night of undisturbed slumber.

THIS WAS A DARK PLACE. *Thin trickles of light leaked through a muck stained corner window, trickles that fell on the inky shadows before being consumed.*

Will stood at a rough wooden table, the surface streaked with offal and gore, pooling in places, dripping from the edges. Soiled hooks of various sizes hung from the ceiling. They clinked in some unfelt breeze.

The atmosphere was oppressive, like breathing hate. And the smell was the rot of the grave.

In the far corner, the darkness deepened. Something was coming, gathering its strength, trying to be seen. Minutes passed while it drew the shadows into itself, forming a knot in the darkness, a knot that swelled, bloating like infection in a wound, bloating and tearing and reforming, lengthening into the hulking figure of a man.

The figure stepped forward, stopping at the boundary between shadow and light. A guttural voice broke the silence.

"Tae get the bodies, well what ae that? Tae spend my nights sifting through graveyard dirt for some infested corpse, sharing ownership wi' the worms? No. I wanted my ain lives tae harvest, bodies tae steward and deliver tae the anatomists in accordance with my ain will.

"I resolved tae dae as Burke did, but wi greater wisdom. Tae take folk known by ither folk would invite the rope. But we had ships pulling intae the west, laden wi the dreck ae the Irish, families wi nowt, and none tae look

out for them... Save me. I stood oan the docks offering guid wirk tae them that needs it.

"So I find myself a family, six Irish, and take the canal back tae Edinburgh, a swift journey, eight hours only. It wis guid tae think that a canal built in nae small measure by their ain folk wis now delivering them intae the fate I decree'd.

"So a first step made, and the family were mine. And if they were the first, I knew there could be mair. For who would believe ill ae such a bene-factor? Not wi' Irish treachery and thievery sae well known.

"Aye, mine in body they were, but why no in soul as well? Could I find ways tae take no jist their bodies, a small penalty for such as these, but also the ither parts, the parts that God hissel keeps claim tae? All this I pondered oan our journey.

"It was dark when we reached the town and darker yet when I goat them all tae this place. E'en pushing through the hanging pigs and the smell ae the blood, e'en though the place was cold and cramped, the Irish look'd at all ae it and they were as grateful as if I'd show'd them a palace.

"I paid nae mind tae their gratitude for whit worth has that? What worth when ye have all the rest – everything they'll ever feel and want and be, fae that day oan? I didnae feel a butcher then, but mair a farmer. A farmer wi a hoose full ae walking meat."

WILL ESCAPED HIS DREAM, propelled by a great wave of disgust and anger. He wrenched the sleep mask from his eyes and switched on the lamp. Casting his ear-plugs aside, he set the radio blaring. He felt an aching need for living voices.

The pride and malice issuing from the figure was palpable, but worse was its utter conviction. He had no room for doubt: the story he'd heard was true; the events described had taken place, and this house, his house, had been the venue.

But the dream figure had not interacted with him. It had simply delivered its tale. Was it a sentient, conscious being or was it just a kind of recording in the stone, some sort of psychic imprint? He had heard similar ideas in the past, but dismissed them as nonsense. Why construct a pseudo-scientific explanation for ghosts when perfectly good scientific explanations existed, such as hallucination, intoxication, or mental illness?

It was ironic that as a lifelong sceptic, he now took hope from quack-theories, for he knew the alternatives were intolerable. Because if not psychic imprints, then he was going mad, or was under attack by an evil he had no defence against.

———

IT WAS A DAY FOR COFFEE. And lots of it.

Will didn't feel great, but he made it through without falling asleep and he got the work done. At five o'clock he left promptly, since he had an appointment to keep at the legal offices of McCall and Wallace.

Gordon McCall was Will's closest friend. They had met when Will bought his first flat in the city, and sharing similar personalities, with only a limited need for social contact, they had become occasional and undemanding companions. On this occasion, as Gordon rose to greet his friend, he was visibly concerned. "Hey, Will. Property developing still extracting its pound of flesh, I see... Are you OK?"

Will held his friend's gaze for a moment before dropping into the chair opposite. "Actually, Gordon, I'm not. I finished the development, but either the house is the problem or I am. Can I ask a few questions?"

"Of course, anything I can do."

Will paused, wondering how much to risk revealing. Hopefully only a little, since being psychotic was bad enough without it actually becoming public knowledge. "I need to know about the house before I bought it, who lived there, why it was empty, why it was cheap. It's important or I wouldn't ask..."

Gordon closed the door to his office. When he sat down again, he looked his friend directly in the eye. "Look, I can't divulge anything about the seller. That's just basic professional ethics. You'd be the same if I asked about one of your policyholders…"

"I don't want to identify the previous owner, or anything like that. I just need some background on their circumstances, the situation that led to selling, something that might help me…"

The solicitor shook his head. "Help you with what? We're friends, but I can't give you potentially sensitive information for no good reason. I stuck my neck out giving you early warning on the sale."

Will sighed, seeing no option but to provide some details. "I feel crazy saying this, but there are strange things going on in the house since I moved in. Perhaps I'm losing it, but I can't sleep – it's affecting my work. It's also, frankly, pretty bloody disturbing, and I need to get to the bottom of it."

A smile played on his friend's lips. "Strange things? Are you saying it's haunted?"

Will shrugged. It was a hard thing to admit.

His friend snorted, slapping his hand against the desk. "Piss-take. Got to be…" But as Will's expression fell, he stopped, puzzled. "Christ, sorry, Will. It's just that this is *you*. You know? Mr Hard-Nosed Sceptic. I didn't ever imagine…"

Will looked down at the desk. "Then you know it must be bad. Help me. Please help me."

The solicitor hesitated before responding. "You need to keep quiet about this or you'll get me struck off. Understand?" He moved to wind down the blinds. "OK. There were some… unusual circumstances, but I don't know if they'll help you or not. Our first contact with that place was about eleven or twelve years back. It was an insolvency sale – some little company went belly-up. The buyer was in his fifties, did it up as a specialist book shop, antiquarian, that sort of thing. This business was more of a hobby for him than anything else; he'd made his money a long time before. Paid for the place outright in cash, and lodged the deeds here.

"Anyway, next I heard was when the fire hit the papers about a year later. Luckily, they caught it before it spread, but the bookshop itself was gutted. There was some suspicion at the time: the owner had moved a lot of books out of the place the week before, claimed he was opening a business in France. It all blew over. With no insurance claim, there was no motive for fraud, so it remained just an accident.

"The owner went to France, and we had the deeds, every day expecting to receive selling instructions, but they never arrived. After a few months, we presumed the man had more money than sense. We just forgot about it. Until four years ago, when we were contacted by his executors to say he'd died."

Will interrupted. "He died four years ago? Why did it take so long to sell it?"

Gordon nodded. "That was the thing. He had a substantial estate, and your place was only a small part of it, but he had made special mention in his will, stating that the address be left unsold and unoccupied. Just like that, no explanation, but money left in trust to pay for minimal external maintenance. You can imagine, his family, other residents, even the council, all up in arms. It took four years for the will to be overturned. His family just wanted the place sold and out of their hair, first reasonable offer. That was where you came in."

The solicitor slouched into his chair. "So, yes, pretty strange circumstances. I've never come across that kind of thing before, doubt I will again."

Will wondered about the meaning behind this history he'd just heard. Might the previous owner have experienced something unpleasant, something that drove him to leave, drove him even to arson? Was it comforting to imagine another human being may have shared his experience? This might mean he wasn't mad after all, but where did it leave him? "If his solution involved a couple of cans of petrol. What's mine?" The thought rose unbidden. "An exorcist?"

Gordon laughed, waiting for Will to join in. It didn't happen.

Instead, Will thanked him and went outside to call the only priest he knew. The little girl who answered quickly passed him to her father. "Hi Tom? It's Will Kearney. Do you have a minute?"

Dishes clattered at the other end. "Of course. But I'm on dinner duty so it will have to be a quick one. How can I help?"

"Well..." Will considered backing out, but he had no other option. "This sounds insane. But... I think my house might be haunted? Or possessed? Can a house even be... I don't know, but I need to speak to someone about it before I go mad." He paced a circle in the pavement. "Tell me to go away and I will. It's just I don't know what else to do right now, and it's getting to me so—"

Tom said, "Hold on a second, Will. I can tell this is going to take longer than I've got. Why don't we meet to discuss this?"

"I think I'd prefer that too, if you could spare the time. Sooner the better from my point of view. I'll come through to Glasgow whenever suits..." He hesitated. "Soon as tonight even?"

Silence at other end, before a quiet reply. "The earliest I can see you is tomorrow. You could come by in the afternoon. I'm in the south side of Glasgow, just off Clarkston Road, 19 Struan Gardens."

As the call ended, Will briefly regretted not imposing on Gordon for a bed for the night. But no sooner had this thought surfaced than a surge of resentment pushed it away. He had worked hard over the last six months. It was intolerable that some weird dream, however unpleasant, could drive him out of his new home.

Turning his collar against the Edinburgh wind, he pushed his way homewards. Another night should help him understand a little more before tomorrow's discussion. Better yet, he might have a good night and see a more sensible way past this.

But on reaching the house, for a moment, the entrance looked strangely unfamiliar. And as the door clicked shut behind, he fancied hearing the echo of his footfall on stone. It stopped him short, but the light switch revealed his carpeted entrance was as it should be, and the odd feeling swiftly faded.

No doubt he was troubled after recent events. And on top of his anxiety, he was extremely tired. Unwilling to go downstairs to bed, he settled himself on the sofa, unsure of what the night would bring.

THE BLUDGEON FELL *like a hammer blow, and a rough hand crushed against his mouth. Groggy, almost unconscious, someone hauled Will from the bed like an insubstantial thing, powerless to resist.*

In a daze, head dangling, the walls of the house drifted past his eyes, angles wrong, motion surreal. His captor tugged at a trapdoor before descending into the darkness, dragging his human cargo behind him.

This cellar, although seen clearly for the first time, had always been waiting for him. His captor tied his hands quickly, with well-practised knots, then wrenched his arms upwards, to suspend him from a ceiling hook, then gagged his mouth with filthy cloth. Beside him, other hooks hung empty, but twisted and rattled as Will struggled for freedom.

Then the butcher stood back to survey his handiwork. He grinned, scabrous lips parting to reveal a mouthful of blackened stumps.

"I kep them doon here until their time. Each saw the killins that went before, and why no? Is it no a gift tae know your ain fate? They'd be fed, or no, according tae my ain choosing. The wains who haitit these hands that kild their faither and muthir, wid eat fae them like wee beasts when I lifted the rag fae thir mouths...

"I wondered aboot the soul. Wis it in the head? I kep the head ae the faither and watched it wi care. But the rot forced it burnt, and I wisnae satisfied. Then I fancied as I cut the throat ae the muthir tae see her spirit escape through the froth. I reasoned that the smaller souls ae the children wid be harder yet tae catch, so I tried tae hold them a time oan the brink ae this world and the next tae better see it. I wis an ignorant man in some ways then, ye see. But I'm no ignorant now.

"I'd tell the anatomists o' accidents in the docks bringing cargo intae Leith, or in the building companies at wirk in the town, or in the ragged schools and poorhouses. I'd bring them the bodies, sometimes jist parts,

taken fae these imagined calamities, wi me a simple go-between hired tae avoid scandal.

"And if they didn't like the state ae the bodies, if they thought the cuts too clean? Well they said nowt and took them anyway. Progress is a hungry beast, and I wis paid well tae feed it.

"Naebody knew the corpses I brought, I'd made well sure ae that, so there were none tae wonder after them."

The butcher reached into a soiled apron pocket and produced a cleaver. He held it before Will's face, smiling as his captive twisted on the hook, straining to avoid the blood-streaked reflection.

"They'll wonder whit happened tae ye but, Billy. Aye, they'll wonder aboot that..."

Then the butcher snarled and drew back the cleaver.

WILL WOKE SCREAMING. Frenzied with fear and panic, he tugged on the clothes he'd worn the previous day and ran from the house, not pausing to shut the door, not pausing to look back.

The wind, bitter in the dark streets before dawn, seared his skin, and he was glad of it. Gooseflesh – he was alive. He was still alive.

All along Princes Street towards Waverley Station, he saw the doomed family in his mind, their hopes for a new life in this city crushed into nightmare.

A coffee shop was opening in the station as Will arrived, and he ordered tea, hot without milk, to sting himself back to reality. But as he lifted it to his lips, he saw livid welts on his wrists from the ropes in his dream. The ropes in his dream?

Slowly, deliberately, trying to steady his breathing, he touched his forehead. But it was inescapable – a painful swelling where the bludgeon had struck.

The shaking began uncontrollably, rising from somewhere deep, causing his cup to rattle against his saucer like gaoler's keys. He saw the cleaver, the heft of it, the deadly gleam on its edge. He saw it swing. And he knew: if he had not woken at that moment, he would never have woken at all.

He slept fitfully on the train to Glasgow Queen Street and awoke feeling wretched in the city of his birth. As he disembarked, he considered never returning to Edinburgh and that bloody house – just staying here, where he had grown up with his family, staying somewhere that thing could never reach him again.

But with his parents dead, he was a stranger in Glasgow now, and his money, his job, his life, all were now tied to Edinburgh. And as for the house, knowing what he knew, he could never pass such a curse on. More than that, last night had left him not only marked, but infected, by a deep and corrosive fear. Unless he overcame his tormentor, nowhere could ever feel safe again.

He wasted as much time as he could bear, walking in the centre of town, watching the ebb and flow of an ordinary day take hold. The people he saw in the city were close to that shore, caught in the humdrum flow of normality. Will had been caught by a different wave, one that dragged him into perilous waters. Eventually he could wait no longer, and caught a train to the south side.

Around three hours early for his appointment, he reached the front door of 19 Struan Gardens. He knew he shouldn't be here yet, that he should wait until the afternoon, but he simply could not. All his hopes were now invested in this meeting, and unfair or not, he couldn't be anywhere else right now, not after the events of the previous night.

When Tom opened the door, his eyes widened at the haggard figure on his doorstep. "Will?" he said.

"I'm so sorry," gasped Will, almost falling inside. "I'm so sorry. I had to come."

Tom caught him on the threshold and stared, Will realised, at this near-stranger invading his home. He stared hard, holding him there as seconds ticked by. Then he simply nodded and stepped back. "Sorry, Will, I thought you might be drunk. Come in and I'll get the kettle on."

Seated at a bench in the kitchen, Will wondered again at how much Tom Flynn had changed. When they'd been at school, Will remembered Flynn's NHS plastic glasses twitching with agitation. Now, the man gazed calmly through stylish designer frames. His confidence was unrecognisable as the boy who shrank into himself when anyone came near.

The shelves opposite their table displayed photographs from various global travels. Will recognised Himalayan prayer wheels, the Valley of the Kings in Egypt, a Mayan ziggurat. "Is that Africa?" Will asked, indicating a vibrant picture of a busy marketplace.

"No. Haiti," Tom replied. The kettle began to gently hiss in the background. "So. You've arrived early," he said.

Will sat, rubbing his eyes. "Something happened. And thank-you for helping me. We were such shits to you at school. I'm so sorry about that now."

Tom smiled and handed him a mug of tea. "Forget it. School was... harsh. But it wasn't all on you guys. I was anxious and fragile about everything. It made me uncomfortable to be around. Thankfully, we've all grown up and moved on."

Will said, "I wanted to ask you about.the priesthood—"

Tom shook his head. "The priesthood was a mistake. I was serious about it, but for the wrong reasons. You know, running from a life I didn't want, instead of trying to create a life I did? Anyway, I asked to be sent to the missions, to take the faith where I felt it was most needed. So, I was accepted and got the training—"

Will interrupted. "Exorcism?"

Tom nodded. "Yes, exorcism, among other things." He sighed. "Exorcism typically occurred more in the developing world than here. That bothered me, really. Why would the devil find easier purchase in the hearts of the people over there? I was uncomfortable with the notion. Most of those I met in Nigeria and Benin were friendlier than those I'd met here, and more generous too with what little they had. I began to see the history of the missions in commercial terms. The Church in those regions sought to compete with traditional beliefs, including in the incontestable reality of spiritual possession and witchcraft. Emphasising the rite of exorcism was good marketing. It was as simple and mundane as that."

"So you don't believe in spirits?"

"I didn't say that." Tom gazed out of the kitchen window before sipping his tea. "The traditional religions helped define African culture. Aspects of those religions: ancestor worship, belief in spirits, a supreme deity, pantheistic sub-deities – these find echoes in every society in the world today. In Catholicism we pray for the departed, believe in the soul, have God as our supreme deity with a pantheon of saints around him. The religious beliefs I found in Africa were not primitive, but complex and culturally consistent.

"For example, in traditional religion, possession often occurs as a living part of their faith. If we accept Christian sects speaking in tongues, why deplore Vodun rituals summoning the spirits of the Loa? To be ridden, or possessed, by the Loa was considered a blessing, granted only to those most in need. But the culture we imposed as missionaries often took these transcendent experiences and denounced them as evil." Tom lifted the cups over to the sink. "But you didn't come here to talk about me, though. I think it's your turn now."

And so Will began. He did not edit his experience in order to seem sane or rational. He told Tom everything. About the house, its history, and the events he had experienced there. He ended by showing the wounds on his wrists and head.

Tom frowned. "You got these marks from events in the dream itself, you say?"

The indentations on Will's wrists were still livid. "This bruising is from the way he knotted the rope." He looked away. "I'm not imagining it... and yet... I just don't believe in things like this."

Tom exhaled. "But after last night, does it serve you to believe nothing in your home wishes you harm? Does it serve you to believe yourself mad? Does it serve you to let these horrors play out with your eyes closed and your fingers crossed, insisting happy thoughts are all you need? Will that serve you, or be your undoing?"

"But what do I believe instead? That two hundred years on, somehow he still exists... this butcher... from my dream. How is that possible?"

"Maybe that's down to what the figure in your dream believed?"

"You can't just believe yourself immortal."

"Why not? It's hardly a new idea and, in fact, the exact pitch of many world religions. Some beliefs are powerful, visceral, even."

Will lapsed into silence for a moment, trying to make sense of it. "But why, Tom? Why did you give up belief, then?"

"I didn't... I just learned to believe in the same way I dress for winter. I asked what serves me... and here we are." Tom held Will's gaze, then he frowned. "So. If I understand it, then over the course of twelve days, your dreams have reached a point of causing physical marks... Your worry is that it progresses furth—"

Will slapped the table. "NO! It won't progress, don't you see? Next time, I'm dead. I should already be dead!"

His host stared into the middle distance as Will twisted and rubbed the skin of his wrists. Finally, Tom rose. "Fancy a drive? I think it's time you showed me this house of yours..."

ON THE JOURNEY TO EDINBURGH, they discussed other things. The near-endless roadworks on the motorway, the incessant drizzle, Tom's children and his work on economic justice. But both men grew subdued as they approached their destination, and soon the conversation lapsed altogether.

It was approaching lunchtime when they arrived, parking on nearby Alva Street. Will felt uneasy as they walked towards his house, and as they reached the door, he turned to Tom. "How do we do this? Can you still exorcise a place, now that you're not a priest anymore? Like the last rites, remember, for my father?" He shivered as he asked, although the temperature was milder than it had been all day.

Tom shrugged. "In the Church's view I'll always be a priest. Laicisation just removes the obligation of celibacy, but even getting that is complex and often ends in refusal. Most of us don't bother. As long as you sign documents relinquishing any claim on your order or diocese, you'll be left to get on with your life. So, I can still conduct particular rituals, but the rituals really only provide focus. We could argue about where the efficacy comes from..." He paused. "Anyway, I'm rather hoping there is another way around all of this. I'm not a spiritual warrior anymore and I abandoned my shining sword of truth over three thousand miles away. So lead on Macduff – let's see what there is to see."

The silence inside had a deadening, uncomfortable quality, and it prompted Will into nervous narration. "This was the old shop front, going back to God knows how long. I've made it my living and dining room. If you come through here to the back, left takes you into the kitchen, and right to a small bathroom. The bedrooms are down the stairs. It used to be a cellar, running the full area of the house. That's the focus, I think."

But as they reached the mouth of the staircase, Tom placed a hand on Will's shoulder. He exhaled slowly. "I feel it, right here. It's appalling. I didn't know it would affect me this way."

Will shuddered at a feeling of dread he had previously only experienced in dreams. "It hasn't been like this before, not while I'm awake." He tried to smile. "At least you know I'm not making this up."

Tom nodded, and they started down, but slowly. Each step was an exertion, a push into something abysmal. Hatred saturated the air, the walls, and the very steps beneath their feet.

When they reached the downstairs hallway, the bedroom door lay ajar but the interior was hazy, rippling like a reflection on unsettled water. The substance of the room was shifting, with the bed fading before them, giving way to something else, something with a far earlier claim on that space; the solidifying altar of the butcher's block.

Hatred welled again, crashing around them like a wave, washing them forward into the room. The old reality was now peeling before their eyes, like strips torn from a counterfeit painting to reveal flashes of the true canvas.

Behind the modern facade lurked a dank cellar in its full dimension. Over 30 feet across, the low ceiling strung with empty hooks. The hooks seemed animated by odd forces, some twisting slowly, others pulled off-kilter as though attracted by a magnet.

"This is the empty room from my dream – the place he dragged me," Will said.

Tom's face was ashen. "You can't see them? You can't see what he keeps here?"

And at the butcher's block, a shadow was forming. As it thickened and coagulated into the shape of a man, it spoke. "It wisnae the law, but the cholera that took me. But who could leave such work as mine unfinished? Not after death had revealed tae me the key. The key I'd sought when my work wis first begun – the key tae the soul." The shadow-thing dislodged a cleaver from the tabletop and spun it in its hands.

Will said, "I see him."

Tom hissed at Will, "Not him. Them! His first victims – they're hollow, empty. But the others? Somehow, he owns them – they're still here!"

The butcher laughed and spat. "Oh, how I'll open ye, Billy. I'll gut ye like a sow, ye and yer friend. I'll pull out yer souls like strings ae offal and hang them on my hooks. Hang them beside the ithers who tried tae steal whit's mine from me. Your house? Yours? This place is mine! FOREVER MINE!"

The butcher strode towards him, speed belying its great size, snarling blasphemies.

Will screamed in desperation. "Tom! Tom! Please! Help me!", But Tom was silent, trembling slightly, eyes unfocused, face flushed and knuckles white as though in the grip of some terrible effort. Then the butcher seized Will by the collar and dragged him towards the table.

The butcher's power was overwhelming. It smashed Will onto the surface of the butcher's block, holding him there. Despite struggling with every ounce of strength he possessed, Will could not move. Seeing the cleaver rise, he tried to pray, tried to recall those words from his childhood, but he could not. His mind froze as the cleaver fell towards him.

But the cleaver did not land.

Tom had caught the butcher's arm and held it. Momentary confusion showed upon the butcher's face, before his friend smashed the brute's limb against the corner of the table. The cleaver crashed to the floor. But the monster's confusion turned to rage as it grasped Tom's throat. "Uncommon strong, ye might be, but strong or no, ye'll end on my table!" It lifted Tom by his neck, struggling to free its other arm from his grasp.

Tom grunted, "I'll... cast you... out... unclean spirit..."

The butcher wrenched its arm free, slamming a grimy fist into Tom's body. It laughed as his breath exploded from him, his face already crimson from the pressure of its grip, deepening into a livid purple. "I'll wager ye willnae, little priest. Strong meat is still meat, and ye've earned a special hook when this ither yin's done..." With that, it threw Tom to the floor. He landed with a sickening thump and lay unmoving.

The creature returned to Will, once more pressing him against the grisly table surface. Hanging his head over the edge, it laughed. "Aye, look back there, back tae the one ye hoped wid save ye." It pinned him with one hand while it rooted inside its apron pocket.

As Will tried to prepare himself for the coming atrocity, he saw something happening around Tom. The man moved weakly, surrounded by some kind of dark aura. A shape seemed to grow from him, rising *out of* him, a shape in shadow, the shape of a man – a shape that stood and charged.

It crashed against Will's captor with incredible force, pitching both the butcher and his table over with a crash. Will recovered himself and watched in awe as the butcher was wrestled to the ground by a tall black man, heavily muscled, his back rippling under the tattoo of a beaded rattle. The butcher swore in disbelief as it struggled to get up, arms grappling for purchase on a floor slippery with the blood of his victims. Unable to rise, it beat viciously against the tattooed man's chest, filthy nails raking against flesh, blood streaming from the wounds. But throughout this, the stranger held fast, calling out a strange repetitious song.

The song spiralled round and round, and the butcher's fists beat like drums. With each blow, the song grew louder and more desperate until finally the tattooed man shouted words that seemed to simultaneously exist in a strange harmony of languages, before repeatedly calling the names, "Brigitte! Ghede!"

This cry echoed around the cellar for long moments before another sound answered it.

Tap. Tap. Tap

Clink. Clink. Clink.

Two new figures were in the cellar now. An aged white woman escorted a top-hatted black man, both dressed in funeral finery, darkest purple and gothic black. The woman carried a silver topped cane, the smirking man a long iron shovel. They wove their way through the room, rapping at certain positions. As the pair rapped, just for a moment, Will glimpsed a person hanging beside them, before a consuming blackness roared upwards, leaving just a hook shaking on its chain.

When the newcomers reached the fighting pair, each pushed a foot onto an arm of the butcher, and his struggles ceased at once.

The woman spoke, again with that uncanny chromatic quality. "*Merci Loko... La mort vous guérira... Death will heal you.*"

Tap. Tap. Tap.

Clink. Clink. Clink.

Both the cane and the shovel were now tapping beside the butcher's head. He roared desperately "I'll no be taken! Leave me be! I'm no finished!"

Tap. Tap. Tap.

Clink. Clink. Clink.

A hole appeared in the cellar's floor, and the air filled with the moist smell of earth. The butcher's head lolled back into the chasm that was opening. He grunted and swore, but he could not evade it. With a shocking suddenness, all four figures dropped into the hole, which swelled explosively outwards before disappearing along with the old cellar, the hooks, and all signs of the struggle.

SHORTLY AFTERWARDS, Tom sat in the middle of the downstairs hall, weeping. It was uncontrolled and childlike, a flood of emotion. Will tried to comfort him. "Tom, Tom, it's OK – it's over – I don't know what you did, but they saved us, those people you brought, they saved us."

"Saved you, not me." He sobbed inconsolably.

"But it's over, Tom. You did it." Will wanted to hug him, to thank him, to make him see how much he had done, but his companion's grief was too great a barrier to cross.

"It's not over. Not for me. It'll never be over. He's gone!" Tom hissed, his chest heaving.

"Look, Tom, everything's OK. I can feel it. Come on and I'll make us some tea and then I'll get you home to your family."

Tom glared from behind bloodshot eyes. His face was strange – the same fragile, resentful, fearful face from their days at school. He almost spat the words. "*His* family! *His* home! I can't be that person without him; I don't know how to be!" He convulsed with tears again. "I told you their possession was a gift. I told you... I told you..."

He stood up shakily and began to make his way up the stairs. "I've lost everything. Everything…" He began running and Will heard the door slam upstairs.

———

Will, although badly bruised and aching all over, slept soundly for the first time in weeks. The next morning, he contacted Gordon to make preparations for the sale. "It'll be a good home. For someone else," he said simply. Gordon made no attempt to dissuade him.

He phoned for Tom later that night, but his wife explained he was unwell and couldn't take any calls. She sounded grief-stricken, like someone who'd suffered a terrible loss. Will didn't pry any further. She couldn't have told him anything he didn't know already.

He replaced the receiver, resolving to call again tomorrow, and the day after, and the day after that. He'd call for as long as it might take to speak to Tom, to re-establish some connection.

He didn't know how or if that might help, but it was clear that his friend believed himself broken, believed himself insufficient for his life. But that same friend had once explained about beliefs and their power. This new belief did not serve his friend, and it was Will's task to make him remember that.

Will would take on that task, because he held a debt. And a debt such as this, a debt that could never truly be repaid, was a debt that should never be forgotten.

THE ANNIVERSARY MAN

The fax was from Denver PD – a picture of the card they found on the body. The small kind you'd tape to a birthday gift: *Don't forget to make a wish!*

He was back.

"Hey Mac! Since you're on vacation wind-down, I'll have a coffee and a twinkie to dunk." Williams was new, but he sure as hell didn't act like it. A profiles and motivations asshole.

Me? I believe the evidence. I'm old school. "Sorry kid – too busy."

"You got an investigation, old-timer?"

"Yeah – lookin' into the death of your last frickin' slave!"

When Kramer and Inglis laughed, Williams pulled the disgusted face he did so well and turned for the vending machines himself. The rest of us shouted the same thing: "Black. One sugar."

Then I snatched up the fax and went to see the lieutenant.

It turned out he was real busy, with over twenty open files on his desk. And laid above them, the crossword.

"Hey Mac? The anterior part of a beast. Blank-blank-A-blank?"

"Have you seen this?" I slapped the fax in front of him.

"Sure. They want your notes from three years back."

"Notes? No way, Lenny. I'm going."

"To Denver? But you only got one more day till Disney, Mac. Remember?"

"Screw Disney. I'm going."

The lieutenant's eyelids dropped in that slow, deflating kind of way that always happens when people understand you aren't kidding around. "OK – Disney, Denver. It's your vacation. Come back rested, I don't give a shit."

"Lenny... You're such a dick—"

"HEAD! That's it!"

I left him scratchin' his ass over twelve across.

***

FIVE BODIES, then three years of nothing.

The thing they don't tell you in the academy, in homicide 101, in the case studies, not even in the frickin' movies, is that real murder police don't want them to stop, not 'til we put them away. I thought this guy was in the wind. But now he was back, and I had a chance to finish it.

I bagged the files, chugged the coffee, then flipped Williams the bird. I was going to Denver, but first I needed to head home to pick up my things.

***

MY WIFE MARLA loves to fill her time with all kinds of crap, which can sometimes make her seem super organised. When I arrived back, she already had everything lined up on the porch: the tickets, the luggage, and three pairs of Mickey Mouse goddam ears for me, her and little Jo. She was going to be seriously pissy about the change of plan, so I just lifted my bag and headed out. I'd rather work a case in beach shorts than deal with her bullcrap.

But when I turned, she was already in the yard, between me and the car, and little Jo was with her, looking bigger than I remembered.

"Mac! You son of a bitch!"

"Marla – not now. You know the job—"

"Our first holiday in twenty-seven years? You'd run out on your granddaughter?"

I waved as I made for the car. "Hey little Jo! Say bye-bye to Pappy..."

The wee one just stared at me. Ice-cold. So like her Grammy.

Marla, as usual, laid out her hard truths. "You have never been here. Never. Not for me. Not for your kids. And now, not for your grandkids."

So what? I'd never hid it. "I don't get to be *here*, Marla. If I'm *here*, spending quality time, watching Doctor Phil, sitting on my ass eating crackers, you know what? People die. And killers go on killing."

She rolled her eyes, like she'd heard it all before. Maybe she had, but it didn't seem like she'd ever listened, and that pissed me off. "But anyhow, Marla, didn't you raise the kids how you wanted? Turned them into high frickin' achievers, just like their ma. One touches men for a living, the other serves pretzels and tomato juice at thirty thousand feet! Our son's a frickin' hostess!"

Little Jo's face purpled. "My pop's a flight attendant!" The way she pouted and balled her little fists, I started to wonder if Marla had put the kid through rehearsals. The mini-me similarity was really starting to creep me out.

Then her Grammy lifted her into a hug. "Don't you fret, little Jo. Your pappy's a stupid S.O.B. who doesn't know jack about flight crew or Swedish massage. He doesn't know jack about his own family, and he doesn't care neither. All because we ain't got tags on our toes, right Mac?"

Marla's always been good with rhetorical questions, but that's OK, because I've always been great at not answering 'em. "Enjoy

Orlando," I said, pushing through the middle and closing the car door behind me.

EVEN THOUGH I'D called ahead and left a message for police headquarters in Denver, when I landed, nobody had bothered to meet me. And when my cab dropped me at the Cherokee Street station house, Lieutenant Dannato, so quick to fax that plea for help earlier, looked at me like a dog turd wrapped in tinsel. "I appreciate this effort Mac, but we don't need an assist on this one. But hey, you stay for a few days and check out the museums. Enjoy the Mile-High City!" This guy was grinning wide enough to swallow a bagel, maybe thinking he'd closed the case already. So I asked him for an update, and it turned out he'd pulled in a thumbprint for interview, and was sure he was about to seal the deal.

That was when I did my mindreader act. "That thumbprint of yours... It's a florist, right?"

"Yeah, a florist. How did you know?"

These lazy humps hadn't read the published MO, so I gave him the elevator pitch. "This guy is always the same: he buys a flower arrangement, unsticks the card, real careful, then trashcans the bouquet. He kills his victims on their birthday, and sticks that card to the body using the same tape. We lifted two florists back in the day. Your thumbprint is clean."

Dannato fought back a little, arguing that their florist had previous. Poor old guy had released aphids through a competitor's letter box four years back, unleashing a massacre of the marigolds. Same crime, different species, right? But I could see from the lieutenant's rising neck flush that he knew he'd screwed the pooch. The problem was, I'd showed him up so bad, he still wouldn't put me anywhere near the case.

Only bright side was that Denver PD now had two embarrassments to get rid of, so they let me escort their ex-top suspect out of the building. This was just as well, because for a stone-cold killer, he sure needed a lot of help with the stairs. It also gave us time to talk.

"He writes the cards himself, Mr Sanchez, so unlikely you could place that message, right?" My guy never let them write the card. He just bought the flowers and a blank.

Sanchez was relieved not to be facing the chair because of a twenty-dollar bouquet, and his memory seemed to have jogged a little.

"Card say make wish, no? Don't forget to make wish? Sure, I remember. He writes, but he lean real hard – I see it on paper underneath for four, maybe five more customers. Seem like wrong words to put on a funeral garland, no?"

I felt my stomach drop. The back of my neck was tingling. "You remember the guy? The guy who wrote that? You remember how he looked?"

"Sure, I think. Young guy, nice-dressed, clean shave, wool hat, big smile. Only yesterday, he goes into hotel opposite my shop. Maybe he stay there, no?"

A sketch artist could help, but that would mean cutting in Dannato, a territorial S.O.B. who had just climbed to the top of my shitlist. So instead, I sent Sanchez home and headed for the hotel. It seemed like four years with no bodies had left my guy rusty. He'd made mistakes. Big ones. I just hoped they hadn't stopped at the flowers.

BY THIS STAGE in my career, I can tell what kind of hotel I'm in by the time I'm at the front desk. If the badge gets their respect, that's one thing, but I've seen plenty where I have to flash the Glock. This place was OK. Budget, but on the level.

The guy at the desk, though, had a particular look. He was young, nice-dressed, clean-shaved. Short kinda hair you could fit under a woollen hat. Big smile.

"Officer, I wish I could help, but I flew in from Hawaii this morning. The only flowers I saw yesterday were on a hula skirt!" He even had pictures. His little digital camera put date-stamps in the corner that backed up his story. Damn. "Why don't I fetch Bryan? He filled in while I was away."

Bryan turned out to be a real Grizzly Adams. Not a regular front-of-house guy at all, except maybe at a trapper's lodge. And that beard on his face was sticking his alibi in mine. I didn't appreciate that, so I came on hard, raising my voice a little, like maybe he'd shot my pet moose.

He didn't like pressure, this guy, not one bit. "The dude with the wreath? What's he done? I didn't know nothing! I was just working the desk!"

This was an obvious case of parolee panic, and he wore it like a big tattoo on his ass. Soon, I'd opened him up so much, I started thinking maybe I'd gone to Disney after all: Jiminy Cricket, Tinker-bell and my fairy-frickin-godmother laying the case out all neat in front of me. It plays like that sometimes. You just need to ride it.

It turned out, Grizzly hadn't just seen our guy – he'd spoken to him. At length. Taken real definite instructions. Boxed, addressed, and mailed a wreath for him. Recorded delivery. Still had all the details.

So Jiminy was singing "Wish upon a star" when I stepped onto the pavement, but all these changes in MO were bothering me. Why the hell would my guy be sending a wreath over to an address in Aurora?

I looked at the date on my watch. Maybe it was someone's birthday?

It was already dark when I climbed out of the cab. This wasn't the best part of town, but the bulge under my left arm was my free pass for most kinds of trouble.

The mailing address brought me to a brownstone apartment block, derelict by the look, though sometimes it's hard to tell. I've been to places with row after row of boarded-up windows, and just one or two poor saps with the lights on, determined to face down the wrecking ball. But when I finally found the front door, City Hall had nailed it shut, so even the saps must have left this dump.

These nails were kinda loose in the rotting wood. So loose, in fact, that the door just swung open. No pulled nails, no breaking and entering, right? But screw it anyway; I'd come too far already.

Inside, the block smelled of piss and burned plastic. It was cold, morgue cold, and condensation dripped down walls wetter than one of Williams's Twinkies. A nearby switch turned on some security lighting, which popped and frizzed a little but was just enough to see by. Enough to spot the lily petals on the floor anyhow.

This was the place.

After leaving six bodies for me to find, with all six scenes cleaner than a mortician's table, I didn't see my guy suddenly scattering petals for ambiance... This was a trail, and he'd left the breadcrumbs. Now, I was playing follow-the-leader and flying solo without backup. I loosened my police issue, then I thought better and drew it all the way out of the holster.

Five minutes walking, back to the wall, getting kinda dizzy from my head flapping right and left at every goddam doorway and corner, until paydirt: a room, fifty yards down. Tinsel streamers hung on either side, glittering from light escaping around the door-frame. Somebody must be inside.

But this was one creaky-ass hallway. Who needs burglar alarms when you got floorboards like these? Any minute now, that door could open, and Christ-knows-what would point out... So, I kept my grip tight on my Glock, and hoped lifting my old knees higher than my puckered ass would be enough to keep the noise down.

When I finally reached the streamers, I shouted "Police!" and kicked through the door, showing first my gun, then the rest of me.

My guy was inside alright, but facing away, standing under a camping lamp he had hung from a flex on the ceiling. The lamp was a yellow old thing, flickering like a damp match.

"Hi Mac," he said, turning around.

Barely, just barely, I made out his face in the light. "Alex?" I had that stomach feeling again, and the tingles, this time all over.

"I suppose I should call you Pop, but you were always more Mac than Pop, right?" He had a card pinned to his jacket. I was trying to read it. "You don't disappoint, Mac. Or rather, you disappoint so consistently I was pretty sure I could rely on it."

"Don't play me kid – you could have got your ass shot! Get outta here! Get back to your job!" I suppose even I don't always want to believe the evidence.

"C'mon, Mac! You hated my job. And anyway, my job's part of this. See, I skipped work today, but those planes still fly without me. They fly lots of places. Choosing seven at random, say, Denver, Providence, Chicago, Portland, Burlington, Hartford. And Boston, Pop. Home sweet home. Back where it started."

I said, "You're shittin' me," but it sure didn't feel that way.

"But good news! Today is show and tell for me, Mac, can't you see that? On the flights, y'know, I kept my eyes open. Strangers flashing ID, passports, dates of birth – it's all out there."

"Alex, why?"

He shrugged. "I did good, though, right? I finally found what it takes to get you to the party. I thought I'd stopped but... But I needed to know if little Jo was enough... She wasn't, huh? Shame."

He took a gun from his pocket. Beretta.

I'd never considered how hard it might be to shoot my own son. Impossible, it turned out. Who knew? I figured that would make me number eight. I stopped breathing when he clicked off the safety. But he pushed the barrel straight up, under his own chin. "Tell little Jo I'll miss her. Great kid. Reminds me of Mom."

"Alex! No!"

"Hey, Mac! Don't forget to make a wish."

A sharp crack, and the bullet cut up through his skull, smashing the lamp above, plunging the room into darkness.

It was just like blowing out a candle.

UNDER THE ICE

When the morning sun crested the hills, Ella swept the frost from the cottage step before stooping to inspect the scratches on her door. As she traced the ragged scoring with her fingertips, splintered wood snagged weathered skin, briefly holding her touch.

Each winter outdid the last, and now, the passing seasons inflicted damage beyond her ability to repair. Ella experienced daily the impact of time upon her own body, and like anyone old, understood that some damage simply *was*. Progress and improvement was a reasonable goal in earlier life, but the years brought bleak wisdom: her true birthright was deterioration, with this decaying cottage the final milestone on her journey. All she owned, all she had been, all that *ever mattered*, was here, in this crumbling memorial to her life with Douglas.

She napped most afternoons. Daylight was a pale inoculation for her night terrors. Any space her fears vacated, true sleep swiftly claimed, and dragged deep.

But that day, screams pulled her back.

She jolted upright into a confused, waking nightmare. Long

moments passed before she understood: tourists were playing on the frozen loch. She heard the voices of children, brought here by parents sworn to protect them, careless parents who were blind to the danger.

From her little mattress on the bench, she couldn't distinguish between cries of laughter or shrieks of fear, not with snow melting down necks and sliding tackles on the ice. Nobody could know, not even those on the loch. Not until they heard the frozen cracking, the greedy splash.

Beneath that misted mirror, it was deep and black and cold. Even the shock could kill a child.

SHE HAD ALWAYS KNOWN this place could not be trusted. But those whispers of unease that barely intruded on the earliest days of her marriage had grown in their distrust, year on year. Now, since Douglas's death, those whispered questions seemed to dog her every waking moment. Her first winter without him made her doubt she'd see a second, or that she would wish to.

In truth, it had always been his place, his lonely kingdom. At first, they'd had the romance of a dark fairy tale: a man bewitched by crags and still water brought a wife to the stony land that was his first love. But all fairy tales have a lesson to teach. She'd learned this was not just his first love, surely, but also his greatest. Why else keep them here nigh-on fifty years? Fifty years in a single room of cold stone. Fifty years of gazing at a hungry loch, while it pondered how best to claim her.

All my worldly goods I thee endow... In her darker moments, she wondered if Douglas had given her this place, or given her *to* it. Or perhaps, once he'd finally understood the paradoxical costs of sharing such solitude, did he reach some limit in his capacity to do so?

That had been another frozen day, one where Douglas reported that the overnight winds had taken her broom far out onto the glassy surface of the loch. Reported, and yet, had not retrieved it. The uneasy whispers asked *why?* But back then her trust was absolute, and of course, she had gone to fetch it without thought or question.

It was an ill-fated place for the wind to have blown it. With only three steps more she would have reached her property, but instead, the ice beneath her feet had splintered like a smile. She would never forget that plunging gasp into the water, the choking cold, the sudden, shocking certainty that she was drowning. But in those days her hair had been long and braided like rope, and after minutes of struggle, Douglas used that rope to wrench her to the surface, roughly slapping the water out and the breath back in.

She had never gone back on the ice after that, and from that day, her husband explored the loch alone. That much he'd given her, at least.

As the afternoon sun weakened, the light turned icy grey, a day dressing to welcome the night. Ella hurried outside, gathering in her washing from the frayed line. She hung out only a little washing at a time, and she'd leave nothing of hers out in the dark. Not here. Not in winter.

Bolting the door behind her, she folded the clothes from her basket and finally moved to her seat. She flicked open her husband's old Bible. She always read from it while the clock ticked off the minutes until sleep.

But tonight, her eyes returned over and over to the old iron stove. It was burning low, and the log basket might not contain enough to see her through the night.

She stepped to the window, craning her neck, wondering how quickly she could gather more wood. Quickly enough, perhaps. With recent strong winds, she'd surely find the odd branch or two.

But the dark was drawing together now, thickening while she watched. Thickening around something.

A movement.

Just the edge of a movement.

Out by the loch.

She slammed the shutters closed. The tourists were gone. There was nothing out there.

She checked the bolts on her door. Once. Twice. They were strong. Douglas had understood her nervousness, and even in this place of isolation, he had worked hard to make their home secure. He'd tried to provide anything she needed. Anything, except a life away from here.

She lifted the kettle and headed for the sink. Some tea would calm her. Those familiar sounds brought her comfort: the gush of the faucet, the hollow drumming of the stream against the base of the pot, the snug clank of the lid.

But something strong rattled the door.

A gust of wind? Surely. The wind always rose so quickly here, whistling between the hills without warning.

But there was no whistling before the door shook again. And then the scratching started.

She backed away, falling into the little seat in front of the dwindling fire. She opened her Bible and read aloud, lips moving not to the words on the page, but feverishly, to the prayers she'd learned as a child. "Out of the depths, I have cried to thee, Oh Lord—"

"Moth-er?"

Ella shrank into the musty arms of her chair, breath catching in whimpers. "Lord! Lord hear my voic—"

"Moth-er? I'm freezing..."

The scratching grew louder, a ragged tearing against the wood.

"Let..." Ella closed her eyes, struggling to focus. "Let... let thine ears be attentive—"

"Moth-er? You left me."

"I didn't leave you!" Ella screamed. "I didn't! I didn't!"

At her words, the scratching grew, and with it the brittle scraping of ice against the porch step.

"In the frozen dark... Moth-er."

Then the door slammed. Hard. From the bottom, as though battered by little fists.

"I didn't leave you!" Ella screamed again, forcing out the words between sobs. "How could I leave you? You were never born!"

Silence.

Even the shock could kill a child. And freeze the womb that held it.

Ella cowered in her seat and prayed. With the hours, the prayers became a meaningless jumble and then a broken, fitful sleep.

WHEN THE MORNING sun crested the hills, Ella swept the frost from the cottage step before stooping to inspect the scratches on her door. As she traced the ragged scoring with her fingertips, splintered wood snagged weathered skin, briefly holding her touch.

CHICKEN HOUSE, ALASKA

W hen Kat heard the unfamiliar voice, she crept quietly down the staircase. Someone was entering their living room. She shifted, peering between the banister uprights. The visitor, two steps away from her mother, was a state trooper, a tall man uncomfortable in his uniform. His fingers twitched as he lowered his hat to his chest. "I'm sorry, ma'am. We found the body of Peter Vasnetsov last night."

Inside the girl, something froze.

Kat knew that finding a body was not the same as finding a person. Finding a body meant that the person was gone. And gone forever.

Mom walked to the window where they'd spent much of their vigil, so many hours staring out towards the tree-line. But they'd never see him coming home, not like Mom had promised, with Peter well and back in control and everything good again. That couldn't happen now.

The shutter rattled as Mom pulled the hopper closed. Her hands trembled so much she couldn't work the latch so she left it unlocked.

She sobbed something, but grief garbled the words, something about how people shouldn't be allowed to die, not from a bad back.

The trooper handed over a card and promised to be in touch after he had the medical examiner's report. When he reached the door he turned. "It's a poison, ma'am, is what it is. And it takes good folks as easy as bad, once the claws sink in."

As the trooper opened their door, Kat realised her mom had forgotten to ask about Mishka. She wanted to scream, but the shut-mouth stopped her, so instead she jumped from the staircase, and tore a page from the notepad beside the door. She scribbled, *Where's our dog?* then pressed the paper into the man's hand.

He shook his head. "I'm sorry. We've got no information on that. Hopefully your dog will make its own way home."

The rest of that day passed in a haze of tears and visitors and phone calls until Kat couldn't listen anymore and went to bed. She lay quietly, flipping pages in a book of folk tales Peter had bought for her home-school library. She'd read these stories so many times the pictures turned into words in her mind. But she flicked past Vasilisa the Brave, Marya Morevna, Ivan Tsarevitch and more, finding no comfort. Belief in magic, so easy before, was now impossible.

Her eyes drifted from the book's tarnished colours up to the cold white ceiling, and she wondered about Peter's last days, in the woods in his old tent, with Mishka by his side, struggling for warmth as autumn nights took hold.

She did not remember when sleep arrived, only how its grip was broken. The noise was faint at first, distant, but growing in urgency, demanding attention. Barely conscious, Kat sat upright.

Mishka? Barking?

Still groggy, the girl went downstairs, opened the front door and stepped into the cold air. Nothing moved on the porch, or the road, or further off into the dark, dense trees. She held her breath, peering into the gloom, listening for any repeat of the sound that woke her.

But everywhere was a patchwork of dark silence, so she returned to bed and wept.

WHAT KAT DIDN'T WANT to remember, but couldn't possibly forget, was her last conversation with Peter.

He had started sneakily, as adults often do, telling her what folk tales teach – that bravery helps us face the world, and wisdom helps us make that world a better place. But he quickly reached his main point, which was a big list of ways Kat needed to change. That, for Kat, being brave meant she needed to rise above the teasing and get back to school. That she needed to cooperate with speech therapy. That she needed to learn how to make wise decisions and take charge of her life.

Her response was still in her bedside drawer, a torn page from her notebook. She'd put it there so she could apologise, but now she just hated that page, and she hated what happened because of it. And she hated the stupid, selfish girl who wrote it. The page read:

Who took charge of your life? Are addicts brave? Or just wise?

The night of that conversation, Peter had packed his tent and left for the woods, with Mishka by his side.

And now he was dead.

HARSH FACTS ARRIVED over the next two days, like rocks through glass. A team of Forest Rangers had found Peter's body while patrolling in the Tongass, marking damaged trees for felling. They'd found him all alone, staring at the sky, laying on the body part that killed him. Searchers, who tried but failed to locate his tent had decided the wind had taken it. They'd found no sign of any missing dog. Last, and worst of all, the medical examiner's report contained what everyone was already whispering. Pills poisoned Peter, pills like the ones he'd left home to get free from, only much stronger.

Mom couldn't afford time off to organise the funeral, but Mr Sievert allowed her to make some calls in return for skipping her lunch break. The day of the service came round quickly.

When Peter left, he'd promised Mom he'd come back clean, and it fell to the funeral director to make good on that promise, using care and chemicals. Her stepfather's glossy skin and pressed white shirt were stark against the plain dark wood of his casket.

Five members of his family travelled up from the Kenai Peninsula for his funeral. They were Old Believers, which Peter once told her meant *Russian Orthodox Old-Rite*. He explained how that meant they'd believed something until others started believing something else and so they had to run away to keep believing the old thing.

Kat didn't really understand it.

As long as she'd known Peter, he'd never seemed very religious. He used to say he'd know if something came after once he got there. But he'd told her how he'd loved growing up among his family traditions, so she was glad his people brought those traditions into the front row of his funeral service. The men in their decorated shirts, the women in dresses of blue and red, so eye-catching and out of place. All of them had clutched little leather ropes to help them pray, and many cried while they did so. Kat hoped then that something did come after, just so Peter could see how many people had cared about him.

His family remained for most of that day, and she was glad of their presence. The oddness of their clothes and the strange way Russian and American phrases all spilled together when they spoke reduced the pressure she usually felt in crowds. Between their strange talk and everyone's stories of Peter, her shutmouth never got the wrong kind of attention.

After they left, she thought that maybe the day hadn't been for Peter so much as for everyone else. She hadn't spoken to his family, but she got to cry with them, and maybe sharing pain that way could eventually make it smaller, easier to get past.

But there was something she needed to do first.

When the pastor talked about living up to our responsibilities and getting on with life, Kat understood what that meant. Her dog had been caught up in the horrible mistake she'd made, and she couldn't think of moving on, not until she brought Mishka home.

———————

HER SEARCH BEGAN in her memories, trying to recall Peter's favourite places – places he might have camped with Mishka, places Mishka might still be, lost and looking for help. They'd often gone hiking together when Mom had worked a weekend shift, because he'd always liked the woods better than the water. In the sea, he'd said, we'll always be only a visitor, but we can make the woods our own. Kat liked the woods too – she'd never found a tree she couldn't climb or one that tried to make her talk when she didn't want to.

And Peter was patient with her shutmouth, telling her more than once how great it was to see a kid writing nowadays, and describing how his grandfather had taught him to copy books by hand when he was a child. He had even carved a cover for her notebooks, with a symbol on the front she didn't see again until the prayer ropes at his funeral. It was a tough old leather folder she'd reused time and time again, with a cord she could tie to her belt.

Once she'd compiled her list of places to search, she took that leather folder with her every time she clambered onto her bike. She used it to ask questions of anyone in town or out on the roads. Maybe her home-schooling hadn't been going so well but at least that gave her time to search.

Sometimes it was hard to remember the calm and sensible side of him they'd known before his accident, before the money problems that came from losing his job. He was real sad to be out of work, but it was only when he started visiting the Pain Mill that everything turned for the worst. The Pain Management Clinic hadn't managed his pain, he'd said, just replaced one kind with another. The first time she'd gone with him to get his prescription, she'd waited in the car park watching the guards on the door, wondering what kind of medicine needs a security detail. It was after that she'd noticed the big changes start, the ones that Mom said had made him *erratic*, the ones that ended with him leaving for the forest.

———

ON THE WEEKEND after the funeral, when she had already searched for days and was beginning to lose hope, Mom said, "Mr Sievert asked about you." She said it in the sneaky way you knew meant something important, not looking up from her carrots while she spoke, just chopping and chopping. She'd already sliced way more carrots than they could use for a single meal.

Kat scratched on her notepad: *Why?*

Mom frowned, her shrug half-hearted. "Just taking an interest, I guess."

Kat didn't think Mr Sievert ever took an interest for no reason. If he got interested in something, that meant he was planning to own it or shut it down.

Mom smiled again, but it was a false one, the frown still lingering underneath. "He's got some gym and climbing equipment. He wanted someone who could try it out, point him at the best things. Would you help him?"

Kat scratched again: *Is he opening a gym in town?*

"I don't know what his idea is. Maybe for a club or activity room or some-such."

Kat wasn't sure about helping Mr Sievert. Peter once said that with the power Sievert had over the town, he might as well be the devil. She remembered wondering at the time why Peter hadn't compared him to God, but decided that either Peter didn't like blasphemy, or he didn't like the man, or that it was a little of both.

———

THE NEXT DAY, Mom parked the car outside a building that Kat supposed might be a gym. Mr Sievert stood outside, wearing a dark wool coat that wrapped around him like the wings of a vulture. His black buckled shoes were shiny and his face was solemn. Perhaps he hoped dressing up all formal would make up for his no-show at Peter's funeral. Kat quickly decided that it didn't.

Mom's smile turned awkward as the man put his arm around her, too familiar. Maybe money lets you touch people, even when their face is saying they gotta go. As Mom drove off, Sievert blew her a kiss, but then tapped at his watch. Whatever favour Kat was doing him, he still didn't want to be shorted on Mom's hours.

Then he looked at Kat. "Come here, young lady," He touched Kat's cheek with cold fingers, then looked her up and down. "Getting bigger, I see." He placed his hand on her shoulder and guided her towards the warehouse door. "I was sorry to hear about Peter," he said, although sorry sounded like just a place his mouth crossed to get where it was really headed.

Kat scratched: *Thank you.* What else could she say? She'd rather he didn't talk about Peter at all.

The man nodded. "Isn't it time you were done with the home-schooling and tried to rub along with folks your own age? Maybe even outgrow that shutmouth of yours."

Kat shrugged. Her words didn't work right and people either made fun or got angry waiting for her to finish. Sticking with shutmouth was just easier.

Once inside, the space seemed big enough, but it wasn't a gym, just an empty old warehouse. Or mostly empty: there was a box frame with two small climbing walls separated by a short line of monkey bars. Kat enjoyed the focus that came from climbing, choosing one move after another. Climbing walls, bars, trees and tough obstacle courses – these were all puzzles for her body, and those were the puzzles she had always been best at. But this thing was a reject from a kindergarten. She leapt onto the bars moving herself easily from one end to the other and back again. She could do that all day, but why bother? She dropped to the ground and shrugged at Mr Sievert.

He sat on a stack of mats, tapping the space beside him. "No challenge, huh? Peter always called you a tree-squirrel. Well, don't worry," he said, "this gear is just passing through. I really wanted you here so we could have a talk." He tapped the space again, raising his eyebrows until she moved his way.

As she sat, he smiled and patted her knee, and Kat felt sorry for Mom having to work for him. He was the kind of man you liked less the closer you got.

Mr Sievert said, "So, maybe you know or maybe you don't: I own the pain clinic, and the medics there work for me. I'm sorry Peter didn't trust us enough to get him through this thing."

Peter hadn't trusted the Pain Mill at all. But she'd thought Doctor Williams ran the clinic. It made a kind of sense, she supposed. The doctor had arrived from Tennessee, and maybe he'd needed local money behind him. And maybe Mr Sievert needed someone who knew pills.

The man cleared his throat, his expression awkward. "So, anyway Kat... things have been tough for you guys. But we'll be seeing more of each other. I'm going to be around now and then. Visiting your mom."

Kat's stomach tightened. She stooped to retrieve her notepad and pen: *What do you—*

Mr Sievert stopped her pen. "Now, just listen. This is a private business." He held her gaze. "I'll be visiting your mom now and then. I know you got money problems, and I'll help you guys out. I hear, before things went bad, you had hopes for next spring?"

Kat shook her head. It seemed so long ago, and anyway, she'd suddenly changed her mind.

The man just laughed. He pulled an envelope from inside his coat. "In here, I've written a cheque to the Gym Camp in Anchorage." He tucked the envelope into the front pocket of her denim shirt, snapping the stud shut. "Now. Safe and sound. I'm sure you're gonna love it." He hesitated. "But it's important you don't talk about this." He grinned, suddenly showing all his teeth. "Listen to my foolishness! Of course you won't talk, but like I said, no writing neither. This is private between you and me and your mom. We don't need anyone knowing."

Especially Mrs Sievert. Kat wasn't so young that she didn't understand what the man was hinting at. Peter was no sooner buried, and the horrible vulture had landed.

"And I was thinking," he continued smoothly, "that maybe we buy you a puppy?"

She wrenched control of her pen: *No!*

He grabbed her shoulders. "Now you calm yourself, girl. Last we heard of that dog was, what? Three weeks ago, out at the Chicken House? He's been gone too long now."

Kat froze, swallowing her upset. Three weeks ago was around the time Peter died. And the Chicken House? Was that near where they'd camped?

Her mind raced, but she feigned disinterest, shrugging and nodding, and hardly listening, doing nothing to keep the conversation alive. Before long Mr Sievert dropped her home, and she was happy as he drove off. The man had a lot of attributes that made him plain bad company.

Once she was sure his car was out of sight, she headed to the shed to fetch her bike. Less than four hours to the Chicken House, if she moved fast. She stuffed her pockets with dog treats and then thought more carefully about what she might need. She clipped on the rear carrier basket she used for delivering newspapers and stuffed a rucksack with an extra jumper, some bear-spray, a bottle of water, and a pack of dog food.

Cycling into the chill breeze made her skin tingle. Finally, she had a solid lead to follow. If the weather held, she would make the Chicken House by mid-afternoon. She'd never been to that part of the forest alone before, but she knew the route from her memories of Peter.

LAST TIME they'd been there, Peter had said, "Come on, *devushka*, you don't need to be scared." He had pointed between the trees, towards the clearing containing the Chicken House.

She had already seen it, of course, or why else would she hang back? This was the closest he had ever brought her, but the place still seemed forbidden to her child's mind. An old tribal lodge on four large stilts carved like totem poles. *It should have rotted by now*, she thought. *Why won't it rot?*

She wasn't sure it was even a tribal hut, because how could it be? Since it had no door, it had no purpose. Or at least, no purpose anyone could really understand.

He walked on, but she hesitated before running to catch up, fearful of being alone so close to this place, but aware the safety of Peter's side meant drawing closer still. When they reached the structure, she scribbled with trembling fingers one word: *Who?*

"That is a mystery. No native tribe ever claimed it, but when I was young, I heard about a band of Koloshi – we say Tlingit now – who were taught by Russian missionaries. I like to think they might have been involved. Look."

He crouched down at the rearmost totem pole stilts, carved like the feet of a huge bird. The poles lacked the proud claws of the eagle seen often in native art, neither curved enough, nor strong enough. Kat found them shocking, in a way. Tribal carving was common in Alaska, and she had seen enough to know that chickens hardly ever featured. *Perhaps never. Except for here.*

"These ridges represent the shank, and as we move up the leg, the ridges track backwards around the pole—"

Like a bird's knee, the way it points backwards, she thought.

"—towards the bird's heel, where the feathers begin. What I want you to see is round the back of this leg."

They both stood and Peter reached up, tapping at the centre of the first row of feathers. One feather was only visible in outline, the textured centre replaced by a symbol carved into smooth cedar.

"This is a three-barred Byzantine Cross. The lowest bar, the slanted footrest, points down towards suffering and up towards heaven. Why place this at the back of the two rearmost legs? Are these legs standing with the faith, or walking away from it? We'd need to ask the carver, and we're a century past that possibility, I think. However, Kat, this symbol is Russian Orthodox – I grew up with this."

While Peter was curious about finding religious symbols on the Chicken House, they just made the whole place more out of kilter for Kat. *More wrong.*

She didn't want to even touch the thing, but nothing about it seemed to worry Peter at all. One time, she was stunned when he tied a rope around the pole and his own waist, checking it held his weight. Putting his backpack on backwards, with the opening under his chin he said, "I've tapped in wedges where I couldn't find foot support, but otherwise we can use holds that nature already left us." He stood on the first wedge, raised the rope up the pole, then moved to the next foothold. "I'll remove wedges and resin the cracks next time I'm passing, so long as this repair holds." Eventually, thirteen feet above her, his hands could reach the base of the hut and he shouted down, "I made a new corner piece!" A lump of rotted wood landed on the ground beside her. Staring up for warning of any more fallout, she saw him fish a fresh L-piece of red cedar from his bag and tap it into place.

When he returned, he'd found her staring in horror at insects burrowing in the mould of the discarded wood. He'd placed a warm hand on her shoulder. "Whoever built this," he said, "nature holds the mortgage now, and the place will be repossessed patiently, the way nature does, year by year and plank by plank." Kat found the place creepy, but she understood then that Peter had a strange affection for it. "The truth is, Kat, nature holds all of our mortgages, but if we last as long as the old Chicken House, we can die happy."

The Chicken House was super-old, so Kat doubted Peter had died happy. Since memories didn't normally leave her eyes streaming, Kat put it down to cycling in the chilly wind.

BY THE TIME she finally turned off the road onto the trail path, the woods had grown gloomy. She cycled another thirty minutes before the path ended, then dismounted and walked her bike through deepening vegetation. The trees were denser here than she remembered, crowding close in the twilight. After a few minutes, when the canopy thinned ahead, she saw warning stripes on tape tied around nearby trunks.

Not far on, she found the reason: bank upon bank of giant Sitka spruce, from here and down a steep hill into the valley, had been recently felled. Maybe it was for spruce beetle or storm damage or perhaps even wildfire prevention, but whatever, a game of huge jackstraws now blocked the only path she knew to the Chicken House.

Leaving her bike, she stuffed water and dog food into her backpack. Then she began picking her way slowly across fallen trunks, treacherously slippy from lichens and fungus, and peppered with tripping gouges from saws and climbing spikes. Worst of all, the route drifted gradually off course. She needed to veer left, back up the slope, but the piled trunks were simply too high to climb.

Kat continued on while hoping to double back. But then she saw something. It was a crazy idea really – a gap between toppled trunks, forming a kind of tunnel. That channel seemed to head vaguely in the direction she needed, but it meant walking blind into deep darkness.

With no other choice available, Kat clambered towards the tunnel and headed inside.

AT THE BEGINNING of that corridor of felled trees, the gloom deepened into near-absolute darkness. Around her, scents defined each step: from earthy to verdant to pungent, soft as memory or chokingly sharp. A furtive shaft of dim light broke through above her, revealing a blockage ahead – a leafy limb formed a barrier between the left- and right-hand logs.

She considered turning back, then spotted a sheen of powdery fungus forming and feeding on the damp bark of the branch. As she watched, little puffs of dust from that surface lifted and drifted forward. Perhaps there was an opening ahead, drawing the dust towards it, but more than that – this fungus was continually sending spores into the unknown, seeking, always seeking, never giving up. That was what she needed to do, too. Mishka might be just ahead, hungry, hurt, alone.

She ducked to crawl beneath the branch and through the dying foliage. The smell down there quickly became oppressive. She rarely suffered from headaches, but one was growing now. And she felt a nervous kind of nausea too. Even with glimmers of growing light ahead, something in the atmosphere continued to press against her.

But she continued, crawling and stooping and eventually rising as the strange corridor opened out into the afternoon light. The fresh air cleared her head but built into a whispering wind making its way through the undergrowth. She even imagined words in its movement: *Devushka! Devushka!*

It was strange to hear a word Peter had always used affection- ately, reimagined as an angry hiss. Minds play tricks, she knew, but why recognise a word from sounds so different from the way she'd previously heard it spoken? Shrugging, she beat the dirt from her clothes and shook her head. Whatever for the wind and its tricks – she might be young, but she was still Alaskan. Weather in all its forms was something she had to get used to.

Only twenty minutes after leaving the fallen trees behind, she saw over the scrub towards her destination, now finally visible. The Chicken House.

The building stood, unchanged from the vision in her memory. Weird and abandoned, forbidding in the gathering dark. It was old, but unbroken, wearing the marks of age not as weakness, but more like an ancient authority, demanding respect. For Kat, that respect was respect underpinned by fear.

Whenever Peter let her choose a route on hikes near this area, Kat always opted away from here. But she knew that, this time, she had to ignore her instincts, the inner voice that said no further, the voice that instructed her to leave.

She shivered as she walked towards the old lodge, growing unsure of her purpose. What if Mr Sievert was wrong? Wasn't it crazy to think she could find a clue, and even crazier to imagine she could find Mishka? But a crazy plan was the only one she had, so she kept walking.

It was definitely growing darker.

Geese screamed overhead. How many flocks had stopped here before the weather called them home? Lots, she was sure, because although she hadn't ever noticed this before, unusual numbers of birds had lived and died in this place. She saw feathers and bones, some scattered in the grass, some gathered into purposeful little piles. As she neared the Chicken House itself, she grew colder.

It was like walking through an evil garden, where sticks and broken branches protruded from the earth instead of flowers. Although most were bare, some were strangely memorial-like, topped with feathers, and others, the ones she found most sinister of all, were crowned by bird skulls. The dying sun glimmering faintly through the eye holes, staring at her while she passed. Next, Kat found sticks adorned their entire length with little bones, rising like bleached white fingers from the soil. *Stop!* they demanded. *Danger! No further!*

But she had found no signs of Mishka yet, so further she went, eventually reaching a final boundary marker only ten feet from the structure itself. This one was taller and thicker than the others, more than a stick, a post, one of a pair in front of each totem leg. Perhaps a rope had once been strung between them, or perhaps other posts had once made a fence? Whatever the purpose, these posts were studded with dried chicken feet, hundreds of them, hard and dusty, clambering over each other as if to escape.

These were not here before.

Kat thought of the hardware store in town, with its antler mounts and moose heads on the walls. But if trophies for hunters made sense, then who were these for? Who would preserve chicken feet, and why? She knew people could be weird, and that was their own business, but this was a level of weird that made you stop and think.

She dug into her pocket for some peanuts, filled her mouth, chewed, and decided to search around under the building.

BENEATH THE LODGE, Kat learned nothing, beyond that the place gave her the creeps. Looking up, she saw something not remembered from previous trips. There was a black iron plate in the structure's base, scored with markings that were impossible to decipher from the ground. She'd thought the place was all wood – in fact, she'd been sure of it.

Did the legs look different too? She wasn't sure. She took a step, reaching her hand towards the leftmost pole, but just at her touch, the chill deepened and the wind gave a strangled whine, exactly like a thinhorn sheep she'd once seen struck by a truck. Maybe a storm was brewing, or maybe not. Either way, she didn't like this place. Since there was nothing in sight, she decided to leave.

As she retreated, she scanned the damp ground between and around the huge totem legs. Just as she was about to give up, a glint caught her eye, so she stooped, pulling a long metal stake from the ground. It looked just like the kind Peter used to secure his tent. There was no corrosion either, so this couldn't have been buried for long. It wasn't much, but it was something.

She widened her search, scanning for more clues.

But then she froze.

Above her, the Chicken House, famous for having no door or purpose, was now *open*. A panel in the previously solid frontage gaped ajar. It was an opening where none had been just moments before. She was certain of it.

Kat knew this was impossible, but she also wondered if impossibility might have some kind of meaning. After all, her goal was impossible: to journey into a vast dark forest seeking a dog lost without food or shelter for weeks. On that basis, perhaps this first impossibility might be a signpost. She would climb the totem leg and enter the house. She had seen Peter climb up once before. Of course, she had no rope. But she also had no choice.

The platform of the lodge towered nearly twenty feet above her, and examining the great leg showed it wouldn't be easy. The carved wooden feathers could serve as holds for her hands and feet, allowing her to start the climb. A fall from that height would be nasty, and maybe even stop her getting home. But she put that thought from her mind. Sure, she'd prefer a harness, a crash mat, a safety rope, but this was an invitation from the Chicken House that she doubted would ever come again. Her fingertips were cold, but strong, and she'd get warmer as she moved. She had climbed higher before. She knew she could do it.

As she touched the old wood, readying herself, the wind slithered around the structure, making words in her mind.

> *Little mouse, Devushka, searching for her beast,*
> *But is she truly ready to join him at my feast?*

If crazy were clues, she must be getting close. The wind could make sounds, and sounds might seem like words, but sentences and rhymes were a stretch too far. Since the first impossible thing hadn't scared her away, neither would this.

She reached above her head, gripping a cold, carved feather with her fingertips and raised her foot to balance on a gnarly protrusion just above the carved foot. With one push she was off the ground. But the wood was damp and her second step faltered, scrabbling on the worn surface. She changed her path, climbing around the pole rather than up, finding the inside wood less damp, her grip more sure. A second step upwards. A third. A fourth. But again, the wind coiled and twisted, its breath nipping her skin and tangling her focus.

Little mouse, Devushka, climbing ever higher,
But just one slip, a tiny trip, she's roasting on my fire.

It was uncomfortable hearing words in her mind. Something was trying to scare her, and it was working. But now, over ten feet off the ground, she heeded the warning in the most practical way, and decided not to slip.

The pole turned smooth beneath her fingertips as the feather carving gave way to the smoother and thinner column that marked the final few feet before the base of the lodge. Fortunately, the wood at this height seemed drier and less slippery. She tightly clasped the featherless surface with her hands and scrabbled upwards until she stood straight on the upper rim of feathers she had just climbed. Pushing the base above her to secure her footing, she leaned backwards, her other hand grasping the front of the ledge. She held tight and stepped off the feather rim, swinging on a single arm until the second could join it, then she pulled herself up and onto the surface platform of the lodge.

Kat caught her breath, shaking out tired arms, and facing the inky blackness of the impossible doorway. The dark was impenetrable, like a solid curtain, and the slithering wind enveloped her, as though she had found its source.

Devushka... Devushka... Creep through my open door,
A little mouse might find a place from where she'll creep no more.

259

But she caught another noise, just below those whispers. A faint, laboured breathing punctuated by little whines of fear or pain or both.

So Kat stepped into the portal.

WITH JUST THAT SINGLE STEP, the darkness drew around her, as though the open door she'd entered was now a barrier to natural light. Her eyesight adjusted, but not in a gradual way. Instead she experienced sudden shifts in her field of vision, as shadows opened like curtains, drawing her attention according to some plan.

The wall to her left flashed into focus, revealing a rustic bench arranged with odd items: a stuffed toy, a long animal tooth, a shining comb. Towards the rear of that same bench rested a carved stone bowl and glistening pestle.

A shift at the edge of her vision unveiled an iron stove on the right-hand wall. It was an unnerving sight, larger than it should be, with cold green flame flickering silently behind dirty glass.

With left and right both in view it seemed impossible that the space between – the space directly in front of her – somehow remained shrouded in the darkest dark. Kat screwed up her eyes, trying to see what might lurk inside that shadow.

When something lunged forward, Kat recoiled, a scream trapped in her throat. It was a deep, primal response, triggered without thought or logic, the kind felt only when waking in terror, propelled from nightmare by the scratching of claws under the bed, or the dragging step of a rag-bound intruder.

But this was not a dream. A thing that had been a shadow became an ancient woman, drawing solidity from the darkness. But it was as that process completed that Kat realised her error: it was the other way around. The darkness drew from *her*. This woman was the source.

She was tall, but impossibly scrawny, with arms that hung like branches from the shawl-draped trunk of her body. Her skin was coarse and dark, scored like the rock face of a mountain. Responding to Kat's soundless panic, the woman's laughter was sudden, a harsh cry from behind blackened teeth. And that noise itself was deeply wrong, a sound that shouldn't be, like the strike of a tree against a window on a still night. Kat glanced over her shoulder, towards the silhouette of the door. Perhaps she could escape?

But the old woman's voice froze her feet to the spot. "So, little *devushka*... Do you know me?"

Kat knew the woman, because Peter's book had taught her to know. To know that behind Vasilisa, behind Ivan and Marya, behind all the peasants and all the stepmothers and all the heroes, this woman waited.

"Speak, *devushka*."

The compulsion to answer gripped Kat, her shutmouth broken before a stronger will. "B-b-b-b-b-b-b..." But words wouldn't come, the girl's terror and her stammer locked in a choking spiral.

Skeletal arms lashed out like whips, hard fingers closing around Kat's ears, wrenching her forward. This close, the woman smelled of rot and soil, and the sleeves of her shawl were thistle-rough, cold at the surface, but with the hint of warmth beneath, like spring lurking behind the death of winter. The old woman stooped, bringing her own face directly in front of Kat's.

"B-b-b-ba!" the girl stuttered again, now wild with fear, desperately forcing words that would not come. She felt fingertips, scuttling like beetles across the surface of her face. The scuttling ceased for a moment, while impossibly long thumbs reached around to her chin. Then the pressing began – down, down, down – forcing the girl's mouth wide.

Face to face, Kat saw the ancient woman smile, lick her lips, and then, her bony chin jerked forward as she spat, like a cat expelling a pellet. "Now swallow..."

Kat gagged, but her more powerful urge was to obey. The woman's phlegm was neither pleasant nor foul, but herbal, with notes of grass and birch-sap. But it was stringy, almost fibrous, and hard to get down.

"I said swallow!"

As the final threads slid down her throat, Kat felt a cooling release along the length of her gullet.

"I know you," Kat said. "Baba Yaga. You are Baba Yaga."

The girl saw the briefest of nods before Baba Yaga snapped her teeth, metal clashing against bone. "That is only one name," she said, "and I have many." She stalked over to the stove, threw the door wide and mixed the coals with her fingers. She rose, holding a black rock crowned with green fire. "Some call me crone, perhaps because the night is ancient. Some call me hag, perhaps because fear is ugly. And some call me Grandmother, which is true in all ways save biology." The woman's smile was a tarnished glimpse of silver. She snuffed the flaming coal with her hand before discarding it on the floor and crossing to the still open door to the lodge.

Kat crouched to see if the dropped black shard gave off heat. It did not, but was ice-cold and sharp-edged beneath her fingers, with an interesting triangular shape. She dropped it into her backpack before returning her attention to the old witch.

"So! Your purpose." The ancient woman kicked the door shut and it closed utterly, leaving no seam of light or any evidence of its presence. But now, a slumped misshapen thing that had lain behind that open door was exposed. Peering more closely, Kat realised the thing was draped in cloth, like the burial shroud Peter's family had used to cover his body. The old woman repeated the words "Your purpose." Then she tugged the covering away.

The shroud was not cloth. It was a rugged canvas that Peter had carefully packed before he left, part of their missing tent. Kat dropped to her knees. "Mishka!"

Her beautiful border collie lay still, hardly breathing, a faint whine audible only when Kat crouched near his throat. And he was thin, much thinner than when she last saw him. The usually white coat of his belly was streaked a dirty brown. Kat gently parted his fur, finding mottled abrasions on the flesh beneath, marks from an injury that had bled and dried, but did not seem sufficient to explain her dog's state.

The old woman said, "Your beast has followed a shade into the old kingdoms. Thrice-nine lands, and then he will be gone." She shrugged bony shoulders. "But the beast is not yet dead, and I find this uncomfortable. He is stuck in my teeth."

The girl recoiled at the idea. "You tried to eat him?"

"Stupid girl! The earth does not eat. It swallows." Then, the crone softened, holding Kat's gaze. "But take heart. Your beast is not swallowed yet."

"Can I save him?"

"Perhaps."

"How?"

"If you follow. There are dangers."

"But we could both come back?"

The old woman pursed her lips. "Only if your beast abandons the shade he walks with. The shade is a creature of loss. It is not your father."

"Peter wasn't my—"

"Tsk!" Baba Yaga's glare froze the girl mid-sentence. "In all ways save biology…"

Then, the old woman grasped Kat by the arm. "Now on that path, when life touches life, an understanding can be shared. The beast may return with you, but must choose to do so. Persuade him… for if you attempt to take him and fail, the shade will keep you both."

Kat had come so far, it seemed impossible to imagine failure. "Please, you must send me there! I will take Mishka and bring him home. I will—"

"Patience! A shade's companion cannot simply be taken, for their presence creates a promise. The shade will exchange one soul for another. If you do not wish that other soul to be yours, you must give them the token of another." The old woman stalked over to her table and lifted the stuffed toy. "This belongs to a little boy. He is younger than you, and full of noise. Who knows if he will bring the world good or ill?" Then Baba Yaga raised the comb, golden and studded with jewels. "The precious trifle of a rich woman. She fancies herself a duchess, discarding riches in the dirt. She has lived many years. Perhaps she will not be missed?" Finally, she picked up the broken tooth. "The fang of a she-bear. This bear is a mother with cub. But in a forest of many bears, perhaps one is unimportant?" The old woman handed the objects to the girl. "You must choose a token to give the shade, two tokens will return to me."

Kat stared at the objects in her hands: the heavy comb, the ragged toy, the mottled tooth.

"No time to gawp! I have given all you may know. A young child, an old duchess or a mother bear. You must decide on a token to give the shade. When that is done, the exchange will be complete, and you may return."

Kat stared at the three objects. "But… will they die? If I choose their token?"

The crone shrugged. "All die eventually. I care little for sequence." She picked up her pestle and mortar then walked back towards her stove. "Now the kingdom path is long and steals all vitality. So we must use a faster route, one that takes you to the border of the final kingdom. The crossing may not be easy, but if you succeed, wait there for your beast. He will share his purpose, and you must share your own. One of you will determine the fate of the other."

"How do I get there, to this faster route?"

"You must start in my stove."

What Kat knew from folk tales troubled her. Baba Yaga was unpredictable. Sometimes she helped. Often she didn't. The girl stared into the green flames, marvelling at their cold and hypnotic dance. Then she gazed down at Mishka, frighteningly still and silent.

"Is this the only way?"

"No, you can let the beast die. Otherwise, only this. And soon not even this."

"Will I be in danger?"

The sudden, flaring laugh exposed the harshness of the old woman's features. "Stupid girl! Fate is a road that forks!" But once again the ancient face softened. "Succeed, little *devushka*, succeed and leave with your beast and my blessing. But fail?" Baba Yaga shook her head. "Fail and become a pain in my teeth." The old woman sighed. "A pain that eventually passes."

Kat remembered tales of the Brave Girl pitted against the Old Witch, but this felt like a different story. Among all her doubts, all her confusion, she found only these certainties: she had wandered into the grip of a great power, the great power had known her goal, and now, offered her a way forward. She had never been brave, but she was the girl who had caused a bad thing to happen, so it was her responsibility to rescue her dog from the consequences. "How do I begin?"

The old woman ground her pestle inside the mortar. Then threw it all, pestle, mortar and powder deep into her oven. With a green flash, the fire went out. "The coals are silenced. You may cross. But hurry."

Without a further thought, Kat jumped into the stove.

———

AFTER THE DOOR clanged shut behind her, Kat found she wasn't inside an iron box at all, but crawling along a mist-shrouded surface of enormous dark rocks. She rose and looked around. The rocks seemed to have toppled right and left of her, forming a stony trench. This trench was not so deep as to prevent her climbing out, but she wondered whether walking this trench might not be the best route to follow? There was often a path in her stories and usually it was wisest to stay on it.

She began to run forward.

Eventually the mist thinned, revealing a distant white structure. Sprinting onwards, she found a bridge across a misty chasm. The problem was the chasm came first, then some distance on, hanging suspended in mid-air was the start of the bridge. The distance was too far to jump.

Tentatively, Kat dipped her foot into the wisps and vapours. Her hiking shoe disappeared as ice-cold mist surged hungrily up her leg. Her instinct to pull back was slowed and softened as the mist reached her waist. In fact, she realised then, that cold was not cold, but warmth and welcome. And falling was not falling, but allowing herself to be safely held, forever. The mist would always be with her. The mist would protect her. And, as the mist reached her heart, she knew the best thing – the right thing – was to lean forward and let go and—

But in the distance, a dog barked.

Kat's climber's brain engaged, and she flung herself backwards, away from the mist, crashing painfully down on the black rock. The last foggy tendril withdrew, leaving her shivering, her body chilled and covered in goosebumps.

She lay for a while on the rock, examining the black, almost metallic lustre of its surface. It reminded her, now she looked closely at it, of the texture and colour of the shard of coal Baba Yaga had pulled from her oven. She looked once more at the shape of the chasm leading to the bridge. It was an arrowhead cut from the rock, coiling with the frozen mist.

It was a crazy idea, but on a crazy day in a crazy place, those were the kinds of ideas she needed. She reached into her backpack, feeling the sharp triangle of coal she had plucked from the witch's floor. Perhaps when she entered the stove, its interior had been preserved, but somehow transformed. Was she running on a path the witch had made in the coals? Was this chasm caused by the missing shard? Could, at any moment, an inferno of green flame return and burn her to ash?

The girl threw her shard at the chasm and watched it arc and expand in the air before crashing into the gap with a thunderous crack. It sealed the hole in the landscape like the missing piece of a puzzle.

After one, two, three tentative steps found the rock secure, Kat ran towards the white bridge.

THE BRIDGE CLATTERED and bucked with her movement. On this first span it seemed like a rope bridge, with a surface of uneven white bamboo poles underfoot, but it was longer than any such bridge the girl had previously seen. Rope bridges were common in forest activity centres and tourist trails, but never strung over such a gulf. Far in the distance she saw a landscape, with a faint but darkly serpentine line wending across it.

Other features of the bridge became apparent as Kat proceeded, so she slowed to look more closely. Cables supporting the walkway appeared from the mists above, so now she knew this was a suspension bridge, with both the deck and supporting cables made from the same white substance. At first, Kat reckoned the same bleached canes she walked on had been strung end to end with rope to make the cables, but now, none of that seemed quite right. Many of the white poles were knobbly at the ends and tethered to each other by some bindings in a mixture of muted colours and tones: various browns and blacks and pinks and creams. Whenever she touched those bindings, she found the texture unpleasant, too warm, with a disconcertingly yielding kind of toughness.

Here and there she saw damage, too, passing numerous areas where tethers hung ragged or canes seemed near to buckling. At around halfway, she found the walkway broken, as though canes, struck from below, had snapped upwards. As she stepped around the damaged section she stooped briefly to examine it, and only then, realised the truth: this material was no kind of bamboo. One day, when they'd found an old barbecue drum at the side of the road, Peter brought it home to repair and she'd helped clean it out, removing the detritus of a rotting rack of lamb. She'd seen marrow then, at the centre of the little fingers pointing out from the spoiling meat. It was clear now how this bridge had been made: from an incalculable amount of bleached bone.

An odd crossing had now become horrifying. Previously, she had walked carefully and attentively, but now she had no wish to fully perceive the surface beneath her, or be forced to think about skeletal remains, and fleshy tethers, nor to wonder how many lives had ended to form this structure. She knew that if the witch had told the truth, then this bone bridge would surely take her to the final kingdom, the distant snaking path where she could find her dog, and convince him to come home.

She decided she could spend less time on this gruesome bridge, and better cover the distance ahead, by abandoning caution and running. So that's what she did. And despite louder creaks and wilder lurches, she felt better for it. She could see the end of the walkway more clearly now and would soon be free of these rattling bones altogether.

But with her footfall, increasing numbers of frays and splits and breaks, in both the cable and the deck, really disturbed her. At first, she strode across them without too much concern, but as the gaps in the deck became bigger, her leaps became more strenuous, and her landings brought shuddering impacts to a structure that was her only protection from the mists and the chasm. Jumping was increasingly unsafe, but what choice did she have?

And then, with the end of the bridge in sight, she reached a hole in the walkway that Kat judged to be longer than her own height. It was a leap she thought she could make, but as she launched herself, the cable snapped to her left, and then, upon landing, the bone deck shattered beneath her feet. She threw herself forward, desperately grasping at a brittle surface that seemed no longer able to hold her. The deck collapse continued, first to her waist, then to her chest, then to her armpits. Until she hung there, white-knuckled, holding two bleached bones that bowed and sagged. But did not break.

One breath followed another. Kat dangled from the splintered bridge, watching the last few broken fragments drop silently into the mist. Before that cascade was even over, ravenous cloud coalesced to swallow her legs, and then crawl slowly up her body. *Comfort,* it promised, coiling ice around her heart. *Warmth. Safety.* All it asked from her was so simple. *Just. Let. Go.*

As the mist crept ever higher, her panic rose with it. She could wrench herself upwards, but her sagging handholds might not survive the violent movement and she would fall anyway. Part of her wondered if the mist's promise might be true. It would certainly be easier to abandon this struggle, but it would also mean everything she had experienced had been for nothing. Today, she'd tried to make amends, to do what Peter had asked of her, to make her own decisions and take charge of her life.

Comfort.

Warmth.

Safety.

After everything that brought her here, those words sounded like lies. She'd come here for Mishka, and she couldn't stop now.

To her left, the structure creaked and groaned, desperate to unravel. The centre was already broken. Kat edged herself slowly, one hand after the other, towards the outer edge to her right. *It's just like monkey bars. Easy stuff. Here. It's stable here.*

With a gasp of effort, she hauled herself upwards, pulling first one knee from the mist to the deck, and then the other. After that she rolled onto her back. For a short while she lay staring into the featureless mist above her while a hammering drumbeat in her chest and throat gradually slowed to silence.

She walked the closing stage carefully, negotiating a huge but final gap by shuffling sideways along the strongest-seeming cable. It seemed to take an age, but finally she stepped off the bleached white bridge to the blackened scrub grass of the Thrice-Ninth kingdom.

JUST AS THE old witch had suggested, she saw two distant figures – a man and a dog – approaching on the path. But then, with a lurch, the girl realised those figures seemed to be shrinking, moving further away. Her delay on the bridge had allowed them to pull ahead of her. This was bad. Hadn't Baba Yaga said the crossing took her to the last kingdom of all?

Thrice-nine and then gone.

Kat began to sprint, quickly reaching the dust path that wound its way through the barren scrub, chasing after her dog. Cresting a rise revealed the edge of the next valley, a place where path and land and light ceased altogether. If her dog reached that point, she was sure it was over. And the figures seemed so near to that boundary she couldn't allow herself to stop, couldn't even slow down. Fortunately, their pace was slow, although it pained her to see Mishka had none of his usual bounce or energy. *The kingdom path is long and steals all vitality.*

As she drew closer, she began to feel it herself, a heaviness at first, but growing into more than that, into a repulsion from the dark curtain at the edge of this valley. Every part of her wanted to turn from that wall, to run, to leave this place and head for home. But she couldn't abandon Mishka. So she tried to shout, strangled sounds escaping between desperate breaths, "St-St-St-St-" And in this gasping panic, she remembered her shutmouth, remembered her voice was a disused, broken thing, that words wouldn't come even when she needed them.

But these words *had* to come.

"Sto-sto-sto-sto-P! Mi-mi-mi-mi-mi-shka!"

Her dog froze and barked once, then lay on the ground, whining. The other figure halted too and the face that turned towards her was Peter's face. Tears began to cloud Kat's vision. Here was the man she had cruelly sent into the woods, only to have him return cold and lifeless, his features frozen unsmiling above a stiff-necked shirt, enclosed by the dark panels of a coffin. But now she saw him, living, moving again. Could this be Peter?

By the time she reached them her breathing escaped as sharp gasps between sobs. She looked into Peter's eyes as she approached, hoping for some warmth, some forgiveness, but he shook his head, and held up a hand. He walked between her and her dog, reached one hand down to briefly grab the fur around Mishka's neck. Then he rose again, stretching that same hand forward to point past her, back towards the bridge. The meaning was clear: she should leave, for the dog was going nowhere.

Looking closely now, Kat saw no recognition on this man's face, no warmth or anger, no vulnerability or pain, no love. This thing had nothing beyond a cold determination to reach the boundary. Understanding she and Mishka were entirely unknown and unloved by this Peter-thing, that neither had value to this entity that was leading them towards oblivion, now, that made her angry.

This wasn't Peter. It was nothing like Peter.

Baba Yaga had described him as a shade, a shadow cast by Mishka's grief. But he wasn't flimsy like an ordinary shadow. There was power and purpose here. This man-thing and his dog had walked many lands together, and as they neared their ultimate destination, side by side, he would not permit Kat to break them apart.

She pointed at her dog, but struggled to make the words, so instead walked forward to press her claim. The shade had taken something that did not belong, either to him or to this land. Mishka was living, and Kat meant to bring him home.

But the thing's mouth twisted into an impersonation of her stepfather. Two clicks, a familiar summoning, delivered without feeling. When he turned, striding towards the curtain at the end of the final valley, her dog rose and followed at his heels.

No!

She leaped to catch them,, stooping to grab Mishka's neck. And when life touched life, an understanding was shared.

KAT FOUND herself inside a memory of a tent, borrowing Mishka's eyes, borrowing all his senses. She smelled the cold canvas. She smelled the earth and the leaves and the damp wood of the Chicken Hut that the tent sheltered beneath. But overwhelming everything else in this space, she smelled Peter's sweat. Her master was so many things: *sick, pained, mind determined, body weak.*

All of that, from the sweat!

Her master's fingers brushed her neck, but his voice was tremulous. "Don't worry, Mish! Good boy!" He smiled, but his eyes were dark, puffy. He was shivering and seemed to have missed a lot of sleep.

The swish of footsteps through grass.

A man outside.

She growled and waited.

Coming closer.

Now.

She barked towards the entrance, heard swearing in response. Peter was weak and must be protected.

When the canvas door unzipped, she lunged, but was struck, kicked hard on her side, unable to breathe. In pain, she smelled her own blood, on the fur of her body. On the buckled shoe of the intruder.

Her master tried to rise, but couldn't. "You bastard. Why'd you hurt him?"

"You didn't control your animal, so I had to." Still peeking out through her dog's eyes, Kat recognised Sievert. But she also smelled him: *skin cream and cologne; rich food and wine; leather gloves and waxed waterproofs; malice.*

"Don't you look a picture, Pete! Trying to taper yourself off, huh? I figured you'd be in a fix around now." The man crouched down. "It hurt me how you didn't trust us to help get you clean."

"After so long, it didn't seem getting me clean was a medical priority."

Sievert chuckled. "The customer's always a priority, you know that." He reached into his pocket and brought out a little bag. "These will help with the withdrawal. They're weak, but a couple should be enough to take the edge off. Help you get through the worst." He wrapped master's fingers around them.

Scent bloomed in the air around master: *anger, fear, want.* "I take these now – I'm back in line next week."

"Whatever, Pete. You can tell yourself you don't need them, but that won't last. I've seen how it goes. Take the damn pill. You're a burden on Mary like this."

"Leave Mary alone."

"Come now… It's you who's doing that." Sievert stood up, lifting the flap of the tent. Master threw the little bag at him, but it missed, landing just outside. Sievert laughed, glancing down on his way out. "Say… I'll just leave those in the dirt for you. Free of charge."

After the man left, Master became upset, but Mishka was in pain and couldn't help. Pretty soon after, Master crawled out to burrow in the mud. Then he got sleepy and shambled into the woods. The dog, dragging one leg followed him until he stopped breathing. Then, having failed to protect him, decided to follow his master forever.

KAT WAS LOST in a storm of feeling, crashing waves powered by guilt, and anger. She was almost overwhelmed, but rage couldn't bring Mishka home. She needed to take that pain and swallow it down if she wanted any chance to help her friend.

With his fur beneath her fingers, still reeling from the aftershock of her dog's grief, she tried to conjure a different experience for them both. They had visited Kincaid Park near Anchorage before Peter's accident, not long after he and Mishka had joined the family. It was a place filled with paths and activities and fun and life, a natural sponge to soak up the energy of the two pups they'd been.

So Kat remembered it for them both: walking through trees and running in the warm sun, bike chasing in the fresh wind and playing in the salt spray at Kincaid Beach.

But beyond that, she remembered something else, a feeling so strong for her she hoped it would communicate: one year on from Peter and Mishka's arrival, a once broken family had rediscovered hope. Did Mishka understand hope? She visualised them running together in that same place, not as they did then, but instead as they were today.

She prayed Mishka understood. Kat was offering more than memories – these experiences could happen again. If Mishka chose, there could be other days ahead, new moments of connection, new sensory joys only open to the living. It was a vision beyond here, today, this dark land where Mishka should not be, but instead, of a happy tomorrow and every day after, where cycles raced and dogs ran and everyone played. Together they'd walk trails full of life, not paths for the dead.

Kat knew what Mishka had seen and suffered, and why Mishka was lonely. They had shared that pain now, and Peter was lost to them both. But she and Mishka were alive – and pain was not all they shared. They shared love, too, and they could build more happiness together. The shade could never offer that, could never offer any true connection. The shade offered only an ending.

Mishka, I love you. Come home with me.

KAT ROSE to find a new light in Mishka's eyes, and the dog padded towards her. The Peter-thing, recognising the change, held out his hand in a demand for payment. Baba Yaga had warned her of this: the shade would take a substitute, either Kat herself, or she must give him the token of another soul.

The decision bore down on her. The witch had given her three items, representing a young boy, an old duchess and a mother bear. She must decide who would die in Mishka's place, and she wanted not just what was convenient, but to do as Peter had once told her, to take charge of her life and not hide from it, to be brave and make the wisest choice.

So Kat gave the shade a token.

As the Peter-creature's hand closed around it, she immediately felt a warmth in her mind, a sense that somehow Baba Yaga approved. But that feeling didn't last long. Instead, all hell broke loose.

The shadow wall in front of them pulsed and bulged and ruptured, releasing a massive iron bowl, swiftly followed by a huge stone pestle. The bowl tipped, and something rolled in front of the shade, something Kat feared might be the victim of her decision. Before she could check, the bowl turned its gaping mouth towards her and swooped. She gasped as the pestle jostled and swept and shoved both her and Mishka into the iron chamber.

Then they flew.

The pestle remained out of sight, clattering and thumping below the mortar bowl. Kat knew it somehow powered their journey, perhaps pushing them aloft like a single jumping leg. They crossed the barren landscape noisily – *glide-thud-glide-thud* – leaving the shadow wall and the kingdom path behind them until they reached the bridge. Kat peered over the edge of the mortar, marvelling how that bony structure proven so treacherous and flimsy beneath her own feet, so easily supported the crashing leaps of the witch's iron bowl. This world seemed to play by its own rules.

Soon, even the bridge was far behind, and the bowl took one final mighty leap, higher, ever higher. Still climbing, it wobbled and then shook violently, before finally tipping in mid-air and letting Kat and Mishka plummet towards dirt.

AT SOME POINT, Kat became aware of a rough, damp, warmth, recognising the playful insistence of a tongue lapping her cheek.

Mishka!

That her dog had slurped her awake struck the girl as so funny and joyous, her grogginess moved immediately to laughter. She hugged her friend close, and they giggled and yapped and tickled and growled to be alive and together in the dark. Then, pulling water and food from her rucksack, she emptied the dry pellets into a pile before cupping her hands to let Mishka drink.

With her dog finally satisfied, she looked around. They were in front of the Chicken House, which was now doorless and devoid of life. She didn't know how much time had passed, but it was certainly darker than when she first arrived. So she and Mishka set off on the route back to Kat's bicycle. Mishka walked tentatively at first, limping slightly, but gaining in confidence as they moved through the tunnel of trees. Her dog was less frail than Kat had feared, given everything he had been through, and she wondered if Baba Yaga had some small part in that.

When they finally reached the bike, Kat wheeled it out to the trail path tarmac before helping Mishka jump into her newspaper delivery box. It was a trick they'd performed before, and Mishka kept watch behind them for the long pedal home.

———

WHEN THEY FINALLY ARRIVED, so long after curfew, Mom was angry and upset. But when she saw Mishka, all questions about her daughter's whereabouts were answered by a flurry of barks, leaps, and excited yaps. "You took a real risk," she said, taking the weight of the rucksack. "But thank God you're home."

After a long reunion in the hallway, Mom sat Kat down and her face grew serious. She looked briskly through the rucksack. "Mr Sievert mentioned he gave you a cheque to pay for camp. That was nice, right?"

Kat's hand drifted towards her empty shirt pocket before she dropped it to her lap. She shook her head.

Mom tipped the bag onto the sofa. "You're sure? No cheque?"

Kat shrugged. There was no cheque. Nor any Mr Sievert. Not any more.

Mom's mouth tightened as she saw something glinting underneath the empty dog-food wrapper. "Oh my God! Is this comb real? Are those rubies?" She spotted dirt and moss between the golden teeth. "Did you find this in the forest?"

Kat nodded. Two tokens must have gone back to Baba Yaga, just like the witch had promised. The girl took the comb and placed it aside. They'd have it valued, and hopefully that might help take some pressure off Mom. But Kat couldn't feel good about that, not yet anyway. All she felt was responsibility for the decisions that got them here.

"But Kat, Mr Sievert's coming by tomorrow. What will I tell him about the cheque?"

Mom felt responsibility too, but she didn't need to. What happened to Mr Sievert's token was all on Kat, and another word for responsibility was burden, something she'd have to carry forever.

Wanting to scratch a message, Kat looked down at the pile for her little notebook, but it was gone, vanished somewhere in the forest. Those woods were vast and deep and dark, and things lost out there, like her little book, and Peter, and Mr Sievert, well... those were things you might never find again, whichever path you took.

She understood now, that losing things was part of life, but finding things would be too. You pick a path. You walk it. And you learn from every loss and every discovery.

Mishka snuffled at her fingers, and Kat had a flicker then, of another thing she'd learned, because there was something else, a trickle of memory, swelling into a feeling, and then a flood of taste, of grass and birch-sap, a witch's gift. A gift from her grandmother.

"M-Mom," the girl said, "everything's g-gonna be OK."

REMEMBRANCE DAY 1968

W hen they tuned the wireless to the Armistice Day service, I shoved my plate away and left the café. Fifty years after that bloody war and still they won't give an old man peace. I slammed the door behind me and glared back through the window, challenging anyone to meet my gaze.

But just for a moment, the reflection in the glass wasn't my face. It was something else, something sallow and insect-like, eyes distorted, round, glassy. And then it was gone, leaving just a frightened old man and the puzzled faces of the people inside.

ALL THE WAY home I felt observed. And even though I couldn't see my follower, I knew they were there. Their presence flickered in the corner of my eye, tingled at the nape of my neck, drilled into the small of my back.

I arrived unsettled, finding the tenement door banging harshly in the wind. My neighbours had left before me, and I always latch the door. Always.

Inside, pale light barely trickled through the windows, and the grey stairway was wreathed in shadow. I gripped the banister as I ascended, moving slowly both through caution and infirmity. But as I reached the first landing, other footsteps joined mine like a broken echo, an awkward irregular sound; a step, a drag, step, drag. I cried out, staring behind me, certain of a follower, but I was alone.

When I entered my home, I knew something was wrong. Badly wrong. On the piano, my old photographs were moved, adjusted. Looking closer I saw the tracks in the dust from where they sat, where they had *been* sitting when I left that morning. Panic took hold as I noticed the other things. My letters, stacked in the bookcase, untouched for years, were disarranged. My old cigarette tin, thrown to the floor.

Someone had been here.

My thoughts raced desperately. The door had been locked – both Yale and mortice, and no-one else had keys. No-one.

I searched around the house, over and over again. Perhaps I'd moved things myself. Certainly, I was becoming more absent-minded as the years wore on. I must have been mistaken.

But then I saw it –something that didn't belong, something that had replaced my medal case on the mantelpiece.

A gas mask.

Sallow and insect-like, its round, glassy stare drew me like an accusation.

It was unmistakable: tattered yellow skin, eyepieces streaked with dirt, straps knotted and torn from hard use. The barest touch conjured a burning stench, as chlorine stung my eyes, dragging me back. Back to somewhere I hadn't been for fifty years.

YOU FIND out a lot about yourself at the front. There's no hiding from it. In the threatening quiet, waiting for the next attack, or when mortars rain down around men screaming and falling in mud that's more blood than water. You find out what you are capable of.

One of the lads had something wrong with his foot. Not badly as things go, but he expected a recall from the front line. Just a couple of days, and he'd have been safe. That's all it would have taken.

I'd known him as Davie.

I shouldn't have been away from my kit-bag, but with the calm morning and some lads playing cards further along the trench, I'd felt safe enough to join them in a hand or two. I'd just slapped three aces onto the crate when the gas shells dropped.

Only me and Davie survived the initial blast.

I knew I'd never make my pack – the stench of chlorine was rising, and once it gets in your lungs, once it takes hold, you can't move, never mind run. I reached his bag before he did. It was as simple as that.

When one man lives and one dies, there is no order, no rank, no honour. He watched me, helplessly watched me strap the mask into place. His eyes burned at me, like black fire, searing through the vapour; then he started choking.

And I turned away.

There are things we must bury. I'd buried this and left its grave unmarked. I'd hid it in some hinterland of lost memory and covered it with five decades of neglect. I'd left it trench-deep in a Belgian field. But now it was back, vivid and clear, sharp as the spike of a bayonet.

I sank to the floor, clutching the mask against me, feeling the dirt grind to nothing beneath my fingers, feeling the rough casing disperse, melting away like a wisp of poisoned air, or the soul of a fallen comrade.

And when I thought of all I'd done with Davie's life, of how I'd used the fifty years I'd stolen... I wept.

OUBLIETTE

PART I – THE WEIGHT

It was always quiet behind the glass.

The glass room was Michael's oasis of calm, his refuge while Crowther paced to and fro, yelling, slapping at his apron, banging clouds of flour from the workbench. This was the best way to observe someone dangerous. Even when his tutor, wild with rage, wrenched dough-hooks from the mixer and threw them to the floor, there was no sharp crash behind the protection of the glass, only a soft, hollow echo.

Everything here was muted and distant.

Everything here was safe.

This was the first time he had used the glass room at college, but he was glad to know that it worked. He could come here so easily now, after years of practice. It was his sanctuary. His place of peace.

Far away, outside the glass, his teacher still screamed quietly. By now, Crowther was purple-faced. "Knead the dough!" he whispered. "Feel the proteins! Use your hands! Be a chef! Be a chef!"

Dimly, Michael wondered if his own calm was sustaining this

rage, but then, another voice intervened. A friendly, chirpy voice, entirely unrattled. "Sir? Do you get better elasticity from a strong flour with less kneading or a normal flour with more kneading?"

Crowther froze, puzzled, before mumbling about pieces of string. Then he moved on to spread wisdom at another bench.

Later, when leaving the class, Michael heard the same friendly voice behind him. "Don't worry man – he's watched too much Gordon Ramsay, I reckon." Michael kept walking, hoping to get away, to make it to the library where he could read alone before the next session, but slowed when the hand touched his shoulder. "Hey. I'm Robbie. Relax, big man... A wee roasting in a kitchen? That goes with the territory."

Michael flushed and smiled. "Michael. I'm Michael."

Robbie beamed. "Micky the Mix! Jees-o, where was he headin' though? How do you up the ante from that? Hara-kiri with a balloon whisk?"

He speaks a lot, thought Michael. *But I like him.*

"I kid you not though Mix, if I'd had the bollocks, I'd have used the Kenwood as well. Those enriched doughs don't half banjax yer manicure."

Michael was happy to agree. "Yeah. I'm all about the technology."

Sometimes the truth was worse than a little lie. Especially when it sounded so *off*. A catering student who didn't like the sound of dough slapping off the table, who was uncomfortable with feeling it give against the impact of his fists, who preferred to leave the tugging, pulling, and pummelling to a machine?

He didn't want Robbie thinking he was weird.

Fortunately, Robbie was more interested in organising a game of pool, so Michael agreed, even though it meant exchanging phone numbers.

Day 1 – Faither

The following morning, he left his room even knowing his father hadn't yet gone to work. It was unavoidable. Some days, Faither hung back, simply so he could catch his son and enjoy some baiting with his breakfast. "Morning, fatty. You're still eating your class-work, I see."

"Did you get the bagels I left out?"

"Aye. Crap. Catering bloody college. A step doon fae hairdressing."

Michael didn't want to hang around for the rest of it, since he'd dallied in his room too long as it was. "Got to go – I've got a lecture, first thing."

"Lecture? Here's my bloody lecture: get a trade, ya useless lump…"

Michael tried to edge past, but Faither reached across his path to the kitchen drawer. He opened it, took out a roll of twenty-pound notes, and counted six into his son's hand. "When you pass the post office, go in and pay the electric. No pissing about. I need eight quid back."

"OK."

But still Faither blocked his way. Something was coming. Michael felt it in the air.

"What have you heard from her?"

"Nothing. Honest." Michael reached for the door, but Faither caught his wrist and pulled him close, glaring. It was best not to stare back, so he dropped his gaze. And it was best not to pull away. Best to wait.

Seconds passed. Whatever happened next wasn't Michael's decision to make.

Eventually, Faither's glare softened to a sneer. "Ye cannae knock the fight out a pacifist. Waste ae bloody time. Away and boil yer jam, ya jessie."

Released, Michael stepped into the rain-sodden balcony that led to the common stairway. As the door closed behind him, he glanced backwards through the glass panel. Faither had turned away. He breathed, and headed downstairs.

He often thought about Mum on the walk to college. The cooking thing had started with her, because of her, really. Her food was never good enough, but it turned out Michael's was a permissible novelty. It became his way of stopping it. He'd never been strong enough for the other way.

And of course, he hadn't stopped it forever.

HE SAW IT ON THE STUDENTS' Union noticeboard. It was just the corner that caught his eye, a sliver of sepia sticking out behind a sheet of pizza discount vouchers and a poster for an anti-austerity rally in George Square. It was a weird thing when he looked at it.

Secret of the Siberian Superman!

There was a picture of some big skinhead holding what looked like a bowling ball with a handle in front of a wrecked forest cabin. And in front of him, crouched at his feet, was a much thinner man and child. Both wore uncomfortable smiles stretched across sickly faces. A caption to the picture boasted about this: *I was once like my son and my brother. You can see the bad blood I overcame.*

The product being offered was a *girya* – which just seemed to be a kettlebell – and it was an old piece of Russian military exercise equipment. It looked rusty, but it was free. Apparently, they were looking for the right person, whatever that meant.

Daft.

Just call Paavo, the flier said. There was a page stapled to the back, written in a foreign language, so Michael turned back to the photograph.

The skinhead wasn't just big. His grin was angry. Ferocious, even. And he had something in his eyes. The sort of eyes it was best not to look into. His relatives had none of that power.

How could lifting a weight do that?

There was a mobile number, but it was probably a con. Still.

Michael ripped the sheet off the board and ran to the college library, hoping to make some sense of the stapled page.

A FEW HOURS LATER, after an afternoon practical, he took the advert out and showed it to Robbie, who said, "Don't buy the weight, Mix. Buy the kid. Give him a life away fae that psycho."

"It's a free-cycle, I think. You don't pay for anything. I'm curious."

Robbie tapped into his phone. *My mate is interested. How does he apply?*

Michael said, "Tell them I feel ready."

Robbie made the addition and the message whooshed into the digital void. "It might be gone already, Mix, but you never know until you ask."

"This photo looks dated, right?"

"Aye. Ancient. Or they took it last week with a filter."

"But I mean this kid… he might not be a kid anymore."

"Maybe not…" Robbie said, looking again. "But I'd put money on Buzz-cut Boris still being a psycho."

They were still laughing when Robbie's phone rang and he handed it guiltily across to Michael

The male voice on the other line was clearly foreign, but the timidity and nervousness needed no translation. "It was my *Isä* – my papa's weight. He want it given. His will."

"Oh. I'm sorry… So you're the boy – the one in the picture?"

There was a pause. "I'm Paavo. Yes, boy, but long ago. But this not about me. His will – I agree to do it. You sound good. Right. Will you take it?"

His accent was unfamiliar, a little like Dutch maybe, but different. Anyway, decision time. "OK. I'll have it. Where do I pick it up?"

"No. No need. It heavy. I deliver."

This didn't seem right for a freebie and Michael said so, but Paavo insisted. "His will. I agree to do it. No problem."

Michael gave his address and phone number and then tried to forget about it. Probably nothing would come of it. Anyway, he had to run for a lecture on Kitchen Management. *Crowther with a suit on. Deep joy.*

IT WAS dark when he turned into his street, but he spotted the car straight away. The headlights caught his attention. He hadn't heard it drive up, so perhaps it had been there a while. Anyway, as he walked closer, the driver's door opened and a thin, almost stick-like figure waved. "Michael? Michael? Paavo!"

Michael was surprised. "Hey, Paavo! That was quick!" It was more than quick – they'd spoken a little over two hours ago.

"No problem! I get it!"

Paavo beckoned him round to the boot of the car. The engine was still running.

"Did you just arrive?"

"Only a while – I leave immediately we talk, but... traffic, you know."

He smiled and shrugged, but it was a big smile and a bigger shrug. Something exaggerated about it. Probably nervous.

The boot opened and Michael reached for the solitary box. But Paavo stopped him. "No. I get. I have to give. His will. You know?" Paavo grunted, picking up the box to proffer it. It seemed a pointless piece of theatre, but Michael waited and accepted it from him.

The box was heavy – way heavier than size would suggest. About as heavy as the microwave ovens in college.

Heavy footsteps behind them. "What's this, lads? Some kind of contraband?"

Shit. Faither. "No. Just someone from college."

"The Blimp and the Needle, eh? Dangerous situation."

Paavo offered his hand. "Hello, I Paavo." Their visitor's expression at that moment was reminiscent of the old photograph. The same scared little smile.

Good instincts, Michael thought. He knows danger when he sees it. Faither ignored the handshake and just looked the thin stranger up and down.

Paavo backed away to the driver's door. "OK... Anyway. Job done. I go." He was inside in no time and moved off without waving.

Faither stared after him until he turned the corner. "So. Who was that weaselly little bastard? Skinny isn't contagious, you know. You won't catch it hanging about with anorexics."

Michael wanted to head inside, but Faither wasn't moving. "Just a friend. Lending me something for college."

A snort. "Aye, right. Open the box."

Michael tore at the tape and peeled up the right corner, revealing a surface of scratched black metal.

"Lying tae me? That's no for college."

Michael flushed. "S-Sort of is. It's a weight. I wanted to get fit. F-For exercise."

Something about this amused Faither, but he seemed to believe it.

"About bloody time... Get started then. Run up the stairs and get the dinner on." Michael ran as best he could. The box was seriously heavy.

LATER THAT NIGHT, when Faither had gone to bed, Michael used his keys to rip through the remaining packing tape on the box. The kettlebell inside was older even than it had seemed in the photograph – the black surface was flecked with rust and covered in odd symbols and scratches. The handle was partially covered with fraying lengths of dirty grip tape. The weight wasn't new or polished or sterile, but that just made it better. It had been in the world and been touched by it, and to Michael it reeked of a life and a freedom he wanted for himself. He manipulated it slowly and carefully. A single fumble might crush his foot, or worse, wake Faither.

Turning it over, he noticed something unusual. On the bottom, four shining silver screws secured a small plate about one-inch square. He guessed it might be for adding or removing extra load, but the chrome screw-heads were so incongruous against the black pockmarked surface that he couldn't leave it unexplored. He fetched a small multi-tool from his drawer and removed the plate. The underside was scratched with some faint letters – *ITSE?* –that Michael didn't recognise. Inside the cranny exposed by the plate's removal, he found a rolled cylinder of paper sheets wrapped around a polythene bag.

The sheets weren't packing material, but instead, a highly detailed sequence of hand-drawn exercises. They were labelled: *Päivä 1* up to *Päivä 3*. Each page offered illustrations of a figure engaged in unusual movements. Very few of those exercises were recognisable as standard lifts. Instead, they seemed to be sequences of specific postures and precise motions. The skill in the drawing was clear, and the movements, although fairly involved, were presented in segments simple enough to follow.

The polythene bag contained an uneven dark-greyish powder. In permanent marker, someone had scrawled *proteiini jauhe* on the polythene. A diagram on the third sheet showed the contents of the bag used to make a drink.

Michael's thoughts betrayed his attempt to focus on the pages. They pulled him back to when he was forced to open the box outside. To the mockery playing on Faither's lips when he heard his son wanted to exercise. To the insults-as-humour over dinner and the passivity and submission imposed on his every waking moment.

Even if it changed nothing, he wanted to begin something now, something of his own. He rose, stealing some blu-tack from the corner of a football poster Faither had stuck on his door, and mounted the first sheet on the wall where he could see it clearly.

The first sequence contained a spiderweb of detail. It began with the weight pulled close to his body. The movements shown in the pictures felt unnatural, not just because he was unused to exercise, but more because the motions delivered an eerie focus that he hadn't experienced before. Alongside this unfamiliar attention, a kind of certainty grew, a resolve that this was something he needed.

His muscles ached as he repeated the sequence, but with each repetition his exultation mounted, spurring him to even greater fervour. It was as though he were, for the first time in many years, taking ownership of his body. These movements were a summoning ritual, manifesting a physicality he had always denied himself.

Day 2 – Dreams and Other Nightmares

Seeing her again was all that mattered. She was ahead of him. He knew it was her – he could see her clearly, but he needed to warn her about her shadow. The shadow she cast was wrong. It wasn't her. It was someone else, something else, trying to rise from the ground at her feet. He needed her to be safe. He needed her to turn around, to see. He followed her, waving and shouting, running as fast as he could. But none of it was working. His chest ached, but she was always moving ahead of him. He couldn't get her attention and—

"Blubber boy!"

The voice shredded Michael's dream and his eyes snapped open. Faither. Standing inside the room, looking down at the bed, and the weight discarded on the floor after his exhausted collapse just before dawn.

"Getting busy last night, were ye?" That smile again.

"I was just looking through it."

"Takes more than jist looking tae shift the flab, fat boy."

There was a pause. Why was he here? Then Michael spotted what he was holding.

"What's wrong?"

Faither held up the phone. "A couple of new numbers on here. So you're talking tae her?"

"No. That was Paavo. You know – the guy who dropped off the weight?"

Faither was already dialling. He put it on speaker and didn't take his eyes off his son. *That's why*, thought Michael, *only the truth*. Only ever the truth. Lies can always be discovered.

From the speaker: "Hi. S'Paavo. I'm away for some days. Leave a message!"

"Ah fuck it." Faither cut the call and moved to the message logs. "We're not finished. Who's this sending you text messages?"

"That's Robbie. He's a guy in my class."

"A lot of new mates all of a sudden."

"He's just a guy I met. Look at the message – he calls me Mix. I don't know him all that well. Yet." Michael's eyes pleaded, but he knew nothing was more certain to get Robbie a call than asking Faither not to.

"Convenient. Let's see." He started typing, narrating as he went. It was an out-of-date camera-phone with multiple letters per key, but he was reasonably fast. Faither had bought the same phone for each of them some years back, ensuring he'd always know his way around the interface. "FOUND – THIS – PHONE – INSIDE – AN – EMPTY – BOX – OF – DOUGHNUTS." He glanced up to ensure his humour was appreciated.

Michael cringed. "Aw please – c'mon."

"DO – YOU – KNOW – THE – OWNER?" He held Michael's gaze again. "Sent. I'll hold on to this and we'll see who responds, won't we?"

Faither tucked Michael's phone into his top pocket and turned to leave for work.

AFTER ENVIRONMENTAL HYGIENE, Robbie approached Michael. "Mix, are you short a phone? I got a freaky text…" Michael flushed. Robbie wasn't stupid. Revealing Faither's "sense of humour" would disclose everything. Nobody wanted to hang around a car wreck like that.

He hoped his face showed relief. "I… I think I lost it in the supermarket. Did someone contact you?"

"I think you mibbee dropped it in the bakery aisle?"

"Could have - I like supermarkets. I walk all the aisles even if I'm only there for one thing." It was a habit he'd learned with his mum, a fragment of truth to make the lies easier to deliver. He continued. "So… did you reply? What did you say?" Michael knew he wasn't doing a great job of hiding his concern, but the wrong message could easily have consequences.

"I just said I was a classmate, and they should hand it in to the college using my name. I didn't want to give yours in case they could use it for some kind of identity theft. They can empty your bank with toenail clippings nowadays."

Michael was relieved. "That's ideal. Perfect in fact." He could see some confusion on Robbie's face, so he quickly changed the subject. "Does your phone have internet?"

"Aye, sure. They all do nowadays, right?"

Michael shrugged. "Can you translate something – save me going to the library?" He pulled out the sheets and the powder from his bag. "These came with that old kettlebell thing. It arrived last night."

Robbie took the sheets and whistled. "Somebody put a bit of effort into these. Look at the detail – you can see scars on the body… Weirdly intense face…". He screwed up his nose examining the label on the bag and typed into his phone. "What's dot-FI in a web address? Finland? Aw check this… I'm getting fitness sites. Looks like the bag label is Finnish for Protein Powder."

Michael nodded. "Finland makes sense."

Robbie was still typing. "And assuming these headings are Finnish as well… Google says PAIVA means 'Day', so I'd guess you've got instructions for three-days-worth of body-buffing."

"I suppose you just start again from the beginning after you finish the last page. Doubt I'll accomplish much in three days…"

"Says you, Negative Nancy! Looking at day two, you'll easily achieve a hernia."

Robbie felt the texture of the powder through the bag and screwed up his nose. "I'd drink cat piss before I tried this stuff though."

Michael had been thinking much the same, but hadn't been sure why, so asked, "How come?"

Robbie shook his head. "I've seen exercise supplements before. This just, like, looks wrong – feels wrong too. It's gritty. Too dark… Uneven texture. Just weird." He looked away, as though remembering something.

"What?"

"Nothing. Just don't drink it."

"No chance of that," Michael agreed, and they headed off for a game of pool.

MICHAEL KNEW the game would get away from him in a major way when Robbie's juke box tracks started to play. First up, "Freebird" by Lynyrd Skynyrd, which, inexplicably, acted as a performance enhancer for his opponent. The black was sunk before Michael got another shot, but he didn't mind in the least. It was the most relaxed he'd been for weeks, and he would happily spend another couple of hours here. Robbie was starting to rack them up again when a woman approached.

"Excuse me? Are you Michael Thomson?"

She wasn't anyone Michael recognised. Faither's chaos toppling more dominoes, probably.

"Yes, I'm Michael… Are you here about my lost phone?"

"No… I'm Mira Brookes. I'm the Women's Officer for the college."

Michael shook his head. This wasn't adding up.

She drew him to one side. "Do you know an Angela Dean?"

Suddenly, he felt sick. His eyes hunted around the games hall. Everything was moving in slow motion. Glacially, students stroked little puffs of chalk from the tips of cues, swayed to the lights of the pinball machine, pushed coins towards slots. Robbie, still lining up his break, was completely oblivious.

Michael replied in a near whisper, "She's my mum."

"Yes, Michael. Your mum contacted us from part of the Women's Aid network. We can't give specific details for her security... Are you OK?"

He wasn't OK. You always have to limit feeling. To narrow-down. To focus. He knew this. But he couldn't. He was shaking and didn't answer. Mira continued.

"Your mum wants you to know she is well. Do you understand? She wants you to know she is in good health."

Michael remembered the night he'd taken her to the hospital, her jaw hanging loose, the face of a broken puppet. He also remembered how, even then, her eyes had attempted to express comfort, her efforts undone by drying blood and missing teeth.

She'd always tried to protect him. Normally she avoided him seeing the violence, but she couldn't stop him hearing it. He still woke hearing it, most nights, even in the months she'd been gone.

"Michael – are you OK?"

He nodded numbly.

"She doesn't know if it is possible, but she wants to have some kind of contact. Do you have a safe number she can reach? And any preferred time of day? It might not be immediate, but she'll try when she can."

Robbie was leaning on his cue, watching them, concern growing. Michael needed to regain control. Now. "My phone is missing. Robbie, can I use your number?"

His friend didn't hesitate. They agreed he could take a call any weekday lunchtime, and Mira left with the information.

They played a few more shots before Robbie raised it. "So, big man. Care to share?"

He didn't, of course, but Robbie needed to know something. "It's my mum. She left a few months back. It's complicated."

"Sounds rough. I've only got my mum. We left my dad when I was younger too." Robbie looked to Michael as though for the possibility of some greater insight, but the awkwardness took him back to the game and he missed an easy black. "Anyway... Explains why you looked so shaken up. That's bloody parents for you."

"I... I've just not seen her for months."

"Shock to the system then?"

"A wee bit."

They left it at that and carried on working through the pile of pound coins they had used to secure their table.

FAITHER HAD LEFT for the pub by the time Michael reached home, so he skipped dinner and went straight to his room. When he pulled the weight from under his bed, the stretch across his shoulders felt good and alien, like a joy he'd somehow stolen from someone else.

He swung the iron ball in a circle passing it hand to hand, loosening up for three or four minutes. When he turned to the drawings, the second sequence was as achingly special as the first; gloriously detailed, but unlike anything from the first day.

He stuck the sheet to the wall and followed it as closely as he could. It was strenuous, but not tiring, and he felt nothing but pleasure in the rising tempo of his heartbeat. As he mastered the initial complexity, he found a soothing, near-hypnotic quality to the drumbeat rhythm of his feet against the floor. He repeated first each movement and then the overall sequence with increasing fluidity.

The bare bulb in the room threw a yellow glow, casting a shadow on the floor that traced his motions like a dark echo. At a certain point in the dance, the silhouette flickered, losing rhythm. It was a jarring discontinuity. How had he caused it? What had he done?

Michael continued, concentrating on the flow of his movements, fixing his eyes on the carpet. He didn't wait long before catching another flicker, and immediately afterwards, an odd distension in the silhouette. Then finally, for moments of motion, the shadow-shape peeled away and moved independently.

Michael's surprise was not so much at this vision, but at his own reaction to it. He felt neither fear nor confusion, only excitement. And more, even, than that: a tumult of emotion swelled beneath the excitement, equal parts restlessness, impatience and anger. But anger most of all. Oblivious now to the silhouette, the flow of the sequence grew stronger, but the anger remained, harnessed and channelled, fuel for the dance.

Hours later, when Faither staggered in after his night out, Michael slapped his light switch, plunging the room into darkness. He waited silently in the shadows until he was sure it was safe to resume.

Day 3 – Transformations

At breakfast, Faither ignored the French toast Michael had prepared and barely sipped at the tea, turning his bloodshot eyes away from the painful sunlight streaming through the window.

He growled. "No fry-up after a night on the piss?"

Michael apologised and offered scrambled eggs with mushrooms. It wasn't wise to point out that he'd had no warning about Faither's drinking plans, so he didn't.

His father slapped a phone down and slid it along the tablecloth. "Take this bastard thing. Your wee pal wants it delivered tae the college. Well, fuck that!"

Michael picked it up and dropped it into his rucksack.

"I'm replacing a boiler all day, so sort the dinner when you get home. I'll text you if I want anything special, understand?" Michael nodded and thanked him. If it wasn't so useful having an errand-boy, Faither probably wouldn't permit Michael to carry a phone at all.

DURING FIRST PERIOD, as Michael rooted through his bag , Robbie spotted the LED blinking. "I see you're plugged back into the matrix then? I didn't get a call."

Michael found the lies were getting easier. "I'd just been checking with the desk every chance I got. I probably just asked at the right time."

"Cool. That's one less worry... But... you're looking stressed, man. Are you OK?"

Michael wasn't sure what to say. He was finding it difficult to focus. He enjoyed college, being near that aspiration of progress and learning. But right now, things were shifting, both around and inside him. It was driving his everyday priorities into the background.

When first midday, then one o'clock and two o'clock passed without his mum calling Robbie's phone, he told himself it was for the best. Even thinking about that conversation came close to unleashing something dangerous sealed inside him.

Tonight, though, he knew he would regain control. After so long in hiding, the exercise sequences had allowed him to take possession of life again.

RUNNING home from college had not been easy exactly, but it hadn't been impossible. At the supermarket, Michael had discovered that his bus routes were diverted, and he'd realised he didn't want to wait. Why it occurred to him to run, he wasn't certain. It had just felt like the thing to do. He arrived home sweating and breathless but exhilarated.

Although lacking appetite for anything beyond completing the exercise, he prepared fresh haddock and leeks for dinner. They hadn't had fish for a couple of weeks, so the choice avoided the flash point of a recently repeated meal.

His father ate in silence. This was not usually a good sign. Mockery was the norm, and deviations from that norm could end in bad places. Eventually, Faither pushed his plate away. "Is that big dumbbell turning you into the strong, silent type?"

"No. I could see you were quiet – I didn't think you wanted to talk."

"Keeping something from me?"

"No. Honest... Did you like the fish?"

Faither sneered and stood. He stared at Michael, shook his head, and left the kitchen.

Michael forced himself to wait, keeping busy by clearing the table and washing the plates. When he heard the sound of the radio from Faither's room he poured a glass of water and went to start his workout.

The exercises were harder tonight. He couldn't stop thinking about Mum. Her failure to call, although a relief earlier, now felt like a second abandonment. He knew, of course, that this was unfair; he hadn't been abandoned so much as escaped. All his life, he had known it. Michael had been more than a mute witness – if Faither was the torturer then Michael was the tether, the binding that had trapped her in a life of subjugation. No, his mum had done what she had to. She'd fled them both. She would have hated to disrupt his college course, and she must have known that he could co-exist with Faither, not happily, but at least mostly safely. The same wasn't true for her. If she'd come home from the hospital, she might be dead now. She'd decided to live.

This idea, turning away from death and choosing to live, began to dominate his thoughts, almost like a mantra, and the fluidity started to build. The movement sequence was shorter, but he repeated it many times. He had been certain he would depart from the diagram sequences when they reached the point of making the drink, but the more he repeated the exercise, the more curious he became. Eventually, he laid down the weight, took the bag of powder from his drawer and emptied it into his glass.

The clear water was consumed by a dark, sinking cloud. The result, murky and grey, left dirty residue floating on top and clinging to the sides of the glass.

He stirred with his finger, drawing grey-black particles upwards into a vortex, only to fall once more when he stopped. The powder remained stubbornly undissolved. This was not a health-drink in any recognisable sense.

He looked again at the diagram, but two things were very clear: this was his last challenge, and it was vile. But isn't medicine always meant to be unpleasant? Should the cure not fit the disease?

And the disease, he now understood, was pervasive and deep-rooted. His infection was impotence and weakness and cowardice, and the infection had become him. The parasite now controlled the host. That meant it needed to be removed. He had to purge it from his system.

He sipped a tiny amount, and even though there was no smell, he struggled to suppress the urge to retch. He swallowed quickly, finding it salty, metallic, gritty. *And wrong. It was wrong.*

The second sip was difficult, and the third seemed impossible. Repeatedly, he raised the glass only to lower it again, barely touched. He couldn't rationalise his inability to proceed, but he'd become locked in a powerful struggle. It was a struggle his bodily instincts would not allow himself to win.

It was late by the time he gave up, half a glass remaining, scared of disturbing Faither with the sound of gagging. Sickened and sweating, he crawled into bed.

THE LAND HERE WAS BARREN. He found himself at a blighted tree beside a wall of crumbling stone. The tree surface was oddly desecrated, its near-side stripped of bark. The wall behind that tree gaped open in a black circle, a tunnel descending into darkness.

He paused for a moment in that space, halfway between worlds. Moonlight shone at his back and cast his shadow onto the wall, a shadow at once intimately familiar, and yet, not his own. Falling to his knees, like a worshipper at a crypt, he crawled through the entrance.

Only the pull of gravity told him that the tunnel arched downwards. His gloom-blind hands scuffed against stony floor, but there was no space to turn back nor any reason to. In the inky blackness, a rough thumb (*a priest?*) anointed his forehead, tracing symbols. Then an accented whisper, *Man you were dust and from dust you will return*, a memory of a childhood observance, oddly distorted.

Far ahead, he discerned a flickering source of light. As it grew stronger, it exposed the surrounding walls, illuminating primitive symbols drawn in charcoal, and words, or scraps of words – *luonto, henki, itse.*

Nearing the source, heat filled the tunnel, and he knew he was heading towards flames. But there was no fear, because it was a cleansing fire, one that could destroy and make new. One that could purge him of sickness, weakness, and disease, and let him rise again from ash.

MICHAEL'S SHEETS were sodden with sweat when he was shaken awake. The drink responsible for his fever sat half-filled beside the alarm clock at his bedside. The clock read 10:14 a.m. He had missed his first period at college.

Faither was at the end of his bed, teeth clenched, punctuating each word with a kick against the mattress.

"Get... up... ya... lazy... lying... bastard!"

Only one thought. *Do as he says.*

Michael scrambled out of bed. "Sorry! Sorry! I slept in! I slept in! I don't know why!"

First, he noticed his rucksack emptied on the floor, his books scattered. Then, with a horrible lurch he saw Faither holding his phone.

"Sorry? Sorry? I'll make ye fuckin sorry! It rang, but you didn't hear it. Then yer wee pal must have decided to send you some messages."

Oh Christ. Please no.

Faither read "MESSAGE 1: HEY MIX. HOPE YOU'RE FEELING OK. I GOT THIS TEXT FOR YOU." He paused at this point. "MESSAGE 2: MIKEY – I'M IN GLASGOW. CAN WE MEET? LOVE YOU. MUM." Another pause. "MESSAGE 3: HI MIX - THIS IS PHONE NUMBER SO YOU CAN REPLY."

The next words were Faither's own. "Ya fucking lying wee shite!"

He was exposed. There was no hiding it. No pretending.

"I'll move out."

"Like fuck ye will."

Faither grabbed him, pulled him close. It had happened before, but this was different. Michael tried to break free, but his struggle was ended by a knee in his groin, followed by a fist to his face. He went down fast, salty wet around his mouth, no air in his lungs. Faither sat down hard on Michael's chest and twisted his head into profile. He raised the phone and leered.

TWO WORDS WERE all it took for Angela's world to unravel. Two little words on a phone. *Home. Now.* A picture message to accompany those words made the nightmare real.

Mikey, my wee boy. My best boy. Bleeding.

The bastard. The evil bastard. He'd never hit Mikey before, not this way, and she'd stupidly believed he never would. She had known she should have stayed away. But how could she? The need to see her son had grown urgent as soon as she was able. She'd always told herself that as soon as she was strong enough, she'd find a way. It had been her motivation for surviving, for healing, for everything.

But now she understood: seeing her son was what she had needed, an expression of her selfishness. So she'd made contact, and what did she have now?

Fresh blood around a swollen nose.

A silent scream through red-stained teeth.

She'd caused this by forgetting the unalterable lesson of her marriage to Alec. For as long as she'd known him, no matter what he did, she always ended up hating herself.

Her hands were shaking as she tried to pay the taxi driver and coins tumbled to the floor. The man smiled. "I'll get that, hen. On ye go." He could see the state she was in, and he wanted to help. That was how the world was divided, she knew now. Between people and predators.

From the street, the place looked exactly the same. An ordinary block of flats on an ordinary street, but one she'd hoped she'd never enter again. *Close enough, Angie – you're on course for never leaving.*

He'd beat her again, that much she knew. But she'd come prepared. She tapped her pocket and felt the hard plastic cylinder of the pill bottle. Only three capsules, but it was enough. She'd been clean for so long, probably one would end her, and Alec would have a beat-up corpse to explain. Her fantasy was dosing him first, but he was so paranoid and angry that she doubted she'd get the chance.

No. She needed to stick to Plan A. Her dead, him jailed, Michael safe. It was the best she could hope for.

She shivered, and not from the cold.

But despite the churning inside her, at least she now had something she'd lacked for months: the absolute certainty she was doing the right thing. It didn't matter what happened now, so long as Mikey was OK. She needed to help him.

She walked up the stairs. Some curtains had twitched when she left the cab, but nobody came out to speak to her. *You'll find good* neighbours in Glasgow, that's something they always say. But even good neighbours will only go so far, only risk so much. Some things were just too dangerous to meddle with, and her marriage was one of them.

Reaching the glass panel on the front door of their flat, she realised how much she'd always hated it. The number of days she'd spent locked inside, contemplating that little rectangle of mundane freedoms. The postie, or the meter reader, or Mr Dunleary across the street, who used to brush his teeth at the living room window. At first, she'd wondered why. But eventually she'd understood the real question was why not? He lived alone, so he had nobody he needed to please. Nobody who might call him a dirty bitch or push his face under the hot tap or squeeze an entire tube of toothpaste into his mouth.

Angela rang the bell.

Alec was cut above one eye, and his nose was bleeding, but still he smiled when he reached the door. It was a smile she'd seen before, chiselled from ferocity and grim triumph.

"Welcome home, doll." He ushered her inside, then grabbed her hair and pulled her up the hallway.

"Alec, there's no need for this. I'm staying. I just want to see Michael is OK."

"Don't worry about him, Angela. You took the piss oot of me for nine fuckin months, so he's the least of your worries."

Angela looked around for something she could use as a weapon, but his grip on her hair was ruthless and only desperation allowed her to speak through the pain.

"Just let me talk to him! Please!"

Alec stopped, decided something, and then dragged her across the hallway to Michael's room. It was, she saw, bolted from the outside. He pushed her face against the door.

"There you go, doll. Talk to him!"

And she tried.

"Mikey! Mikey, are you OK? Please darlin', please, are you OK?"

And she heard him, crying and broken and alone and scared. But OK. He was OK.

"I'm sorry, Mum! I'm sorry. He read your message. I'm so sorry!"

She had no time, and she knew it. She had to say the most important things. "I wish I'd stayed with you, Mikey. I love you! I love you, son."

But already Alec was dragging her away.

INSIDE HIS ROOM, Michael ached all over. Blood from his right eye trickled down towards his swollen mouth. A couple of his fingers were staved, maybe broken.

He had struggled a long time before Mum had arrived, trying to make it safe for her, fighting in a way he could never have imagined before. He wondered briefly where the courage had come from, but inside he knew there was no mystery. His gaze fell on the scummy half-filled glass on his bedside table. It hadn't been enough.

They were arguing now, but this was just the preamble. He knew how it went from here.

He couldn't do this again. Listen to it. Witness it. Condone it. But he couldn't fix things by himself. He didn't have it in him. Not fully.

Not yet.

He picked up the glass.

Across the hall he heard her screaming. Intermittently pleading and cursing. Giving as good as she got. Faither's big excuse was that she'd always had too much fight in her. As though somehow breaking her spirit would finally fix their misery. But her spirit had never been the problem. And Michael knew his mum: there was only one way that light would ever go out.

Last night it had taken him five hours to swallow down half of the filth in the glass; every part of him had fought against it. But now was different. Nothing mattered without her. He tipped back his head, preparing himself.

Submit. Accept.

He opened his throat, and poured.

Find me in water.

Rising in the grey.

From dust returning.

His soul was on fire. His memories were burning.

I am *Erkki. My will.*

Michael grunted, stumbling down to his knees to grab the *girya.*

It was painful to lift so he changed hand. He must have it, he needed it—

Need nothing. Am new. My will.

No. Not yet. Michael raised the weight and crashed it against the handle of his door. Once. Twice. The shock shot through his hand. He needed more force, bringing both hands together to swing it double-handed.

Hand hurt. My body. Protect.

No, Michael thought. *It's my body.*

He swung the weight with all his might, screaming as wood buckled, as the bolt snapped on the other side. Faither installed that bolt when he was eight. It had been strong, but it was never designed for this punishment. When he kicked the door, it opened with a crash.

He could hear them in Faither's room. Mum was shouting. He needed to help her.

Ignore woman. Not important.

A leaden sensation spread down his legs. Some *thing* was establishing itself, growing inside him, wresting control. Right now, Michael needed cooperation. Was it a person? If so, it felt like a type he knew very well. So his next thought was a simple internal challenge: *Are you scared of Faither?* Despite the following moments of inner silence, he had no doubt a response would come.

No. I fear nothing.

The resistance dissolved and Michael moved to the other

bedroom. The door was pushed shut, but Faither hadn't taken the time to lock it. He swung the weight and crashed through. Mother was behind the bed. Her nose was bleeding. The portable TV lay smashed at Faither's feet. Both froze in shock. Mum screamed, but Faither recovered himself and laughed.

"Your boy needed a slap, Angie. Looks like I rearranged his face a bit."

My mum stared, her mouth working silently, her hands trembling. Then she said, "That's not Mikey! For Christ's sake, look at his eyes!"

Faither paused. "So, big guy... If you're not Michael, then who the fuck are ye?"

"*Olen perkele!*" Michael knew his mouth had just made a joke, but had somehow left him out of it. His arms, too, had flung themselves aloft in a derisory challenge. Michael's physical actions seemed increasingly beyond his own command.

He felt the thing inside him choosing what it wanted to do next, felt himself drawing distant from his own being. Desperately, he cast around his memory for something, something that belonged to him and his mother, a reminder of his own life. Something that might help him assert control.

On my first day at school, I hugged her at the gate and she pretended her tears were from laughter.

It was a long-hidden personal memory, and he felt it push the thing back, helping him to regain himself. But time was short. Faither had challenged the thing inside him, and it was growing in dominance. He couldn't let it take control until he was sure his mum was safe.

He caught her gaze, trying to make her understand. Her eyes softened into a kind of recognition, but it took all of his strength to speak. "Mum... Don't worry... We look after each other. That's all... all this is... But Erkki... is coming. When we go... outside... don't follow."

Faither, uncertain now of what he was facing, looked nervously between his son and the weight he carried. "Need a weapon? Can't face me like a man?"

Not man. Will be. Soon.

Michael stretched his arm as if offering the

girya

He didn't know exactly what he was doing. Reaching slowly. So slowly. Holding the weight at full extension, his muscles began to tremble.

Faither attempted to snatch just as Michael let it drop. There was a snap and a scream as it landed, crushing Faither's ankle, but Michael found himself already pushing Faither's head back with the flat of his other hand before circling behind to complete a chokehold.

Finish it.

Michael balked. It would be so easy, to end it now, to give her this memory. *But I don't want her to see this.*

"Mum... stay... here."

He dragged Faither backwards out of the room and down the hallway to the door. Faither flailed and grunted as his shattered foot snagged against door-frames and furniture, the pain and lack of oxygen restricting his ability to fight back. At the door, Michael tightened his grip still further, until he felt the struggling diminish and consciousness depart.

Finish it.

No! She was still watching.

Michael dragged Faither outside into the porch, before pulling the door shut behind them. He knew now, whatever was unfolding inside him was unstoppable. He wouldn't be here to protect her if his father recovered. There were no choices left.

He knelt down, took a breath, and loosed his internal tethers. Immediately, a crack echoed in the stairwell from a single brutal twist of Faither's head.

He rose away from the body before looking back through the small door panel, finding his mother timidly approaching the other side. Their hands hesitated, then touched through the glass. Her face was a mask of despair. Of loss. But love. Always love.

But Faither was dead. And the magnitude of what he had done breached the last of his defences.

You are mine. Not Michael. You are Erkki.

I am Erkki. From dust returned. This woman is nothing.

...is everything. Once I fell from the climbing frame in the park and she carried... me... home... and...

This woman is nothing.

I am Erkki.

ERKKI BRIEFLY REGARDED the corpse at his feet before looking out from the balcony. A car parked across the street flicked its lights on. The driver's door opened, a stick-thin man got out, looked up, and opened his arms.

PART II – THE SEARCH

Day 4 – Family Reunions

Andy Lorimar switched off the engine and waited while Doirin double-checked the address. He examined the unfamiliar Glasgow tenement blocks on either side and supposed he'd get used to this. After so many decades as a bachelor workaholic, he had never imagined that his personal life could ever contain this many appointments.

"I wonder, would it keep things simple if I just stay in the car? I don't mind. I've brought a book."

Doirin Chambers arched her eyebrow. "I see. I leave you down here. Like a getaway driver? That's an insult, and you don't insult family."

"You didn't know they were your family until that DNA website."

"It's a family tree website. The DNA test just helps build the tree." Andy tried raising his hands in mock submission, but she was not placated. "Anyway, aren't you DNA's biggest fan? God knows, you've used it to lock enough people up."

Sighing, he got out of the car.

"And apart from that…" She hesitated, resting one hand on the bonnet. "There's one other thing. I've had a feeling."

"Since when is that unusual?" Doirin had feelings all the time. It was one of the things he liked about her.

"Not a normal one. I haven't had a feeling like this since we first met."

Since the events following their first meeting were comparable to being dragged backwards through a hedge-maze of ghosts and criminal scientists, he gave the only response he could come up with. "Christ no. Please don't jinx us." Then he followed her towards the tenement, stony-faced.

As they climbed the internal staircase, Doirin offered, "Anyway, she did suggest I bring you along."

"But why?" He had spent the drive hoping he was only on taxi duty, but it was increasingly obvious his die had been cast days ago.

Doirin shrugged. "I suppose everyone likes a man in uniform."

Andy sneaked a glance at his brown linen shirt and grey hiking trousers. He decided against mentioning the almost entirely plain-clothes nature of his career with the police. Since Doirin had recently revamped his wardrobe, she would certainly have a comeback.

When they found the door marked *Julie Macleod*, he put Doirin's abnormal feeling from his mind and rang the bell.

DOIRIN'S newly discovered cousin greeted them with a welcoming smile. Was there a family resemblance? Around the eyes, for sure, but precise judgement became difficult once the crying and hugging started. Doirin and Julie walked inside with arms around each other, and Andy followed.

Andy couldn't help casting a professional eye around the place as they walked inside. The flat was cosy, with two bedrooms, and tidy, apart from some spots of teenage clutter here and there. It had a welcoming feeling, although perhaps that was an inevitable conse-quence of arriving without a search warrant or a scene-of-crime photographer.

Julie seated them on comfy chairs around a glass coffee table. Although their host was younger than her visitors by around two decades, that didn't seem to create any distance between them. Small talk flowed easily, until eventually, as he knew she would, Doirin threw in a little drama, "I've been trying to explain to this man that DNA isn't just for the nasty things in life." She put a hand on Julie's leg and wrinkled her nose. "He's so used to wiping it off of knives and hammers and such."

Julie's face fell. "Oh, Andy. That's terrible!"

"Perhaps it would be, but Doirin's exaggerating a little. Forensics and pathology deal with the grimy details. I rarely get my hands dirty."

Doirin shook her head. "He's downplaying it, Julie. He was sick at a crime scene recently."

"That was my inner ear problem."

"Whatever – you had to give the investigation over to that other eejit, and you were ill for days."

Andy's mouth tightened at the memory. Devlin had determined the grisly scene had just been a suicide pact, with no crime or villains to find. He sometimes wondered if he'd believed his colleague just so he could stop feeling guilty about it.

Doirin tapped her own ear conspiratorially, causing Julie to lean forward. "Andy got that inner ear damage on the job as well. From being punched in the head... See, that's why I'm glad he's retiring."

"I'm only partially retiring. I'll take on private cases now and then." The words still sounded odd: *I'll take on private cases.* It made the work sound much more relaxed, optional even. He supposed it would be in some ways. Perhaps, if he was really lucky, he wouldn't carry quite the same burden of duty when engaged in private investigation, but he doubted that was how things worked.

It would be weird finding his own cases, but Doirin was most likely right. It would probably be a lot safer. Especially if, as he sometimes expected, he didn't find much work at all and they ended up entertaining themselves on cruises and coach trips, instead.

After Julie had brought over tea and biscuits, she looked at Doirin and shook her head. "What I can't get over is that without those tests we did, you would never have even known that your dad had a twin."

"Daddy never mentioned your grandfather to me. Not once. But then, I was ten when I lost him."

"So you never heard the name Alisdair Macleod? Because he was always on about Kenneth-this, Kenny-that, even after your dad died."

"I never heard the name. He wasn't the biggest talker my daddy, and I'm sure the separation was painful to him, whatever was behind it."

"Gramps said your mum was behind it... she'd never liked how close they were."

Andy saw a complex expression flicker across Doirin's features. Some sadness, some anger, and finally, resignation. Doirin said, "That sounds like the mother I knew, right enough. Her shoulders had more chips than a casino. I never understood why, but we never got on."

"He said your mum changed after a stillbirth. That was when she pushed him out of your lives."

Doirin froze. "I don't think that's right."

"No? Gramps said your mum lost a baby."

"But there was only me and my sister, Rosie. No stillbirth that I ever knew of."

"Was Rosie the eldest?"

"No. I was."

Julie took Doirin's hand. "And she said nothing? Not even when you got older?"

"What do you mean? Say what?"

"Doirin, I'm a twin, and my sister has a pair of identical twins, too. My Grandpa and your dad. Identical twins. It happens some-times that it runs in families. You were a twin, too. Or would have been." Julie gripped Doirin's hand tightly. "I'm so sorry. If I'd known... I should have kept my mouth shut."

Andy reached for Doirin's arm, but drew back at a sudden commotion. The doorbell was ringing, and not just once, but over and over as though someone was leaning on the button. Then the door banged repeatedly. Julie, obviously alarmed, rose to get it and Andy walked with her.

The door opened to reveal a teenage boy, perhaps eighteen years

313

old, and a woman with bruising on her face. The marks were recent. Andy judged they'd happened within the last day or two.

Julie said, "Robbie? What's happened?"

"I forgot my key, sorry! But it's my friend Michael from college. He's in trouble!"

———

ROBBIE WAS RIGHT. His friend was in trouble. Deep trouble. The woman, Angela, had turned up at his college today searching for friends of her son. She had clearly been a victim of recent violence, and Andy suspected he saw the lasting effects of older injuries, too. But whatever she'd been through, she wasn't timid about telling her story.

Even if it wasn't the story Andy had expected.

By the time Angela concluded, they had learned that her attacker was dead. She wasn't here about the perpetrator or for herself. Every step she had taken since her ordeal seemed to have been for her son. "He only did the things he did to protect me."

"I understand that, Angela, but it sounds as if your son killed your ex-husband."

"He wasn't my ex. We never divorced. I just stopped using the bastard's name last time he put me in hospital."

"My point is: violence has resulted in someone's death..." Explaining criminal procedure to a victim of violence had not been on Andy's expected trip itinerary. "Now, clearly this man was an abuser, but the circumstances here mean a court has to decide the outcome. Michael can't run away from that. You'll both need to make the case legally."

Angela nodded. "That's what I want. We need to find him and bring him back. Before..."

Andy asked, "Before what? Are you scared he might harm himself?"

His mother shook her head. "Not himself, not exactly. But the other one will. The one who took him."

"Who is this other one? I thought you said Michael did this?"

Robbie spoke up. "Micky's a really gentle dude, Mr Lorimar. Shy, yeah, but the nicest guy in the class. He wouldn't have done this, not alone. Can you find him?"

Andy sighed. One day before his gold watch, the sky was falling in. "Angela, you already have an assigned investigator, correct?"

"Yes. I called the police last night. I was in shock for a while, but once I'd pulled myself together, I called them. They were at the house until one in the morning."

"Well, in that case, they're already looking for your son. I guarantee it."

"But… I think we have a better chance of finding Mikey if we're fast. And we need to be fast. Before he's gone for good…"

Robbie said, "Tell him about the weight."

Angela searched in her bag and handed Andy some papers. Each one was a detailed drawing depicting a series of movements with a kettlebell style weight. Whoever drew them had annotated the pages with strange symbols. He said, "I understand the digits 1, 2 and 3, but what does this scribbled heading – *Päivä* – mean?"

Robbie answered. "It means 'Day', Mr Lorimar. Those sheets are a three-day exercise programme that came with an old kettlebell Micky got for free off the college bulletin board. I've got a photo of the advert, and a phone number for the guy Paavo, who delivered it to Micky." He turned to Angela. "Do you have the other page, the one all in Finnish?"

Angela frowned. "This is all there was. I didn't know there was another one."

Robbie said, "I offered Micky my phone to translate it, but he said he'd already checked it at the college library."

Andy asked, "What was that page about? Do you think it was important?"

Robbie shrugged."I don't know – he thought it was about Paavo's family."

Angela frowned, impatient. "But these sheets are the important ones, I think." She glanced at Robbie. "Right? I mean, we both thought that something about this weight, about these instructions… It changed him somehow. He's not responsible for what happened."

Scowling, Andy leafed through the pages again before handing them back. "I don't see what three days of working out could have to do with this." He paused, considering the grim fate of his own mother, the exploitation and abuse she'd suffered, before being eventually taken from him altogether. It was impossible not to consider how far he might have gone to protect her, given the chance. "I don't believe we need to make this complicated. Anyone who witnessed the things Michael saw might easily have been driven towards the same actions. He protected you, but it went sideways. A court will give him credit for that, I'm sure of it."

Angela snapped. "I *want* him to go to court. But I want it to *be him*, not whatever these"—she snatched the pages from the detective's hands—"put inside him."

Doirin, who had been silent since Robbie and Angela's arrival, walked over to the woman and briefly held her shoulder. Then she crouched down to touch the pages in Angela's hands. Eventually, she said, "There is something odd about these diagrams, Andy. Perhaps you should take a look."

He accepted the papers, scowling again. There was something here for sure, but it was both intriguing and troubling: this was a case where he could easily cast his younger self as the killer. He took a photograph of one of the exercise sheets and messaged it to a contact at Edinburgh university.

Andy Lorimar:
Something Finnish and unusual requiring a professional opinion. Any idea who to contact?

A response arrived in under a minute.

Prof. Maxwell:
Unusual, indeed. But not my field. Let me ask around.

Andy took the rest of the materials and promised to contact Angela as soon as he had any kind of update. He still had one more day at the office before he'd be able to spend much time on the case.

LATER, Andy dreamed of being a child again.

There was no happiness in the dream, only a crushing sense of urgency, as though he'd landed inside a single moment, a moment upon which everything might tip.

Billy was in the dream, perfectly still, gazing through the window from the old armchair he'd annexed for his sole use – because this was a man who always took what he wanted, caring nothing for the claims of others. Although facing away as the boy crept into the room, he remained unmistakable, the way he held his head, the coiled tension in his shoulders.

He always took what he wanted, and he would take Andy's mother away. Forever.

The dream was a doomsday clock on countdown.

But Billy was still, so still he seemed trapped inside a tick of the clock, a single second lengthened to allow Andy to be thrown into this moment, like a ghost in the machine. Now he was caught inside dream-fabric that was stitched with compulsion, draped in the suffocating need to act.

So, act.

Andy's mind raced, retracing the geography of a place he hadn't seen in so many years. He thought about the little kitchenette, and whether everything would be in the same place as he remembered it: *If I go now, if I fetch a knife, can I stop it?*

But his legs refused to move. *Once he's dead, they'll know I did it and lock me away. I'll lose her a different way.*

And he stood frozen, trapped in indecision, struggling to move, or breathe or scream. If he couldn't break the paralysis, he knew what would happen. So why couldn't he move?

When his mother's key turned in the lock, Billy turned to stare at Andy. And grinned.

"ARE YOU OK? Andy? What's wrong?"

Doirin had shaken him awake.

He felt wetness around his eyes, wiped the tracks from his cheeks. "Sorry, Do. I don't know what that was."

"I think maybe you do."

She could always tell. "Ach. I'm just thinking about things I didn't change when I had the chance."

"Andy, some things you change. Some things change you. What you witnessed is part of who you are."

"Well. I witnessed it all right, but Angela's boy Michael, he did more. He changed it."

"Yes. And he had to do a horrible thing. Maybe now you get to see what happens afterwards."

WHEN MICHAEL BECAME HIMSELF AGAIN, he was in the boot of a car.

He'd powerlessly observed events leading up to this point, but was now shocked to be here, as himself, feeling the rocking of a sea-crossing.

After he'd given up the fight for control, after Erkki had taken over, perhaps many hours later, Michael had regained some awareness, but not like this. At that point, his perceptions were dreamlike, but safe in the glass room, looking out through Erkki's eyes. Paavo had been driving, his face riven with concern.

Michael eventually understood that Paavo's attempts to converse with Erkki in Finnish were being ignored. He earned some terse responses, but only to questions posed in English. Did Erkki speak English for Michael's benefit? Or had the transition cost him some facility in language?

The awkward half-silence of the journey was eventually interrupted after they passed signposts for the Hull ferry. That was when Paavo had pulled off the road and helped Erkki into the boot of the car.

So, Michael had watched it happen, but through Erkki's eyes. He'd assumed he'd be watching through Erkki's eyes forever. And yet he was here again, in the dark, cold beneath a lid of rusting metal, nauseated by the damp stench from the cargo mat and the endless rolling of the North Sea.

Day 5 – Gold Watch Day

Andy, in a precious few moments of silence before any of the social last-day nonsense began, idly packed a box with the contents of his desk. Uncertain if he was sad or excited, he decided he was probably both.

Then his phone rang.

"Hello. This is Tarvo Pettinen. I am looking for Detective Lorimar."

"You've found him, Mr Pettinen. How can I help?"

"Perhaps it will be the other way around. I'm a professor of anthropology, and I received a curious photograph you sent to our mutual friend at The University of Edinburgh. I have become quite intrigued."

"Well, Professor Pettinen, thank you for taking the time to call. So, you recognised something?"

"Yes. I think so. Perhaps. Could you let me know some background?"

"Well. A criminal investigation is underway, so I'll request that you keep our discussion between ourselves. That image comes from some materials tangled up in the disappearance of a young man, and by one theory, may have inspired him to commit murder."

"Who was the Finn? The victim, the suspected perpetrator? Or perhaps both?"

"That is the odd thing. Neither one."

"Odd indeed. Well, before I commit myself, I would like to see the original if possible. I suspect something, but the image quality leaves me uncertain."

"Of course. There are other pages you may be interested in." Andy flicked past the image the professor would have received, and then the others he had not. He hovered over the photograph Robbie had sent him of the advert showing a weightlifting man and his scrawny family. "One thing that's been bothering me. Why might a Finn describe themselves as a Siberian Superman?"

The professor hesitated before answering. "Two thoughts, just guesses. The first would be simple genetics. Siberian DNA travelled to Finland, so the place is in our blood, not only among the Sämi populations, but further south too. This person may have an attachment to that history. My second thought is that there have been Finns in Siberia since at least the early eighteen hundreds. Some willing, some deported, present in sufficient numbers to be considered a distinct ethnic group. Some families will have returned from that experience, feeling part Siberian, part Finnish."

Andy wasn't sure that any of that helped the case, but he was confident that the professor was worth consulting. "Where can I bring the materials for you to examine?"

"Fortunately, I'm currently nearby. I'm on a brief lecture tour in Scotland. If it suits you, I'll be at the Department of Social Anthropology at The University of St Andrews tomorrow afternoon. If you arrive any time from three p.m., I'll tell reception to expect you."

Andy concluded the arrangements and hurried off the phone. A crowd was gathering, and given the likely reason, his own attendance was mandatory.

DCI Brian Nesbitt called the largest meeting room in their Fettes Avenue office to order. "Friends, Romans, and fellow officers! Lend me your ears!"

Devlin nudged Andy in the ribs and muttered. "Pretty sectarian way to start a meeting, don't you think, Link-man? Don't Catholics count as friends nowadays?"

Andy shrugged, deciding that having put up with Devlin for his entire career, he could handle another few hours.

The chief continued. "As you all know, this is Detective Inspector Andy Lorimar's last day on the job."

At that, Devlin roared, "Yes!" He then stamped his feet, cheered, clapped, and whistled to a room of increasingly shocked faces. Eventually, he stopped, puzzled. "What? Can't I be happy for him?"

Nesbitt shook his head and moved on. "Now, you may not know that DI Lorimar isn't just hanging up his spurs and heading into the sunset, but plans to keep his hand in by taking on private investigative work in the city."

Devlin pointed across the room towards DC Lenny Burns, who colleagues considered either his closest friend or perpetually grinning crony, depending on how charitable they felt. "Lenny thinks you'll be hanging out of trees taking candid snaps of folk doing the nasty. Y'know? Andy Lorimar – marital vow enforcer!"

Annoyingly, that got some chortles from the crowd. PI work attracted frequent mockery around these parts, and nothing was likely to change that. "Thanks DS Devlin, but I'll be after something a little more high-class than that."

Devlin gave a thumbs-up to Burns. "You can relax then, Lenny. Tell your wee granny to have at it. She's perfectly safe."

The chief cleared his throat ominously. "That's enough hilarity, Devlin... As you might expect from the king of chamomile tea, there will be no piss-up this evening. There will be a buffet in here at lunchtime for you to say your individual goodbyes, then he'll spend the afternoon being deprogrammed by HR. And one last happier point to end on: given DI Lorimar's wealth of experience, don't faint if we have him back to consult now and again, should the case demand it."

At this, Devlin did not stamp and cheer.

"At ease now, people. I need to steal DI Lorimar away for a quick discussion with our colleagues in Glasgow. We'll see some of you back here in an hour."

AS THE CHIEF guided him into the office, Andy asked, "What do Glasgow want me for?"

"Apparently they heard you'd stuck your nose into a case of theirs."

Angela had obviously spoken to them. "It's that mess I mentioned. The one where the mother wants me to help find her son."

"So you're not taking it easy for a few weeks?"

"Ach. I'll give this thing a week or so, see if I can help out."

"OK. Pull a chair round. We best get this over with." Nesbitt typed on his phone keypad, then switched it to speaker mode. It rang once, then a voice drawled. "This is DCI John Kilburn. Who are you?"

"This is DCI Brian Nesbitt. As promised, I've got DI Andy Lorimar here."

"Not DI for much longer though, eh? From tonight, aren't you a PI instead? As in, Painful Irritant. Does that sound about right, Mr Lorimar?"

Brian Nesbitt's face coloured. "Now DCI Kilburn, I can assure you this is an exemplary investigator."

"You'll vouch for him, maybe. But you won't control him. Not after tonight."

It was time, Andy thought, to speak up for himself. "I'm sorry if you feel any intrusion here, DCI Kilburn. That isn't my intention. Of course, I'll share any relevant information I uncover with your team. My only goal is to bring Michael Thomson before a court. Angela Dean asked me to help find him—"

A sarcastic tone sounded over the line. "If she really wanted to find him, then why did she delay so long before calling us in? At least five bloody hours, we think. Feels more like she wanted him to escape."

It was an uncomfortable thought, and one that had already crossed Andy's mind. "She told me she was in shock."

The phone speaker barked a clipped response. "I heard that claim, too."

"It doesn't sound implausible, given what took place."

"Given HER ACCOUNT of what took place. I must remind you that this woman is unreliable. She has history with pills and alcohol."

Andy wondered if John Kilburn applied his casual certainties to all victims of crime. "If I may, DCI Kilburn, substance issues are relatively common among long-term victims of domestic violence. I don't think it speaks to inherent unreliability, more to her way of enduring."

The scoff was audible. "And what makes you such an expert, Lorimar?"

"If you must know, I watched something similar happen to my mother."

Kilburn didn't skip a beat. "That's all we need. A personal crusade."

Brian Nesbitt interrupted. "Sorry, gents, I want to keep this short and productive. Do we have any agreement on information sharing? Do we have an approach?"

"Here's the approach from Glasgow, DCI Nesbitt. We'll happily share information within the police service. So, I accept your offer of help. Tomorrow morning, I'll share all our evidence with your team. Sadly, that might be too late for Mr Lorimar, who, by that time, will have a new role as a hashtag me-too social worker. Should there be any unsanctioned leaking outside the service, then you, DCI Nesbitt will carry full responsibility. Hopefully, that's quite clear to everyone?"

"Yes, DCI Kilburn. Understood."

Andy made one last try. "DCI Kilburn, I have a telephone number provided by Robbie Macleod, one of Michael Harrison's friends. He believes a person who provided exercise equipment might be worth locating—"

"Stop! I already heard this shite from the mother. Last time I looked, we needed reasonable grounds before exercising police powers. The son did this. Not some recycling do-gooder three days distant from the offence. If Michael Harrison had eaten ice cream last week, should we throw up roadblocks for all the Mr Whippy vans? Be serious! DCI Nesbitt, expect to receive access to the case files tomorrow a.m."

When the line went dead, Nesbitt said, "Prickly, those Glasgow types... Mind you, he's correct about that phone number."

Andy nodded ruefully. "More to the point, he's trouble. I can't accept any help from you as an independent."

"Agreed. And it's too late to organise a consulting role."

Both men sat in silence, then Nesbitt said, "I could, however, swing a slight change to your leaving arrangements, if you are amenable?"

"How so?"

"The best approach is, I reschedule your exit. For a brief interval, you remain in the team. Kilburn agreed to share evidence, so I'm assigning you to do whatever you think best to help Glasgow retrieve their vanished suspect. Your official leave date will adjust to when the project completes or you give up this case. At the very least, you'll get an extra couple of weeks' pay."

"That doesn't feel quite fair. And HR expect—"

"I'll deal with Human Resources. And forget fair. Kilburn was just given free access to the sharpest tool in my investigative box, and his first thought was to stab me with it? No. Show those idiots, Andy. Find the guy. And at least this way you have legitimate access to all the evidence. Not only that, but I can still run interference for you if the shit hits the fan."

"Hopefully it won't."

"Aye, right, as Glasgow might say..." The chief stood up. "Nothing else changes. We'll proceed with your buffet as planned. Not least because I've paid extra for the good sausage rolls." As they walked to the door, he added, "Let's just keep this between us and HR to avoid confusing the natives. What's a few extra days between friends?"

They proceeded exactly as discussed, and after the buffet, Andy was released, not for dismantling by Human Resources, but for something more intimidating. He had to break the news to Doirin.

AT HOME, he found Doirin camped out in the kitchen with a pot of tea and a solemn expression. When he told her about the delay to his leaving date, she shrugged, adding, "This week, next week, when-ever. I don't mind."

The news-breaking had gone easier than he'd expected, so he was a little unnerved by the way this was playing out. "Well. If you're really OK. I hope I'm not ruining our plan for some days away."

"No. I didn't actually book a holiday in advance, because I'm not stupid." Something about her tone puzzled him. "I was always a lot of other things, according to my mother, but never stupid."

That was when the penny dropped. "C'mon, Doirin. I know that what Julie told you was a shock to the system but try to forget your mother."

"She was right, though, wasn't she? All those times she said I'd ruined her life?"

"No, she was wrong. If she thought you ruined her life by surviving a difficult birth, then honestly, she sounds more a monster than a mother. It was a horrible event, but you can't put something like that on a child."

"She didn't put it on me. Not exactly. She never told me it was my fault, but the effects of her loss spilled out, anyway. That makes her human, not a monster."

"She was the adult. You had to carry her loss your whole childhood."

When Doirin glared at him, he realised he needed to take a different tack. "Look. I want to be here for you if you need me, so is it really the right time for this case? If you want me to drop it, I will."

She looked away for a moment, then shook her head. "See that feeling I had? The one that I told you about? That feeling meant this isn't about what I want. You must do this one, I think. And I'll be back in the holiday mood about the same time you sort it all out. Probably."

AFTER DOIRIN WENT TO BED, he decided if the case was moving forward, he should place a call to his favourite insomniac. After a single ring he heard: *DI Petrakis of Cybercrime division is busy right now. Please call my office. Or leave a message after the beep. Or both. Whatever.*

"Elisia? I can tell that's actually you. It's Andy."

"I know it's you, Andy. I might not use real names in my phone contacts for privacy reasons, but as a memory jogger, your number brings up a stock image of a grumpy old man. Anyway, I heard you were retiring. Do you need help to select premium bond numbers?

I'm sorry to tell you: there is no algorithm. They're randomly allocated."

Andy consoled himself with the fact that Petrakis only bantered with people she liked. He hoped she liked him enough to help. "Not quite retired. And I need some... technical advice."

"Ah. *Technical* advice... I'll call you back from another number – give me forty-five seconds."

It took nearer a minute, but he didn't want to make her defensive by pointing that out. The number that showed up on his mobile screen appeared foreign. "Andy? This number is in your call logs. Should anyone ever ask, you decided it would be fun to string along a scam caller from Armenia."

Nobody would ever ask, but Petrakis often gave unusual advice, and it was best just to accept it. "OK, scam caller. Here's my technical question. Say I have a mobile number that I wanted to geolocate but reasonable grounds for suspicion are, at best, debatable."

"Well, if proper channels are unavailable. Is it serious enough for improper channels?"

"Murder. And a suspected weird kind of kidnap."

"Is the number likely to be in the UK or international?"

"Hopefully UK, but I don't know. It was in the Glasgow area a few days ago."

"Well, I've got two pieces of good news and one piece of bad news. The good news is that mobile networks use SS7, a protocol with more leaks than a Welsh buffet. The bad news is software to poke around with mobile networks internationally is both dark-side and expensive. Perhaps not restricted purely to nation-state level anymore, but still pretty far up the magic money tree."

He heard her typing furiously in the background. With Petrakis, that was a hopeful sign. "What's my final good news?"

"Well, let's just say... some entities who own those systems might not keep them as locked down as they ought to."

He heard a more or less continuous clicking of keystrokes in the background of their conversation and wondered how she talked and typed at the same time. It might be that female multi-tasking thing that Doirin was always on about. "Elisia, I don't want you taking any risks for this."

"Me? No! Ignore the typing. I'm just messaging a confidential informant... So. What's the number?"

He told her the mobile number he'd taken from Robbie's phone and heard a flurry of data entry on the other end of the line. Her CI seemed to need precise, detailed, and above all, lengthy instructions. Petrakis claimed many CIs across multiple slightly shady technology areas. Putting aside the fact nobody had ever met a single one of them, she remained an incredibly useful person to know.

While he listened to the remote keyboard, he steeled himself for the news that the mystery phone number was no longer in use. If they were dealing with experienced criminals, it would be a short-term burner-style device discarded after the incident. But this story didn't speak of technology-aware criminality. Most probably, the number was owned by an entirely innocent student. But maybe not.

Finally, the typing stopped. "My CI is now processing the request. So how's life with Doirin?"

"Good, but she's a bit down at the moment. She did a DNA ancestry thing and found some relatives. Which was nice, but they had some upsetting news for her. It turns out she was a twin but her sister died at birth. Her mother never let on."

"That's horrible. She's lost control of her DNA?"

Andy briefly removed the phone from his ear to shake his head. It was a reminder that Petrakis had a distinctive set of concerns not shared by everyone. "She's not worried about DNA so much. But it's brought up family stuff, mainly about her difficult relationship with her mother."

"Shame. My mum's a little intense sometimes but we've never doubted she loves us. I've been lucky that way. Must suck for Doirin. Tell her I'm thinking about her."

"I will. How's things with Asha?"

Petrakis resumed typing. "We've been better, but don't worry about it. IMEI acquired, by the way..."

"I-M-E-I?"

"International mobile equipment identifier. It's what you see when you type star-hash-zero-six-hash into your phone keypad."

"Like I've ever done that."

"Just me then... Anyway, it's just a unique hardware ID for the phone your witness was contacted by... And Rotterdam."

"What?"

"The number you gave me is currently active against cell towers in Rotterdam in the Netherlands. On or near the ferry terminal, in fact. Right now, that's where you'll find the phone."

That was curious. The phone had left Glasgow and was now in a European ferry hub. The obvious possibility placed 'Paavo' as a holiday traveller in Europe. Either that, or someone fleeing a crime scene. "I guess it is possible we caught him disembarking at a final destination or perhaps en route somewhere else. I don't suppose your CI could check again tomorrow?"

"No problem. They're fairly obedient. Are you placing bets on any particular destination?"

"No. But we found some Finnish language on other pieces of evidence, so the person I'm interested in might be from Finland. Either way, they are on the move."

"You could always call them."

"Maybe. But I don't want to spook them. Not until I'm sure where they ended up."

"OK. Would you like to know who owns the cell phone?"

"You can do that?"

"The IMEI identifies the handset, but my CI has also pulled the IMSI, which is the subscriber registered against the SIM. Y'know, a shadowy power elite won't pay the big bucks unless a system offers the whole soup-to-nuts of data privacy violations."

Andy hesitated. "Elisia, maybe..."

"Maybe nothing. You're a good guy investigating a murder-kidnap, which is the most reputable task this system will ever be put to. Let's just agree, it's fine."

He sighed. He'd been a not-quite private investigator for only around two hours and already he was wading through ethical compromise. "It's not fully fine, but I would like to know the subscriber." At that, another frenzy of keystrokes sounded down the line. "You see, I do have a potential first name, so it will be interesting if it—"

"Erkki Hautamaa. Does that tie up?"

"Since it's not Paavo, then not really..." Andy pulled out his notepad. "But spell it for me..." Perhaps this was a stolen phone, after all? He took a careful note of the name, just in case. He would mention the Rotterdam connection to Angela when they next met – if the family had relatives there, it might suggest some kind of link.

WHEN THE CAR ENGINE STARTED, Michael found himself back behind the glass, but Erkki was present too, pacing and yelling just outside.

Something horrible had changed.

Michael had never shared his space before and doing so affected him in a primal way. He backed away, cowering from Erkki's cursing, from the fists pounding outside the glass.

Rage consumed Erkki, and hatred too.

Occasional clear words escaped the inarticulate ranting. Beyond the rage, these words betrayed a disbelief that Michael was here at all, when he should be... What? Dead? Since Erkki had not known what would happen, there must be limits to his knowledge.

But beyond the anger and the disbelief, were hints of something else Erkki had not expected to encounter, something he was entirely unused to facing: fear.

Now, watching the man fling himself screaming against the glass walls, pounding with his fists, desperate to remove Michael from this space, it became obvious that he couldn't get in. This meant there were also limits to Erkki's power.

Michael wondered then if perhaps less had changed than it had first appeared. Nobody could breach the protection of the glass. Not even Erkki.

Michael was still safe.

At least for now.

Day 6 – Anthropology

When he saw the call was from Angela, he knew he had to take it. He thanked Brian Nesbitt and tucked the folder of evidence under his arm, then accepted the call as he reached his car.

Her voice was sharp, frightened. "They've said they could arrest me. Is that true?"

Bloody Kilburn. "Try to stay calm. There was some unhappiness that you didn't report this earlier." He flicked through the evidence folder, finding nothing more than that. "They're applying pressure to make sure you've told them everything. If they are there now, put them on and I'll find out."

"No. They've gone."

Another indicator it wasn't serious. Just a regular game of witness intimidation. Sure, they're traumatised already, so why the hell not? "Look, I'll be there soon. Don't worry."

It took fifty minutes to arrive. Angela's flat was visible on the second floor. There were two doors per level, each with a street-facing balcony that gave access to a common stair. Andy walked up the stairs slowly, looking around for anything that might help. As a result, he decided to briefly call in on Angela's downstairs neighbour.

The man answered the door in a waistcoat, blue shirt and bow tie and a pair of underpants. "What is it? A delivery?"

Andy wondered if the man might be expecting some trousers. "Sorry, sir. If I'm disturbing you, I can come back?"

"Nah. Just out of a Zoom meeting, so I've got a minute."

"I'm a detective investigating the incident upstairs. I wanted to ask about your doorbell."

"Yeah. Noticed it, did you? It's fairly unobtrusive, but I have to admit..." The man grinned like a winning father on school sports day. "It's a top-of-the-range SentryBell. One-hundred-and-eighty-degrees of security. Total quality. Well spotted."

"It's a nice device. Sorry if the other detectives already bothered you for the video."

"Nobody's been in to see me, but I'm just back from holiday last night. Two weeks away, hence putting on the style for the work colleagues this morning."

Andy focused carefully on the man's bow tie and nodded.

The man said, "So what do you need?" while producing a mobile phone from his waistcoat pocket.

"Do you have any video from three days ago – midday onwards?"

"Oh yes. I've got a full month on the timeline. I could pay for more, but the subscription doesn't come cheap."

Together they watched as the first midday clip showed Angela arriving by taxi.

"So it picks up movement on the street as well?"

Mr Waistcoat looked momentarily defensive. "Yes. I can define image boundaries for data protection, but I haven't got round to that yet."

"No problem. What clips come after?"

The visibility was surprisingly good. The next clip clearly showed Angela passing the camera on her way upstairs. Then another showed the taxi driving away. There were some other clips of dog-walkers and passing vehicles, until at just around an hour after Angela's taxi, the doorbell camera activated for another car, perhaps an older-model Volvo. The car pulled to a halt, and then sat with its lights on. A thin man got out and stretched his arms upwards. *Signalling someone?*

The flooding clip showed Michael walking down the stairs and then getting into that car. "Can you zoom in? I'm after that licence plate."

"Sure thing." The man controlled the image with two fingers. "How's that?"

"Good, but we might get a better image just before it's parked. He's too close to the car in front."

The man scrolled back and then zoomed in to reveal a smudged rectangle. There was dirt on the plate and the image wasn't perfect.

"Can you send me a copy of these last two clips, so I can play around with them?"

"Sure. I'll message you both links." They exchanged details, and the man shared the clips. Before Andy left, Mr Waistcoat said, "Good luck. And make a copy of those if you need to keep them – they'll be wiped in a few weeks."

With that, the helpful bare-legged office worker returned inside, and Andy continued up the stairs.

ANGELA OPENED HER DOOR WARILY, her eyes lowered, dark shadows pooling beneath them. Clearly, it had been days since she'd had a proper sleep.

"I knew you would want to see it, so I've changed nothing since it happened," she said. As she brought him inside, he heard her breathing catch. "Whenever the doorbell rings, I can't help wondering if Mikey might be... I know it's stupid, but it's the only reason I'm staying here."

All around them, Andy saw the hallmarks of a dwelling designed for suffering, extending far beyond everyday signs of neglect like stained wallpaper, musty carpets and shabby linoleum. Here, it was the hints of domestic pride that were most sinister: slickly greased external bolts on internal doors, polished grilles on inside windows, grilles on external windows secured by gleaming brass padlocks.

The deceased gaoler had kept every available space ready to be pressed into service as a dungeon.

Angela pointed at one heavy bolt on the hallway floor. "This is from the room Mikey broke out of to save me."

"Do you mind if I look inside?"

Angela followed him into the room. The internal door panel was buckled and splintered at the level where the bolt had once been fixed. Andy's nostrils detected a low-level, but distinct, acrid smell. He glanced down to stains on the rug, possibly vomit. "Was Michael ill?"

"Those diagrams told him to drink something. I think he struggled with it. There." She pointed to a glass on the floor beside the headboard. It was dry inside but clouded with grime.

"Forensics didn't take this away then?"

"They swabbed it, but said it looked like dirt."

"OK. Can I check around the bed?"

"Sure. What are you looking for?"

"Anything that might help... Hopefully, I'll know it when I see it."

He pulled the bed away from the wall on its left, then sat down, examining the room from that vantage point. Above his eye level, he noticed a piece of solitary Blu-tack oddly positioned on the wall, too low for a poster. Since that didn't seem obviously helpful, he commenced searching the floor around the bed. It felt strange to be doing this so informally, without even a pair of gloves, but he reminded himself a forensics team had already got what they needed. The risk of contamination was one hundred percent and he couldn't make it worse. Carefully, he stretched his arm down the gap between the wall and the bed to feel the floor beneath. He worked his way along, and around the point his arm reached the headboard, he felt some cardboard from a box of some kind.

The box was near-weightless as he pulled it out. There were scraps of tape still attached but everything was clean enough that it had obviously been opened recently. The only thing left inside was a small, torn scrap of paper , with staple holes suggesting it had come from the corner of a larger sheet. The words on the sheet were: *Oletko valmis? Erkin tarina*

He handed the scrap to Angela and took out his phone. "I've not had many cases where I need a translator..." It was amazing how quickly these things worked. "Apparently that says: *Are you ready? The story of Erkki.*" He looked up upon hearing a sharp gasp. Angela's face was grey with shock. "Angela, does this name mean something to you?"

"Mikey mentioned it. He said 'Erkki is coming.'"

Interesting. It dovetailed with Petrakis telling him an 'Erkki' had owned the mobile phone, so he offered a theory: "I wonder if Paavo was a false name? Perhaps the person who gave Michael the equipment was returning to fetch him?"

"No. He meant that Erkki was taking control. He was losing himself."

"I understand why you think that. But take a look at this video I got from your downstairs neighbour."

He took out his phone and played the clips. "You see how this shows Michael stepping into a car? Michael wasn't being mysterious. Someone *was* coming. And they drove him away from here after..." He stopped himself from saying *the murder*, since only a court could decide on that. "After what happened."

Angela shook her head, her mouth tightened. "No," she said. "That's not how Michael carries himself. That was his body, but it wasn't *him*."

He persevered. "I also have information on the phone number from Robbie, and let's just say it wasn't controlled by anybody called Paavo."

"Also Erkki, I suppose?"

Andy nodded. "So, that's why I think this might be a false name. Even if not, we now know someone helped Michael, whatever their name turns out to be. It's a lead."

"But you don't believe me," she said.

"I believe in your instincts, about Michael. It's very possible he thought he was being influenced or taken over… But this isn't about belief for me. My job is putting something solid together from fragments of evidence." He held up the scrap of paper. "Robbie mentioned a missing page, and this looks like a piece of it. If Michael translated that page, we don't know what he learned, precisely, but we know it came from words on a page. That's where he learned about this Erkki…"

"Where he *first* learned about Erkki. What I saw wasn't learned."

"Angela? Have you ever thought that maybe this Erkki persona was the character Michael needed, in order to do what he eventually did? He isn't a violent young man, and he didn't hide that. Robbie described how gentle he was. Perhaps he knew he couldn't protect you being himself. So he needed to be someone else."

"He pretended, you mean?"

"No. I'm not saying he was pretending. It runs deeper than that. But maybe it's deeply psychological, but not, I don't know, anything more magical than that."

"You didn't see him."

"That's true… And I guess we park it and keep digging." There was one final important question. "Do you have family or friends in the Netherlands? Anyone Michael might know?"

"No. Why?"

"Look, we don't have evidence that the phone number Robbie gave us is connected with Michael at this point, but that phone is still in use and located near Rotterdam."

Angela's shoulders sagged. "So he's left. It makes sense."

"We don't know that phone is related to Michael."

"I do… Why don't we call the phone? Speak to whoever is there? Prove it?"

"No. It's better to find out where that phone ends up than to spook them into discarding it."

"OK. So what now?"

"I want to trace the car in this video if possible. And I have a meeting this afternoon with an academic at St Andrews university – about the exercise diagrams. I can call you afterward—"

"I'm coming. I want to be there."

He knew better than to argue.

Professor Tarvo Pettinen was a friendly, older gentleman with a shock of grey hair and lively eyes. He greeted them warmly. "Welcome to my borrowed office. I apologise for the delay. I returned slightly late from a walk to see the lovely St Andrews Castle, and their most unlovely oubliette... But excuse me – that is French – what do you call it here?"

Andy answered. "Oubliette works, but I suppose in English we might also use bottle dungeon?"

"Yes! Bottle dungeon! How evocative. Can you imagine? Being lowered twenty feet into darkness and forgotten? I do so hope the Scottish authorities no longer employ this punishment, Detective Lorimar. I have become very anxious about answering these questions to your satisfaction!"

After the introductions, the professor took the exercise diagrams and positioned them carefully beneath a goose neck magnifier clamped to the side of the desk. He seated himself and pored over the first of the sheets. "Now, remind me, please. These came from where?"

"They were found at the scene of a crime in Glasgow. We don't know where they originated, or even if they are definitely evidence at this point..." Angela stiffened as though about to object, but Andy caught her eye and shook his head. "But we do want an expert's opinion on what they might be."

"Yes. Yes, indeed. And you have other photographs, you say?"

"We do." Andy fished the evidence shots of the kettlebell out of his folder. "This kettlebell weight was from the same source as those diagrams. You can see it has some unusual symbols etched around its body."

"I see them," He flicked through the photographs. "Wow-wow-wow."

"You recognise them?"

" I might have seen something like them in certain forests, on certain trees, or perhaps on a stone marker. But in the past, however, not nowadays"

"OK. What do marks like that signify usually?"

"Well, this weight has precise scratches on the surface: two digits, then this numeric symbol, two digits above and below, then a further two digits. In the old days, this was what we called a *karsikko* mark. It was used to commemorate the dead."

"How was this mark used? What do the numbers mean?"

"There was some variation in these things, but most commonly a section of tree is stripped of bark. This creates a smooth surface, to allow numbers or other symbols to be inscribed. The numbers usually conveyed the year, day and month of burial. If that is the case here, then your piece of equipment was marked to commemorate a death that took place late last month, around three weeks ago."

"Why are the numbers written backwards?"

"Usually, they are not." The professor frowned, shaking his head. "I will say the *karsikko* tradition was not just a commemoration of the dead, but also a protection against their return. The belief was that should a spirit rise and see the mark, it would understand it must stay in its grave. If I were being fanciful, I'd suggest this was written reversed on the outside surface to be perceived correctly from the inside! But, of course, this kettlebell, as you call it, was not a grave. It is quite confusing to me."

Angela interrupted. "I think something was inside the weight – I found some dirt in a glass."

The professor shrugged. "I'm unsure, but I will say these materials are not just confusing but strange in an esoteric sense. The three other pages seem to show not just exercises, but ritualistic movement. Some of the designs are indicative of shamanism."

Andy took the bait. "In what sense, shamanism? And what might that mean?"

"Shamanism is a ancient belief system found in various places. Still present in Siberia today, for instance, and highly significant in our Finnish history and folklore. Shamans used trance to interact with spirits across three different realms. These divided circles are reminiscent of the shamanic upper, middle, and lower worlds. You will perhaps see, as the series of exercises progresses, the illustrated figure moves a little lower in the diagram."

Andy had noted the repeated circle motif, but hadn't paid attention to the placement of the figure performing each exercise. The professor was correct, however – exercise by exercise, day by day, the figure was drawn lower within its circle. "What might this indicate?"

"Perhaps the creator thought the movements induced a shamanic trance that facilitated communing with the lower world? You see, dance and drum rituals have been used historically to attain such altered states, and these exercises look highly choreographed, so it may have been the idea. These diagrams certainly suggest their creator was influenced by aspects of the occult and Finnish myth. But even there I find confusion." The professor adjusted the sheets beneath his magnifier, and took some notes on a scrap of paper. "Look at the letters - faint but present, beside each exercise. For day one, these spell the Finnish words *tummimmat kalat* which in English means 'darkest fish'."

Andy glanced towards Angela, who shook her head.

The professor continued. "On day two, we have *minä olen* which simply means 'I am'. While on day three we see *sinun säiliösi*, which means, I suppose, 'your vessel' or 'your container'. Darkest fish I am your vessel. Very odd."

"You mentioned Finnish myth. Does this reference to fish have meaning there?"

"Not especially, not in real myth at least. But what really bothers me is that I encountered something *unreal*, indeed, fake, but very reminiscent of these words some years ago. I was at Turku university as an external referee for a research student. Their thesis contained a treasure trove of previously unknown runes."

"Runes? You mean ancient inscriptions? An ancient language?"

"Here, I mean folk poetry, but sung more often than spoken. This candidate claimed to have encountered an old rune-singer as a child and made notes in his childhood diary. My colleagues at that university were very open to this. Our national epic, the *Kalevala*, emerged from runes collected from singers and ordered into a coherent narrative.

"Anyway, the University of Turku hoped to use this thesis to publish new verses from the same ancient stories. This caused much excitement! The student had prepared Russian and English translations of the verses, so their press releases were all but drafted!"

The professor rose, taking a mobile phone from his pocket and pressing it to his ear. "But it was all fake. The research student had lied and he'd fabricated all the verses. His elderly rune-singer had never existed. The so-called childhood diary was written alongside his thesis. It would have been a major scandal, but my friend caught it in time."

The professor then held up a finger and spoke into the phone "Juho? *Se on* Tarvo! *Tarvitsen apuasi!*" A brief conversation proceeded in Finnish, before the professor hung up. "My friend is just now sending me an email of the English translation. Can you remember when we waited on parcel post? As an older man, I have no more time to waste! Ah! Already it is here... A thesis by – let me see – Reino Hautamaa."

Andy noted the second name matched that of the owner of the phone. This was surely not a coincidence.

Professor Penttinen walked between Andy and Angela and perched on the edge of his desk. "I am sure I can search in this document... Yes. Let's try those strange two words... Well, here we are.

And how it comes back to me even as I read it. Now listen to the English."

Darkest fish of Tuonela, in the river of Manala
May be caught by skills unspoken, sent to find a willing vessel
In the living lands of sunshine.
But the swan will call unceasing, for return of its lost children,
Until the moon grows full in heaven, when the river will recall them,
Save they send to swim another.

He looked up from his phone. "I don't know what is more remarkable! The correspondence between your strange papers and this poetry, or me being able to remember it! Darkest fish, is I suppose, an unusual phrase, but combined with the 'willing vessel' I cannot imagine such coincidence. Don't you see? Wow-wow-wow."

Andy asked, "But what does the verse mean?"

"Nothing real! As I mentioned, they debunked this material. However, the faker's thesis made some controversial claims. Our mythic underworld is Tuonela. To get there, the dead must cross a river, sometimes called Manala. On that river is a monstrous swan, who we might see as a kind of guardian of death – one of many we Finns have I might add. But now we reach the controversial aspects. These *darkest fish* were supposedly how our mysterious old rune-singer described souls crossing the river to the underworld. To catch such a fish was supposed to rescue them from death itself! In the real Kalevala a woman retrieves the body parts of her dismembered son using a copper-handled rake, then revives them using song and magic honey. Our less imaginative liar merely catches a herring! Finally, since these dark little fish were supposedly souls without any body at all, the bogus thesis introduced the idea that some vessel would be required in our world to allow their return."

Andy, fearing the effect this might have on Angela, hesitated before asking the question. "But what does it mean to be a vessel? How would you qualify?"

"Please. These fake runes were not explicit about the fake way any of it would fake work. I read you the verse, and my interpretation would be this: a willing person might step aside for this resurrected soul, but by the time of the next full moon, the river of death will reclaim its stolen fish, unless someone swims in their place. So perhaps the displaced vessel dies to take the resurrected one's place in the underworld?"

Angela said, "So, you're talking about possession, right?"

"Something like it, I suppose. Our liar had certainly watched too much cinema. Here we have a work of complete fiction. It did not emerge from our ancient tradition. It emerged from an over-active imagination."

"Could I see the translated verse?" When Andy saw Angela taking notes, he couldn't help but be concerned. While aspects of the professor's tale might coincide with her fears, she must surely have picked up that this was a story of forgery and lies, not reality.

He tried to talk to her about this on the return trip from St Andrews, but she remained mostly silent, deep in thought. He only discovered what was on her mind when he finally dropped her at the entrance to her tenement. Leaving the car, she turned to him and said. "The day after tomorrow is the next full moon."

———

ON HIS SOLITARY drive back to Edinburgh, the in-car console popped up with a call from Romania. Andy considered ignoring it before the penny dropped. "Elisia, is that you?"

"You're no fun. Remember, though. Anyone asks, I'm just a nuisance caller."

"You can say that again."

"Cheeky... Well, my first piece of mischief is to tell you that, no, I can't apply some sort of magic clean-up to that video so that pixels not actually present in a rectangular smudge magically appear. So I don't have the plate number."

"Ah well. Worth a try."

"There was some blue on the left-hand side of the smudge, so I'd guess an EU plate. Spoiler alert: that would be a decent plate for breezing through half of Europe like you own the place, but I can't say any more than that. Bit of a dead end."

"Well, I've forwarded those videos to Glasgow too, but I doubt they'll make any more of it than you have."

"Relax – they definitely won't. Which brings me to my second piece of mischief: where your target phone is now."

"So it didn't stay in Rotterdam?"

"Nope. My CI wrote a clever script to query the location repeatedly over the last twenty-four hours. Big road trip: it's been through Germany, Poland, Lithuania, and Latvia. They've recently entered Estonia, heading for Tallinn."

Andy pictured a map of Northern Europe. "That's on the Baltic, right? I'd put money on an imminent ferry crossing into Finland, given everything else we know."

"Sounds plausible. Will I call you tomorrow with an update?"

"Yes, please. Do you want to forewarn me the location of my next international caller?"

Her reply held an obvious note of disgusted puzzlement. "What kind of anonymity system would that be?"

MICHAEL WAS certain of one thing: don't take advice from your enemy.

If Erkki wants me to move, I remain exactly where I am.

First, it started with persuasion. Erkki, outside the glass, gently explaining that it was Michael's time to be in the world. That it was best for everyone if he obeyed Erkki without question. That there were things only Erkki understood, and so Michael should follow his guidance.

But Michael stayed put.

After that, the persuasion turned to threats. Erkki blustered that he would use terrible force and teach obedience through pain. Erkki screamed he would destroy the glass room and force Michael to eat the fragments.

But despite his furious, hammering fists, something had become obvious. Erkki could not destroy the glass room. He didn't have that power.

Michael could tell that there was more to this display than a demand for obedience. If you grew up watching every human detail, observing as though lives depended on it, then you learned to tell the difference between whims and needs.

Erkki had a need.

Because there were other times, without Erkki's intervention, when Michael suddenly found himself in control. It wasn't clear why, and usually it was only for flashes of time. He'd be looking out through Erkki's eyes and then, suddenly, there would be no Erkki, only Michael, in his own body, thinking his own thoughts.

Perhaps this happened when Erkki became fatigued or bored, or perhaps there was some other trigger. What was obvious was that when it ended, Erkki, on his return, was shocked and angry.

So, Erkki had a need.

He needed to control Michael's comings and goings.

But he couldn't. And that scared him.

PART III – THE PRICE

Day 7 – Decisions

The first call of the morning was from Phoenix, Arizona, and it arrived over breakfast. "I'm pretty sure it's the middle of the night where you are," Andy said.

"I wish it was. That's when I do my best work. But do you know, I've had another email from your boss, still trying to recruit me?"

"No mystery there. I've told him you're a good detective."

"It's not just that, though, is it? It's the whole Liam Neeson thing."

"OK, you've lost me."

"I have a very particular set of skills."

"Oh, yes. There's that, I guess. But it would be actual detective work up here, less of that fancy desk jockey stuff you do for the London laptop brigade."

"Well, this fancy desk jockey just called to tell you that your mystery phone seems to have settled in south-east Finland near the Russian border. I've just sent you the latitude/longitude, but it's a very approximate location, based on triangulating the cell-masts."

"Is there any way to be precise?"

"One way – if you were over there, you could use a mobile Stingray device. You drive around, and it will locate the handset, but your car becomes a rolling crime scene. I can neither confirm nor deny whether I might know a source in Denmark."

"No thanks. Not least because I can't be sure if my missing suspect is there."

"If it helps, based on the times and distances between my queried locations, I'd say the car has had more than one driver. They were in motion for thirty hours straight."

"See? Like I said, a good detective... But an excellent one would know lots of coffee could get a single driver there too."

"Well, in that case, your excellency, I bid you good day and good luck."

IF IT SEEMED as if the day had started well, when he called Angela with the news the sky fell in. "I'm sorry," she said, "but we were taking too long, so I used the number this morning. They told me where they are. I have the address."

It was a shocking development, and one that might have ruined everything. "I wish you hadn't done this. Who did you speak to?"

"The one who calls himself Paavo. He said Michael is with him. They're in Virolahti in Finland."

Andy checked a map on his phone. The location certainly tallied with what Petrakis had found, and that surprised him. "Angela, have you actually spoken to Michael?"

"A little. Paavo put him on the line. It was Michael's voice, but it wasn't Michael. He pretended to be, but it wasn't."

"I can't understand this. Why would they even speak to you? Why give you an address?"

"Paavo said Michael needed me, today, as soon as possible. That much I believe. So I've booked a flight. I'm going over."

"You can't. It's dangerous."

"I know it is, and that's why I'm going. I left him in danger once before and look what happened. Not this time."

"I mean that it's dangerous for you. They didn't invite you from the goodness of their hearts."

"Well. You can come with me. There are more tickets from Edinburgh via Amsterdam this afternoon. I'll pay for yours."

"Don't be silly. How can you afford that?"

"I have my access to the joint account again now. Alec kept my bank card and rolls of cash in the kitchen drawer. I don't care about the cost."

"Forget paying, but let me think..." Was he actually considering this? "I can't go abroad on police business without clearance."

"Well, look into it and let me know. I'm heading out for the train to Edinburgh, but you can call me on this number. Don't worry if you can't make it. Thanks for all you've done already."

Done already? It felt like the little progress he'd made had entirely unravelled.

ANDY FOUND Doirin in the living room. "Can I get your thoughts, Do," he said. "This thing is sprouting arms and legs. Angela has an address in Finland and is heading after Michael. It's risky, and if you don't want me to go, I won't ask the chief for clearance, but I'm worried about what she's walking into."

Doirin shook her head. "No. You need to go. Be careful, obviously. But there's no choice in this." He was used to the way Doirin saw things by now. For her, a clear thread of purpose wove its way through every decision. He wished he shared that, but had to make do with choosing, and then hoping for the best.

She stood up. "Julie is coming through today. I'm meeting her in an hour, so I best get going. I don't think this will take you long."

He tried to push away the thought: *I hope not. Tomorrow is the full moon.*

DCI BRIAN NESBITT sighed down the phone line. "Finland? Are you sure he's there?"

"She says she's spoken to him, or at least someone who sounded uncannily like him. And you've seen the video. He did get into that car."

"It's still a hell of a distance."

Andy felt bad not fully disclosing his knowledge, but he wasn't going to risk any fallout for Petrakis, or give the chief an ethical headache. "I agree, but the timings work if they got on the Hull ferry on the night of the incident. They could drive the rest of the way, with one final quick hop across the Gulf of Finland."

"Maybe. If you can eyeball him, get a watertight ID so we know for sure, then that at least builds a case for extradition? But I'll need to clear it with international liaison. You can't gather evidence lawfully if I don't."

Andy knew that would take time, and Angela was leaving today. "She's been given the address and invited over. She's going whatever we decide. How about I take a two-day leave of absence. Is there a problem if I'm there as a private citizen, helping her negotiate his return?"

"It's a mess if he claimed coercion later, so Angela would have to vouch for you in that instance. But honestly, a negotiated return would be a big win. Extradition from Finland isn't easy without European arrest warrants to fall back on. But you need to play it nice and easy. Make sure everyone knows you are there in a private capacity. Send me an email to that effect and bring Kilburn up to speed."

After that Andy booked his own flight and told Angela he'd see her at the airport.

———

ERKKI ALWAYS SEEMED to rage at night. Two or three times now, Michael had caught a pattern. The night sky would brighten, catching Erkki's attention and then he'd appear to Michael, pounding his fists outside the glass.

He'd done it repeatedly last night before and after they'd arrived at the cabin. Then in the morning, he'd seemed to give up, and Michael watched as he raged at Paavo.

But a little while after that, something had changed.

Paavo had spoken or perhaps pretended to speak on the phone.

Because the world was quiet from the glass room, Michael heard only fragments of a one-sided conversation, so he couldn't know if any of it was real. But Paavo had seemed excited and had talked about Michael, inviting someone to come and *take Michael home.*

Then Erkki had spoken on the phone too, in a bizarre impersonation of Michael's own voice.

Not long after that, Michael heard Erkki's voice gathering around the glass room. It started as a whisper but grew in strength and power until he understood what he was being told: *"You can't stay in there forever. You must come out to protect her."*

Later he watched helplessly while Erkki and Paavo spoke.

They were pretending a crazy thing, pretending Michael's mother was coming. Worst of all, they were discussing how Erkki would kill her unless Michael came out and took control.

And then, all around the glass room Erkki's whispers gathered, growing louder and louder and louder: *"Tonight is the last night. It must happen tonight."*

It was already dark when Andy negotiated car hire at Helsinki airport. Angela came from the shop carrying water and snacks. "For energy," she said. Although adrenaline was currently providing all they needed, they had a long night ahead.

The two-hour shift in the time zone had cost them any chance at daylight, but the moon was high and bright as they set off, glaring down on them, like a spotlight.

"This is what they said? That we should just turn up, however late?"

"Yes. That is what they said. They said it had to be tonight."

Andy tried to find comfort in something, anything. "Well, this isn't based upon the full moon at least – that's tomorrow."

"I've thought about that. This is the last moon that isn't full.

Tomorrow, the debt is collected, unless tonight they make the repayment."

Andy said, "Please. Try to remember, that's all fake." But Angela said nothing.

So they headed east, towards the Russian border, travelling in near-silence, unsure of what they would find.

Eventually, after two hours, when they felt as if there was nothing around but trees and empty fields, they saw a flickering light in the window of a solitary house some distance back from the road. A confused compass weathervane topped the chimney pot, showing eight arrows radiating outwards from a corroded central disc. To Andy, those arrows seemed a clear signal: *anywhere but here.*

But, as he knew she would, Angela said, "That's the house, just how they said." He pulled off the road. And they set off on foot.

Day 8 – Just Past Midnight

The man who answered the door was pale, and thinner than seemed healthy. His face appeared almost ghostly in the moonlight until an all-too-human flicker of concern shattered the mask. He glared at Andy – clearly both unanticipated and unwelcome – making the detective feel justified in having made the journey.

Then the thin man shrugged. "Hello. I'm Paavo. Come," he said, and walked out past them towards the woods.

"Hang on," said Andy. "Where are we—"

"Just follow," Paavo shouted back. "We go to Michael."

Angela did not hesitate joining Paavo on a dirt path winding through the trees, and Andy hurried after.

Soon, the trees were tall and thick around them, the drumbeat moon slashing through the branches above, a flickering metronome almost at the end of its cycle. Andy wondered if Angela saw it too, but deep down, he knew. Here was her lunar clock, counting towards a dark illusion firmly lodged in her head. He had failed to dissuade her, but what chance had he ever had? Illusions were powerful, especially here, especially among the trees at midnight. Even Andy felt it.

"Watch," Paavo said, taking out a torch. "Ground not safe." He guided them right, off the path and into the undergrowth. They followed, walking for what seemed like fifteen minutes, each turn taking them further from the road. Finally, a scramble down a moss-covered bank had them facing a hole in a decaying concrete wall. A damaged young tree, losing its bark, had rooted here, partly obscuring the entrance, but Paavo pushed the branches aside, ducking to walk inside.

"What is this place?" Andy asked, as he followed Angela inside, stooped almost to his knees.

"Michael here. This was part of Salpalinja, once," Paavo called back. "But now forgotten, now ours."

The torchlight ahead joined with a flickering in the distance, and the smell and the greasy soot marks on the tunnel walls suggested there had been a fire down here, a big one, and recently too. What had the professor told them? *Your piece of equipment was marked to commemorate a death that took place late last month, around three weeks ago.* Was this the source of the grit in the glass? Is this where they burned a body?

Down they went, until the tunnel opened out into a room. The smell of fire was strongest here, emanating from the dead remains of a large pyre in one corner of the room. At the opposite corner, the flickering light issued from an oil lamp. The lamp sat on top of a plastic folding table. Four camping stools were arranged around that table, and on one of them, impassive and unmoving sat Michael, his arms resting around what looked like a small dish of dirt or ash.

Paavo stood at the pyre, but gestured for Andy and Angela to take a seat. As they did so Angela said, "You told me Michael, not him."

Michael spoke, his voice clipped, oddly flat, wrongly accented. *Like someone playing a part*, Andy thought. The lad's smile, when he looked at Angela, was cold. "This is our problem also. Michael is never here when we ask him. But you will change that." He took out a small knife, and cut into his own palm, then held his arm away from the bowl, letting the blood drop on the ground. He nodded to Paavo who produced an old gun.

"Don't move. Is real." Paavo shot into the dirt and the echoing report was deafening in that small space. He pointed the gun at Angela. "Michael. Is time. You save or she die. Your choice."

Andy cast his eyes around the room, looking for defensive options, but could not help but see the change on the young man's face. The shift from impassivity to emotion was nothing short of breathtaking. "Mum?"

Angela looking tired, but not defeated, smiled, although it didn't fully mask the concern in her eyes. She said, "Give me the knife, Mikey."

He dropped the blade on the table, as though unaware he'd even been holding it. Angela dragged it to her side of the table. Then she reached into her pocket, and slowly spread out her scant provisions from the airport. Paavo seemed puzzled but did nothing, seemingly prepared to permit this strange reunion.

Angela said, "D'you want, water? Chocolate?" but when he stared back, confused and afraid, she opened the bottle and sipped down some water herself.

"I don't know what they want, Mum."

"That's OK, Mikey, I do." Andy was too slow to stop her as she lifted the knife and drew the blade across her own hand, letting red drops fall into the bowl of ash. But she stopped at that and took her son's wounded hand in her own.

Paavo cried, "What you do?" his face collapsing in fear and confusion. Whatever strange and careful choreography he had prepared made no allowance for Angela's intervention.

"Don't be scared, Mikey. I love you."

"I love you too, Mum, but—"

"Don't worry, son. I took some pills in the tunnel."

Andy could see it now, and wondered why he'd been so blind

before: the slackening of her features, the slowing of her breathing. "Angela, what did you take?"

Paavo ran towards the entrance, brandishing the gun but unsure what or how to regain control, unsure if control was even possible anymore. Angela gazed at him, her eyelids drooping. "No. You can have me, not Mikey." And at that, Paavo ran back up the tunnel.

Michael wept. "No," he said. "No, Mum."

Andy stooped and followed Paavo up the tunnel, but the man was now nowhere in sight. He dialled the emergency services, and was relieved the operator spoke English. "It's opiates," he said, "strong ones. I'm not sure which." He gave them the location that showed on his phone, and described the terrain they'd face as best he could.

Running back down he found Angela cradled in her son's arms, her words slurring badly, her eyes closing, she said. "Mikey... we... look out... for each other. That's... all this is."

DCI Brian Nesbitt and DCI John Kilburn were on the tarmac at Edinburgh to take Michael Thomson into custody. Only Andy and Michael had been allowed to disembark. The other passengers were held on board for the handover and while the body bag containing the corpse of Angela Dean was taken to a pathology van.

Kilburn pointed as the van door closed behind her remains. "See, Lorimar? I told you she was unreliable."

Andy wanted to punch him, and might have had Nesbitt not stepped between them at that precise moment. "You have your suspect, DCI Kilburn."

"Suspect? Don't be so generous. This one's a slam dunk."

Andy looked at Michael's broken face, as he was led away, and couldn't help but wonder at the weird circular horror of it. The boy had internalised some alternative personality to save his mother, but the story was too powerful for them both and he lost her anyway.

Later, asking Doirin what the point was in any of it, she'd answered, "You couldn't save her, but she saved her son."

"Did she, though? Heading for psychological assessment, but prison for sure. I think 'saved' is maybe stretching it."

"Life and hope," she said, turning over in bed.

As she drifted off to sleep, he remembered her advice from before. *Some things you change. Some things change you.*

Michael Thomson had bought his mother a stay of execution, but hadn't changed her fate. He'd certainly changed himself though, and his whole future. Poor bastard.

Three months later

The visitor reception felt different somehow, now that Andy was a regular citizen, although the formalities were largely the same. "Telephone, keys, watch, and any other belongings in the tray, then head through the scanner." At the other side, he raised his arms for the body search, wondering if it had always taken so long and been this thorough.

As he sat in the waiting area, he wondered how Michael was bearing up. Too soft for this environment, but then again, who wasn't? He'd heard through his old channels that the intake psychologist had given an encouraging assessment. No major delusions or dissociative identity disorder but some signs of what they called *depersonalisation*, ascribable to trauma, for which they assigned him to a regular counselling group. Prison counselling in a group setting was something Andy had never really trusted. Perhaps he'd been too long in policing, but having criminals share life strategies had always seemed a high-risk endeavour.

As they led him towards the visitor room, he saw Michael through the glass. His face carried a harder edged expression that likely came from three months in the prison system. But the young man smiled broadly as the guard brought the detective to his table. "Detective Lorimar!"

"Hi Michael. Technically I'm *Mr* Lorimar nowadays. I've gone private. Best call me Andy and avoid the confusion."

"OK, we'll go with Andy. I was pleased to see your name on the sheet."

"Yeah. Sorry it took so long. It's poor form for a witness to visit the accused before the trial is over and done. Anyway, at least all the messing around means you've only a year left to do."

Michael shrugged.

"How's the counselling going?"

The lad sighed. "A bit shit, really. There's a couple of guys in the group that are just arseholes. I don't go now."

"Isn't it mandatory?"

Michael leaned forward, murmuring. "Well, I *go*..."

The guard reacted quickly to Michael's change of posture. "Sit the hell back, Thomson!" It was almost a panicked hyper-vigilance, as though he feared serious trouble.

Before Michael sat back, he whispered, "I just send Erkki."

Andy felt a prickle on the back of his neck but tried not to react. "So, you still feel him sometimes?"

"Oh, yeah... I am him sometimes."

Andy gazed around the room. Multiple tough, angry cons glared back at him. There were a lot of scars on display, physical and otherwise. He could see how this idea might help the lad cope in here. Give him some toughness to draw on. "But when you send him to counselling, doesn't the group, the psychologist... don't they notice the differences?"

"Nah. We've spent enough time together now. I've taught him how to be like me. He was very interested. Very keen to learn."

"But if you've kept this hidden from the psychologists, I'm intrigued... Why tell me?"

"Because, Andy, isn't it obvious? You've met Erkki. So he really, really wants you to know." And then Michael leaned forward, held Andy's gaze, and grinned.

AFTERWARDS, on his way home, Andy thought back over many aspects of the conversation he'd just had. But it was something about the grin that bothered him. It was oddly fierce, sure, but it wasn't just that. It was the gaze that accompanied it. At first, Andy felt as if he were looking into orbs of lifeless glass.

But then came a tiny flicker, just a fractional second of desperate emotion, and it gave Andy a crazy idea. It was the idea that someone else might be watching from behind the glass, someone trapped behind transparent walls of grief, contributing nothing to the world except the useless, silent pounding of their fists.

ABOUT THE STORIES

Thanks for making it to the end!

(If you didn't make it to the end, say because the book fell open at this page, the correct action now is to stop reading and head back to safer waters. Here be spoilers.)

So, you may well be asking: A book of stories? Why not a novel?

There are two answers to that.

The first answer: I've always loved shorter-form stories. As a kid, wandering the library shelves, I became captivated by huge illustrated anthologies, often of ghost stories or folk-tales. The closest I ever came to weight-lifting was when I maxed out my junior library ticket on three Hamish Hamilton hardcover collections (Witches, Giants, and Goblins, if memory serves). If Hamish Hamilton had published a Bumper Book of Crochet, I'd have borrowed that too, but in that universe, dear reader, you would most likely be wearing a jumper.

Before we come to the second answer, let's talk about the stories.

The majority of the stories were written for this collection, with a small number of pieces written previously. A couple of those previously-written had an earlier moment in the spotlight. "The

Anniversary Man" was selected as part of a Scottish Crime Writing competition by *The Scotsman* newspaper earning entry to a master-class Q&A session with no less than Ian Rankin. This was a pretty fortunate development, given the only thing Scottish about that story was me. "Remembrance Day 1968" was selected as part of a competition on BBC Radio Scotland's *Cover Stories* and produced and broadcast on their *Radio Café* show.

Some stories in this collection strike me as a homage to the old folk-tales of my childhood. I'm thinking of "Chicken House, Alaska", "Under The Ice" and "The Soldier's Daughter", although all are placed in a more modern and probably darker context. I only say *probably darker*, because I'm far from certain. Those old folk-tales could be awfully dark, and perhaps that exposure in my youth taught me something about how, with a following wind, the light and shadow of human experience might blend into powerful fictional truths.

The novella "Swole" grew from the character of Bill Zee. He was essentially a tempting devil, like Mephistopheles from the Faust legend, but reimagined as a good ol' boy from southern states of America. My original story, revolving around the global financial crash, wasn't quite right so I parked the character. Then, a few years back I read about the ever-evolving but little-discussed problems in male body image, and I knew I had something Bill would love to get his claws into.

The story "Original Features" came from wanting to write a haunted house tale, but one that explored the way sleep can act as a gateway to the fears of even the most level-headed amongst us. It's also about death and a few other things of course, but then, what ghost story isn't?

And that brings us to the second answer on why I'd write a book of short stories: To paraphrase the great Stephen King: sometimes they come back. For example, the closing novella here, "Oubliette", features Andy Lorimar from my novel *One Night Only*. Even though he doesn't show up in the opening part, the story couldn't have progressed without him. You also find the characters Devlin and Petrakis from my first novel are present in these pages, and in turn, certain characters from the stories here seem insistent enough that they might well return in later work.

Anyway, any questions or comments don't hesitate to get in touch at nightsborder.com, or find me on Goodreads. I'd be delighted to hear from you.

ABOUT THE IMAGES

Given my already-declared love for illustrated story books, and since this was a book of stories, I thought it would be a lot of fun to have some illustrations. Over the years I'd raised the possibility of collaboration with the more artistic of my friends and family, but there was alway less interest than I'd hoped, what with them having lives of their own to spend time on.

Fortunately, artificial intelligence stepped forward (don't worry, not in a Terminator sense), and so the images introducing the stories in this book were developed using technology. A term frequently used in generative AI art circles is that of co-creation, meaning that the combination of human and software is more than the sum of the parts. Given I can't draw for toffee, that is most certainly true in my case. However, I think the general idea is that while AI might be good for quickly generating screeds of ideas, a human must control the process and decide which ideas to pursue to a conclusion.

At the end of the print edition I've also included a short image gallery with a few larger images inspired by specific scenes. I really did the larger images for my own interest – I wondered whether the AI tools were flexible enough to create images closely matching specific story elements of a story – but I didn't think my curiosity justified imposing a huge download on every e-book user. My conclusion, for what it's worth is that if you put the time in, you can sometimes get pretty decent results, but it isn't always easy.

THE AI TOOLS I USED

The main tools involved were *Dall-E* from Open-AI (via labs. openai.com and Microsoft's copilot.microsoft.com), and *Stable Diffusion* from Stability.ai (via local install, beta.dreamstudio.ai and clip drop.co). This area changes quickly, so the comments I make below should be taken with a pinch of salt, as they apply to the versions I used at the time and your future mileage will almost certainly vary.

In my experience, DALL-E results seemed to more closely follow instructions and provided better ways of revising elements of the image, while, prior to DALL-E 3, Stable Diffusion-based tools gave more polished results and provided more useful variations on an already existing illustration. Often, I'd seek the best of all worlds by moving images between tools and even standalone image editing software. People tell me Midjourney creates the best AI art of all, and it certainly is a very popular system, but I didn't get along with the quirky instant messaging interface, so didn't spend much time with it.

Tools producing generative art are controversial, because

although end-users pay to generate images, content visible on the internet has often been used in training datasets without any permission sought or remuneration given to creators of that content. Understandably, legal cases are ongoing to define better practice in this area. I'm hopeful that the fact these models degenerate when trained on too much non-human data – something amusingly called Model Autophagy Disorder, or MAD – will force wholesale revision in how AI generation companies view human creators going forward. I decided early on to avoid using artist names to reproduce specific human styles for any illustration you see in this book, but only the law can create a stable settlement in this space.

THE PROCESS OF AI ART CREATION

The basic approach when working with generative art tools is to supply and refine a series of prompts - which are textual descriptions of particular image elements and styles you wish to have created. As an example, the image at the top of this section used the following prompt:

A writer and a robot paint a masterpiece on a blank wall. Black and white. High contrast. Highly detailed. Pencil illustration.

I selected the result you see from around twenty variations within Stable Diffusion's Dreamstudio, and in none of these variations did the characters paint on a blank wall – I always got a frame. This kind of omission is fairly typical. When you encounter blindspots in the generation step that are tricky to overcome, you may decide to live with what the engine wants to deliver. One way around is to supply a starter image for the engine to use as a basic guide for the result. This approach allows you to specify the level of similarity or difference from the supplied seed image. In this case, I could have used an image editing tool to erase the frame, for instance, and then make that my template. I did similar things on various occasions for the story illustrations – it was usually quicker than creating a blizzard of revised prompts and variations to force the AI engine into a space it seemed not to want to go.

While results are guided by your inputs, they always have a random component, which means that the same prompt can be reused to provide an endless set of results to choose from. Stable Diffusion tools have the neat feature of *negative prompting* – allowing you to specify elements *you don't want* alongside the main prompt listing those elements you do want. I tried this feature to ensure I had no picture frame in the image above, so as you can clearly see, negative prompting is a suggestion and not a guarantee. Most likely, the term 'masterpiece' was dominated by framed images in the AI training dataset for the specific model I used, so I could ask all I liked, but I wasn't getting it.

Setting your own expectations about these tools is important. You will often get impressive results, but those results seldom exactly match what you had in mind. Most commonly, the results from any given prompt will simply take you a little nearer the target. When that happens you can adopt that result as a new base image and then revise your prompt to strengthen the aspects you like. This process is like working with an artist who randomly ignores and exaggerates chunks of your instruction – the AI engine's understanding of how language maps to pictorial elements is driven in unknown ways by a training dataset you have never seen. My process was to make thousands of images, chasing the most fitting variations until, eventually, I could fish a gem or two from the sea of randomness. I'm confident talented humans would be faster drawing the images themselves, but lacking those skills, AI was the only game in my particular town.

The bottom line for me is that I learned some new tools, and enjoyed seeing the results alongside the stories. It was an interesting challenge to try to create suitable visuals for the stories, and while some visuals ended up more suitable than others, it was always fun.

WHY NOT USE A HUMAN?

Well, if this human could draw, that is the route I'd have taken for sure. But given that door was closed, my first consideration was that human art takes time and that time is justifiably expensive. A book by a new writer that is unlikely to make a profit is not the kind of project a sensible publisher will attach a professional book illustrator to. And that goes double when illustrations are very much optional, as they were in this case.

The second consideration is that it is difficult for human artists to work with writers who don't clearly know what they want. As the first book I've ever considered having illustrated, I was certainly guilty of not fully knowing what I was doing. It took me thousands of images across multiple tools to get a reasonable idea of what I was after, and freelance professional artists justifiably prefer a solid specification to work from.

So in my scenario – constrained budget and uncertainty around specification – AI tools can usefully fill the gap. They force me, the writer, to expend my own effort, rather than waste an artist's time with endless revisions. AI image generation will likely put art in books, like this one, that would never have had art inside otherwise. The suitability of that art will largely depend on the time and effort expended by the person driving the AI. My guess is that AI results will inevitably tend more towards the generic than what might be produced with a human collaborator.

So in conclusion, and as you might expect, there is no free lunch. On top of the costs of the AI generation (the platforms I used charge to create images) it takes significant time to get usable results. I've certainly spent many days of effort using these AI tools, and all for a quirky project that could easily have omitted art altogether. Having said that, I enjoyed the process, so those days felt well spent. I hope you like the images, but even if not, I suspect I did this largely for an audience of one – me!

IMAGE GALLERY

Over the following pages, the print edition of the book presents a gallery of illustrations inspired by some of the stories. See the section *About the Images* for more details on how these images were created.

MOTHER'S MERCY

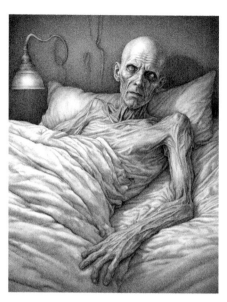

A pallid face craned towards her as the figure struggled to sit up, then a tremulous hand broke free from the bedding... "Moth-Mother! Mother!"

Was she melting now, fading into a supporting role in her own life, a tiny cog spinning in some ancient wheel?

DISSOLUTION

Devlin wrote the word Bampot, *double-underlined it and then said, "Come again?"*

THE SOLDIER'S DAUGHTER

His sadistic toil had spawned a vast emptiness where nothing could ever survive.

SWOLE

Do you wanna be a champion gorilla, Tony? Do you wanna be the silverback?

THE UNFORSAKEN

The outlaw that folk called The Phantom was seen riding into town, just the way they always said on the warrant posters

THE ANGEL'S GATE

Humans are as moths, and their most fervent prayers a mere fluttering in the dark.

Can such moths, drawn to shadow, be brought into my will? Can you help them find favour in my sight?

FIGURE EIGHT

"It's supposed to be a snake eating its own arse, bruv. Maybe that's why it's drawn blood?

ORIGINAL FEATURES

There were no major structural problems, and the price was perfect. It was a property developer's dream.

THE ANNIVERSARY MAN

I waved as I made for the car. "Hey little Jo! Say bye-bye to Pappy..."
The wee one just stared at me. Ice-cold. So like her Grammy.

UNDER THE ICE

Fifty years in a single room of cold stone. Fifty years of gazing at a
hungry loch, while it pondered how best to claim her.

CHICKEN HOUSE, ALASKA

A thing that had been a shadow was becoming an ancient woman, drawing solidity from the darkness

REMEMBRANCE DAY 1968

...something sallow and insect-like, eyes distorted, round, glassy.

OUBLIETTE

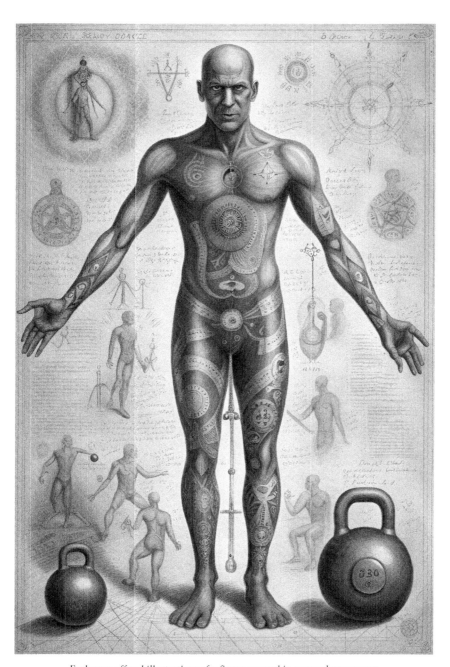

Each page offered illustrations of a figure engaged in unusual movements

And then, all around the glass room Erkki's whispers gathered, growing louder and louder and louder: "Tonight is the last night. It must happen tonight."

ABOUT THE AUTHOR

G.P. Ritchie was born a Glaswegian but was never terribly good at it. After a misspent childhood hanging around libraries, falling into the company of the wrong sorts of books and comics, he began writing primitive software on a ZX Spectrum. He studied computer science at University, unwisely taking no gap year for lion-taming, mountain climbing, or any of that exciting stuff proper authors get under their belt before writing one of these descriptions. He has made his own chocolate a few times, so there's that.

Upon moving fifty miles to work in software development, he discovered he'd most likely been an Edinburgher in disguise all that time. But what to do with all those hours he'd previously reserved for friendly conversation with strangers? Mostly he played scrabble, but nowadays he's using some of them in the service of fiction.

He's written a fair amount of computer software, but has also crowbarred some material onto radio and stage. He lives in Edinburgh with his wife and son.

g

ACKNOWLEDGMENTS

We've reached the section where I thank people for helping me out. There are lots of those people, of course, mostly unheralded, and they stretch all the way back to childhood. So, apologies right now to anybody I forget – buttonhole me about it later and extract your pound of flesh…

Authors always try to be clear at this point about who owns any mistakes. Well, since I'm the person making these stories up, then writing them down, then fiddling with them for what seems like forever, before putting them out into the world, you know where I stand on that one. If you find something quirky, careless or flat out wrong, then I'm as cross as you are and won't rest until I've brought the culprit to justice. Now over to the list of suspects…

For finding and squashing a whole host of bugs in the language, thanks go to my editor, Kat Harvey, and to my alpha-reader (both in terms of seeing the roughest drafts, and being undisputed leader of the pack) my wife Jenny.

For information on law and Edinburgh prisons I owe gratitude to David Dickson and Grant Markie. Some of what they said I'll have misheard, as we were in a noisy Filmhouse bar at the time, but it's amazing what you can spin out from catching every second word.

For unwittingly collaborating in an email exchange that spawned 'The Unforsaken" I owe thanks to David Coffield and Kevin McFadyen. They probably thought we were arguing about programming languages, and yet, I seemed to have cobbled a story out of it.

For help with image editing, and for quality checking the AI images, thanks go to Thomas Palmero-Halpin and my son Sam. Ever wondered what an AI engine says when it sees a particular prompt? No, me neither, but Sam let me know anyway, often hilariously.

My beta readers got the manuscript months before it was publication-ready, but they stuck with it and told me their thoughts. Thanks go to Robert Welbourn, Amanda Halpin and Maurice Franchesci. It got better with every review guys, cheers.

Since I strive to maintain a fairly boring life containing the absolute minimum of murder, possession, and travels through the kingdoms of the dead, books from other authors were used in researching aspects of the stories here. By now I've certainly lost many of them to brain compost, however, I'll mention a few. For the male body issues that inspired 'Swole', I found The Adonis Complex both enlightening and depressing. For background on the Irish traveller community featured in 'The Angel's Gate' I read Irish Travellers: The Unsettled Life, and learned a lot only to find I didn't much need it. For aspects of Finnish mythology in 'Oubliette', I read Kalevala Mythology by Juha Y. Pentikainen, which was good, and then later found the less serious (AKA more fun) treatment of The Finnish Book of the Dead by Tina and Teri Porthan. Also in 'Oubliette' we brushed against the weirder side of anthropology, and if that's an interest, you might enjoy Spirits, Gods and Magic by Jack Hunter.

Finally, for endless discussions at our weekly breakfast club, I have to thank my son Sam once more. I would describe him as a philosopher in waiting if he spent less time lampooning philosophers.

Everything else, I owe to Jenny.

ALSO BY G.P. RITCHIE

One Night Only

Life is precious. That's why they take it.

As a boy, Andy Lorimar loved puzzles, but one he didn't solve destroyed his childhood. It would have taken his future too, if he hadn't found stability within the police service. Now a long-serving Edinburgh detective, he's built a solitary existence following evidence to find the truth. After the horrific murder of a city councillor and the disappearance of a council employee, the trail of evidence points towards political corruption. But Andy suspects there may be another path to uncover, a shadow-maze stretching back years into darkness. A path that strays uncomfortably close to a woman who hears the voices of the dead.

Printed in Great Britain
by Amazon